Witches and Witchcraft

From Matthew Hopkins, The Discoverie of Witches *(1647).*

Witches and Witchcraft

An Anthology of Stories, Poems, and Essays

Edited by Katherine Kerestman and S. T. Joshi

Hippocampus Press

New York

Published by Hippocampus Press
P.O. Box 641, New York, NY 10156
www.hippocampuspress.com

First Edition
1 3 5 7 9 8 6 4 2

ISBN 978-1-61498-482-5 paperback
ISBN 978-1-61498-483-2 ebook

Contents

Introduction

Western civilization has long had a love-hate relationship with witches. From the dawn of time, wise men and wise women have been revered for their superior awareness of the visible and invisible worlds. Whether it is an intuitive or learned ability, their cunning affords them an additional control over our environment that we are lacking: they have privileged information about the cosmos that is dangerous every bit as much as it is beneficial to humankind. These wise ones knew how to improve people's lives—how to calm fever, heal wounds and skin eruptions, and assist in birthing and dying—when few others knew these secrets. Through techniques employing touch, words (spoken, sung, or written), and herbs, often in combination, they could calm an afflicted person's anxiety even as they healed his or her body. For the important help they render, they were, and are, often revered.

These greater abilities, however, have been sometimes turned against the wise ones, for it is a regrettable part of human nature to blame someone when something goes wrong. The randomness of events, it seems, is something the human mind has difficulty accepting. Therefore, whether it is a storm at sea, the burning of a building, an untimely death, a famine, a stillbirth, or an epidemic, people always look for a cause. More often than not, a person or persons are blamed. Did Harold's sin of lechery (or blasphemy) pull down the wrath of God upon himself and the entire community? Did the wrinkled old midwife smother the infant she was pulling from the womb out of envy? Did the Satan-worshipping witches nearly cause the sinking of the ship of King James, in order to bring down the Church?

The idea of witches is titillating. Witches can do things we can't, such as dance sky-clad (naked) in the woods, have sex with the devil, and soar through the air on cats or goats. They can find hidden treasure and kill people they don't like. When we want something and we don't know how else to get it, we often turn to magic—and to the practitioners of magic—to help us, crossing their palms with silver to attain our goals. At the same time, we are afraid of them. And what we are afraid of, we typically want to destroy. These are the themes of the tales contained in this volume.

The witch motif is of incredible antiquity in Western culture—and it is a motif that covers related figures such as the sorceress, the warlock (male witch), and so on. The sorceress Circe, in Homer's *Odyssey* (probably dating to the eighth century B.C.E.), is able both to change human beings into swine and to maintain a romantic (and perhaps sexual) hold on these same men and their leader, Odysseus (Ulysses in Latin). One of the most striking cases of female sorcery occurs in Euripides' *Medea* (c. 431 B.C.E.), where the title character becomes enraged at the infidelity of her husband, Jason, who had led the Argonauts to capture the Golden Fleece, bringing Medea back home to Corinth; she devises a poison that kills not only Jason and his father, Creon, but her own children.

In the Christian culture that dominated the West since the fourth century C.E., witchcraft was intimately connected with Satan; indeed, the belief that witches actually made pacts with the devil and copulated with him became commonplace—and that is why witchcraft was regarded as a heresy. Pope Innocent VIII endorsed (and perhaps commissioned) Heinrich Kramer to publish the first authoritative witch-hunting manual, *Malleus Maleficarum* (1486; usually translated as *The Hammer of Witches*), a book that was actually used in the witchcraft trials that became increasingly common over the next several centuries. Other treatises—Nicholas Rémy's *Daemonolatreiae libri tres* (1595), Henri Boguet's *Examen of Witches* (1602), and many others—all focused on the heretical aspects of the witch, while also spinning wild tales about witches' power over both male and female sexuality. While a few scholars rejected belief in witches and their supernatural powers, the predominant opinion through the seventeenth century was that belief in witches was a central component of Christian belief—a belief resting upon the notorious line in Exodus, "Thou shalt not suffer a witch to live" (22:18). Hundreds of thousands of witches—men, women, even children and infants—were tried and executed throughout Europe, in both Catholic and Protestant countries.

The American colonies were not immune from such persecution. We find ourselves drawn to Salem, time and time again, as we attempt to satisfy an endless desire to penetrate more deeply into the untold parts of the horrible story of neighbors accusing neighbors and causing them to die. It was in Danvers (formerly Salem Village) that the "afflicted girls" first began hurling their accusations—ground zero of the Salem holocaust. Decades after the trials of 1692, which resulted in the execution of a score of men and women, one of the accusers, Ann Putnam, issued a tepid apology that nonetheless blamed Satan—rather than her own religion-infused hysteria—for her actions.

At what point did witchcraft transmogrify from actual belief to the stuff of fiction? The European Enlightenment of the eighteenth century did much to destroy the intellectual foundations of belief in witchcraft, and by the end of the century a Romantic reaction to the rationalism of the period led to the emergence of the Gothic novel. Witches, however, did not loom large as a motif in the hundreds of novels produced between 1764 and 1820. Only gradually did the witch become a baleful figure in weird literature, whether it be in poetry or prose fiction. By the latter half of the nineteenth century, the American satirist Ambrose Bierce could poke fun at the whole topic in "A Fowl Witch" (1874). From a slightly different perspective, L. Frank Baum, in *The Wonderful Wizard of Oz* (1900), produced, in the Wicked Witch of the West, an enduring symbol of the witch's terrifying powers. The chapter included here features numerous grisly episodes not included in the classic 1939 film.

The widespread attribution of witchlike properties to old women (especially those of a solitary or retiring sort, or those who—as in the "wise woman" of Celtic lore, practiced unorthodox medicine) remained a common theme well into the twentieth century, as Eleanor Scott's "The Old Lady" (1929) attests. Witches figure in African American lore as well, as indicated by "A Plantation Witch" (1880) by Joel Chandler Harris. Harris was a white writer with a serious interest in the

9

black culture of the American South; but actual African American writers, such as James Weldon Johnson, also treated the subject.

The witch is a presence in cultures around the world, as we can see in the brief fable "A Visit from the Shades" by the seventeenth-century Korean writer Im Bang. Alice Elizabeth Dracott's "The Old Witch Who Lived in a Forest" (1906) treats of witches in India, as does Helena P. Blavatsky in "A Witch's Den" (1892).

As the twentieth century dawned, pulp writers in *Weird Tales* and other magazines—ranging from Robert E. Howard to Clark Ashton Smith to Frank Belknap Long—all featured witches in their tales and poems. The enduring power of the motif can be seen in the wide array of original stories and poems in this volume by some of today's leading writers of the weird.

But it should never be forgotten that, however entertaining a tale or poem of witches may be, the many centuries during which witchcraft was a terrifying reality led to appalling crimes against innocent people, even if some of them may have indoctrinated themselves into believing that they were witches, capable of flying or hurling curses at their foes. That baleful undercurrent of misguided belief should always temper our enjoyment of any fictional narrative of witches or sorceresses.

—KATHERINE KERESTMAN AND S. T. JOSHI

From *Medea*

Euripides

    Medea: Friends, this long hour I wait on Fortune's eyes,
And strain my senses in a hot surmise
What passeth on that hill.—Ha! even now
There comes . . . 'tis one of Jason's men, I trow.
His wild-perturbèd breath doth warrant me
The tidings of some strange calamity.

                        [*Enter* Messenger.

    Messenger: O dire and ghastly deed! Get thee away,
Medea! Fly! Nor let behind thee stay
One chariot's wing, one keel that sweeps the seas. . . .

    Medea: And what hath chanced, to cause such frights as these?

    Messenger: The maiden princess lieth—and her sire,
The king—both murdered by thy poison-fire.

    Medea: Most happy tiding! Which thy name prefers
Henceforth among my friends and well-wishers.

    Messenger: What say'st thou? Woman, is thy mind within
Clear, and not raving? Thou art found in sin
Most bloody wrought against the king's high head,
And laughest at the tale, and hast no dread?

    Medea: I have words also that could answer well
Thy word. But take thine ease, good friend, and tell,
How died they? Hath it been a very foul
Death, prithee? That were comfort to my soul.

    Messenger: When thy two children, hand in hand entwined,
Came with their father, and passed on to find
The new-made bridal rooms, Oh, we were glad,
We thralls, who ever loved thee well, and had
Grief in thy grief. And straight there passed a word
From ear to ear, that thou and thy false lord
Had poured peace offering upon wrath foregone.

11

A right glad welcome gave we them, and one
Kissed the small hand, and one the shining hair:
Myself, for very joy, I followed where
The women's rooms are. There our mistress . . . she
Whom now we name so . . . thinking not to see
Thy little pair, with glad and eager brow
Sate waiting Jason. Then she saw, and slow
Shrouded her eyes, and backward turned again,
Sick that thy children should come near her. Then
Thy husband quick went forward, to entreat
The young maid's fitful wrath. "Thou wilt not meet
Love's coming with unkindness? Nay, refrain
Thy suddenness, and turn thy face again,
Holding as friends all that to me are dear,
Thine husband. And accept these robes they bear
As gifts: and beg thy father to unmake
His doom of exile on them—for my sake."
When once she saw the raiment, she could still
Her joy no more, but gave him all his will.
And almost ere the father and the two
Children were gone from out the room, she drew
The flowerèd garments forth, and sate her down
To her arraying: bound the golden crown
Through her long curls, and in a mirror fair
Arranged their separate clusters, smiling there
At the dead self that faced her. Then aside
She pushed her seat, and paced those chambers wide
Alone, her white foot poising delicately—
So passing joyful in those gifts was she!—
And many a time would pause, straight-limbed, and wheel
Her head to watch the long fold to her heel
Sweeping. And then came something strange. Her cheek
Seemed pale, and back with crooked steps and weak
Groping of arms she walked, and scarcely found

Her old seat, that she fell not to the ground.

     Among the handmaids was a woman old
And grey, who deemed, I think, that Pan had hold
Upon her, or some spirit, and raised a keen
Awakening shout; till through her lips was seen
A white foam crawling, and her eyeballs back
Twisted, and all her face dead pale for lack
Of life: and while that old dame called, the cry
Turned strangely to its opposite, to die
Sobbing. Oh, swiftly then one woman flew
To seek her father's rooms, one for the new
Bridegroom, to tell the tale. And all the place
Was loud with hurrying feet.

                So long a space
As a swift walker on a measured way
Would pace a furlong's course in, there she lay
Speechless, with veilèd lids. Then wide her eyes
She oped, and wildly, as she strove to rise,
Shrieked: for two diverse waves upon her rolled
Of stabbing death. The carcanet of gold
That gripped her brow was molten in a dire
And wondrous river of devouring fire.
And those fine robes, the gift thy children gave—
God's mercy!—everywhere did lap and lave
The delicate flesh; till up she sprang, and fled,
A fiery pillar, shaking locks and head
This way and that, seeking to cast the crown
Somewhere away. But like a thing nailed down
The burning gold held fast the anadem,
And through her locks, the more she scattered them,
Came fire the fiercer, till to earth she fell
A thing—save to her sire—scarce nameable,
And strove no more. That cheek of royal mien,
Where was it—or the place where eyes had been?

Only from crown and temples came faint blood
Shot through with fire. The very flesh, it stood
Out from the bones, as from a wounded pine
The gum starts, where those gnawing poisons fine
Bit in the dark—a ghastly sight! And touch
The dead we durst not. We had seen too much.

  But that poor father, knowing not, had sped,
Swift to his daughter's room, and there the dead
Lay at his feet. He knelt, and groaning low,
Folded her in his arms, and kissed her: "Oh,
Unhappy child, what thing unnatural hath
So hideously undone thee? Or what wrath
Of gods, to make this old grey sepulchre
Childless of thee? Would God but lay me there
To die with thee, my daughter!" So he cried.
But after, when he stayed from tears, and tried
To uplift his old bent frame, lo, in the folds
Of those fine robes it held, as ivy holds
Strangling among your laurel boughs. Oh, then
A ghastly struggle came! Again, again,
Up on his knee he writhed; but that dead breast
Clung still to his: till, wild, like one possessed,
He dragged himself half free; and, lo, the live
Flesh parted; and he laid him down to strive
No more with death, but perish; for the deep
Had risen above his soul. And there they sleep,
At last, the old proud father and the bride,
Even as his tears had craved it, side by side.

  For thee—Oh, no word more! Thyself will know
How best to baffle vengeance. . . . Long ago
I looked upon man's days, and found a grey
Shadow. And this thing more I surely say,
That those of all men who are counted wise,
Strong wits, devisers of great policies,

Do pay the bitterest toll. Since life began,
Hath there in God's eye stood one happy man?
Fair days roll on, and bear more gifts or less
Of fortune, but to no man happiness.

Francisco Goya y Lucientes, Witches' Flight *(1797–98)*

From *Malleus Maleficarum*

Heinrich Kramer and Jakob Sprenger

We have already shown that they [witches] can take away the male organ, not indeed by actually despoiling the human body of it, but by concealing it with some glamour, in the manner which we have already declared. And of this we shall instance a few examples.

In the town of Ratisbon a certain young man who had an intrigue with a girl, wishing to leave her, lost his member; that is to say, some glamour was cast over it so that he could see or touch nothing but his smooth body. In his worry over this he went to a tavern to drink wine; and after he had sat there for a while he got into conversation with another woman who was there, and told her the cause of his sadness, explaining everything, and demonstrating in his body that it was so. The woman was astute, and asked whether he suspected anyone; and when he named such a one, unfolding the whole matter, she said: "If persuasion is not enough, you must use some violence, to induce her to restore to you your health." So in the evening the young man watched the way by which the witch was in the habit of going, and finding her, prayed her to restore to him the health of his body. And when she maintained that she was innocent and knew nothing about it, he fell upon her, and winding a towel tightly round her neck, choked her, saying: "Unless you give me back my health, you shall die at my hands." Then she, being unable to cry out, and with her face already swelling and growing black, said: "Let me go, and I will heal you." The young man then relaxed the pressure of the towel, and the witch touched him with her hand between the thighs, saying: "Now you have what you desire." And the young man, as he afterwards said, plainly felt, before he had verified it by looking or touching, that his member had been restored to him by the mere touch of the witch.

Dollhouse

Mary A. Turzillo

That dollhouse
you found
in the attic
of your new home:

Beware of invitations
your children may get
of tea-parties with special scones
from the elusive biddy
who lives in its attic.

She's not imaginary.

She is six inches tall,
dresses all in black,
ancient in dress and comportment.
She sweeps the dollhouse with her magical broom,
then pets her diminutive cat.

Those tea-parties:
if your children sip
from the wee hand-made cups
or eat the penny-size scones the Lilliputian woman baked,

they will speak in tongues,
they will gaze sightless at the full moon
until their eyes turn to molten glass,
their hair will grow white and fall out.
Your youngest will wither
tiny and tinier
until the dollhouse witch carries her

like a severed thumb
up to her attic
where she and her cat will spellbind her forever.

Albrecht Dürer, Witch Riding on a Goat *(c. 1500)*

The Search for the Wicked Witch

L. Frank Baum

The soldier with the green whiskers led them through the streets of the Emerald City until they reached the room where the Guardian of the Gates lived. This officer unlocked their spectacles to put them back in his great box, and then he politely opened the gate for our friends.

"Which road leads to the Wicked Witch of the West?" asked Dorothy.

"There is no road," answered the Guardian of the Gates, "no one ever wishes to go that way."

"How, then, are we to find her?" enquired the girl.

"That will be easy," replied the man; "for when she knows you are in the Country of the Winkies she will find you, and make you all her slaves."

"Perhaps not," said the Scarecrow, "for we mean to destroy her."

"Oh, that is different," said the Guardian of the Gates. "No one has ever destroyed her before, so I naturally thought she would make slaves of you, as she has of all the rest. But take care; for she is wicked and fierce, and may not allow you to destroy her. Keep to the West, where the sun sets, and you cannot fail to find her."

They thanked him and bade him goodbye, and turned toward the West, walking over fields of soft grass dotted here and there with daisies and buttercups. Dorothy still wore the pretty silk dress she had put on in the palace, but now, to her surprise, she found it was no longer green, but pure white. The ribbon around Toto's neck had also lost its green color and was as white as Dorothy's dress,

The Emerald City was soon left far behind. As they advanced the ground became rougher and hillier, for there were no farms nor houses in this country of the West, and the ground was untilled.

In the afternoon the sun shone hot in their faces, for there were no trees to offer them shade; so that before night Dorothy and Toto and the Lion were tired, and lay down upon the grass and fell asleep, with the Woodman and the Scarecrow keeping watch.

Now the Wicked Witch of the West had but one eye, yet that was as powerful as a telescope, and could see everywhere. So, as she sat in the door of her castle, she happened to look around and saw Dorothy lying asleep, with her friends all about her. They were a long distance off, but the Wicked Witch was angry to find them in her country; so she blew upon a silver whistle that hung around her neck.

At once there came running to her from all directions a pack of great wolves. They had long legs and fierce eyes and sharp teeth.

"Go to those people," said the Witch, "and tear them to pieces."

"Are you not going to make them your slaves?" asked the leader of the wolves.

"No," she answered, "one is of tin, and one of straw; one is a girl and another a Lion. None of them is fit to work, so you may tear them into small pieces."

"Very well," said the wolf, and he dashed away at full speed, followed by the others.

It was lucky the Scarecrow and the Woodman were wide awake and heard the wolves coming.

"This is my fight," said the Woodman; "so get behind me and I will meet them as they come."

He seized his axe, which he had made very sharp, and as the leader of the wolves came on the Tin Woodman swung his arm and chopped the wolf's head from its body, so that it immediately died. As soon as he could raise his axe another wolf came up, and he also fell under the sharp edge of the Tin Woodman's weapon. There were forty wolves, and forty times a wolf was killed; so that at last they all lay dead in a heap before the Woodman.

Then he put down his axe and sat beside the Scarecrow, who said, "It was a good fight, friend."

They waited until Dorothy awoke the next morning. The little girl was quite frightened when she saw the great pile of shaggy wolves, but the Tin Woodman told her all. She thanked him for saving them and sat down to breakfast, after which they started again upon their journey.

Now this same morning the Wicked Witch came to the door of her castle and looked out with her one eye that could see afar off. She saw all her wolves lying dead, and the strangers still travelling through her country. This made her angrier than before, and she blew her silver whistle twice.

Straightway a great flock of wild crows came flying toward her, enough to darken the sky. And the Wicked Witch said to the King Crow,

"Fly at once to the strangers; peck out their eyes and tear them to pieces."

The wild crows flew in one great flock toward Dorothy and her companions. When the little girl saw them coming she was afraid. But the Scarecrow said,

"This is my battle; so lie dawn beside me and you will not be harmed."

So they all lay upon the ground except the Scarecrow, and he stood up and stretched out his arms. And when the crows saw him they were frightened, as these birds always are by scarecrows, and did not dare to come any nearer. But the King Crow said,

"It is only a stuffed man. I will peck his eyes out."

The King Crow flew at the Scarecrow, who caught it by the head and twisted its neck until it died. And then another crow flew at him, and the Scarecrow twisted its neck also. There were forty crows, and forty times the Scarecrow twisted a neck, until at last all were lying dead beside him. Then he called to his companions to rise, and again they went upon their journey.

When the Wicked Witch looked out again and saw all her crows lying in a heap, she got into a terrible rage, and blew three times upon her silver whistle.

Forthwith there was heard a great buzzing in the air, and a swarm of black bees came flying towards her.

"Go to the strangers and sting them to death!" commanded the Witch, and the bees turned and flew rapidly until they came to where Dorothy and her friends were walking. But the Woodman had seen them coming and the Scarecrow had decided what to do.

"Take out my straw and scatter it over the little girl and the dog and the lion," he said to the Woodman, "and the bees cannot sting them." This the Woodman did, and as Dorothy lay close beside the Lion and held Toto in her arms, the straw covered them entirely.

The bees came and found no one but the Woodman to sting, so they flew at him and broke off all their stings against the tin, without hurting the Woodman at all. And as bees cannot live when their stings are broken that was the end of the black bees, and they lay scattered thick about the Woodman, like little heaps of fine coal.

Then Dorothy and the Lion got up, and the girl helped the Tin Woodman put the straw back into the Scarecrow again, until he was as good as ever. So they started upon their journey once more.

The Wicked Witch was so angry when she saw her black bees in little heaps like fine coal that she stamped her foot and tore her hair and gnashed her teeth. And then she called a dozen of her slaves, who were the Winkies, and gave them sharp spears, telling them to go to the strangers and destroy them.

The Winkies were not a brave people, but they had to do as they were told; so they marched away until they came near to Dorothy. Then the Lion gave a great roar and sprang toward them, and the poor Winkies were so frightened that they ran back as fast as they could.

When they returned to the castle the Wicked Witch beat them well with a strap, and sent them back to their work, after which she sat down to think what she should do next. She could not understand how all her plans to destroy these strangers had failed; but she was a powerful Witch, as well as a wicked one, and she soon made up her mind how to act.

There was, in her cupboard, a Golden Cap, with a circle of diamonds and rubies running round it. This Golden Cap had a charm. Whoever owned it could call three times upon the Winged Monkeys, who would obey any order they were given. But no person could command these strange creatures more than three times. Twice already the Wicked Witch had used the charm of the Cap. Once was when she had made the Winkies her slaves, and set herself to rule over their country. The Winged Monkeys had helped her do this. The second time was when she had fought against the Great Oz himself, and driven him out of the land of the West. The Winged Monkeys had also helped her in doing this. Only once more could she use this Golden Cap, for which reason she did not like to do so until all her other powers were exhausted. But now that her fierce wolves and her wild crows and her stinging bees were gone, and her slaves had been scared away by the Cowardly Lion, she saw there was only one way left to destroy Dorothy and her friends.

So the Wicked Witch took the Golden Cap from her cupboard and placed it upon her head. Then she stood upon her left foot and said, slowly,

"Ep-pe, pep-pe, kak-ke!"

Next she stood upon her right foot said,

"Hil-lo, hol-lo, hel-lo!"

After this she stood upon both feet and cried in a loud voice,

"Ziz-zy, zuz-zy, zik!"

Now the charm began to work. The sky was darkened, and a low rumbling sound was heard in the air. There was a rushing of many wings; a great chattering and laughing; and the sun came out of the dark sky to show the Wicked Witch surrounded by a crowd of monkeys, each with a pair of immense and powerful wings on his shoulders.

One, much bigger than the others, seemed to be their leader. He flew close to the Witch and said,

"You have called us for the third and last time. What do you command?"

"Go to the strangers who are within my land and destroy them all except the Lion," said the Wicked Witch. "Bring that beast to me, for I have a mind to harness him like a horse, and make him work."

"Your commands shall be obeyed," said the leader; and then, with a great deal of chattering and noise, the Winged Monkeys flew away to the place where Dorothy and her friends were walking.

Some of the Monkeys seized the Tin Woodman and carried him through the air until they were over a country thickly covered with sharp rocks. Here they dropped the poor Woodman, who fell a great distance to the rocks, where he lay so battered and dented that he could neither move nor groan.

Others of the Monkeys caught the Scarecrow, and with their long fingers pulled all of the straw out of his clothes and head. They made his hat and boots and clothes into a small bundle and threw it into the top branches of a tall tree.

The remaining Monkeys threw pieces of stout rope around the Lion and wound many coils about his body and head and legs, until he was unable to bite or scratch or struggle in any way. Then they lifted him up and flew away with him to the Witch's castle, where he was placed in a small yard with a high iron fence around it, so that he could not escape.

But Dorothy they did not harm at all. She stood, with Toto in her arms, watching the sad fate of her comrades and thinking it would soon be her turn. The leader of the Winged Monkeys flew up to her, his long, hairy arms stretched out and his ugly face grinning terribly; but he saw the mark of the Good Witch's kiss upon her forehead and stopped short, motioning the others not to touch her.

"We dare not harm this little girl," he said to them, "for she is protected by the Power of Good, and that is greater than the Power of Evil. All we can do is to carry her to the castle of the Wicked Witch and leave her there."

So, carefully and gently, they lifted Dorothy in their arms and carried her swiftly through the air until they came to the castle, where they set her down upon the front door step. Then the leader said to the Witch,

"We have obeyed you as far as we were able. The Tin Woodman and the Scarecrow are destroyed, and the Lion is tied up in your yard.

The little girl we dare not harm, nor the dog she carries in her arms. Your power over our band is now ended, and you will never see us again."

Then all the Winged Monkeys, with much laughing and chattering and noise, flew into the air and were soon out of sight.

The Wicked Witch was both surprised and worried when she saw the mark on Dorothy's forehead, for she knew well that neither the Winged Monkeys nor she, herself, dare hurt the girl in any way. She looked down at Dorothy's feet, and seeing the Silver Shoes, began to tremble with fear, for she knew what a powerful charm belonged to them. At first the Witch was tempted to run away from Dorothy; but she happened to look into the child's eyes and saw how simple the soul behind them was, and that the little girl did not know of the wonderful power the Silver Shoes gave her. So the Wicked Witch laughed to herself, and thought, "I can still make her my slave, for she does not know how to use her power." Then she said to Dorothy, harshly and severely,

"Come with me; and see that you mind everything I tell you, for if you do not I will make an end of you, as I did of the Tin Woodman and the Scarecrow."

Dorothy followed her through many of the beautiful rooms in her castle until they came to the kitchen, where the Witch bade her clean the pots and kettles and sweep the floor and keep the fire fed with wood.

Dorothy went to work meekly, with her mind made up to work as hard as she could; for she was glad the Wicked Witch had decided not to kill her.

With Dorothy hard at work the Witch thought she would go into the court-yard and harness the Cowardly Lion like a horse; it would amuse her, she was sure, to make him draw her chariot whenever she wished to go to drive. But as she opened the gate the Lion gave a loud roar and bounded at her so fiercely that the Witch was afraid, and ran out and shut the gate again.

"If I cannot harness you," said the Witch to the Lion, speaking through the bars of the gate, "I can starve you. You shall have nothing to eat until you do as I wish."

So after that she took no food to the imprisoned Lion; but every day she came to the gate at noon and asked,

"Are you ready to be harnessed like a horse?"

And the Lion would answer,

"No. If you come in this yard I will bite you."

The reason the Lion did not have to do as the Witch wished was that every night, while the woman was asleep, Dorothy carried him food from the cupboard. After he had eaten he would lie down on his bed of straw, and Dorothy would lie beside him and put her head on his soft, shaggy mane, while they talked of their troubles and tried to plan some way to escape. But they could find no way to get out of the castle, for it was constantly guarded by the yellow Winkies, who were the slaves of the Wicked Witch and too afraid of her not to do as she told them.

The girl had to work hard during the day, and often the Witch threatened to beat her with the same old umbrella she always carried in her hand. But, in truth, she did not dare to strike Dorothy, because of the mark upon her forehead. The child did not know this, and was full of fear for herself and Toto. Once the Witch struck Toto a blow with her umbrella and the brave little dog flew at her and bit her leg, in return. The Witch did not bleed where she was bitten, for she was so wicked that the blood in her had dried up many years before.

Dorothy's life became very sad as she grew to understand that it would be harder than ever to get back to Kansas and Aunt Em again. Sometimes she would cry bitterly for hours, with Toto sitting at her feet and looking into her face, whining dismally to show how sorry he was for his little mistress. Toto did not really care whether he was in Kansas or the Land of Oz so long as Dorothy was with him; but he knew the little girl was unhappy, and that made him unhappy too.

Now the Wicked Witch had a great longing to have for her own the Silver Shoes which the girl always wore. Her Bees and her Crows and her Wolves were lying in heaps and drying up, and she had used up all the power of the Golden Cap; but if she could only get hold of the Silver Shoes they would give her more power than all the other things she had lost. She watched Dorothy carefully, to see if she ever took off her shoes, thinking she might steal them. But the child was so proud of her pretty shoes that she never took them off except at night and when she took her bath. The Witch was too much afraid of the dark to dare go in Dorothy's room at night to take the shoes, and her dread of water was greater than her fear of the dark, so she never came near when Dorothy was bathing. Indeed, the old Witch never touched water, nor ever let water touch her in any way.

But the wicked creature was very cunning, and she finally thought of a trick that would give her what she wanted. She placed a bar of iron in the middle of the kitchen floor, and then by her magic arts made the iron invisible to human eyes. So that when Dorothy walked across the floor she stumbled over the bar, not being able to see it, and fell at full length. She was not much hurt, but in her fall one of the Silver Shoes came off, and before she could reach it the Witch had snatched it away and put it on her own skinny foot.

The wicked woman was greatly pleased with the success of her trick, for as long as she had one of the shoes she owned half the power of their charm, and Dorothy could not use it against her, even had she known how to do so.

The little girl, seeing she had lost one of her pretty shoes, grew angry, and said to the Witch,

"Give me back my shoe!"

"I will not," retorted the Witch, "for it is now my shoe, and not yours."

"You are a wicked creature!" cried Dorothy. "You have no right to take my shoe from me."

"I shall keep it, just the same," said the Witch, laughing at her, "and some day I shall get the other one from you, too."

This made Dorothy so very angry that she picked up the bucket of water that stood near and dashed it over the Witch, wetting her from head to foot.

Instantly the wicked woman gave a loud cry of fear; and then, as Dorothy looked at her in wonder, the Witch began to shrink and fall away.

"See what you have done!" she screamed. "In a minute I shall melt away."

"I'm very sorry, indeed," said Dorothy, who was truly frightened to see the Witch actually melting away like brown sugar before her very eyes.

"Didn't you know water would be the end of me?" asked the Witch, in a wailing, despairing voice.

"Of course not," answered Dorothy; "how should I?"

"Well, in a few minutes I shall be all melted, and you will have the castle to yourself. I have been wicked in my day, but I never thought a little girl like you would ever be able to melt me and end my wicked deeds. Look out—here I go!"

With these words the Witch fell down in a brown, melted, shapeless mass and began to spread over the clean boards of the kitchen floor. Seeing that she had really melted away to nothing, Dorothy drew another bucket of water and threw it over the mess. She then swept it all out the door. After picking out the silver shoe, which was all that was left of the old woman, she cleaned and dried it with a cloth, and put it on her foot again. Then, being at last free to do as she chose, she ran out to the court-yard to tell the Lion that the Wicked Witch of the West had come to an end, and that they were no longer prisoners in a strange land.

From *Demonolatry*

Nicholas Rémy

Book II, Chapter III
That Witches make Evil Use of Human Corpses; especially of
Abortive Births, Criminals put to Death by the Law, or any that have
died some Shameful or Dishonourable Death.

We have the authority of Porphyrius, *De Sacrificiis*, and Psellus, *De Daemonibus*, that witches very often make foul use of human corpses in their evil works; the supposition being that, as soon as souls are freed from their earthly connexion, they become endowed with powers of vaticination; but that they still retain some contact with their former house of flesh, and are therefore believed to hover around and haunt their dead bodies. But this seems to me entirely improbable; for no one ever yearns for the prison from which he has escaped, nor can there be any need for a soul that has at last attained to a state of purity to have any dealing with a fetid and putrid corpse; and the separation effected by death between soul and body, until we appear before the judgement seat of Christ, is greater than any that can be wrought or thought (II *Corinthians* v. 10). It is probable, therefore, that this is all a deliberate and malicious invention of the Demons that they may more and more deceive human nature, and still more ignominiously abuse mortal remains in their contrivances for the destruction of the human race. Tacitus (*Annal.* II), speaking of Piso who was suspected of sorcery, says: "There were found the remains of human bodies taken from the ground and their tombs, spells and enchantments, and the name of Germanicus scratched on tablets of lead; decomposed flesh half burned, and other cantrips by which it is believed that souls are doomed to the infernal deities." Apuleius (*Golden Ass,* Bk. II) also touches this point when he assigns the reason for the practice at Larissa in Thessaly of keeping a watch during the night over the bodies of the dead, and says: "Without doubt it was to prevent the witches, who infested that country, from shamefully biting pieces out of them for use in bringing calamity upon the living."

The witches of our own time also use such practices, especially when they can come by the corpse of a man who has been put to death and exposed upon a cross as a public example. For they derive the material for their evil charms not only from the corpse, but even from the instruments of its punishment, such as the rope, the chains, the stake, or the fetters; for it is a common belief among them that there is some virtue and power in such things in the preparation of their magic spells. They can have no other reason for possessing themselves of the abortive births of women; for they make from the skin of these a parchment which they inscribe with some barbarous and unknown characters and afterwards use in the attainment of their dearest wishes. As to this, Agrippa and Petrus de Abano and Weyer, three masters in damnable magic, have left instructions which surpass all human nature. Others again cook the foetus in its entirety until it is either reduced to dry ashes or melted into a mass with which they mix certain other ingredients. Giovanni Battista Porta of Naples, in the Second Book of his *Natural Magic,* observes that this practice was used in his time. Pliny wrote that not only midwives, but harlots also, used thus to dislimb abortions for the purpose of preparing poisons for their crimes. And the practice is common to-day in German Lorraine, as I have often found in my examinations of witches on a capital charge.

Anna Ruffa, at Dieuze, October 1586, acknowledged that she had helped a witch named Lolla to dig up a corpse which had recently been buried by the great Gate of Dieuze, and that from its charred ashes they had concocted a potion which would cause the certain death of those whom they wished to kill. Catharina of Metingow (*ibidem,* Sept. 1586) added that to make it nastier to the taste, she used to mix with the potion lupine, ferns, elecampane, ox-gall, soot, or anything else that was even more bitter; for they force the poison into their victims' mouths against their will and in spite of their utmost struggles, as will be shown later. This is borne out by the testimony of Meg Bricq at Forpach, Aug. 1587, concerning the digging up of the corpse of an infant which had been buried the day before by its father, Faber Wolf. His account differs from the one above in only one respect; for he did not burn the body to ashes, but melted it down into a lump from which he could the more easily prepare his unguent, afterwards reducing the bones to ashes with which to sprinkle the trees that their fruit might fail. This agrees with the statement of Fuxena Eugel at Bulligny, April 1586, that she used to scatter such ashes to the winds with curses and incantations, either to burn off the blossom from the trees or to kill the crops. Maria, the wife of Johann Schneider, who lived in Metzerech, recounted that Joanneta, the wife of Soniaus Mathes, gave premature birth to a child which she secretly buried in the floor of the apartment in which she lived; but certain witches got wind of this and dug it up again shortly afterwards and reduced it to an ointment, with which she herself had at times anointed a besom upon which she sat and was borne up on high to Bruch, the place appointed for the Sabbat by her Little Master, *Rousgen*. Antoine Welsch at Guermingen, Dec. 1589, said that he had been told of similar doings by the wives of Gross Michel and Besskess, each of whom was very well known to him among the confederacy of witches; namely, that not long since they had dug up from the cemetery at Guermingen two such corpses, which had lately been buried by their parents, Bernhardi and Antoine Lerchen, and that after consuming them in fire they had converted them to their magic uses; but first they cut off the right arm with the shoulder and ribs belonging to it, to be used as a light in case they wished to administer poison to anybody at night. This is a marvellous matter which might well appear to be fabulous. The finger-tips of that dismembered limb used to burn with a blue sulphurous flame until they had entirely completed the business which they had in hand; and when the flame was extinguished the fingers would be just as whole and unimpaired as if they had not been providing the tinder for a light; and however often they had cause to use it, the fingers were still found to be undiminished. Not long after he had made this statement, it was confirmed in almost the same words by the wife of that Bernhardi (Guermingen, Jan. 1590); and she did not deny the shameful deeds which she had committed upon her own offspring; how for her hellish purposes she had torn it in pieces, roasted it and destroyed it.

Beautiful Baby Bianka

Debra K. Every

Lena had lived in Salitska all her life—and she hated it. She'd watched with growing jealousy as her brother made ready for an exciting life in Krakow, because she knew that an adventure of that sort was only afforded to men. Once he had gotten settled, one would think he would have opened his home to her, but no. It was a hard truth that the most a farmer's daughter could hope for was to marry a man with five hectares of land and spend her days tending chickens, hauling water, and sweeping dirt from floors that never remained clean.

She had found such a man in Jakub Karwacki—hardworking enough to support her and simple-minded enough to be controlled. There was but one problem. Jakub wanted a child, as did most men in Salitska, who looked at women as keepers of their hearth and breeders of their lineage. The thought of something growing inside her belly was a horror, but it was a bargain Lena had no choice but to make.

The Karwackis settled in a small farmhouse surrounded by six hectares of wheat where Lena spent her days wishing she was anyplace but there. They had no visitors but for the postman who would come from time to time with a letter from her brother in Kraków. Those letters were a bitter reminder of what life could have been like if she had been born a man.

Lena's drudgery was soon interrupted by the unwelcome news that she was with child.

Now, in Salitska there was a time-honored tradition that when a woman found herself in the family way, she would go to Ciotka Albina—Aunt Albina—for a blessing. Ciotka Albina was a fearsome old woman of indeterminate age who lived in a small cottage at the edge of the village that some said was the first to have been built there. Many a tale had been told about those women foolish enough to ignore this tradition. As the warning goes, Auntie Albina's blessing would keep

Baba Osa at bay—an insect-like creature that had the ability to kill with a simple song if not paid the proper respect.

This tradition presented a problem for Lena because of a happenstance many years before. She kept it a secret, not because of regret or shame, but because she saw no sense to expend effort in explaining her actions.

It occurred when she was in her sixteenth year—a shallow, mean-spirited girl; smarter than most; more ambitious than all. Lena had no respect for the backward ways of her neighbors. She especially had no respect for Ciotka Albina, who used folklore to keep the village in thrall. Lena was a modern girl. This was, after all, 1897. In just four years a new century would sweep those old beliefs away.

It was a sunny day in late spring. She had made plans to meet a boy who had mistaken her haughty ways for a mysterious aura. She had no real interest in the boy, but he was not as dull as his friends and there was a possibility that he would someday leave their backward village. Her hope was that he would take her with him.

Lena set off for town wearing her best dress and Sunday shoes, but the only route to Salitska from her parents' farmhouse was through Loda Forest. It was yet another reason to curse where she lived.

She was walking along one of the forest paths, doing her best to keep her shoes unsoiled, when she heard a cry coming from a ravine to her left. She peered over the edge and there was Ciotka Albina, lying in a heap at the bottom.

When the old woman saw Lena she said, "Thank goodness you are here. Please, little *koteczek,* help me. I fear my leg is broken."

Lena stared down at the old woman. Why should she dirty her best dress and Sunday shoes to save someone who had no more than a handful of years left on this planet? Truth be told, the village would be better off without her superstitious ways.

With no more than a backward glance, Lena resumed her walk, leaving Ciotka Albina to the crows. The old woman was finally saved by a woodsman, but her injured leg never healed properly, remaining a painful souvenir from that day in Loda Forest.

Over the years, whenever Lena happened to pass Ciotka Albina on the street, the girl turned her head away. It was not Albina's piercing eyes she was trying to avoid—the eyes that blamed Lena for the pain she endured. Lena felt no contrition for her past deeds. She avoided Aunt Albina's stare as her wordless way of letting the old woman know that she was of no consequence.

It was laughable to imagine that she would go to Ciotka Albina for a blessing, now that she was with child.

Lena's pregnancy was difficult. As her belly swelled, she diminished. Where most women's faces glowed, Lena's grew hollow. Where their limbs ripened, Lena's dwindled into sticks. And while fatigue rules the day for all women as they wait for their babies to arrive, Lena's was magnified a thousandfold.

Jakub, being Jakub, cared for everything. He'd wake even earlier than usual to set the fire and bake the bread. Once the house was in order, he would tend the fields. At night he would prepare the meals. Lena could scarcely keep her food down, and so he took to making simple broths. And all the while he would beg Lena to see Aunt Albina.

"Please, my love, visiting Auntie Albina would take but a moment and it would help with your discomforts."

Lena narrowed her eyes at her husband, feeling nothing but pity for his small-minded ways. "And what, dear husband, could Ciotka Albina do for me? Wave a magic stick? Brew a magic tea? Tend to your farming, Jakub. That is all you are good for."

Jakub was not a brave man. He was, in fact, so cowed by his wife's words that he soon abandoned the duties of a father-to-be and allowed his wife to ignore what he knew in his heart should be done.

The baby came in the dead of night with more pain than Lena could have imagined. By the time the midwife arrived, her mattress was soaked with blood and her head was wild with fever. But after twenty-six hours of labor, the cries of a beautiful baby girl resonated in the small cottage.

And beautiful barely described her. This was no wrinkled baby bird. The child came out uncrying, fully formed, plump and pink. Her eyes were a strikingly pale blue, her skin as smooth as a pitcher of cream. Her rosebud lips were graced with a half-smile. She was an angel incarnate. Jakub named her Bianka.

Lena felt triumph at this perfect child having been born without bothering with Aunt Albina's blessing—and she made sure her husband knew of it.

"Do you now see how useless Ciotka Albina is? There is no more perfect child in all of Salitska."

But proving Auntie Albina wrong was where her joy ended. Lena cared nothing for the child. She allowed Bianka to suckle at her breast for the first few days, but the feel of her daughter's demanding mouth was so disturbing that she took to squeezing her milk into a bottle topped with a nipple fashioned from a sheep's bladder.

"You wanted this baby," she said, thrusting the bottle into Jakub's hand. "You feed it."

Jakub was happy to oblige. He settled into a chair by the hearth with Bianka in his arms and stared down at her beautiful face as she suckled. As the days passed, he spent more and more time with Bianka and less and less time in the fields. It was as if he had been bewitched.

Lena regained her strength and as it grew so did her anger. The start of spring was upon them and still the fields lay unplanted.

"O mój Boże, husband! When will you put that infernal child down and tend to the fields?"

Jakub remained smiling as he kept his eyes on the baby's face. "A moment more, my love. That is all I ask."

But that *moment more* never ended. Day after day, week after week, Jakub remained in the chair by the hearth staring down at his beautiful child. Lena tended the fire and scraped together what little they had for their meals.

After six weeks, enough was enough. Lena had used the last of their wheat and there was but one piece of dried cheese in the larder. She was hungry and frustrated and angrier than she had ever been. This was no life, saddled to a useless husband and even more useless child.

She strode to the chair and snatched the baby from her husband. "Get up, you lazy man!"

But Jakub never moved his gaze from his arms, even after Bianka had been taken away. He remained still and serene with his face smoothed clean of worry. Lena roughly grabbed his shoulder to shake him awake.

But when she did, her hand broke through, as if Jakub's shoulder were nothing more than a shell as thin and as fragile as a hollow egg. Cracks grew, becoming larger as they traveled from his shoulder down to his chest and stomach while Jakub remained looking down with a beatific smile. The cracks became fissures, growing larger, moving to every part of his body until, with a loud crash, Jakub shattered into a thousand shards that fell into a pile on the floor.

Lena stumbled back and in so doing dropped Bianka at her feet. The child's blanket fell open, revealing a body with no legs. From her chest down Bianka twisted like a scale-less snake, smooth and slick, with a tapered point coiling in the air. Lena couldn't break her eyes away.

Bianka smiled widely and then opened her mouth. Two tongues darted out, growing long enough to free themselves from her lips and land on the floor. They divided into four, then eight, then sixteen— multiplying into a pile of squirming, writhing larvae. The pile grew so large that it reached the toe of Lena's foot and made its way up her ankle.

Their first touch roused Lena into action. She reached down to her ankle to swat them away, but as soon as her hand came into contact, the larvae divided yet again and crawled up her wrist.

There was now a swarm of larvae traveling from her legs to her hips and another traveling from her wrist up her arms. Soon the two converged at her chest. Lena became a solid mass of twisting eyeless worms traveling toward her neck in greater and greater number. Her clothes were quickly eaten away. She could feel them now attached to her skin. Lena ran around the room, blindly crashing into chairs and tables. She felt the slime of their bodies as they covered her now-naked breasts, tearing at her nipples until droplets of blood-tinged milk—her blood, her milk—stained the larvae's bodies.

They coursed up to her head and through her scalp, feasting on her hair, leaving her head bald and bleeding. Lena wanted to scream but kept her mouth closed for fear they might crawl down her throat. But there were other ways to enter into her body, as she would soon discover.

It started with a single larva. It reached the edge of her ear and wriggled its way toward the opening. As if it had signaled its brothers, more followed. Lena felt them enter into first one ear and then the other. She could feel them burrowing into her brain.

Lena could control herself no longer and in a cry of anguish opened her mouth and screamed. But the sound did not reach her ears. In its place Lena heard a voice humming. At first the sound was sweet—a beautiful lullaby, lilting back and forth, calming her, until she stopped moving and stood in place like a pillar of stone, listening, listening. Soon the lullaby took over her mind, growing louder, bleeding into her head and then neck and then chest. Lena's body became a single vibrating thing. She swayed in place as her arms and legs trembled. Her eyes grew wide, giving the larvae yet another opening in which to crawl. Then she dropped her jaw, allowing her voice to join in, creating a painfully loud duet that reached into every corner of the room. The sound was so loud and the vibration so great that Lena's body suddenly exploded into a multitude of pieces like a great exploding star in the sky.

The postman had been knocking at the door for no more than a minute when he heard the cry of a baby. When it became clear that no one was tending to the child's distress, he tentatively opened the door.

On the floor was the most beautiful child he had ever seen, crying as if it was the end of the world. He gathered her up; at the sight of him, the baby stopped crying.

He looked around the room and called out.

"Hello? Is anybody home?"

But there was no one.

"My, my little one," he said, gazing down at the child's face. "Whatever shall we do?" He couldn't leave the little mite alone and so decided to take her home until the Karwackis returned.

His wife would be so pleased.

From Matthew Hale, The History of Witches and Wizards *(1720)*

The Hag

Robert Herrick

> The Hag is astride,
> This night for to ride;
> The Devill and shee together:
> Through thick, and through thin,
> Now out, and then in,
> Though ne'r so foule be the weather.

> A Thorn or a Burr
> She takes for a Spurre:
> With a lash of a Bramble she rides now,
> Through Brakes and through Bryars,
> O're Ditches, and Mires,
> She followes the Spirit that guides now.

> No Beast, for his food,
> Dares now range the wood;
> But husht in his laire he lies lurking:
> While mischeifs, by these,
> On Land and on Seas,
> At noone of Night are a working.

> The storme will arise,
> And trouble the skies;
> This night, and more for the wonder,
> The ghost from the Tomb
> Affrighted shall come,
> Cal'd out by the clap of the Thunder.

Foragers

Stephen Mark Rainey

Alamance County, North Carolina
March 6, 1781

The fast-flowing stream was called Alamance Creek, and now that
darkness had fallen it was easier to hear than to see. After so many
hours, Lieutenant William Voss found it impossible to believe that he
and Sergeant Thomas Landrake had yet to emerge from these deep
woods—and that, somehow, they now found themselves alone.

Since breaking camp in Hillsborough—God knew how many days
ago—General Cornwallis had pushed his army at a hard march, with no
provisions other than what each man could carry, so hunger and thirst
had begun to take a deadly toll. This morning Voss and Landrake,
along with eight hand-picked men of the Duke of Wellington's Regiment, had departed their new encampment along the southern banks
of Alamance Creek and followed the stream through the woods, expecting to come upon farms or villages where they might plunder
food, water, tobacco, and whiskey. To their dismay and disbelief, the
damned woods appeared to go on forever.

By mid-afternoon their foray a failure, and the small company had
turned back toward camp. By rights they should have reached it well
before dusk. On their outbound trek they had encountered a single
fork in the stream and followed its southern branch, as northward
might lead them straight to General Greene and his Colonial Army's
encampment. Yet, on their return, they never found the fork again.
Voss knew with absolute certainty that they had not, *could* not have
passed it unawares.

And then . . .

"Where in bloody hell did we get separated?" A burly, powerful
man from Glastonbury, Landrake's voice sounded like a bear's growl.
"And how? We were all together, and then we weren't."

With great effort Voss kept his voice measured. "I wish I knew. But they can't be far away."

"Winters! Carlisle! Pryce! Where the hell are you?"

The stream's gurgling voice could hardly have overpowered Landrake's. But the otherwise silent darkness offered up no reply.

Though the day had been sunny and temperate, the evening air carried a chill. The men's threadbare uniform coats would offer little comfort if the temperature dropped much lower. And in this hostile country, even so deep in the forest, Voss disliked the prospect of building a fire. A gibbous moon hovered above the mostly leafless treetops, but the many tiers of tangled branches permitted only a few pale streamers to filter through. Weary and half-starved, he and Landrake could not proceed much farther.

"Damn Cornwallis to hell anyway," he muttered.

He felt the big man's eyes drilling into the back of his head. "Forgive me, Lieutenant, but it's hardly a well-kept secret that you've had thoughts of, ahem, resigning your commission. I don't suppose there's anything to that. Is there, Lieutenant?"

Voss froze. That Landrake could have heard any such rumor was more than unlikely—a near-impossibility, in fact—but he knew the sergeant to be shrewd and intuitive, and he might well have guessed his commanding officer's intentions. Not one man in Cornwallis's army could deny that, in the past weeks, order and discipline and had gone straight to hell, and unprecedented numbers of men had slipped from their tents under cover of darkness, never to return.

All because, more than a month ago at Ramsour's Mill, that damned fool of a commanding general had burned their provision train and sworn to pursue General Nathanael Greene "to the end of the world."

Voss's tone took on a sharp edge. "I've never condoned gossip in the ranks, Sergeant Landrake."

"Of course not, Lieutenant. However, should *some* officer permanently part ways with this regiment, I wonder whether he might consider the company of a friend?"

Voss considered Landrake a capable soldier and loyal subordinate.

Over their several years together he had developed a certain fondness for the fellow. His voice softened. "If that were the case, Tom, *some* officer might."

"Very good, sir. I shall—" The sergeant broke off and stepped to Voss's side, pointing into the distant darkness. "Is that a light I see?"

Voss had noticed it at the same time. A tiny golden glimmer in the black depths ahead. "That it is. Though most certainly not from our camp." For their foray he had carried no musket, only his razor-sharp spadroon, which he now drew from its scabbard. "We will approach with caution."

They took slow, stealthy steps. The soft gurgle of the stream helped cover the faint but constant crunching of their boots in dry leaves. Soon Voss could smell a faint hint of woodsmoke, and moments later he realized that the light spilled from between the partially drawn curtains of a pair of windows. Once they had closed to within a hundred feet, Voss made out the façade of a small log cabin in the center of a grassy clearing, perhaps forty feet in diameter. A trio of stairs led to a covered verandah and a solid wooden door between the two windows. At the cabin's rightmost end a stone chimney, which oozed a thin plume of pale smoke, jutted above a sharply angled roof.

Hanging above the stairs, a crude, hand-carved sign read, "Gadwick's Tavern."

"A bloody tavern?" Landrake whispered. "In the middle of the forest?"

"We must have reached its edge. Yet we've never strayed from the creek, and we're nowhere near our camp. Most peculiar."

Landrake unslung his musket from his shoulder. "I don't see anyone outside. Or any horses."

Voss moved forward, slipping from tree to tree until he reached a huge sycamore a few feet from the cabin's nearest corner. He took cover behind the thick bole. A moment later Landrake followed in his footsteps and dropped to one knee beside him.

"Do you hear anything?" Voss whispered. "I don't."

The sergeant listened for a few seconds. "Nothing."

"There can't be many men inside, if any. But I'll wager there's water and whiskey, if not food."

"I say we do it."

Voss nodded, lamenting that neither of them possessed a flintlock pistol. He tightened his grip on his sword and directed Landrake to charge his musket and fix his bayonet. "There may be rebel militia men in there. We'll move up and check the windows. If it looks clear, I'll open the door. You go in with the musket and move right, if possible. I'll go around the door to the left."

"Very good, sir."

Making as little noise as possible, Voss led the way up the stairs, positioned himself beside the lefthand window, and leaned forward to peer inside. He could barely see through the grimy glass panes, but in the narrow opening between the curtains he made out a few vague, shifting shadows. From his place beside the other window Landrake nodded, signaling that he deemed the way clear.

With the sergeant poised for action, Voss reached for the metal doorknob, twisted it, and shoved the door open. With two long strides Landrake crossed the threshold and stepped to the right, musket at the ready. In an instant Voss slid inside and pivoted around the door to the left, sword poised to strike at the first sign of aggression. He kicked the door closed.

It took several seconds for his brain to process the tableau before him.

From a huge fireplace to his right a roaring fire cast golden light over the stone hearth and knotty wood floor. Five long, rectangular wooden tables, arbitrarily spaced, occupied the better part of the room. At all but one of the tables a pair of dark, cloaked figures sat on benches across from each other, a flickering lantern between each pair. None of the hidden faces rose to take the slightest notice of the new arrivals. At the room's far end a fair-skinned, raven-haired woman stood behind a wooden counter that ran almost the length of the wall.

She regarded them with surprising indifference, though her irises gleamed with such brilliance that Voss could discern their sapphire color even from twenty feet away. After several seconds her thin, pale lips spread in a perfunctory smile. "Good evening, gentlemen." Her airy voice sounded like notes from an ethereal woodwind. She motioned to the vacant table, farthest from the fireplace, half-hidden in the shadows to their left. "That one is for you. I will bring you refreshment in a moment."

Neither of the men moved. Voss's gaze swept over the cloaked figures, and he noticed before each a tall glass tumbler filled with dark amber liquid. Now and again, with a slow, almost mechanical motion, one would lift his glass to unseen lips and drink.

"You've no need for your weapons," the woman said. "None of us here bear enmity toward your king. Or to you."

"Tories?" came Landrake's gruff whisper.

With another wan smile, she shook her head. "Non-aligned."

Voss lowered his spadroon, but his muscles remained taut, ready to spring at the first hint of movement against them. "What is your name?"

The woman lifted two filled glasses and set them on the wooden surface before her. "These are yours. Please sit, and I shall bring them to you."

Landrake growled. "The lieutenant asked your name."

"I am Lillian Gadwick."

Voss stepped forward, scanned the room again, and threaded his way between the tables to the bar. He could not make out a single face beneath any of the dark hoods, though he sensed that every concealed eye had focused on him. When he reached the counter he stood and looked the woman up and down. She wore a gauzy, dust-gray dress, almost the color and texture of cobwebs. She was hardly unattractive, yet of such ashen pallor that she might have been an animated corpse. He shuddered at the notion.

She pointed to one of the filled glasses and took a step backward. "Very well. Drink, then, sir."

Voss reached for the nearest glass and with two fingers nudged it toward her. "You first."

A bland expression etched on her face, she lifted the glass, took a long swallow, and set it back on the countertop. Her somber eyes held his for some indeterminate spell until, finally, her face brightened with a broad, unaffected smile.

"As you see, I am unharmed."

Now, locking his gaze on her sapphire eyes, he picked up the glass and took a tentative sip. He almost recoiled, for the amber liquid first tickled, then scorched his tongue and throat. When the fiery sensation subsided, he tasted smooth, smoky liquor, and a comforting warmth spread through his entire body. The second sip was like the first, only more intense, more *intimate,* as if his every nerve could both taste and feel the mysterious draught.

His weariness had not left him, yet a new flow of energy, like an infusion of tonic, charged his muscles.

Landrake materialized next to him, clutching his musket in one tense hand. His deep hazel eyes studied Voss with concern before swiveling to regard the barmaid.

"We're hungry," he said. "Do you have any food?"

Lillian Gadwick slid the second glass toward him. "Perhaps this will satisfy your needs."

He glanced at the glass and then at Voss. "Sir?"

Voss felt as if he were peering at himself from some distance above. "As you see, I am unharmed."

Landrake lifted the glass and took a tiny sip. After a pause, as if to savor its deep burn, he drained the glass and set it back on the bar counter.

As Voss watched, the sergeant's face appeared to waver behind a shimmering heat haze. Lillian Gadwick made an expansive gesture, and her voice chimed like mellow musical notes. "The conflict here drew my attention. I have traveled far to find what I need. And desire." Her smile widened until it appeared almost serpentine. "It is my pleasure to make your acquaintance, gentlemen."

"You speak in riddles," Landrake said, his speech slightly slurred. "What is this place? We marched through woods all day where there should have been no woods. We followed a fork in the stream, but when we returned, there was no fork. Our men vanished almost before our eyes—we turned, and they were gone." The sergeant enunciated each short, sharp syllable. "What—is—this—place?"

The viper smile widened. "This is my tavern, Sergeant Landrake."

Despite the warm light that painted his features, the sergeant's face went chalky white. "How the hell did you know my name?" He pointed at Voss. "The lieutenant never spoke my name."

"It is my business to know."

He leaned toward her and sneered. "All right, then. Now, Miss Lillian Gadwick, you'll be answering straight, or this—" He hefted the musket, brandishing its bayonet. "*This* will be doing the asking."

A low, barely audible murmur and shuffling sound crept from behind them. Voss glanced back at the tables and saw several of the figures rise like slow, curling, black smoke from their benches. He placed a firm hand on Landrake's left forearm. "Let's not be hasty, Sergeant." His eyes shifted to the woman's. "I would prefer a more genial conversation. But Sergeant Landrake makes valid points. I suggest you provide more sensible answers." He lifted his sword and pointed it toward the four figures now standing like cloaked statues. "I should hate to be forced to reduce the ranks of your . . . clientele."

The woman paid him no mind but kept her gaze fixed on Landrake. Her expression turned thoughtful. "I need a familiar."

"What the hell does that mean?" the sergeant rumbled.

The rustling among the tables increased, and the remaining cloaked figures rose, their movements awkward, jerky. *Like marionettes,* Voss thought. A tremor of unease shimmied down his spine. No, more than unease: apprehension and disbelief, for now he could see into the dark recesses beneath those hoods.

Only vacant space.

No faces.

"A trick of the light," he whispered. Sheer reflex drew his sword to striking position. The nearest of the ghastly figures lurched toward him, one arm extended, a skeletal, spider-like hand slipping from beneath the billowing sleeve.

Voss's grip on the spadroon's haft nearly slipped.

The bone-white hand was missing its little finger. From the third knuckle, a scar in the shape of an inverted question mark ran down the back of the hand to the wrist.

"Carlisle?"

The name came out as a cough.

The hand, its movements at first slow and tentative, shot forward like the head of a snapping turtle. Voss drew back, swung the spadroon in a tight arc, and brought its blade down and through the bony wrist. He felt the solid contact, yet the blade drew no blood—nor severed the hand. By God, that blow should have removed the hand at the wrist, but the grisly appendage remained whole. Unscathed.

An airy, sing-song voice rose from behind him: Lillian Gadwick, chanting strange syllables in what he took to be a language—yet he knew on some instinctive level that this could be no language devised by any human tongue. Much as when he had tasted that incomparable elixir, he felt as if a swirling fog had enveloped his body and mind. Through a hazy veil he saw the cloaked figure withdraw and again become a statue.

Carlisle.

It *was*—or had been—Private Carlisle! There could no mistaking that hand. The man had lost his finger at Cowpens, in South Carolina, back in January. So what the hell was this *thing* that had once been a man, a private in the Duke of Wellington's Regiment?

A ghost? It must be!

Those eight men. All of them.

Ghosts!

"Lieutenant!" Landrake's voice, sharper and higher than he'd ever heard it.

Voss spun, blade raised, only to see the big, bearlike man staggering backward from the bar counter, with what appeared to be smoke curling from his coat collar. Was it simply the fog in his brain playing tricks on his eyes? No, no, it wasn't. Thick gray and black plumes were swirling up around his neck and over his face, groping like ghostly fingers. The sergeant's musket hit the floor with a heavy *thunk*—and then went off with a deafening *boom,* for he had charged the priming pan. On a high shelf behind the bar a ceramic ale stein exploded into a million fragments.

The gray-garbed figure of Lillian Gadwick slid out from the end of the bar and moved toward the frantic, bellowing Landrake, who batted at his face with both hands. The woman did not walk. She *glided,* her crown now a full head higher than before because her feet, though hidden beneath the long, fluttering hem of her dress, no longer touched the floor.

The woman was a damned witch!

Sergeant Landrake toppled to the floor, thrashing and screaming. Voss saw that his exposed flesh now glowed red-orange, as if a superhot fire blazed *inside* his body. Oily black smoke billowed from his collar, his cuffs, from beneath his long red coat. His body curled into a tight ball, his screams peaking, so loud and shrill that Voss wanted to cover his ears, but his fingers refused to loosen their grip on his sword.

He saw Landrake's body contract and then *compact,* as if in the grip of some vast, invisible fist that clenched and crushed his flesh and bones into a small, tight mass. Now Voss could discern only a writhing, fiery shape, no larger than a full knapsack, belching black smoke like an overheated coal furnace. Beyond the roiling black columns Lillian Gadwick hovered in the air, *inhaling* the smoke, her jaws spread wide, her lips pulled back in a hellish grin that revealed row upon row of gleaming teeth, like the tiered pipes of an organ designed to blare praise to Lucifer himself.

At some point Voss realized the screaming had stopped. The smoke and flame dwindled and vanished, leaving behind a charred, black, ovoid *thing,* no larger than an opossum, which undulated and squirmed, issuing a constant stream of sickening grunting sounds, punctuated by sharp, piercing chatters and chirrups.

Then, at one end of the black ovoid, a pair of gleaming eyes *popped* into existence and swiveled from side to side. Huge hazel eyes that reflected golden firelight.

Sergeant Landrake's eyes.

"My Christ," Voss whispered. His eyes rose to regard the grotesque, still-floating figure of Lillian Gadwick. "You witch! You *devil!*"

With a sickening, ripping sound, four scaled, reptilian appendages—which ended in clawlike hands, neither fully human nor animal—burst from the dark, organic mass and scrabbled at the wooden floor. Then, from the ovoid's posterior end, a scorpion-like tail unfurled and whipped back and forth with sharp snapping sounds.

The lovely, melodic voice of the witch drifted to Voss's ears. "Behold my familiar."

The Landrake-thing's eyes rolled to peer at Voss. Below them a tooth-studded orifice opened and spread in rictus of fury. It unleashed a piercing, almost birdlike screech, and then, on its four lizard-like legs, the thing scuttled toward him and halted at his feet, its hazel, *human* eyes glaring at him with accusatory rage.

He stumbled backward toward the tables, but something cold—frigid—touched his shoulder and halted him. Glancing back, he realized it was the chalk-white hand of the cloaked figure nearest him. Then he saw the woman approaching, her face having returned to its lovely if ashen appearance. The Landrake-thing scuttled into the shadows at the far end of the bar.

Lillian Gadwick's voice slithered into his ears and to his brain. "I welcome you, Lieutenant Voss, to the ranks of *my* king's guard. Your duties are simple." She motioned to the cloaked figures. "You and your men shall serve as sentries along the border of my homeland. In return, when opportunity allows, you may enjoy the hospitality of my tavern. And I shall tolerate your existence. Until I do not."

"You are not sane." His voice came out a ragged whisper. "I cannot be sane. This is all madness. Madness!"

A low moan rose from the far shadows: Sergeant Landrake's tortured voice. A few garbled syllables followed, as if the awful thing he'd become were attempting to speak but had no control of whatever now passed for its mouth.

Voss felt coils of cold force, like an unseen, living shroud, beginning to tighten around him. Although he could still see and hear, something like transparent fabric wound around his eyes, over his ears, and drew painfully taut, as if by invisible hands. His eyes remained focused straight ahead, for he could not move them. Or see his own body.

The woman's airy voice continued. "As you may have perceived, Lieutenant Voss, your very constitution has been altered. Thus, you are now well suited for the crucial task that lies ahead of you. So let us venture . . . elsewhere."

Lillian Gadwick's gray-clad figure slid into his field of vision with the crawling Landrake-thing fawning at her heels. Standing before Voss, she lifted her arms above her head and recited a series of words or syllables he could not comprehend. As if a noonday sun had flared into existence, the nighttime darkness outside the windows dissolved under a sudden, harsh brilliance. A smooth, intricate dance of her hands, and the tavern's heavy wooden door swung inward.

"Proceed."

Some force beyond his will impelled him forward, and it was only when he found himself halfway to the gaping door that he realized his feet had not carried him, for they no longer touched the floor.

He was *gliding* forward.

A chorus of shuffling, whispering sounds rose behind him, and he realized his cloaked companions—his former troops—had fallen into a column behind him. Together they drifted toward the blazing unknown beyond the tavern door.

The witch crossed the threshold first. He followed immediately, and as his vision adjusted to a new, *alien* spectrum of light and color, his heart—or whatever organ now thundered in his chest—nearly exploded.

Chaos reigned in a dizzying sky. Black stars burned in a brilliant, white-gold backdrop, though Voss could see no sun or moon. Before him a vast body of metallic-silver water extended toward the far horizon, above which the contours of innumerable, insanely distant towers and spires shimmered like jewels against the mad sky.

Beyond a long, rocky slope, along the sea's near shore, uncountable masses of wraithlike figures ringed the body of silver water as far as his vision could reach. Before them, treading up the slope like a gigantic, upright insect, came something tall, gangly, unclothed, with glittering, onyx-black skin. Its pounding footsteps sounded like the booming beats of an immense kettle drum.

Lillian Gadwick bowed low before the inhuman figure. Then she straightened, and her now-powerful voice rang out and echoed over the silver sea. "I bring new additions to our king's guard."

The monstrous black thing towered high above the diminutive woman. It bore a tall, oblong head, mounted on a neck so thin it appeared to float above its stick-figure torso.

Like Voss himself—and his parade of cloaked wraiths—the black giant had no face.

But he felt its unseen gaze. And he knew that he and his once-human troops now served *this* ungodly thing, even as the witch, his mistress, also served it.

He had no idea what lay before him, and he despaired, for whatever he and his men had become, he knew, perhaps by way of some second sight, that none of them would ever die, however desperately they might wish it, in the service of Lillian Gadwick or her faceless demonmaster.

Not until *it* or the witch deemed otherwise.

As he and his corps of wraiths moved forward and slid into place, joining the legions of identical figures along the shore of the silver sea, something stirred in the far distance. Drawn by the now-familiar force that had subjugated his will, Voss's arms rose to his sides and stretched outward until his bone-white fingers slipped from his cloak's dark sleeves and touched those of the beings to either side. The hand on his left was missing its endmost digit.

That one had been named Carlisle. Now, like Voss and the rest of his company, he had become a mere cog in the endless, spectral blockade against whatever was coming.

When he saw countless gigantic, conical forms break the surface of the water and advance at incredible speed, all sprouting arrays of thorny, segmented arms that slashed to and fro like living, avaricious scythes, his response would have been to scream.

If only he were able.

Unimaginable worlds away, as he prepared his army to break camp at Alamance Creek and march into battle at Guilford Courthouse, North Carolina, General Charles Cornwallis received an infuriating report of yet more desertions, including Lieutenant William Voss, of the Duke of Wellington's Regiment, and nine of his most outstanding soldiers.

He would have—and had—expected far better of such men.

From Matthew Hale, *The History of Witches and Wizards* (1720)

The Horned Women

Lady Wilde

A rich woman sat up late one night carding and preparing wool, while all the family and servants were asleep. Suddenly a knock was given at the door, and a voice called—"Open! open!"

"Who is there?" said the woman of the house.

"I am the Witch of the One Horn," was answered.

The mistress, supposing that one of her neighbours had called and required assistance, opened the door, and a woman entered, having in her hand a pair of wool carders, and bearing a horn on her forehead, as if growing there. She sat down by the fire in silence, and began to card the wool with violent haste. Suddenly she paused and said aloud: "Where are the women? They delay too long."

Then a second knock came to the door, and a voice called as before—"Open! open!"

The mistress felt herself constrained to rise and open to the call, and immediately a second witch entered, having two horns on her forehead, and in her hand a wheel for spinning the wool.

"Give me place," she said; "I am the Witch of the Two Horns," and she began to spin as quick as lightning.

And so the knocks went on, and the call was heard, and the witches entered, until at last twelve women sat round the fire—the first with one horn, the last with twelve horns. And they carded the thread, and turned their spinning wheels, and wound and wove, all singing together an ancient rhyme, but no word did they speak to the mistress of the house. Strange to hear, and frightful to look upon were these twelve women, with their horns and their wheels; and the mistress felt near to death, and she tried to rise that she might call for help, but she could not move, nor could she utter a word or a cry, for the spell of the witches was upon her.

Then one of them called to her in Irish and said—

"Rise, woman, and make us a cake."

Then the mistress searched for a vessel to bring water from the well that she might mix the meal and make the cake, but she could find none. And they said to her—

"Take a sieve and bring water in it."

And she took the sieve and went to the well; but the water poured from it, and she could fetch none for the cake, and she sat down by the well and wept. Then a voice came by her and said—

"Take yellow clay and moss and bind them together and plaster the sieve so that it will hold."

This she did, and the sieve held the water for the cake. And the voice said again—

"Return, and when thou comest to the north angle of the house, cry aloud three times and say, 'The mountain of the Fenian women and the sky over it is all on fire.'"

And she did so.

When the witches inside heard the call, a great and terrible cry broke from their lips, and they rushed forth with wild lamentations and shrieks, and fled away to Slieve-namon, where was their chief abode. But the Spirit of the Well bade the mistress of the house to enter and prepare her home against the enchantments of the witches if they returned again.

And first, to break their spells, she sprinkled the water in which she had washed her child's feet (the feet-water) outside the door on the threshold; secondly, she took the cake which the witches had made in her absence, of meal mixed with the blood drawn from the sleeping family. And she broke the cake in bits, and placed a bit in the mouth of each sleeper, and they were restored; and she took the cloth they had woven and placed it half in and half out of the chest with the padlock; and lastly, she secured the door with a great cross-beam fastened in the jambs, so that they could not enter. And having done these things she waited.

Not long were the witches in coming back, and they raged and called for vengeance.

"Open! open!" they screamed. "Open, feet-water!"

"I cannot," said the feet-water, "I am scattered on the ground and my path is down to the Lough."

"Open, open, wood and tree and beam!" they cried to the door.

"I cannot," said the door, "for the beam is fixed in the jambs and I have no power to move."

"Open, open, cake that we have made and mingled with blood," they cried again.

"I cannot," said the cake, "for I am broken and bruised, and my blood is on the lips of the sleeping children."

Then the witches rushed through the air with great cries, and fled back to Slieve-namon, uttering strange curses on the Spirit of the Well, who had wished their ruin; but the woman and the house were left in peace, and a mantle dropped by one of the witches in her flight was kept hung up by the mistress as a sign of the night's awful contest; and this mantle was in possession of the same family, from generation to generation for five hundred years after.

From Francisco Maria Guazzo, Compendium Maleficarum *(1608)*

A Lowland Witch Ballad

William Bell Scott

The old witch-wife beside her door
    Sat spinning with a watchful ear,
A horse's hoof upon the road
    Is what she waits for, longs to hear.

The mottled gloaming dusky grew,
    Or else we might a furrow trace,
Sowed with small bones and leaves of yew,
    Across the road from place to place.

Hark he comes! The young bridegroom,
    Singing gaily down the hill,
Rides on, rides blindly to his doom,
    His heart that witch hath sworn to kill.

Up to the fosse he rode so free,
    There his steed stumbled and he fell,
He cannot pass, nor turn, nor flee;
    His song is done, he's in the spell.

She dances round him where he stands,
    Her distaff touches both his feet,
She blows upon his eyes and hands,
    He has no power his fate to cheat.

"Ye cannot visit her to-night,
    Nor ever again," the witch-wife cried;
"But thou shalt do as I think right,
    And do it swift without a guide.

"Upon the top of Tintock hill
        This night there rests the yearly mist,
In silence go, your tongue keep still,
        And find for me the dead man's kist.

"Within the kist there is a cup,
        Thou 'lt find it by the dead man's shine,
Take it thus I thus fold it up,—
        It holds for me the wisdom-wine.

"Go to the top of Tintock hill,
        Grope within that eerie mist,
Whatever happens, keep quite still
        Until ye find the dead man's kist.

"The kist will open, take the cup,
        Heed ye not the dead man's shine,
Take it thus, thus fold it up,
        Bring it to me and I am thine."

He went, he could make answer none,
        He went, he found all as she said,
Before the dawn had well begun
        She had the cup from that strange bed.

Into the hut she fled at once,
        She drank the wine;—forthwith, behold!
A radiant damozel advance
        From that black door in silken fold.

The little Circe flower she held
        Towards the boy with such a smile
Made his heart leap, he was compelled
        To take it gently as a child.

She turned, he followed, passed the door,
    Which closed behind: at noon next day,
    Ambling on his mule that way,
The Abbot found the steed, no more,
    The rest was lost in glamoury.

From L[awrence] P[rice], The Witch of the Woodlands *(1655)*

Why We Don't Dig Up Witches

John Kachuba

Will Shifflet looked up, saw the crows settling in the trees eyeing him intently and thought, I am *not* going to dig up the witch.

He turned up the collar of his jacket against the wind and jammed his hands into his pockets, hunching his shoulders to keep from shivering. A broad belly of gray clouds scudded across the treetops. The chill wind carried upon it the scent of rain. A few moments later, fat drops of icy water splattered on the barren ground.

Fitzpatrick, the new city manager, blathered on about something, but Will paid him no mind. He watched the rain splash upon the weathered gravestone at his feet, the water bleeding over the worn letters, swinging a crazy arc through the "C" in "Cranna" before dropping to the ground.

Fitzpatrick and the town engineer looked down the slope to the road that passed the cemetery as they discussed the project. Will stamped his work boots upon the frozen ground, trying to restore some warmth to his feet. Widen the road? A dumb-ass idea. The details bored him. All he knew was that Fitzpatrick would demand that he dig up the witch.

Will remembered a time from the old days, when he was just a boy, his mother telling him about the witch's last days:

Hannah Cranna lit one last candle and now the tiny cabin was bathed in light, as if it were noon on a summer's day. Outside the dark windows, the winter wind rattled the trees like bones. An occasional puff of wind, soft as a dying man's breath, would sigh into the room and set the candle flames dancing. But Hannah was not in a dancing mood—Old Boreas was dead.

A small wooden box that she had cobbled together lay on a table in the center of the room. Candles surrounded it, dripping wax onto the rough wood. Hannah stood over the box, looking down at her longtime friend and companion. Immense grief washed over her, followed oddly by a sense of relief that it was over, that it would soon be over for her as well.

She stretched her pale, gnarled fingers down to the box and stroked the rooster's ebony feathers one last time. Soft. She thought of him following her everywhere, thought of the comfort he brought her in the long, lonely nights.

A tear fell upon the dead bird. She wiped her eyes, picked up the wooden lid, and laid it across the box, nailing it shut.

She took her shawl from the peg near the fire and wrapped it around her shoulders, pulling it forward to cover her head. She picked up the box, opened the door, and stepped out into the cold night.

The trees waved skeletal limbs against the starry sky as she passed below. An owl hooted. Beneath a large elm was a hole she had dug earlier that day. Hannah carefully placed the box in the earth. The shovel stood nearby in a pile of dirt. She refilled the hole and now the tears came. She couldn't stop them.

Will sat in the Public Works garage, sipping coffee, his feet propped on the desk. DeMarco and some of the others were watching TV in the back room, but he had no interest in that. Through the window he watched a windblown curtain of water ripple over the street, slowing the traffic along the town green to a crawl. Gray clouds hunkered over town. Mist swallowed the steeple of the Congregational Church across the street. There wouldn't be much work done today. That was okay with him.

He wasn't eager to get back to the cemetery. He wasn't superstitious, but it didn't seem right to go around disturbing dead people, especially dead people who were also witches. And one, a witch who, according to his mother, could possibly be his ancestor. It was a stupid idea, anyway, widening the road. Who needed that? The town had been around since 1639 and Turkey Roost Road had been there all that time. The road didn't need anything except resurfacing every now and then.

But Will knew that things were changing in his town. Despite the objections of almost everyone, this Fitzpatrick, with his big ideas about development, his expensive suits and shiny new BMW, would have the town covered over with condos and shopping centers if he had his way.

Will took a swallow of coffee. Sure, easy for him, he thought. He doesn't have to dig up a witch.

Will had plenty of doubts about Fitzpatrick. He had heard the rumors and figured there was probably something to them. Embezzling. Bribery. He wasn't surprised. It seemed that's how business was done these days. *Progress.* Were people so dishonest, so morally bankrupt in the old days? Would Hannah have stood for that?

Will's mother had said:

The first thing young Mrs. Peterson noticed when Hannah opened the cabin door was the absence of the old witch's cantankerous rooster. Still, she set the bundle of firewood on the hearth quickly, expecting the ghastly bird to fly at her out of nowhere. She nodded to Hannah and turned to go but the old woman caught her by the arm.

Hannah dragged the frightened woman to a chair and sat her in it. She did not smile or even thank Mrs. Peterson for her gift, having grown accustomed to the kindnesses of the townsfolk who held her in awe, if not outright fear.

"Now you listen, girl," Hannah said, as though lecturing a schoolgirl. "Old Boreas is dead and I'm bound to follow him."

The young woman was speechless. She stared at Hannah, her eyes wide with fright. The witch shook her roughly by the shoulders.

"Pay attention! Don't go stupid on me, girl. When I am dead you must not bury me until after sundown. Not a moment before, do you hear?"

Mrs. Peterson nodded.

"Speak up! Do you understand me? Not one moment!"

The witch's face was inches from her own. "Yes," Mrs. Peterson whispered.

"Good girl. And another thing: my coffin is to be hand-carried to the burial ground. That's the only way." Hannah shook the young woman one more time for good measure. "Mind me, girl! Do as I say."

Mrs. Peterson swallowed hard and said she would. Who would cross a witch?

Without saying another word, Hannah opened the door. Mrs. Peterson didn't linger.

They got an early start the next morning. The storm had finally blown itself out and now the sky was a hard, clear blue. Will felt he could reach up and rap his knuckles against it. He bounced along in the high seat of the truck next to Haines, the kid. Will didn't drive much anymore: eyes too weak. He didn't care. Now he had more time to look around, to see where they were going, even though after all these years he could see the route perfectly with his eyes shut.

The kid was also bouncing on the torn seat, drumming skinny fingers on the wheel in time to music he heard in his ear buds. A hole in the grimy dashboard marked where the radio used to be. Will watched the kid bopping to his music and smiled to himself, barely remembering what it had been like to be nineteen.

The road rolled beneath the broad yellow hood of the truck as if the vehicle were sucking it in. That would keep everyone busy, wouldn't it? Trucks that ate the highway so PW could get back out there and repave. Will thought that if such a truck could be invented, Fitzpatrick would figure out a way to make a quick buck on it.

They were driving down Turkey Roost Road. The ancient oaks and maples marching down from the hillsides revealed a few houses, but the landscape hadn't changed much in the three centuries since settlers came up from the New Haven colony. Will knew all about these stalwart settlers. His ancestors had been among them, including one who may have been a distant relation to Hannah Cranna herself. His knowledge was gleaned from family stories and rumors, legends and gossip. He knew the history of this place, heard its rhythm in his bones.

Haines slowed the truck, waited for a minivan engorged with kids to pass, then turned left into the cemetery. Will and the kid climbed down from the cab. They didn't take tools from the truck. This trip was merely an inspection. Will's thirty-plus years in Public Works had taught him the value of several inspections before doing any work.

A fringe of trees bordered the burial ground on three sides. The road edged the fourth. There wasn't much left of the cemetery, no more than two dozen or so stones leaning in the yellow grass, most of them illegible, some mere stumps, like broken teeth set in the rotting earth. The witch's grave was in the near corner of the lot, on a little knoll that rolled down to the road. The frozen grass crunched beneath their boots.

They stood before the stone, the kid bobbing and dipping his head to his internal music.

Ice crystals glittered in the letters chiseled into the stone.

HANNAH CRANNA
1783 – 1860
Wife of Capt. Joseph Hovey

Will wondered why she had invented a new name for herself after her husband, the captain, mysteriously fell from a cliff, widowing her at a young age. Some said she changed her name when she sealed a pact with the devil; others said she just wanted to start anew. As for her husband's mysterious fall from a cliffside path he had walked so often he could navigate it with his eyes shut? Well, it was said—and probably *known* by more than a few—that he was not scrupulous about his marriage vows and was plowing at least one other man's field.

Hannah believed in vows.

A chill wind blew across the cemetery, rocking the barren trees. Will noticed a dozen or more crows perched high in the branches, riding the wind as though sailing a Yankee clipper. The kid watched the birds too, standing still for once, his hands in his overalls.

Will turned his attention back to the grave. It was parallel to the road, on a knoll that had eroded extensively. He was surprised the witch hadn't already rolled out of her grave into the street—what was left of her, that is. Two other graves were set in line with Hannah's. Will shook his head. Those graves would have to be moved as well.

"That's *progress*, Will," Fitzpatrick had said. "You can't stop it."

"It ain't right, though," Will said. "We have no business messing around with dead folks."

"You'll move them, or I'll get someone who will."

If Will had had his way he would have settled things with Fitzpatrick out behind the garage, man to man, but things weren't done that way anymore. *Progress.* Fighting would result in a lawsuit and jail time.

He wasn't having any of it. He tried to think of ways to sabotage the task but couldn't come up with anything. Maybe the kid had some ideas, but when he saw Haines wandering around the cemetery like a pup sniffing his way through a junkyard, he decided he would be useless. As he walked between the graves, Will felt the ground beginning to soften. It had been a mild winter so far, courtesy of El Niño and climate change. Sunshine aided the thaw.

He stopped beside Hannah's stone. He noticed the crack snaking diagonally across the stone, a new one he realized, probably caused by the latest thaw.

It's up to you now, old girl, he thought. *I can't stop them.*

Something spooked the crows roosting in the trees. They rose up in a frenzy of flapping wings and raucous cries. Their shadows streamed over the grave. That's when Will noticed the thin rivulet of black fluid oozing from below the grave, meandering down to the street.

He remembered his mother's story:

Mrs. Peterson trudged through the new-fallen snow, a wicker basket of freshly baked bread slung from one arm. She could see Hannah's cabin in the distance, tucked in a hollow beneath a grove of towering hemlocks. She dragged her feet through the deep snow, breaking the first path to the cabin. It was clear from the unblemished drift piled against the door that the old woman had not yet ventured outside.

Mrs. Peterson knocked. No answer. Snow feathers floated from the hemlock branches, reminding Mrs. Peterson of Hannah's ferocious rooster. The bird was dead, but she could somehow sense its presence. She nervously scanned the woods for any sign of it.

She knocked once more. Silence. She slowly pushed the door open.

A single candle was burning on the table, barely illuminating the room. Mrs. Peterson set the basket on the floor near the door. In a dark corner of the cabin she saw the bed and the body lying on it. When she drew closer to the bed, Mrs. Peterson realized the witch was dead.

Within a few hours the undertaker had Hannah's body safely secured in a simple pine box. Despite Mrs. Peterson's objections, the men wasted no time remov-

ing the witch from her home. A hazy winter sun stood in the silver sky as a party of men slogged through the snow with the coffin. It was an uphill climb to where the wagon stood waiting in the lane, and the men were panting by the time they placed the coffin in the back of it.

The undertaker, muffled in a black cloak, flicked the reins and whistled the horses up. At first the two horses danced in their traces, steam blowing from their nostrils, their ears laid flat back. A second snap of the reins got them moving through the snow.

The men silently followed the wagon.

The lane rose where it met Turkey Roost Road. The men heard the scraping sound even before they saw the coffin sliding from the back of the wagon. One of them rushed forward to catch it, but not quickly enough. The box lurched from the wagon bed and shot out onto the road. All the men could think to do was jump out of its path. As it hit the snowy lane, the coffin picked up speed and flew back down the slope.

The men, dumbstruck, watched the coffin recede in the distance. By the time they came to their senses and took off after it, the coffin had come to rest against the cabin door.

The men once again took hold of the coffin and once again wrestled it up to the wagon. The wagon had proceeded only about twenty yards before the coffin burst forth a second time. This time the men were able to grab it before it slid too far and hoisted it up into the wagon bed. They stood around the wagon, worn out by their task. The sun was low in the sky, a pale-yellow smudge on the western horizon. When the men had recovered their wind, the wagon started up again. Now two of them sat on the coffin.

As the wagon made Turkey Roost Road, the coffin began to shake. The two men, eyes wide with fright, held on as best they could as the pine box bucked and heaved beneath them. The others jumped into the wagon and piled on top of the coffin, but still it quaked and trembled, threatening to pitch them all into the road.

The panicked undertaker lashed the reins. The horses bolted, the wagon slewing wildly on the slippery road, the men jostling in the back like popping corn.

By the time the wagon reached the cemetery, the sun had disappeared from the sky. The coffin lay quietly in the rear of the wagon while the men dug the grave. It

65

was dark when the men finally carried the coffin into the cemetery and lowered it into the earth by the light of the gravediggers' lanterns.

As the exhausted burial party headed back into town, they noticed a reddish-glow in the woods down the lane. Hannah's cabin was in flames. No one moved to put the fire out.

Will didn't always attend town meetings, but he had no choice tonight. Fitzpatrick wanted all the PW guys present. Why? Did he think the town was out to lynch him?

Will, the kid, and a few others sat in the rear of the packed meeting room. The Public Works boss, DeMarco, sat beside Fitzpatrick at a table up front. Will thought the city manager looked nervous as he fiddled with the knot of his tie, but DeMarco, sitting back in his chair with his arms folded across his chest, looked formidable.

After the meeting was called to order, Fitzpatrick gave a long-winded presentation, complete with a slick video, about widening Turkey Roost Road. The video showed its present condition, especially where it passed the cemetery, and an artist's rendering depicted the future roadway, a highway of *progress.*

The crowd wasn't impressed. Too expensive, they said. Too much traffic. Too many people. The city manager's face turned scarlet as he tried to defend his plan. Will thought the man was having a heart attack.

But the next morning Fitzpatrick was his old self again, strutting through the Public Works parking lot.

"Looks like somebody got lucky last night," one of the men said.

Someone else snickered. Ugly rumors said Fitzpatrick would screw anything that held still long enough. Including the mayor's wife. Will didn't doubt them.

That's what *progress* brought. No morality anymore, anywhere. Will guessed it wasn't that way in Hannah's time. If she wanted things orderly and peaceful, *moral,* who would argue with her? Who would dare cross a witch?

Later that morning, while spreading sand on an icy patch of Turkey Hill Road, Will noticed black fluid dribbling down the slope beneath the cemetery, saw it pooling at the side of the road. He thought it was oil at first, maybe leaking from some old tank buried under the ground, but closer inspection told him it wasn't oil. He didn't know what it was. And it had a terrible odor. He threw a shovelful of sand over the puddle.

By the time he got back to the garage, everyone had left for the day. That's all right; he could use the overtime, he thought, while washing up in the restroom. He took a shortcut through the administration building, heading for the parking lot behind the building. It was dark inside, but he knew his way around.

Something thumped against a wall.

He stopped.

He heard the thumping again.

He saw a faint light glowing beneath the city manager's office door, and when he drew closer he heard other sounds. He wasn't so old that he didn't recognize the sounds of love. All right, *lust*. He didn't know who the woman was. It didn't matter.

Damn, he thought, right in the office! Had the man no shame? No morality at all? He left the building and stepped into the night, wondering about Fitzpatrick's poor wife. It troubled him all the way home, this nasty business with the city manager.

Outsider.

Troublemaker.

Sleazeball.

He was angry that his little town, this place where his family had lived for centuries, was being corrupted by something foul. Polluted. Hannah would have been furious. He tried to think again of ways he could sabotage the road project.

Two days later he was sitting in the Public Works garage, eating a sandwich, when he saw Fitzpatrick leave the building in his BMW. Will had the police scanner on as usual but wasn't paying much attention to it. It was the kid, Haines, who came in later and told him they had a

67

mess to clean up on Turkey Roost Road. Didn't seem too important, the kid said, so you could probably finish your sandwich.

But when they drove out a few minutes later and saw the red and blue flashing lights of the emergency vehicles, Will knew the kid was wrong, as usual. It was much worse than he had said. It was obvious there wasn't anything the paramedics could do for Fitzpatrick, who lay in the street beside what used to be a silver BMW but was now nothing more than a corrugated piece of scrap-metal wedged up against an old oak tree.

Will walked away from the police and paramedics, as they covered the body. He stood on the edge of the oily, black slick that lay across the road. Tire tracks skittered through it. He looked at the slick for some time, wondering, before lifting his eyes to the knoll below the cemetery. It was clean now, no trace of fluid oozing down the slope. Whatever it was, it had emptied itself out.

From Matthew Hale, The History of Witches and Wizards *(1720)*

From *An Examen of Witches*

Henri Boguet

Chapter XI
Of the Copulation of the Devil with Male and Female Witches

The third point in Françoise Secretain's confession was that she had had carnal relations with Satan. Clauda Jamprost, Jacquema Paget, Antoine Tornier, Antoine Gandillon, Clauda Janguillaume, Thievenne Paget, Rollande du Vernois, Janne Platet and Clauda Paget confessed the same thing; and it has been revealed in the examinations of witches that they all have this connexion with Satan. The Devil uses them so because he knows that women love carnal pleasures, and he means to bind them to his allegiance by such agreeable provocations. Moreover, there is nothing which makes a woman more subject and loyal to a man than that he should abuse her body.

And since male witches are addicted no less than female to this pleasure, the Devil also appears as a woman to satisfy them. This he does chiefly at the Sabbat, according to the reports of the father and son, George and Pierre Gandillon, and of those women whom I have several times named, who all agree in saying that in their assemblies there are many demons, of whom some take the form of women for the men, and others that of men for the women. These demons are called Incubi and Succubi. And it is no new thing for Satan to draw us to him by these means; for we read that, in order to tempt St. Anthony, St. Jerome and other devout persons, who passed their life in the solitude of the desert, he commonly appeared to them in the form of a courtesan.

There is also another reason for the coupling of the Devil with a witch, which is that the sin may thereby become the more grievous. For if God abominates the coupling of an infidel with a Christian, how much more shall He detest that of a man with the Devil? Moreover, by this means man's natural semen is wasted, with the result that the love between man and wife is often turned to hatred, than which no worse a misfortune could happen to the state of matrimony.

Chapter XII
Whether Such Copulation Exists in the Imagination Only

But since there are some who maintain that the coupling of which we have just spoken exists in the imagination only, it will be well to say something here on this subject. For some treat the matter with derision, some are doubtful about it, and others firmly believe it to be a fact. St. Augustine appears to be among these last, as also St. Thomas Aquinas and several other later learned authorities. But the witches' confessions which I have had make me think that there is truth in this matter; for they have all admitted that they have coupled with the Devil, and that his semen was very cold; and this is confirmed by the reports of Paul Grilland and the Inquisitors of the Faith. Jacquema Paget added that she had several times taken in her hand the member of the Demon which lay with her, and that it was as cold as ice and a good finger's length, but not so thick as that of a man. Thievenne Paget and Antoine Tornier also added that the members of their demons were as long and big as one of their fingers; and Thievenne Paget said, moreover, that when Satan coupled with her she had as much pain as a woman in travail. Françoise Secretain said that, whilst she was in the act, she felt something burning in her stomach; and nearly all witches affirm that this coupling is by no means pleasurable to them, both because of Satan's ugliness and deformity, and because of the physical pain which it causes them, as we have just said.

The ugliness and deformity lies in the fact that Satan couples with witches sometimes in the form of a black man, sometimes in that of some animal, as a dog or a cat or a ram. With Thievenne Paget and Antoine Tornier he lay in the form of a black man; and when he coupled with Jacquema Paget and Antoine Gandillon he took the shape of a black ram with horns: Françoise Secretain confessed that her demon appeared sometimes as a dog, sometimes as a cat, and sometimes as a fowl when he wished to have carnal intercourse with her. For all these

70

reasons I am convinced that there is real and actual copulation between a witch and a demon; for what is there to prevent the Devil, when he has taken the form of an animal, from coition with a witch? In Toulouse and Paris women have been known to make sexual abuse of a natural dog; and it seems to me quite to the point to refer here to the legends of Pasiphaë and other such women.

Another matter that I must mention, which is as strange as it is true, concerns one Antide Colas of Betoncourt in the district of Baume. She was imprisoned at that place for witchcraft, and it was found when visiting her that she had a hole beneath her navel, quite contrary to nature. This hole was examined on the eleventh of July, 1598, by Master Nicolas Milliere of Regnaucourt, Chirurgeon, who thrust his probe deeply into it in the presence of his servant, and of Antoinette Mongin, Jannette Bolet and Claudine Menestrey, who were required to be there as witnesses; and then the witch confessed that her Devil, whom she called Lizabet, had sexual connexion with her through this hole, and her husband through the natural hole; but afterwards, when she was taken by order of the Court to the prison of Dôle, and they wished to examine this hole, it was found to be closed up, and there remained nothing but a scar. This woman was burned alive on the twentieth of February, 1599. But who would believe that Satan even lies with witches in prison? Yet this woman of whom we have just told confessed that he did so; as also did Thievenne Paget, who said that the Devil had lain with her three times while she was in prison.

When Satan means to lie with a witch in the form of a man, he takes to himself the body of some man who has been hanged. But even if he has only a body formed from the air, there is still nothing to prevent him from intercourse with a witch; for in that case he makes the body of air so dense that it is palpable (for air is, of itself, palpable), and consequently capable of coition with, and even defloration of a woman. And why should not this be easy for him, seeing that he is powerful enough to overthrow a town or a city or a kingdom? And as for his semen, he has but too plentiful a supply, even were there no other source of it, in that which he receives when he acts as a Succubus.

And therefore I thoroughly believe all that has been written of Fauns, Satyrs and woodland gods, which were no more than demons, and were inordinately lustful and lascivious. Also I think that we may consider under this head the stories we are told of the wantonnesses of Numa, and of the nymph Egeria, and of several others whom the poets have particularly mentioned.

Similarly we find in the West Indies that their gods, which they call Cocoto, lay with women and had sexual intercourse with them; unless it was really certain lickerish men who abused them, as Decius Mundus, a Roman knight, whose story Josephus tells in his Antiquities, did to Paulina under pretence of being the God Anubis.

But to return to Françoise Secretain, it is a strange thing that Satan lay with her in the shape of a fowl. I am of opinion that she meant to say a gander instead of a fowl, for that is a form which Satan often takes, and therefore we have the proverb that Satan has feet like a goose. Yet it would be as easy for him to take the shape of a fowl as that of a gander. For we know that he has at different times assumed the shape of a dog for the same purpose, and we have two remarkable examples of this: one of a dog, said to be a demon, which used to lift up the robes of the nuns in a convent of the diocese of Cologne in order to abuse them; the other, of certain dogs found on the beds of the nuns of a convent on Mount Hesse in Germany.

Song of Fae-Land

Dmitri Akers

The elder witches sing the songs of Fae,
That echo in an otherworldly clime,
Beyond the ears of men and light of day,
Beneath those ancient graves of rot and rime,
That wake with wights and sprites that stirred from time,
Within the shadows, pupae break their shells,
As Butterflies may raise their wings of lime,
And dry their bodies in the flaming hells,
To fly towards the skies, to knolls of deaf'ning knells.

Along the hues of Zephyrus' own breath,
The Butterflies are flying o'er the graves
To cast their spectres o'er those sites of death
That Fae had built with ancient stones and staves
Beside the wood of wyrds and satyrs' caves,
The magick realms that birth the death of change;
The tombs and headstones, etched with glaives,
Contain remains of Faerie, which derange
Design with horrid shapes, that witchery arrange.

Upon the Butterflies' own quiv'ring wings,
A charnel dust begins to slough—as death
May slough the former husks of living things—
Against the busts of Sobek, Ra, and Seth,
With hieroglyphs that dwarf *aleph* and *beth;*
The Underworld is spewing what it holds,
As fleeing souls have oped the Gates, they sing!
They fling and loose the chains of hellish folds,
They flee those azure fires, they flee the Pharoah's moulds!

The Butterflies are hov'ring o'er the ranks
Of souls, and plunge to drink the wine of *Death;*

Thro' Gates of Hell, they fly and find the banks
Of flowing streams of bile—that rotting Lethe!
A Fae is breathing but the death of breath,
The Butterflies have swooped and heard its whine,
They sink their mouths into the Faerie's shanks,
To sounds of choral din, they drink the wine,
Beneath the singing souls, that bore the witches' sign.

From [James Carmichael?], Newes from Scotland *(1591)*

Dolls

Ramsey Campbell

Cold as the February wind, the full moon blazed over the fields. Anne Norton heard the wind ruffle the wheat a moment before it plucked at her naked body. She shivered, but not from the cold, which hardly touched her. Already the power was coursing through her; already the belladonna and the aconite were shivering through her genitals and her legs. She ran behind her husband John through the gate in their stone wall.

Once out of the garden she glanced back at the cottages of Camside. Some were empty, she knew, and so was the Cooper farmhouse at the edge of the village. The rest were dark and sleeping, without the faintest gleam of a rush-light. Across the common, the high voice of a sheep joined her in derisive mirth. Ahead of her, John had reached the edge of the wood. Shadows streamed down his naked back.

The wood was quiet, muffled. Only the Cambrook stream gossiped incessantly in the darkness. The others must already be waiting at the meeting-place. Now the ointment seemed to pour hotly down her legs. She ran more swiftly, gliding through splashes of moonlight, as the trees began to toss in their sleep. The wind stroked her genitals, which gulped eagerly.

She plunged into the Cambrook, shattering the agitated ropes of moonlight. Beneath her feet pebbles gnashed shrilly, with a hard yet liquid sound. When she reached the bank she looked back sharply, for she'd heard the stream stir with more life than belonged to water. But the water was flowing innocently by.

As if the gnashing of the pebbles had been the earth's last snatch at her she felt herself leave the ground. She saw the luminous ground race by beneath the skimming blur of her feet. Ranks of trees danced beside her, huge and slow but increasingly wild, branches about one another's shoulders. She felt all the strength and abandon of the trees flood through her.

In a moment, or perhaps an hour—for the wood seemed to have swelled like fire, to cover the whole countryside—she had reached the glade.

Everyone was there. The four Coopers were standing in a row at the edge of the glade, waiting impatiently, restless as the trees. Elizabeth Cooper glared at Anne with open hostility. Anne grimaced at her; she knew it was John at whom the old woman wanted to glare, jealous of his power. The Coopers had preserved the witchcraft for so long alone that now they were unwilling to allow power to anyone else. But they dared not oppose John. Giddy with borrowed power and borne up by the fierce ointment, Anne strode into the glade, feeling her feet sink to earth.

John had been halted by Robert Allen. The man's eyes were rolling out of focus, so that he seemed to address someone behind John's shoulder. "Celia Poole called my Nell a witch," he said. "She meant it as a joke, till she saw how Nell looked. She thinks slowly, but she'll come to the truth."

John nodded. He seemed to withdraw from his eyes, sinking down to a secret center of himself, leaving his eyes glazed by moonlight. Watching, Anne flinched away. Though his power sustained her, it was unthinkably terrifying; it was something she dared not ponder, just as her wedding night had been. "Celia Poole," he said. "By the time she is sure, she will be unable to tell."

Adam Cooper stepped forward, defiantly impatient, almost interrupting. "Introibo," he shouted.

At once Elizabeth Cooper began to chant. It was in no language Anne knew, she wasn't sure it was even composed of words: a howling and yodelling, a clogged gurgle. Sometimes sounds were repeated monotonously, sometimes Anne recognized no sound that she'd heard from the previous meeting. She suspected the old woman of making up the chant. None of this mattered, for the Coopers had linked arms and were dancing wildly around the glade, the outermost dragging the bystanders into the dance as they passed.

Anne was snatched away by Adam, almost overbalancing. John

had been caught by Jane Cooper, scarcely fifteen but already plumply rounded. Anne felt a hot pang of jealousy. But now that John had joined the dance they were whirling faster, spinning her away from her jealousy, from everything but the linked circle of thirteen turning about the axis of the center of the glade, whizzing above the ground.

Clouds shrank back from the moon; light washed over the glade, and the shadows of the capering trees grasped at the earth. Anne felt her husband's power surging through the circle, lifting her free of the ground. When she opened her mouth the chant spilled out, incomprehensible yet exhilarating. Beside her Adam's penis reared up, unsheathing its tip, enticing her gaze.

Suddenly the dance had spun her out of the circle; she rolled panting over the damp grass. The circle was breaking up, and Adam ran to the edge of the glade, where he'd hidden a basket. From the basket he produced a black hen, which he decapitated, squeezing the body between his thighs to pump the gory fountain higher. "Corpus domini nostri," he shouted, elevating the head toward the moon.

He'd changed the ritual again, Anne realized; last time they'd eaten fish which he'd consecrated, and the time before there had been biscuits like flattened communion wafers. All the Coopers' magic changed from month to month, largely because of Elizabeth's failing memory. In this case it didn't matter, for the meaning of the ritual remained the same. "Amen!" Anne cried with the rest as they lay on the ground, hearts pounding. That would show Parson Jenner how frightened she was of him.

"Amen!" they shouted. "Domini nostri! Domini nostri!" And nodding to Robert Allen, John rose to his feet and left the glade. The twelve fell silent. The moon hung still and clear. Even the trees were subdued, like uneasy spectators holding their breath. Their shadows wavered to stillness, as if the frightened anticipation of the twelve had gripped them fast. Anne's heart scurried as time paced, slow, slower.

Before John returned his power had filled the glade, cold and inhuman as the moonlight. Nobody looked at his face. Everyone gazed at his hands, where all his power was focused. His hands displayed a knife and a faceless wooden doll.

Robert Allen refused to take the doll at first. He gazed at it, and at the immobile moon-bright hand that held it out to him, with something like dread. Not until Nell gestured furiously at him did he clutch the doll, closing his eyes and squeezing his face tight about a silent curse.

As soon as Robert handed back the doll, John slashed at its head half-a-dozen times with the knife. His movements seemed casual, negligent, practically aimless. But now there was a face on the doll: low brow, long blunt nose, high cheekbones and wide mouth: Celia Poole's face.

Though she had watched him carving before he had turned to witchcraft, Anne was terrified. His carving had the economy and skill of pure hatred. That, and more: carving, he became a total stranger— not the man who had courted her, not the man she'd lain coldly beneath on their wedding night, not the man their marriage had made of him. When he strode away into the trees, gazing at the doll, she felt exhausted with relief. Even had he not forbidden them to watch his curse, she could never have followed.

John was hardly out of the glade when Elizabeth Cooper seized Robert Allen. She slid down his belly and thrust her head hungrily between his legs. To Anne it looked as if a gray hairy spider had fastened itself beneath Robert's belly and was plucking at its web. His entire body strained back like a bow from the arrow of his genitals. His face glowed coldly with moonlight as his mouth gaped wider, wider.

Elizabeth's action released them all from their dread. Adam pushed Jenny Carter against a tree and thrust into her from behind as she clawed at the trunk. James Carter was tripped by Alice Young and Nell, who fastened on him with their genitals as if they were famished mouths. Arthur Young had pinioned Mary Cooper to the ground with her arms stretched wide, but she lifted her hips higher to shackle him too, gasping.

Jane Cooper lay on top of Thomas Small, her plump young breasts crushed against his chest as his thick arm pressed her to him. He'd torn up a bunch of nettles and was flailing her round buttocks with them.

Her buttocks churned, pumping him, as her hands yanked frantically at his hair. She cried out as he did, almost lifting herself free of him.

Elizabeth lifted her head and looked at Anne as Robert Allen slumped to the ground, spent. "Your John never shows his face now, does he?" she taunted. "Does without, does he? You mark my words. No man has that kind of power."

There was nothing behind her words but envy, Anne knew. Envy had made her seize Robert Allen as soon as John had gone. Nevertheless, Anne suddenly felt rejected by the others, as she had tried not to admit to herself while she waited for a partner. She grabbed Adam as he left Jenny Carter still' clinging to the tree, and dragged him on top of herself. Deeper in the wood she heard a creaking, as of trees flexing in the wind. But there was no wind.

Her body closed on Adam's penis, sucking him deeper, quickening his thrust. Her thighs crushed his ribs, her toes arched upward, straining him closer still. Her buttocks rolled against the damp grass, and the ointment blazed through her legs, exploding in her genitals almost at once. At her third orgasm his penis seemed to double its size, pumping long and uncontrollably.

As she lay beneath him she heard the tread approaching through the wood, creaking.

She tried not to think. She tried to feel nothing but Adam's heavy body crushing her against the grass; but he pushed himself away and sat waiting, suddenly subdued. She tried to hold the cold bleached glade still, empty except for the twelve. She tried to fend off what was approaching. What the orgiasts had been trying to ignore was unthinkable. Since she couldn't think it, it couldn't happen.

She was trying to convince herself when the devil stalked creaking into the glade.

He surveyed the twelve, sneering, and his head brandished horns that could gore a bull. His eyes, his wide mouth and the hollows of his cheeks were thick with shadow. So much Anne saw before she wrenched her gaze away. But it was no use averting her eyes, for she could feel his body massive as an oak dominating the glade, and smell the fetid leather of him. She looked up.

He was beckoning. One finger thick and knotted as a branch hooked toward them, creaking faintly. Perhaps that was the most terrible aspect of him: that he never spoke, because he had no need. Anne felt a sudden wound gouged out where her stomach had been. It must be her turn now. Then she realized he was not beckoning to her, but to Jane. His enormous penis stood ready before his featureless belly, glistening with moonlight.

He waited, finger hooked, while Jane went trembling to him in the center of the glade. His presence seemed to weigh down time; her paces were hours long. When she reached him and at last touched his shoulders timidly, he threw her to the ground.

At once he was on her, his knotted fingers pinning her shoulders down. As the huge penis entered her she gasped as though it had clubbed all the breath from her. Her stinging buttocks struggled wildly beneath him, on the grass. He drove himself deeper into her, with long slow deliberate strokes. Even when she tore at his back with her nails and bruised her thighs against his sides, his sneering mouth neither spoke nor moved.

When she fell back exhausted he thrust her away and strode out of the glade, creaking slowly and massively as the trees.

Parson Jenner was screaming.

"The carnal mind," he screamed, "is enmity against God! To be carnally minded is death!"

The church hurled his voice back behind Anne. She dwindled into herself. He wasn't looking at her. He couldn't know.

"That is God's word," the parson said quietly, intensely; then screamed "Will you silence him with the words of men? Will you tell him lust is natural, God-given? Wallowing in filth is in the nature of animals! Is that your nature? Will you glorify your own slime and call it Christian love?"

Anne wished she dared cover her burning face. She knew he was right. She knew it more certainly every time he preached on the subject. She'd known it on her wedding night, as soon as she'd seen John's uplifting penis. She'd known as he drove it into her, dry and hard and rough, for no better reason than that Parson Jenner had licensed him to. Her body had stiffened against the intrusion and grown cold, and so it always behaved with John.

Yet it hadn't behaved so when she was sixteen, when she'd joined (she had to hurry her mind past the words, lest God and Parson Jenner overhear) the coven. The ointment had helped her then, initiating her into ecstasy; it had always done so since. Only at home, on her bed with John, did her body feel rigid and grimy. After much thought she had decided why. In the village the parson's power was everywhere. She was free of his power only in (she thought it loudly, defiantly) the coven.

The entire coven was here in church, subdued by Jenner's power. Anne glanced about surreptitiously. There was Adam, sitting stiffly upright as if held to attention by his long black jacket, his genitals muffled beneath the folds of its full skirts. There—Anne felt an inexplicable violent surge of jealousy—was Jane, her breasts laced tightly into a corset-bodice, her buttocks surely throbbing still beneath the many petticoats and long skirt and apron; they could hardly have recovered in less than a day. And there were all the others, hiding behind their intent respectful faces. In the gallery at the west end Anne saw Robert Allen and Arthur Young, Robert's oboe and Arthur's horn at their sides ready to accompany the next hymn.

"Did Jesus Christ Our Lord," Parson Jenner screamed, "bring shame upon His Blessed Mother's virgin flesh by lusting after woman?"

This must be the only time he ever felt passion, Anne thought in a bid to reassure herself. But that made it worse. It meant that the force of the whole man was behind his words. She snatched her gaze back to the altar, trying to pretend she'd never looked away.

His power was too strong for them. By hiding their bodies and their thoughts from him they had acknowledged his power. The coven was nothing but an escape from him, an escape dictated to them by the whims of the full moon. The rest of the month they were his.

She knew that the Carters and the Youngs had joined the coven simply in order to escape the sermons by which Jenner had restricted their marriages. She imagined his furious contempt if he ever found them out. She felt diminished, ashamed. She could hear him telling her that the coven was nothing but a delusion.

She shook her head; at least, it trembled. Her thoughts were confused. She tried to force her way through the gray mist which always descended on her mind after each coven and hung about her until the next full moon. There was more to their witchcraft than delusion. Once, running through the Cambrook at midnight, she'd heard the entire stream rise up behind her, a glittering mantle coldly boiling in the moonlight, sweeping forward to follow her to the coven; but when she'd turned the water had been playing aimlessly between its banks. She was sure she'd heard that.

And there was something she had seen. Once, at the height of the coven's ecstasy, she had looked up to see a gigantic white moonlit face grinning at them from the sky. Its eyes and mouth had been full of night; their tattered rims had smoked slowly. As it had gradually spread to encompass the whole of the sky, still gazing down and grinning, horns had streamed from its forehead.

"Lust is a delusion, a trick played on us by the devil!" Parson Jenner screamed. "Did Our Lord Jesus Christ feel lust? Did His Blessed Mother?"

A delusion, Anne thought. If the devil could make her feel what she felt at the coven, he could certainly make her see faces in the sky. Her mind grew ashen. The coven had no power except the power of delusion.

But it had, she thought suddenly. It had real power, terrifying power. For the first time that day she was able to look up at Parson Jenner's face. "We shall sing in praise of God," he declared. She rose to her feet, buoyed up beyond the music. The coven and the parson had battled within her. And the coven had won, because it had John's power.

Color flooded back into her mind and into the church, and for the rest of the service she felt as if she were caught in a blaze of light: until,

82

as she emerged from the church, she saw Celia Poole walking ahead of her, unharmed.

At once John, strolling beside her powerful and secret behind his calm face, became what the others had been in the church: a hollow puppet skulking behind a God-fearing expression. He'd said Celia Poole would be struck down before she could speak. But how could he be sure unless he silenced her immediately? His power had failed. Parson Jenner had won.

At their cottage she sat wordlessly. The parson's power was here too. While others enjoyed a Sunday stroll she and John must sit at home, insisting on their piety. Her stomach ached dully. Having starved herself for the coven she must now abstain on the Sabbath. She gazed toward her spinning-wheel, then looked away. She could not even mend their clothes, lest the parson chance to call.

Her mind felt dark as the earth floor. The grandfather clock marked off the approach of the evening service, loudly, lethargically. She imagined Celia Poole springing to her feet in the church, not for a public penance but to denounce Nell. Then Nell would break down and implicate them all. And Parson Jenner would have them, his voice surrounding them, binding them with a noose of villagers. Never mind George II's Witchcraft Act. That kind of leniency wasn't for Jenner, nor for the village he had made his own.

She watched John place wood on the fire, carefully, untroubled. She refused to be deluded by his calm. Behind his discreetly secretive face there was nothing. He was the only one who could have saved her from Jenner. She'd thought the parson's first victory over him, years ago, had filled him with cold hatred—the source of his power. But that power had faded.

He sat opposite her, his face unchanging. For a moment she realized that his days outside the coven might be as gray as hers. But at least she had her ecstasies beneath the moon. What pleasure could he have that carried him through life?

It didn't matter, she thought, shrugging dully away before the thought took shape. Neither of them could look forward to pleasure, now that Jenner had won. A wind forced smoke out of the fireplace toward them, billowing darkly up to the rafters.

On her way to the later service she stumbled continually in the deep ruts of the road. It was as though they were forcing her feet toward the church. The red-brick cottages stood back from her in their large gardens. The sun hung low over the wheat, and her shadow bumped over the ruts, dragging her along.

Before she reached her appointed place in the pew she passed the Coopers. None of them looked at her and John, nor did she dare look directly at them. The parson's power was absolute; they dared not even acknowledge each other. She wondered whether they were as numb with dread as she.

Then she saw that the Pooles' places were empty.

She didn't dare hope yet. But she felt the possibility of hope for the first time in church since Jenner had taken up residence. The Pooles were almost always half-an-hour early for the service; they preferred not to suffer each other's awkward silences alone.

Kneeling, she gazed about. The church had been neglected in the previous parson's day. Then Jenner had come and blamed them all, fastening his words deep in their most secret flaws. Some of the villagers had welcomed him, as the solution to what they saw as the laxity of the time; the others had not dared oppose him, for his contempt was spreading through the villagers like an epidemic. Most of the villagers infected themselves before the contempt could be turned against them.

Then Jenner had called them to clean and renovate the church, to renew its whitewash. It gleamed around Anne, in the evening light. But now she felt that perhaps this was not the victory Jenner thought it was. After all, it was Jenner who preached the unimportance of earthly things. The real victory was over Celia Poole, and that was John's—

When Anne heard the footsteps approaching down the aisle she knew without turning that it was Celia Poole.

Turning with the rest as they disapproved of the latecomer, Anne saw Celia take her place unruffled in her pew—in the pew which, like the rest, had been built to Jenner's order by John. In Celia's eyes, bid-ing its time, Anne saw the denunciation. Beside her Richard sat, red-faced and puffed up by their recent argument. Celia's eyes showed that she had won.

As if he had been awaiting his moment of triumph Jenner strode to the altar, robes flying. His Latin rang through the church, hard and imperative. Anne responded dully, though the words were virtually meaningless to her. They sprang from her, bypassing conscious thought, as the chant at the coven had done. But these words were closing on her like a trap. Each word Jenner or the congregation spoke held her more tightly, binding her in readiness for Celia's accusation. She felt Celia behind her, ready to pounce to her feet.

There was a clattering and a heavy thud.

The Latin broke off. Everyone looked round. There was something in the aisle, writhing helplessly as a baby. Its face was black and strained about a protruding silent tongue; the mouth worked, but only foam emerged. It was Celia Poole.

"Be vigilant!" Jenner screamed, pointing. "Because your adversary the devil, as a roaring lion, walketh about, seeking whom he may devour!"

Anne could hardly contain her smile. She knew this was not the devil's victory. It was the coven's.

Then, as Richard looked up from his writhing wife, his eyes blank and moist with fury, she realized he knew also.

It was the day before the next full moon that Elizabeth Cooper's words began to grow into Anne's suspicion.

Anne was mending clothes. Unafraid now, her mind moved smoothly as her needle through her memories. For the first time since her marriage she found herself spontaneously enjoying her work. She dwelt on it. She remembered the initiations of the Carters and the Youngs, remembered their wild writhing and cavorting as they had experienced their own untrammelled sexuality.

Her mind snagged on that. Suddenly she wondered what had happened to John's sexuality.

She tried to think. John wasn't sexless, quite the contrary; his fierce desire had terrified her on their wedding night, when sex had confronted her unsteady with rush-light rather than luminous beneath the full moon. When he knew he was unable to coax or bludgeon a response from her he had withdrawn his desire into himself, but she couldn't believe it had vanished entirely. "No man has that kind of power," Elizabeth had said.

Of course. That was where his sexuality had gone: into his magic power. Elizabeth's jealous words had inadvertently shown Anne the truth. But somehow Anne wasn't entirely convinced. She heard John in his room, finishing a piece of furniture. She'd often caught him looking at her when he thought she was unaware; she'd seen the desire in his eyes. She'd shudder then: she couldn't, that was all, it was no use trying to force her. Now, thinking about it instead of hurrying past, she couldn't believe that he had managed to translate his desire so easily into his power. Surely the ecstasy of the coven must inflame him beyond control.

Besides, she was sure John had always had the power. It had been Parson Jenner who had channelled it into hatred. John was an expert furniture-maker, as his father had been; he worked cheaply yet with style, and many of the farm laborers boasted a canopied bed rather than a trestle or a flock mattress on the floor. But John's genius had been for the figures he carved; tiny riders, shepherds, farmers, animals—even, in his room, an entire miniature Camside populated with minute replicas of the villagers. He'd used to take some of his carvings to Brichester; he had seldom brought any home.

Near Christmas he had used to display his work at the edge of the road outside their cottage. Since their marriage he had devoted more time to his carvings; that last Christmas he had displayed more work than was likely to be bought even by the villagers and the folk who made a special journey from Brichester.

He had been standing by his display, and almost the entire population of Camside had been admiring his work, when Parson Jenner stalked up. He stared at the display as if it confirmed the rumor of some awful sin. "Thou shalt not make unto thee any graven image!" he'd shouted at John. "Do you not understand the word of God? A graven image is a carved image. It is not for man to steal perfection from God."

Anne had felt the crowd change in an instant from admiring to condemning John's work, had felt their disapproval seize her too, almost palpably. She'd felt frightened but safe; John would overcome them. But then he'd betrayed her. He had given in to Jenner and had asked what he could do. "Burn them," Jenner had said, "and give thanks to Almighty God for your salvation."

Half-an-hour later John's work had been a cone of flame. Anne had felt contemptible, hollow. When John had retreated into the cottage she had thought he'd gone to hide his miniature Camside, or mope over it; but he'd brought it out in pieces and had thrown it on the fire.

Since their marriage she had avoided the coven, for she'd thought that John was becoming suspicious. The Coopers had let her lapse, for the other couples had recently been initiated. But that month, desperately pursuing her sense of self, Anne had obtained the ointment from the Coopers and had gone to the meeting. Running through the nodding wood, leaving behind the cottage and its air of terrible defeat, she felt released at last. Behind her, urging her on, she'd heard the faint padding of the wood's heart—except that when she'd reached the glade and had turned to see what everyone was looking at, she'd realized the sound had been John's footsteps.

"I thought so," he'd said, though he'd gazed in surprise at some of them. "Well, I have more reason to hate the pratings of the religious than any of you. You had better let me join you."

"And then we shall be thirteen at last," Anne had said, suddenly sure that he'd saved himself for this victory over Jenner.

"You would have been more use to us," Elizabeth had said, "when you had it in you to carve your dolls. They would have given us power over the ones you carved."

He'd taken a knife from his pocket; Anne had seen decision flood his eyes, like the moonlight that spilled over the blade. "Perhaps they still may," he'd said.

Within the week Jonas Miller had smashed both knees beneath his wheel. Jonas had helped John throw his dolls on the fire, with virtuous relish; John had carefully gouged out both knees from the image of Jonas he'd carved in the glade. After that, the coven had called John to strike down their enemies at whim, but he had cursed a victim only for good reason, lest a spate of injuries and afflictions betray the presence of the coven. Roger Place, the Brichester landlord, had been prevented from enclosing land in Camside by a chronic urinary infection that had confined him to his house, so that Arthur Young had kept his job day-laboring on the widow Taylor's land. And those who John heard had begun to suspect the witches were silenced: most recently, Celia Poole.

As she remembered Celia's fate Anne's doubt faded. To wield such power John must draw on the whole of himself, on his frustrated de-sires too. Such power must be capable of subsuming all of him into itself. Her needle moved easily again.

Musing on Celia, Anne felt pity for Richard Poole: a timid man, anxious to avoid unpleasantness and bad feeling; no doubt he had tried to argue Celia out of her proposed denunciation. Now that his wife had been stricken with epilepsy, Anne imagined that he would with-draw further into himself, poor man. Still, the coven had had to pro-tect itself. Able to feel comfortable again, Anne encouraged the fire with the bellows.

She was warming her hands gratefully when Jane Cooper arrived to collect the chair that John had finished. Anne felt an almost habitual jealousy at the sight of the girl. A moment later, when Jane had gone into John's room, Anne felt ashamed; she was too much at peace with the world to spoil it with such unworthy emotions.

One luxury John's work afforded them was tea, something Jane was unlikely ever to have tasted. A pot full of water stood ready by the hearth, and Anne hung it over the fire. Then she hurried to tell Jane to wait.

When Anne entered the room John scarcely bothered to conceal his expression. He was gazing at Jane, his eyes full of the memory of coupling and the promise of more. After what felt to Anne like many minutes, he glanced at her with weary impatience and put away his feelings, like a master brusquely hiding a book when a maid enters.

Jane went out, the upturned chair on her back. Anne returned to her own room, stumbling, and stood aimlessly. For a moment she battled with the truth. John couldn't have touched the girl. He never had done so at the coven, and the elder Coopers would never allow it under any other circumstances. They were as strict as Jenner on that point. Indeed, she thought (or almost thought, for her mind shied away), if they were able to take each other at will, there would be no need for the coven.

But the truth was waiting patiently for her to look at. John was the devil that appeared at the coven; that was how he gratified his sexuality.

Even now, urged on by that insight, she had to struggle in order to think of the devil. He had appeared eight full moons ago, creaking out of the wood as if the trees and wind and moonlight had combined in him. Since then he had always appeared at the height of their ecstasy. He had never been seen before John had joined the coven; they had taken that as proof of the power of thirteen, and of John's power. The women had cried that his penis was hard and unyielding, as Elizabeth had said it would be, remembering covens of her childhood. Everything had seemed to show the old magic had returned to them. Now Anne saw there was another explanation.

The devil had never taken her. She had been unthinkingly grateful to be spared, so grateful that she dared not think of her good fortune lest thinking bring the devil upon her next time. Sometimes she moaned and writhed in her sleep as the massive sneering face weighed on hers, the enormous penis conquered her. At the last two covens she had been sure the devil must take her, and she'd locked away dread deep in her mind; but he had chosen Nell and Jane again. At last she knew why she had felt instinctively jealous of Jane.

Within her mind, memories bound themselves into a certainty. The devil never appeared until John had vanished into the wood to curse his dolls. Even when nobody had petitioned him to curse, he said he must renew the existing curses so that their power would not weaken. Always the devil appeared from the direction in which John vanished. And—remembering this, Anne realized that the truth had always been in her mind—whomever John danced with before the sacrifice, the devil later chose.

Before she had time to be terrified of him, she strode into his room. He was carving the leg of a chair, with a lover's delicacy. "The devil who comes at the full moon," she said, tightly aware that they had never discussed the coven outside its time before. "I know who he is."

"He is our master," he said, not looking up.

"He is not mine. He is you in disguise, so that you can have all the women at your mercy. That's how you get your fucking."

"I would not touch any of them," he said with a contempt as profound as Jenner's.

She recoiled, back into her own room. Yet somehow, when she reflected, his words hadn't quite the power she was sure he intended. He hadn't said he wasn't the devil. Of course he wouldn't touch other women, since his head-to-toe disguise would always intervene between their touching bodies: not if he meant "touch" that way.

She might have contented herself with that, with the sense that he was having to strain at his words in order to deceive her, since that was a kind of victory: she'd trapped him into a position where he couldn't use his power directly. But all at once "I would not touch any of them" turned and insulted her. Not "any of you"; he excluded her out of pity, out of indifference; she was beneath even his contempt. She was sure in her bitterness that there could be no other reason. The water rose up in the pot, hissing, brimming over. She snatched it away from the fire, coldly, calmly. She knew what she was going to do.

Later she told John that she was going to church. Jenner had been looking at her oddly, she said, and she wanted to head off his suspicions. She hurried down the road, toward the church. As soon as she was out of sight of the cottage she doubled back, into the wood.

She strode into the coven's glade and halted, confused. The sun was a silver wafer decomposing into a gray pond, and beneath its light the glade looked bare and cramped, hemmed in by denuded trees: not at all like the expanse of ground about which the trees danced deasil. But she recognized the gnarls of the trees between which the devil always emerged. She hurried toward them, calming her heart. Around her the wood creaked slowly and deliberately, like the pendulum of an enormous wooden clock.

She knew that John never brought his dolls with him to the coven: that he hid them and his knife beforehand, somewhere in this area. The devil-disguise was here also, she was sure. That was the proof she needed.

Someone was coming toward her through the wood. She hushed the creaking trees frantically with an unthinking gesture, but they swayed slowly on, interrupting her view of the depths of the wood with a dense net of branches. The branches made passes over each other, like the hands of a conjurer she'd seen in her childhood. Within the slow net of sound and black wood, someone was approaching.

After a long breathless time she told herself that it must have been a stroller, and went on. She peered between the trunks, anxious to find John's disguise, anxious to be gone. The trunks moved apart stolidly as she walked, revealing trunks beyond. Twigs groped blackly against the dull blurred sky. The trees swayed in unison, creaking with the effort, but their roots stayed firmly buried. Someone was following Anne through the wood.

She twisted around, glaring through the trees. There was nobody. At last she turned back, and came face to face with the devil.

He was sneering sightlessly out between two close-grown trees. He was almost hidden within a pile of twigs and branches, which had slipped down from his cheeks and left his face protruding, as from an impossible beard. His fixed mouth sneered; his eyes were sockets from which all but deep darkness had been gouged.

Even immobilized as he was, his massiveness was terrifying. But she forced herself closer and began to pull away the branches. At once she realized that the devil's leather hide was stretched over a wooden frame. No wonder he was massive. She remembered the tale she'd heard that a large quantity of leather had been stolen from a Brichester cobbler's; she didn't need to wonder where the wooden frame came from. As she separated the branches, she saw that the devil had no pe-

91

nis, only an orifice. She nodded grimly.

She was preparing to touch the devil, to prove that she could do so, when a movement back in the direction of the coven's glade caught her attention. Her imagination had not deceived her, after all; someone else was in the wood. It was Richard Poole.

She wrenched the branches together over the devil, and shrank back behind the trees. Peering out, she glimpsed Richard's face. He was no longer timid. His gaze was blazing with hatred. She knew he was searching for signs of the coven.

As she slipped between the trees and fled, she heard a creaking as if the devil had stirred in its sleep. Startled, she stumbled, snapping a branch. When she regained her balance she saw Richard staring at her. She nodded casually to him and strode away, ignoring her frantic heart.

When her heart slowed she found she was able to plan, and smiled wildly. Everything had fallen in her favor. She felt powerful enough to be reckless. She had hidden the devil completely; she had been too far from it when she stumbled to have betrayed it to Richard. She could afford to wait until tomorrow night. Already she had two plans, and she wanted to enjoy them both to the full.

It was the next night. Anne was running behind John. The full moon had cleared the sky; its light seeped through the hard ground, the starved trees, the restless grass furred with frost. When the branches stirred their movements lingered on Anne's eyes, like trails of luminous mist. Even John seemed to glow coldly from within. The weeks since the previous coven felt like a dream from which she had awakened at last.

But the weeks weren't so dreamlike that she could not interpret them, or plan from them. As she entered the glade she saw that everyone was waiting again, and realized why she and John always arrived last: in order that the others should feel bound to wait, to confirm their faith in his power. Very well, she thought. She could make an entrance too.

Loudly enough for everyone to hear she said to John "Make me a doll of Parson Jenner."

Before he turned inward, toward the core of his hatred, she

thought he looked at her in something like admiration. "Why should you curse him?" he demanded.

"He saw how I smiled when Celia Poole was taken by her fits," she said. "Now he watches for me to betray myself. Every night I dream that I have. Soon it will be true."

John's eyes stared at her, and within them was someone old and overwhelmingly vicious, famished of everything save hatred. "He will never watch you again," he said.

A confusion of emotions welled up through her: satisfaction, terror, admiration, a poignant sense that they could admire each other only in this moment of inhuman power. She had often wondered why he had never cursed Jenner. At times, with a contempt as deep as that she'd felt when he'd burned his carvings, she had believed he was terrified of the parson. But perhaps, she had thought yesterday, he was too afraid of being engulfed by his own power ever to use it for himself. Yesterday she had seen that she could both test him in this and render Richard Poole harmless. If Jenner were destroyed, the villagers would never dare move against the coven. She smiled at the cold bland moon.

Elizabeth Cooper was chanting impatiently, almost shouting— scared, Anne thought, of the enormity John had undertaken to perform. The Coopers were dancing, stamping defiantly like animals. She ran to join the chain of dancers, holding fast to Jane's arm. Elizabeth frowned spitefully down the chain at her; it had always been the Coopers who chose the order of dancers. But Anne smiled back triumphantly and dragging the others with her, danced to John and took his arm. She let the chant seethe through her and pour from her mouth.

Her legs felt aflame with the ointment, urging her to dance more wildly. She gripped John's arm and capered, anxious to exhaust the dance, willing him to go in order to return to her —as the devil, if he must. Her heavy breasts rolled with the dance, their nipples taut and tingling; her genitals smacked their lips eagerly. She looked down at herself as her hips flexed powerfully. She would make him forget Jane and the rest. Beyond John she saw the circle of dancers close, as he took Alice's hand.

Anne was lying at the edge of the glade, legs loose and trembling. Adam had ripped open a fish and was displaying it to the moon. "Domini nostri," they shouted. All of a sudden John wasn't there; they were all huddled close to the trees, waiting amid the rusty creaking of the wood, and Anne's stomach suddenly felt as empty and cold as the glade.

John was striding toward her through the trees. His face was fixed and bland as the moon. His glowing colorless hand thrust a doll toward her. As she grasped the doll she stifled a cry. It had seemed to move in her grasp, as if Jenner were trapped in the wood, struggling frantically within her curse, his buried struggles making the surface crawl.

She closed her eyes to curse, and found panic waiting. If they tried to curse Jenner he would know; God would tell him; he would destroy them. She gripped the doll fast, hearing it creak. She entrusted herself to John's power. She squeezed everything from her sight except burning red, and cursed.

When John had taken the doll from her she opened her eyes. She didn't see him carve the face; Jenner was already there when she looked, glaring up from the wooden head, tiny but vastly contemptuous of her. It was as if the core of Jenner had burst out of the wood and was staring at her from John's hand, all the denser and more concentrated for its size. For a second she felt its power take hold of her. Then she stared back at the paralyzed mannequin, and felt colossal with triumph.

John vanished into the wood, fading as he walked, only feebly luminous now, entirely dark, gone. Silenced by what he had done, the twelve waited unmoving. They needed their master to appear, to reassure them that their presumption had not destroyed him; all except Anne, who lay untroubled as her excitement grew, spreading through her thighs. When she heard the creaking among the still trees she knew it was John, returning to take her. Her genitals gasped with excitement.

The devil stalked into the glade, bearing his immobile sneering face toward them, beneath the moon. His deep eyes rolled with shadow. For the first time Anne dared look closely enough to see that his feet were cloven. The leather of his limbs gleamed dully as it wrinkled, creaking.

Above his thighs his penis stood like a swollen rod of moonlight.

Anne was on her feet before she saw that he was beckoning to Alice Young.

As Alice rose Anne knocked her sprawling and strode toward the devil. The others gasped in outrage, more loudly as she took hold of his penis with her hands. It was far bulkier than any of the men's, and stiffer; it seemed wholly unlike John's, as she remembered it from the beginning of their marriage. The inhumanly still face leaned toward her, the shadows of its great horns drooping over its forehead. Within the staring sockets she could see no eyes at all.

Then the devil gripped her shoulders, bruising them cruelly. He twisted her about and threw her down. The thawing grass struggled beneath her breasts and legs. She felt his icy knees forcing her thighs apart, and strove to hold them closed. But his hands closed on her shoulders like vices, trapping her before she tried to crawl away, and his penis thrust peremptorily between her buttocks.

She began to cry with pain and rage—with a frustration she hadn't felt since her wedding night. Her legs shoved helplessly at the earth; her feet clawed at the crackling grass. He was riding her, butting deeper into her, his body creaking stiffly as the trees. The heavy smell of leather clogged her nostrils. His movements rubbed her nipples against the ground. She sobbed, for the ointment was responding to him in defiance of her will, causing her to squeeze him deeper into herself. She could not distinguish the blaze of her pain from the fire of the ointment.

Suddenly he withdrew and released her shoulders. She began to crawl swiftly toward the edge of the glade. When she heard him creaking slyly above her she turned on her back to fend him off. He had been waiting for her to do so. As she kicked out he lifted her knees and forced them wide, then, as her genitals and her mouth gaped, he slid himself into her.

She shouted in protest, writhing like an impaled moth. She felt stretched to breaking, on the lip of pain, but as she waited for the pain, a slow explosion began to spread through her from her genitals. The huge unyielding bludgeon rubbed within her, lifting her from the ground at each stroke. The sneering mask pressed against her face. She pummelled his unresponsive chest with the heels of her hands.

Suddenly something broke deep within her, in her mind, as the explosion reached it. It was as if the pent-up blaze of the ointment had engulfed her all at once. She was inundated by the force of the explosion, blinded. She tore at the brittle grass and earth with her hands as her knees dragged him closer again, again.

She fell back, drawing long slow hungry breaths. The devil was raising himself from her when she saw Richard Poole rush into the glade.

She screamed a warning, but the devil still moved slowly, unheeding. The watching eleven stared blankly at her, then at the man who had already dashed through their midst. Moonlight streaked across the blade of Richard's axe.

The devil regained his feet, and was turning when the axe swooped. Perhaps the sight of the sneering shadow-eyed face reminded Richard he was timid after all; for the axe, which had been aimed at the devil's neck, faltered aside and lopped off the devil's right arm.

The coven screamed, and Anne screamed the loudest. The arm fell across her legs. Richard whirled the axe and buried it between the devil's shoulders; then he fled into the wood, snapping branches. The devil tottered and began to fall beside Anne. She kicked the severed arm away hysterically. Then she stared at her legs, searching for spilt blood. There was none, for the arm was made entirely of wood.

She was so furious at the deception, furious with herself for having responded to this dummy, for having even feared for its life, that she gave herself no chance to wonder how it had been made to move. She turned on the devil, lying on its back next to her. She wrenched at its brandished penis. It was a shaft of young wood carefully pared to smoothness. As she twisted it violently, it turned in the socket and came away in her hand.

He'd made sure the wood was as moist as possible by renewing it each time, she explained to her startled heart. How thoughtful of him, she thought viciously. In her hand the penis now felt exactly like wood.

96

But a sound was intruding on her musings. As the clamor of Richard's flight faded, they all heard someone moaning nearby.

John had ceased moaning by the time they found him. He lay on the ground close to where Anne had discovered the devil. He seemed to be sinking into what at first looked like an enormous expanding shadow, that surrounded him completely. He was lying on his right side in the undergrowth; they could not see his right arm. His left hand was gripped deep in his crotch, and the blood pulsed uncontrollably between the fingers.

He was not quite dead. He gazed at them with a last surge of power, and Anne felt his contempt condemn them all. She hadn't believed him when he'd said he would never touch any of them. She saw him watch her realization, and begin to smile mirthlessly. Then all the power drained from his eyes, and it was as if the entire wood drooped.

A chill wind carried to them the sound of Richard fleeing toward the village, shouting Parson Jenner's name.

From Francisco Maria Guazzo, Compendium Maleficarum *(1608)*

From *Wonders of the Invisible World*

Cotton Mather

The *New-Englanders* are a People of God settled in those, which were once the *Devil's* Territories; and it may easily be supposed that the *Devil* was exceedingly disturbed, when he perceived such a People here accomplishing the Promise of old made unto our Blessed Jesus, *That He should have the Utmost parts of the Earth for his Possession.* There was not a greater Uproar among the *Ephesians,* when the Gospel was first brought among them, than there was among, *The Powers of the Air* (after whom those *Ephesians* walked) when first the *Silver Trumpets* of the Gospel here made the *Joyful Sound.* The Devil thus Irritated, immediately try'd all sorts of Methods to overturn this poor Plantation: and so much of the Church, as was *Fled into this Wilderness,* immediately found, *The Serpent cast out of his Mouth a Flood for the carrying of it away.* I believe, that never were more *Satanical Devices* used for the Unsetling of any People under the Sun, than what have been Employ'd for the Extirpation of the *Vine* which God has here *Planted, Casting out the Heathen, and preparing a Room before it, and causing it to take deep Root, and fill the Land, so that it sent its Boughs unto the* Atlantic *Sea* Eastward, *and its Branches unto the* Connecticut *River* Westward, *and the Hills were covered with the shadow thereof.* But, All those Attempts of Hell have hitherto been Abortive, many an *Ebenezer* has been Erected unto the Praise of God, by his Poor People here; and, *Having obtained Help from God, we continue to this Day.* Wherefore the Devil is now making one Attempt more upon us; an Attempt more Difficult, more Surprizing, more snarl'd with unintelligible Circumstances than any that we have hitherto Encountred; an Attempt so *Critical,* that if we get well through, we shall soon Enjoy *Halcyon* Days with all the *Vultures* of Hell *Trodden under our Feet.* He has wanted his *Incarnate Legions* to Persecute us, as the People of God have in the other Hemisphere been Persecuted: he has therefore drawn forth his more *Spiritual* ones to make an Attacque upon us. We have been advised by some Credible Christians yet alive, that a Malefactor, accused of *Witchcraft* as well as *Murder,* and Executed in this place more than Forty Years ago, did then give Notice of, *An Horrible* PLOT *against the Country by* WITCHCRAFT, *and a Foundation of* WITCHCRAFT *then laid, which if it were not seasonally discovered, would probably Blow up, and pull down all the Churches in the Country.* And we have now with Horror seen the *Discovery* of such a *Witchcraft!* An Army of *Devils* is horribly broke in upon the place which is the *Center,* and after a sort, the *First-born* of our *English* Settlements: and the Houses of the Good People there are fill'd with the doleful Shrieks of their Children and Servants, Tormented by Invisible Hands, with Tortures altogether preternatural. After the Mischiefs there Endeavoured, and since in part Conquered, the terrible Plague, of *Evil Angels,* hath made its Progress into some other places, where other Persons have been in like manner Diabolically handled. These our poor Afflicted Neighbours, quickly after they become *Infected* and *Infested* with these *Dæmons,* arrive to a Capacity of Discerning those which they conceive the *Shapes* of their Troublers; and notwithstanding the Great and Just Suspicion, that the *Dæmons* might Impose the *Shapes* of Innocent Persons in their *Spectral Exhibitions* upon the Sufferers, (which may perhaps prove no small part of the *Witch-Plot* in the issue) yet many of the Persons thus Represented, being Examined, several of them have been Convicted of a very Damnable *Witchcraft:* yea, more than One *Twenty* have *Confessed,* that they have Signed unto a *Book,* which the Devil show'd them, and Engaged in his Hellish Design of *Bewitching,* and *Ruining* our Land. *We* know not, at least *I* know not, how far the *Delusions* of *Satan* may be Interwoven into some Circumstances of the *Confessions;* but one would think, all the Rules of Understanding Humane Affairs are at an end, if after so many most Voluntary Harmonious *Confessions,* made by Intelligent Persons of all Ages, in sundry Towns, at several Times, we must not Believe the *main strokes* wherein those *Confessions* all agree: especially when we have a thousand preternatural Things every day before our eyes, wherein the *Confessors* do acknowledge their Concernment, and give Demonstration of their being so Concerned. If the Devils now can strike the minds of men with any *Poisons* of so fine a Composition and Operation, that

Scores of Innocent People shall Unite, in *Confessions* of a Crime, which we see actually committed, it is a thing prodigious, beyond the Wonders of the former Ages, and it threatens no less than a sort of a Dissolution upon the World. Now, by these *Confessions* 'tis Agreed, *That* the Devil has made a dreadful Knot of *Witches* in the Country, and by the help of *Witches* has dreadfully increased that Knot: *That* these *Witches* have driven a Trade of Commissioning their *Confederate Spirits,* to do all sorts of Mischiefs to the Neighbours, whereupon there have ensued such Mischievous consequences upon the Bodies and Estates of the Neighbourhood, as could not otherwise be accounted for: yea, *That* at prodigious *Witch-Meetings,* the Wretches have proceeded so far, as to Concert and Consult the Methods of Rooting out the Christian Religion from this Country, and setting up instead of it, perhaps a more gross *Diabolism,* than ever the World saw before. And yet it will be a thing little short of *Miracle,* if in so *spread* a Business as this, the Devil should not get in some of his Juggles, to confound the Discovery of all the rest.

Cotton Mather and the Witches

Donald Tyson

In 1688 Cotton Mather (1663–1728) took a young girl named Martha Goodwin into his household to live with his family. The girl was the second eldest child of John Goodwin, a mason of the town of Boston who was believed to have recently come under the curse of a witch, an elderly Irish woman named Ann Glover, known by her neighbors as Goody Glover. The affliction struck four of the six children in the house but passed over the eldest boy and the baby, who were not troubled by it. It caused the middle four (two girls and two boys) to fall into fits in which they screamed like wild animals, went temporarily blind, deaf, or dumb, ran around flapping their arms like geese, and contorted their bodies in seemingly impossible postures. Sometimes when they tried to eat, they could not do so because their teeth remained set together and would not part.

The manner of their flying, as described by Mather, seems more than natural. He wrote that they would be

> carried with an incredible Swiftness thro' the Air, having but just their Toes now and then upon the ground, and their Arms waved like the Wings of a Bird. One of them, in the House of a kind Neighbour and Gentlemen (Mr. Willis) flew the length of the Room, about 20 foot, and flew just into an infants high armed Chair; (as 'tis affirmed) none seeing her feet all the way touch the floor.[1]

Their afflictions took a religious bent. When two ministers of the church tried to give a Goodwin boy good counsel, he suddenly went deaf and could not hear anything said to him except only the last word. When prayers to God were spoken to the children or the Bible read to them, Mather wrote:

---

1. Cotton Mather, *Late Memorable Providences Relating to Witchcrafts and Possessions*, 2nd impression (London: Printed for Tho. Parkhurst at the Bible and Three Crowns in Cheapside near Mercers-Chapel, 1691), 14–15.

They would then stop their own Ears with their own Hands; and roar, and shriek, and holla, to drown the Voice of the Devotion. Yea, if any one in the Room took up a Bible to look into it, tho' the Children could see nothing of it, as being in a croud of Spectators, or having their Faces another way, yet would they be in wonderful Miseries, till the Bible were laid aside.[2]

The troubles began around midsummer, 1688, when Martha Goodwin, who was thirteen years old at the time, accused Mary Glover of stealing an article of clothing from the laundry. Mary worked as a servant in the Goodwin house, and her mother, Goody Glover, was a washer-woman. Mary denied the charge, and a heated argument took place. Shortly thereafter four of the six Goodwin children began to fall into fits in which they behaved as though they were possessed by demons. The demons would force the children to commit acts of evil, but the children would warn those present when they felt compelled to do some mischief, so that they could be forcibly prevented. The ministers of the town and other good men went to the Goodwin house, which Mather referred to as "haunted," to pray for the possessed children. The youngest child, a boy, was delivered from affliction by this Day of Prayer, but the other three continued as before.

The Goodwin children had suffered this demonic possession for three months when Mather decided to accept the girl Martha into his house. His reasons for doing so were pious and sincere. He believed such demonic possession, induced by witchcraft, could be cured by prayer. But he was also motivated by a fascination for the subjects of witchcraft and possession and wished to observe the progress of the girl's affliction. This interest he had inherited from the researches of his father, the renowned minister of North Church and president of Harvard College, Increase Mather (1639–1723), who had written about witchcraft and other supernatural wonders in his books, notable among them his work *An Essay for the Recording of Illustrious Providences,* published in 1684 in Boston.

---

2. Cotton Mather, *Memorable Providences* 17–18.

Cottonus Matherus

*S. Theologiæ Doctor Regiæ Societatis Londinensis Socius,
et Ecclesiæ apud Bostonum Nov-Anglorum nuper Præpositus.*

Ætatis Suæ LXV, MDCCXXVII.   P. Pelham ad vivum pinxit & Crispi Fecit 1728.

103

In the text of that work Increase Mather specified what he intended by the term "illustrious providences."

> Such Divine Judgements, Tempests, Floods, Earth-quakes, Thunders as are unusual, strange Apparitions, or what ever else shall happen that is Prodigious, Witchcrafts, Diabolical Possessions, Remarkable Judgements upon noted Sinners: eminent Deliverances and Answers of Prayer, are to be reckoned among Illustrious Providences.[3]

There are chapters on preternatural events and demonic possession, both of which Increase Mather believed were often caused by witchcraft. He wrote: "Sometimes (as Voetius and others observe) bodily possessions by evil Spirits are an effect of Witch-craft."[4]

Increase Mather made frequent mention in his book of the demonologists, as they were called—men such as Johannes Weir (1515–1588), Nicholas Rémy (1530–1616), and Joseph Glanvill (1636–1680), who had written first-hand observations on the nature of witchcraft and demonic possession. These works were regarded as textbooks on how witches were to be recognized, exposed, neutralized, and prosecuted. Cotton Mather saw himself as a champion of God, engaged in mortal combat against the forces of evil that threatened to overwhelm New England. In the "Author's Defence" section of his 1693 book, *Wonders of the Invisible World,* he wrote, "I have indeed set my self to countermine the whole PLOT of the Devil, against New-England, in every Branch of it, as far as one of my darkness, can comprehend such a Work of darkness."[5]

To understand Cotton Mather's personal zeal against the witches, it is necessary to know something about his family history and the attitudes of his contemporaries. The pilgrims who fled England in the seventeenth century and settled in the Boston area of New England

---

3. Increase Mather, *An Essay for the Recording of Illustrious Providences* (Boston: 1684), the Preface (unpaginated).

4. Increase Mather, *Illustrious Providences* 198.

5. Cotton Mather, *Wonders of the Invisible World,* 2nd ed. (Boston & London, 1693), Author's Defence (unpaginated).

were given the pejorative descriptive title "Puritans" as a mockery of their life purpose—to stand pure and without stain before God. They fled England to escape what they regarded as the corruption and decadence of English Protestantism. None of the Protestant sects flourishing in England at the time was strict enough or pure enough to meet their exacting standards of holiness. For example, they regarded the Quakers as riotous sinners and scrupulously avoided their company.

Six decades after their arrival, Cotton Mather would write about those early pilgrims who had fled persecution in their homeland to establish a spiritual Utopia in America, "they embraced a voluntary Exile in a squalid, horrid, American Desart, rather than to live in Contentions with their Brethren."[6] Boston and its surrounding villages quickly grew and prospered under their severe work ethic. So well did the Puritans succeed in their endeavor that Cotton Mather was able to record the words of a visitor to New England from a sermon the visitor later delivered before the English Parliament: "I have now been seven Years in a Countrey, where I never saw one Man drunk, or heard one Oath sworen, or beheld one Beggar in the Streets all the while."[7]

This achievement was all the more remarkable in that the Puritans had not regarded New England as a desirable destination when they had sailed from England. On the contrary, in their eyes America was a wasteland, a desert, a wilderness filled with fiendish, godless heathens and devils of every description. It was quite literally the refuge of Satan himself. The belief was current at the time that Satan had fled from Europe to escape the dominance of Christianity, and had sought security in the vast wildness of the New World, where he could rule uncontested over men who had never been touched by the words of Christ.

Rebecca Jane Estey wrote in her 1928 Boston University Masters of Arts thesis on Cotton Mather:

> In New England, furthermore, there was a popular theory that the legions of the devil, largely driven out of Christian Europe, had taken refuge in

---

6. Cotton Mather, *Wonders of the Invisible World* 11.
7. Cotton Mather, *Wonders of the Invisible World* 11.

the wilds of America; and that dismayed and furious at the Puritans' attack upon their final stronghold, they had marshalled their forces for one desperate assault upon the New England theocracy. In the supposed degeneracy of the New England churches of his day Cotton Mather saw the special hand of the devil; and the witches were soldiers of the prince of darkness in the same great campaign.[8]

The first Puritans believed they were entering into Satan's domain and establishing their colony in its black heart, surrounded by evils of every description that ceaselessly sought to corrupt and destroy them. They might as well have been trying to found a colony inside the very gates of Hell itself. Estey wrote, "In the view of the Puritans, the Indians were the wretched remnant of a race seduced to the western hemisphere by the devil himself, that he might rule them undisturbed. The landing of the Pilgrims was an invasion of the devil's own territory; the missionary work of the ministers was a direct storming of his strongholds."[9] Among the many fearsome devils and monsters lurking in the American wilderness were the witches, Satan's most loyal and faithful shock troops. If witches could flourish in Europe, in the midst of Christendom, how much easier was it for them to ply their evil works in New England, so far removed from the centers of the faith in the Old World.

One of the early Puritan settlers was Richard Mather, a deacon of the English church who was suspended for nonconformity in 1633 and again in 1634 when the Archbishop of York, Richard Niele, learned that he had never worn a surplice while preaching. Niele told Mather, "it had been better for him that he had begotten seven bastards."[10] Richard Mather was persuaded in the spring of the following year to

---

8. Rebecca Jane Estey, "Cotton Mather and the Superstitions of the Early Period of American Literature" (M.A. thesis: Boston University, 1928), 10. See also Charles W. Upham, Salem Witchcraft (Boston: Wiggin and Lunt, 1867), 1.393–94.

9. Estey, "Superstitions of the Early Period" 12.

10. Richard Webster, "Richard Mather," Encyclopaedia Britannica, 11th ed. (Cambridge: Cambridge University Press, 1910–11), 17.885.

set sail for the New World in the hope that he could preach in his own way, without censure or repression. He established a church in Dorchester, a Puritan town near Boston that had been founded in 1630.

The family name of Mather prospered in New England. Richard Mather had six sons, four of whom became ministers of Christ. One of his sons, Increase Mather, gained great prominence in the town of Boston as the minister of the North Church and the president of Harvard College. He also attained notoriety as a writer, particularly for his 1684 book *An Essay for the Recording of Illustrious Providences,* referred to earlier. This work collected various supernatural and uncanny happenings that Increase Mather believed to support the existence of God and the authenticity of Jesus Christ. That was the primary purpose of the work in its author's mind, although the sensational and titillating nature of its subject no doubt played a large part in its success.

Increase Mather passed his fascination for prodigies and wonders on to his son, Cotton Mather, who was a prodigy in his own right. The boy was not named after the useful textile product of Southern plantations, as might be supposed, but was given the maiden name of his mother, Maria Cotton. By all accounts his intellect was remarkable. He entered Harvard College at age twelve and graduated with a Bachelor of Arts at age sixteen. Two years later he received his Master of Arts from his own father, who was president of Harvard College at the time. He had an astonishing gift for languages and taught himself Hebrew while at Harvard. Cotton was generally disliked by his schoolmates. The other students resented such brilliance in a boy so much younger than themselves, and shunned him.

Cotton followed his father's profession and became a minister of the North Church of Boston, where his father was minister. He also became a popular writer, particularly of books and pamphlets concerned with witchcraft and wonders of the spirit world. In this regard he outdid his father, more than doubling his father's output of sermons, tracts, essays and books. It is impossible to consider Cotton Mather without at the same time considering his father, Increase Mather. They two are almost clones of each other. They believed the same things, wrote on the same subjects, held the same profession, preached in the same church, went to the same school, became renowned popular writers, and espoused the same views regarding the reality and dangers of witchcraft and demonic possession.

While the possessed girl Martha Goodwin was living under Mather's roof, the old Irish washer-woman Goody Glover was arrested and examined for witchcraft.

> It was long before she could with any direct Answers plead unto her Indictment; and when she did plead, it was with Confession rather than Denial of her Guilt. Order was given to search the old womans house, from whence there were brought into Court, several small Images, or Puppets, or Babies, made of Raggs, and stufft with Goats-hair, and other such Ingredients. When these were produced, the vile Woman acknowledged, that her way to torment the Objects of her malice, was by wetting of her Finger with her Spittle, and stroaking of those little Images. The abused Children were then present, and the Woman still kept stooping and shrinking as one that was almost prest to Death with a mighty Weight upon her. But, one of the Images being brought unto her, immediately she started up after an odd manner, and took it into her hand; but she had no sooner taken it, than one of the Children fell into sad Fits, before the whole Assembly. This the Judges had their just Apprehensions at; and carefully causing the Repetition of the Experiment, found again the same event of it.[11]

The small rag dolls were what are known as witches' poppets. Their use by witches was common in Britain and Europe at the time. They operated on the principle of sympathetic magic. The doll was made to represent the target of the witch's malice, and then whatever torment the witch inflicted on the doll was believed to fall upon the person it represented. Most commonly, poppets were stuck through with pins or nails, although they might also be roasted over a fire to induce a fever in the victim. The application of spittle to the poppet by Goody Glover is interesting, in that spittle is magically associated with the in-

---

11. Cotton Mather, *Memorable Providences* 7–8.

tellect and with language, coming as it does from the mouth, the organ of speech. Glover seems to have used spittle to convey her malicious incantations, which may have been muttered under her breath, or may only have been silently held in her mind.

Cotton Mather interviewed the old woman twice while she was in jail but got little satisfaction from it, because Glover refused to speak English and would answer his questions only in Irish Gaelic, a language that Mather confessed he did not know. This was a strange affectation, since prior to her arrest the old woman had been able to speak perfectly good English. Although she would not speak English, she understood Mather when he spoke to her in that language. She would not deny to Mather the charge of witchcraft leveled against her. When Mather questioned her about the nature of her witchcraft, she told him she would be happy to answer him, but her spirits would not allow her to speak. She referred to them as her two Mistresses.

Mather told her he would pray for her, but Glover replied that if she wanted prayer she could pray for herself. He prayed for her anyway against her will. He wrote, "When I had done, she thank'd me with many good words; but I was no sooner out of her sight, than she took a Stone, a long and slender Stone, and with her Finger and Spittle fell to tormenting it; tho' whom or what she meant, I had the mercy never to understand."[12]

Ann Glover was hanged for witchcraft on 16 November 1688 at Boston. In New England witches were always hanged according to English law, never burned as they were in Scotland and other European countries. She was the last witch executed at Boston, though by no means the last witch to be hanged in New England. While being led to the scaffold she was heard to say that her death would not end the suffering of the three Goodwin children, who continued to fall into fits and exhibit the symptoms of demonic possession. According to Glover, other witches were involved in their tormenting. The ordeal of the accusations, trial, and execution of her mother proved too much for Mary Glover, who went raving mad and had to be locked away.

---

12. Cotton Mather, *Memorable Providences* 12.

Ann Glover's words proved prophetic. The three Goodwin children still afflicted by demonic possession continued to suffer great torments. These fits were not continuous, but came in clusters. For a time the children would be normal, then some incident would set them off and cause them to exhibit all the classic symptoms of demonic possession. The girl Mather took into his house, Martha Goodwin, was fine for four days following the execution of Goody Glover, but on 20 November she suddenly cried out, "Ah [They] have found me out! I thought it would be so!"[13] and fell into a fit. When Mather prayed for her, she would clap her hands over her ears, and if her hands were pulled away she would cry out, "[They] make such a noise, I cannot hear a word!"[14] She could not stand to read the Bible or any religious text, but had no trouble reading secular works.

All this while, the girl was surrounded by invisible spirits that she referred to as "them" or "her company." These spirits appear to be similar in their behavior to the fairies of English folklore. They acted in a capricious and malicious manner. At one time they gave her an invisible horse to ride, which she would mount and ride in her imagination to gatherings of these spirits. At another time they told her to dive into a well to retrieve silver plate that had been hidden there, and they promised to protect her from harm. Mather reported that she would hold long conversations with these spirits, although he could only hear her words, not the words the spirits gave in response to her questions.

Mather recorded her words in one of these one-sided conversations.

> Well what do you say? How many Fits more am I to have?—pray, can you tell how long it shall be before you are hang'd for what you have done?—You are filthy Witches to my knowledge, I shall see some of you go after your Sister; You would have killed me, but you can't, I don't fear you.—You would have thrown Mr. Mather down stairs, but you could not.—Well, How shall I be To morrow?—Pray, What do you think of To

---

13. Cotton Mather, *Memorable Providences* 18. The square brackets are Mather's.
14. Cotton Mather, *Memorable Providences* 19. The brackets are Mather's.

morrow?—Fare ye well—You have brought me such an ugly Horse, I am angry at you; I could find in my heart to tell all.[15]

It is clear from this that the girl regarded the spirits tormenting her as familiars of witches. Mather believed that witches had numerous spirits or spectres who served them as agents in works of evil. He wrote in *Wonders of the Invisible World,* "The Witches, which by their Covenant with the Devil, are become Owners of Spectres, are often times by their own Spectres required and compelled to give their Consent, for the molestation of some, which they had no mind otherwise to fall upon."[16] These spectres were able to assume various forms, some frightening or horrifying, others the images of the witches who sent them, or the images of innocent townspeople.

The reference to Mather being thrown down stairs refers to an incident in which the girl warned Mather that one of these spirits intended to cause him to fall backwards down a flight of stairs. Mather wrote, "she cry'd out, Mr. M.—— One of them is going to push you down the stairs, have a care. I remember not that I felt any Thrust or Blow; but I think I was unaccountably made to step down backward two or three stairs."[17]

Mather discovered that when the girl entered the study of a young man of the household, she suddenly became completely free of her demons. She told him, "They are gone; they are gone! They say that they cannot,—God won't let 'em come here!"[18] It seemed that the young man's holiness had imbued his study with that same essence, which repelled the tormenting devils. If there was any other emotional dynamic between the girl and the young man, Mather refrained from writing about it. When the girl left the study she immediately became possessed once again. At times Mather would take her there to give her a respite from the torments of her possession.

Mather kept the girl in his house all winter. Gradually her fits be-

---

15. Cotton Mather, *Memorable Providences* 30.
16. Cotton Mather, *Wonders of the Invisible World* 18.
17. Cotton Mather, *Memorable Providences* 29.
18. Cotton Mather, *Memorable Providences* 27.

came less frequent, and for periods of weeks she would be more or less normal in her behavior. In her final fit in Mather's house her company of spirits made her think that she was dying. She so well simulated a dying person that those around her believed that she truly was going to die. But when the fit was over she was her normal self once again. The three afflicted children continued to suffer occasional minor relapses, but eventually, through the repeated application of prayer, they were all delivered from their torments.

Mather closed the main part of his *Memorable Providences* with the following observation: "But I am resolv'd after this, never to use but just one grain of patience with any man that shall go to impose upon me, a denial of Devils, or of Witches. I shall count that man Ignorant who shall suspect, but I shall count him down-right Impudent if he Assert the Non-Existence of things which we have had such palpable Convictions of."[19]

It was a brief three years after the events of the Ann Glover trial and the demonic possession of the Goodwin children that New England was shocked by another visitation of witches, this time in the quiet little hamlet known as Salem Village, at no great distance from Boston. It is presently an historic district within the town of Danvers. Mather naturally took a keen interest in the proceedings of the trials, given his recent experiences. He wrote a book about the Salem witchcraft shortly after the affair came to its sad termination, and it is from the pages of this book, *Wonders of the Invisible World,* that we chiefly know about his part in the sorry business.

In the opening of his book Mather laid forth his understanding of what was taking place in the hamlets of New England. Satan, enraged by the piety of the Puritans, decided to make yet another attempt to destroy them. Mather wrote, "Wherefore the Devil is now makeing one Atempt more upon us; an Attempt more Difficult, more Surprizing, more snarl'd with unintelligible Circumstances than any that we have hitherto Encountred."[20]

---

19. Cotton Mather, *Memorable Providences* 41.
20. Cotton Mather, *Wonders of the Invisible World* 12.

This assault had been predicted more than forty years earlier by a person accused of witchcraft and murder, who had given forth the prophecy of "An Horrible PLOT against the Country by WITCH-CRAFT, and a Foundation of WITCHCRAFT then laid, which if it were not seasonably discovered, would probably Blow up, and pull down all the Churches in the Country."[21] Mather did not name the witch, but it appears to have been Mary Parsons, who was tried in Boston in 1651 for witchcraft and acquitted, then shortly thereafter tried for the murder of her own young son, Joshua Parsons, at the age of five months, and convicted. However, she does not seem to have ever been executed.[22]

Mather took this prophecy by the acquitted witch and condemned child murderer, whom he did not name, seriously and truly believed that the recent eruption of witchcraft in Salem Village proved its fulfillment.

> And we have now with Horror seen the Discovery of such a Witchcraft! An Army of Devils is horribly broke in upon the place which is the Center, and after a sort, the First-born of our English Settlements: and the Houses of the Good People there are filled with the doleful Shrieks of their Children and Servants, Tormented by Invisible Hands, with Tortures altogether preternatural.[23]

Mather believed that the plague of witchcraft was spreading beyond Salem, and so took it upon himself, as his duty before God, to alert New England to this danger by writing his book.

The form of the threat was this: 120 persons had been accused and had confessed to signing a book presented to them by the Devil, and then agreeing to carry out his plot to destroy the Puritan colonies by bewitching and ruining the land. Mather introduced a caution to the reader:

---

21. Cotton Mather, *Wonders of the Invisible World* 13.
22. Henry Martyn Burt, *The First Century of the History of Springfield: The Official Records from 1636 to 1736* (Springfield, MA: Henry M. Burt, 1898), 1.73–79.
23. Cotton Mather, *Wonders of the Invisible World* 13.

We know not, at least I know not, how far the Delusions of Satan may be Interwoven into some Circumstances of the Confessions; but one would think all the Rules of Understanding Humane Affairs are at an end, If after so many most Voluntary Harmonious Confessions, made by Intelligent persons of all Ages in sundry Towns, at several Times, we must not Believe the main strokes wherein those Confessions all agree. . . . If the Devils now can strike the Minds of Men with any Poysons of so fine a composition and Operation, that scores of Innocent People shall Unite, in Confessions of a Crime, which we see actually Committed, it is a thing prodigious, beyond the Wonders of the former Ages, and it threatens no less than a sort of a Dissolution upon the World.[24]

The book presented to the new witches by the Devil is the book of the so-called Black Pact, in which the acolytes of Satan swear to serve the Dark Lord for the rest of their lives, and sign their names, or make their marks, in their own blood to seal the formal contract. In return for this servitude they are given the power to harm and destroy, and thus terrorize their neighbors. The Devil was usually described in these meetings as a black man. Mather described him as a "small Black Man."[25] He may have intended a negro dwarf by this characterization, although when the Devil was described as a "black man" in England and Scotland, a Caucasian of dark complexion, black hair, and dark eyes was probably intended, not a negro.

The quotation above indicates two things. First, that Cotton Mather was absolutely convinced that a plot by Satan was underway to destroy the Puritan settlements and erase them from the land using witches as his agents; but second, that Mather did not automatically accept all the testimony of the accused witches as factual. Indeed, in several places in his writings he expressed doubts as to the veracity of their accounts, if only because what they described struck him as impossible and contrary to the laws of God and nature.

He was conscious of the possibility that witches would accuse innocent people of witchcraft, since this would sow confusion and des-

---

24. Cotton Mather, *Wonders of the Invisible World* 13–14.
25. Cotton Mather, *Wonders of the Invisible World* 17.

pair throughout the community. Against this suspicion was the general belief that the pious were protected from witchcraft by God, and that witches could not send spirit familiars to assume their appearance in order to implicate them falsely. Mather was not at all convinced of this belief. He suspected that the agents of witches did indeed have the ability to simulate the appearance of good men and women, and could appear in these guises before those they tormented, so that the sufferers would accuse their innocent neighbors of witchcraft. He wrote about "The multitude and quality of Persons accused of an Interest in this Witchcraft, by the Efficacy of the Spectres Which take their Name and Shape upon them; causing very many good and wise Men to fear, That many innocent, yea, and some vertuous Persons, are by the Devils in this matter imposed upon."[26]

This led Mather to write against the practice of accepting what was known as "spectral evidence"—testimony by witnesses that the accused had appeared to them in dreams or visions engaging in witchcraft. Such evidence was used during the witch trials at Salem Village in 1692, and was in part responsible for the conviction and execution by hanging of nineteen individuals. There are usually said to have been twenty men and women executed during the Salem witch hysteria, but Giles Corey died while being interrogated under the torture of pressing: increasingly heavy weights were placed on his chest to force him to declare a plea of guilty or not guilty. He refused to plead and died. His death cannot be termed an execution.

Spectral evidence had not been accepted in the court proceedings in New England prior to the Salem witch trials. It was introduced by the recently appointed Lieutenant Governor of Massachusetts, William Stoughton, who served as the chief justice during the Salem trials. Stoughton had been impressed by the use of spectral evidence in the 1662 witch trial at Bury St. Edmunds, a town in West Suffolk, England. A published account of that trial[27] was circulated among the Sa-

---

26. Cotton Mather, *Wonders of the Invisible World* 19.
27. The title of the work is *A Tryal of Witches* taken from a contemporaneous report of the proceedings of the Bury St. Edmunds witch trial of 1662.

lem judges and was used as a justification for the introduction of spectral evidence. Following the Salem trials, spectral evidence was discredited and was not used again in any court proceeding in New England—at least, not in any formal way. Cotton Mather did not wholly deny the validity of spectral evidence, but he wrote that it should be used with caution. He believed it was sufficient to indict a witch, but not to secure a conviction.[28]

Despite slanders to the contrary, Cotton Mather's role in the Salem witch trials was not significant. He took a keen interest in the affair, and he prayed with some of those who were condemned as witches prior to their executions. At one point he offered to take six possessed children into his own household, as he had done with Martha Goodwin, but the families involved refused his offer. He took no active part in the trials themselves and did not attend any of them, but did write a letter to one of the magistrates, John Richards, cautioning against a too ready acceptance of spectral evidence. Mather's mind was very much divided on this topic. He believed wholeheartedly in the reality of witchcraft and witches, and thought spectral evidence had a place in exposing the truth of their doings, but at the same time he recognized that it might prove unreliable if the witches were able to simulate the appearance of innocent men and women, as he suspected to be the case.

The Salem witch trials began in February 1692 and ended in May of the following year. When they were finally over, five men and fourteen women had been hanged, one man pressed to death for refusing to enter a plea before the court, ten others condemned but not executed, an unknown number of deaths of those hundred or so being held in prison, and two hundred more accused. As is not uncommon in witchcraft cases, the earliest accusers were young girls. The mania began in Salem Village, but the trials were held in Salem Town, as it was then called. During the hysteria there was widespread fear among the population as to which of them would be the next to be accused and

---

28. Wendel D. Craker, "Spectral Evidence, Non-Spectral Acts of Witchcraft, and Confession at Salem in 1692," *Historical Journal* 40 (June 1997): 336.

imprisoned. Accusations generally multiplied in witchcraft trials, because each person accused was encouraged to name accomplices. In this way the madness spread.

Cotton Mather's greatest critic was his contemporary Robert Calef (1648–1719), who wrote a book shortly after the publication in 1693 of Mather's *Wonders of the Invisible World*. Calef's book, titled *More Wonders of the Invisible World*, was completed in 1697 but not published until 1700. In it Calef accused Mather of being the prime driver of the witchcraft hysteria at Salem Village. By the time of the book's writing, five years after the executions, remorse had set in, and the good people of Massachusetts were embarrassed and ashamed at what they had done. Mather's hitherto sterling reputation as a divine was greatly tarnished by Calef's imputations, and for the remainder of his life he was never entirely able to escape from their shadow.

Calef's animus against Cotton Mather seems to have begun when Calef wrote an account of how Cotton and his father, Increase Mather, had together visited a seventeen-year-old girl named Margaret Rule who was possessed, as they believed, by the spectres of witches. This possession first began on 10 September 1693, some months after the hysteria of the Salem witches had died down. Calef was not himself a witness of the events, but received his information from observers who were said to be present. His account was thus hearsay.

Calef's narration of the visit by Cotton and Increase Mather to the girl's bedside was written on 13 September. Calef sent a copy of it to Cotton Mather, ostensibly to get Mather to correct its errors. Mather was infuriated by some of its contents, particularly the imputation that both he and his father had laid their hands on the body of the girl in a manner that was too familiar. They had rubbed her stomach several times in an effort to restore her to consciousness when she had passed out and apparently stopped breathing. Calef wrote of it in these terms: "He laid his hand upon her Face and Nose, but, as he said, without perceiving Breath; then he brush'd her on the Face with his Glove, and rubb'd her Stomach (her Breast not covered with the Bed-cloaths) and bid others do so too, and said it eased her, then she revived."[29]

When Cotton Mather did not respond to Calef's first letter, Calef showed his written accounts of the events to several of Mather's friends. Mather was not amused. Calef wrote in a letter dated 19 September, "I showed them to some of your particular Friends that so I might have the greater certainty: But was much surprized with the Message you sent me, that I should be Arrested for Slander, and at your calling me one of the worst of Lyars."[30]

Cotton Mather decided to let the matter drop and did not take Calef to court, but he was greatly offended both by the insinuations in Calef's account and by its many factual errors. He wrote to Calef on 15 January 1694:

> As false a representation 'tis, that I rub'd Rule's Stomach, her Breast not being covered. The Oath of the nearest Spectators, giving a true account of that matter will prove this to be little less than a gross (if not a doubled) Lie; and to be somewhat plainer, it carries the Face of a Lie contrived on purpose (by them at least, to whom you are beholden for the Narrative) Wickedly and Basely to expose me. For you cannot but know how much this Representation hath contributed, to make People believe a Smutty thing of me.[31]

Calef began a correspondence in which he badgered Mather for explanations and justifications for his beliefs and actions. In modern times we would characterize Calef as a stalker. He was obsessed with Mather. Mather eventually stopped replying to Calef's letters, and Calef took offense at this. This was the root of Calef's personal animus against Cotton Mather. On 18 March 1694, Calef wrote in a general letter to the ministers of Boston concerning Mather: "his Strenuous and Zealous asserting his opinions, has been one cause of the dismal

---

29. Robert Calef, *More Wonders of the Invisible World* (London: Printed for Nath. Hillar and Joseph Collyer, 1700), 13–14.

30. Calef, *More Wonders of the Invisible World* 16.

31. Calef, *More Wonders of the Invisible World* 20–21.

Convulsions we have here lately fallen into; Supposing that his Books of *Memorable Providences*, relating to Witchcraft, as also his *Wonders of the Invisible World*, did contain in them things not warrantable, and very dangerous."[32]

To fully understand what was going on between these men, it is necessary to know that this occurred at the turning of the tide. The executions of the nineteen Salem witches in 1692 marked the end of the witch hysteria. Calmer and more rational voices began to prevail, and there was a general embarrassment among the ministers of Boston and surrounding communities over their excessive zeal in persecuting witches. Mather's opinions, which had ridden the swelling tide of witchcraft mania, were now out of fashion, and Calef's cautions against a too ready acceptance of the devilishness of witchcraft were finding greater acceptance. Calef wrote:

> And that our Salem Witchcraft, either respecting the Judges and Juries, their tenderness of Life, or the Multitude and pertinency of witnesses, both Afflicted and Confessors, or the Integrity of the Historians, are as Authentic, and made as certain as any ever of that kind in the World; and yet who is it that now see not through it, and that these were the Sentiments that have procured the sorest Affliction, and most lasting infamy that ever befel this Countrey, and most like so to do again, if the same notions be still entertain'd.[33]

Calef saw Mather as a promoter of the old ideas that had provoked the Salem witch trials and subsequent executions, and he did not believe that Mather had changed his ideas. He felt it his duty to discredit Mather personally as a way of discrediting his ideas about witchcraft. To a large extent he succeeded. Cotton Mather was never again held in the same high regard in Boston as had been the case prior to the Salem trials. The great men of the town were embarrassed that they had embraced Mather's views with such uncritical enthusiasm.

---

32. Calef, *More Wonders of the Invisible World* 33.
33. Calef, *More Wonders of the Invisible World* 37.

A little more than a century after Cotton Mather's death, an historian of the Salem witch trials named Charles Upham would echo Calef's sentiments regarding the motives and moral shortcomings of Mather.

> Dr Cotton Mather aspired to be considered the leading champion of the church, and the most successful combatant against the prince of the power of the air. He seems to have longed for an opportunity to signalize himself in this particular kind of warfare; seized upon every occurrence that would admit of such a coloring to represent it as the result of diabolical agency; circulated in his numerous publications as many tales of witchcraft as he could collect through out New and Old England, and repeatedly endeavored to get up a delusion of this kind in Boston. He succeeded to some extent. An instance of witchcraft was brought about in that place by his management in 1688. There is some ground for suspicion that he was instrumental in causing the delusion in Salem; at any rate, he took a leading part in conducting it. And while there is evidence that he endeavored, after the delusion subsided, to escape the disgrace of having approved of the proceedings, and pretended to have been in some measure opposed to them, it can be too clearly shown that he was secretly and cunningly endeavoring to renew them during the next year in his own parish in Boston. I know no thing more artful and Jesuitical than his attempts, to avoid the reproach of having been active in carrying on the delusion in Salem, and elsewhere, and, at the same time, to keep up such a degree of credulity and superstition in the minds of the people, as to render it easy to plunge them into it again at the first favorable moment.[34]

Upham's opinion, so obviously shaded by that of Calef, would define the general consensus on Cotton Mather throughout the nineteenth and twentieth centuries. But more recently a reaction has occurred, and historians are inclined to see Mather as merely a man of his time who believed what all other men then believed, although perhaps with more enthusiasm than most. Mather was not "instrumental in causing the delusion at Salem," nor did he take a "leading part in conducting it." If Mather had a fault, it was in not seeing which way

---

34. Charles Upham, *Lectures on Witchcraft* (Boston: I. R. Butts, 1831), 106–8.

the wind was blowing on the subject of witchcraft, and not allowing himself to be blown along with it. He maintained his sincere opinion that witchcraft was real, that it was an operation of the Devil against Christendom, and that it was necessary to fight it with every resource lest it overwhelm the civilized world and plunge it into endless darkness.

From *Macbeth*

William Shakespeare

ACT III

Scene 5. *A Heath.*

Thunder. Enter the three Witches, *meeting* HECATE.

First Witch. Why, how now, Hecate! you look angerly.
Hecate. Have I not reason, beldams as you are,
Saucy and overbold? How did you dare
To trade and traffic with Macbeth
In riddles and affairs of death;
And I, the mistress of your charms,
The close contriver of all harms,
Was never call'd to bear my part,
Or show the glory of our art?
And, which is worse, all you have done
Hath been but for a wayward son,
Spiteful and wrathful, who, as others do,
Loves for his own ends, not for you.
But make amends now: get you gone,
And at the pit of Acheron
Meet me i' the morning: thither he
Will come to know his destiny;
Your vessels and your spells provide,
Your charms and everything beside.
I am for the air; this night I'll spend
Unto a dismal and a fatal end:
Great business must be wrought ere noon.
Upon the corner of the moon
There hangs a vaporous drop profound;
I'll catch it ere it come to ground:
And that distill'd by magic sleights

Shall raise such artificial sprites
As by the strength of their illusion
Shall draw him on to his confusion:
He shall spurn fate, scorn death, and bear
His hopes 'bove wisdom, grace, and fear:
And you all know, security
Is mortals' chiefest enemy.

    [*Music and a song within:* "Come away, come away," etc.
Hark! I am call'd; my little spirit, see,
Sits in a foggy cloud, and stays for me.   [*Exit.*

    First Witch. Come, let's make haste; she'll soon be back again.

                            [*Exeunt.*

ACT IV.
Scene 1. *A Cavern. In the Middle a Boiling Caldron.*
Thunder. Enter the three Witches.

    First Witch. Thrice the brinded cat hath mew'd.
    Second Witch. Thrice and once the hedgepig whin'd.
    Third Witch. Harpier cries, "'Tis time, 'tis time."
    First Witch. Round about the caldron go;
In the poison'd entrails throw.
Toad, that under the cold stone
Days and nights has thirty-one
Swelter'd venom sleeping got,
Boil thou first i' the charmed pot.

    All. Double, double toil and trouble;
Fire burn, and caldron bubble.

    Second Witch. Fillet of a fenny snake,
In the caldron boil and bake;
Eye of newt and toe of frog,
Wool of bat and tongue of dog,
Adder's fork and blindworm's sting,
Lizard's leg and howlet's wing,
For a charm of powerful trouble,

Like a hellbroth boil and bubble.

    All. Double, double toil and trouble;
Fire burn, and caldron bubble.

    Third Witch. Scale of dragon, tooth of wolf,
Witches' mummy, maw and gulf
Of the ravin'd salt-sea shark,
Root of hemlock digg'd i' the dark,
Liver of blaspheming Jew,
Gall of goat, and slips of yew
Sliver'd in the moon's eclipse,
Nose of Turk and Tartar's lips,
Finger of birth-strangled babe
Ditch-deliver'd by a drab,
Make the gruel thick and slab:
Add thereto a tiger's chawdron,
For the ingredients of our caldron.

    All. Double, double toil and trouble;
Fire burn, and caldron bubble.

    Second Witch. Cool it with a baboon's blood,
Then the charm is firm and good.

                Enter HECATE *to the other three* Witches.

    Hecate. O, well done! I commend your pains;
And every one shall share i' the gains:
And now about the caldron sing,
Like elves and fairies in a ring,
Enchanting all that you put in.

    [*Music and a song:* "Black spirits," *etc. Hecate retires.*

    Second Witch. By the pricking of my thumbs,
Something wicked this way comes.

    Open, locks,
    Whoever knocks!

                Enter MACBETH.

    Macbeth. How now, you secret, black, and midnight hags!
What is't you do?

All.   A deed without a name.

Macbeth. I conjure you, by that which you profess,
Howe'er you come to know it, answer me:
Though you untie the winds and let them fight
Against the churches; though the yeasty waves
Confound and swallow navigation up;
Though bladed corn be lodg'd and trees blown down;
Though castles topple on their warders' heads;
Though palaces and pyramids do slope
Their heads to their foundations; though the treasure
Of nature's germens tumble altogether,
Even till destruction sicken; answer me
To what I ask you.

First Witch.   Speak.

Second Witch.   Demand.

Third Witch.   We'll answer.

First Witch. Say if thou'dst rather hear it from our mouths,
Or from our masters'?

Macbeth.   Call 'em; let me see 'em.

First Witch. Pour in sow's blood, that hath eaten
Her nine farrow: grease that's sweaten
From the murderer's gibbet throw
Into the flame.

All. Come, high or low;
Thyself and office deftly show!

> *Thunder. First* Apparition: *an armed Head.*

Macbeth. Tell me, thou unknown power,—

First Witch.   He knows thy thought:
Hear his speech, but say thou naught.

First Apparition. Macbeth! Macbeth! Macbeth! beware Macduff;
Beware the Thane of Fife. Dismiss me. Enough.

> [*Descends.*

Macbeth. Whate'er thou art, for thy good caution, thanks;
Thou hast harp'd my fear aright: but one word more,—

First Witch. He will not be commanded: here's another,
More potent than the first.

> *Thunder. Second* Apparition: *a bloody Child.*

Second Apparition. Macbeth! Macbeth! Macbeth!

Macbeth. Had I three ears I'd hear thee.

Second Apparition. Be bloody, bold, and resolute; laugh to scorn
The power of man, for none of woman born
Shall harm Macbeth.   [*Descends.*

Macbeth. Then live, Macduff: what need I fear of thee?
But yet I'll make assurance double sure,
And take a bond of fate: thou shalt not live;
That I may tell pale-hearted fear it lies,
And sleep in spite of thunder.

> *Thunder. Third* Apparition: *a Child crowned, with a tree in his hand.*

> What is this
That rises like the issue of a king,
And wears upon his baby brow the round
And top of sovereignty?

All.   Listen, but speak not to't.

Third Apparition. Be lion-mettled, proud; and take no care
Who chafes, who frets, or where conspirers are:
Macbeth shall never vanquish'd be until
Great Birnam Wood to high Dunsinane Hill
Shall come against him.   [*Descends.*

Macbeth.   That will never be:
Who can impress the forest, bid the tree
Unfix his earth-bound root? Sweet bodements! good!
Rebellion's head rise never till the wood
Of Birnam rise, and our high-plac'd Macbeth
Shall live the lease of nature, pay his breath
To time and mortal custom. Yet my heart
Throbs to know one thing: tell me, if your art
Can tell so much, shall Banquo's issue ever
Reign in this kingdom?

All.   Seek to know no more,
Macbeth. I will be satisfied: deny me this
And an eternal curse fall on you! Let me know.
Why sinks that caldron? and what noise is this?

                                                    [*Hautboys.*

First Witch. Show!
Second Witch. Show!
Third Witch. Show!
All. Show his eyes, and grieve his heart;
Come like shadows, so depart!
                A show of eight Kings, the last with a glass in his hand;
                        Banquo's Ghost *following.*
Macbeth. Thou art too like the spirit of Banquo; down!
Thy crown does sear mine eyeballs. And thy hair,
Thou other gold-bound brow, is like the first.
A third is like the former. Filthy hags!
Why do you show me this? A fourth! Start, eyes!
What! will the line stretch out to the crack of doom?
Another yet! A seventh! I'll see no more:
And yet the eighth appears, who bears a glass
Which shows me many more; and some I see
That twofold balls and treble scepters carry:
Horrible sight! Now, I see, 'tis true;
For the blood-bolter'd Banquo smiles upon me,
And points at them for his. [*Apparitions vanish.*] What, is this so?
First Witch. Ay, sir, all this is so: but why
Stands Macbeth thus amazedly?
Come, sisters, cheer we up his sprights,
And show the best of our delights:
I'll charm the air to give a sound,
While you perform your antic round;
That this great king may kindly say,
Our duties did his welcome pay.
    [*Music. The Witches dance, and then vanish, with Hecate.*

Burnt Ghost

Simon MacCulloch

The woman who burned came last night.
The child is now under sedation.
The gradual incineration
Of charring flesh isn't a sight
For unprepared, innocent eyes.
A witch, we think, burnt at the stake,
And horribly eager to take
Revenge for the child-spiteful lies
Of youngsters who said she had hexed them,
When ugly demeanour and gait
Were really the grounds for their hate
And agedness all that had vexed them.
So now she assails us at will,
Tormenting each fresh generation
Of townsfolk, her manifestation
A screaming raw spectacle still.
A medium tried to persuade her
To let her long agony cease;
A spattering with hot human grease
Was how the roast spectre repaid her.
An exorcist's garments caught fire;
A psychic detective was choked;
She laughed and she howled and she smoked
And writhed in the reek of her pyre.
That's why we believe it is time,
Myself and these other men here,
To pay, though the price may be dear,
The debt of that long-ago crime.

A lottery gave us the names
(Your Bobbie, alas, being one)
To end it as it was begun
With the children this time in the flames.

Donna and the Yaga

Robert P. Ottone

Donna lit another cigarette and tucked herself into the motorcycle jacket she picked up last spring at the second-hand shop on the corner of Fifth and Garfield. It was heavy, but it kept her warm in the fall breeze whistling through the elevated train platform. She was at the station just off Sunset Park and could see from her vantage point the 9/11 memorial grove, the pool, and the playground, even under the dark of the night sky.

She checked her watch, then her phone to make sure the time was correct. Her sister often made fun of her for carrying both an iPhone and wearing a watch, since both essentially did the same thing, but Donna couldn't help that she was a creature of habit. The cigarettes were such a habit. So was being on time.

Which was why, when the trains ran late, she found herself annoyed. Not that she had anywhere to be; she'd spent the evening getting drinks with friends after work at Velour's down the street from the office, and had the entire weekend to relax and get caught up on paperwork, but she just wanted to get home already.

"Damn it," she muttered, turning from the tracks and looking east, further down. No trains were coming from either direction, and Donna rolled her eyes. She checked the MTA app and noted the green font stating that everything was, in fact, running on time.

She took another drag of the cigarette and turned toward the park again.

This time she noticed something different.

A house.

Standing above the trees near the center of the park, beside where Donna knew were basketball courts and a baseball field.

A house. *Floating.*

"What the hell?" she said softly, taking a step toward the chain-link fence that ran along the upper platform of the train station. She squinted and stared into the park.

There was a light on in one of the windows of the house.

Donna walked down the steps from the platform and started toward Sunset Park. It wasn't a far walk, maybe three minutes, yet she was thankful that along with the leather jacket she had her Uggs on. The drinks after work weren't about looking stylish; it was about unwinding after a particularly hectic week at the accounting firm. She bristled against a colder-than-normal breeze as she came to the metal gate leading into the park.

She pulled on the gate, but it wouldn't budge. She could still see the house from this new vantage point, its sloped A-frame looking sharp in the distance against the dark blue, starless sky.

Looking around, Donna found purchase on the gate and began climbing over, her curiosity getting the better of her. She knew the danger of being caught in the park at night. She could pay the fine. She needed to know what exactly this house *was,* and how it had seemingly gone up overnight.

All the times she'd passed Sunset Park, there hadn't been anything like this. It was just a park. A heavily used, well-funded part of New York City's infrastructure, providing a green oasis in a sea of gray. Donna had been to concerts there, had gone to art exhibitions, been on dates.

Never once had she seen a house, floating or otherwise, in the center of the park.

Once over the fence, she tucked herself into her jacket more and started along the dimly lit path toward the basketball court. She'd played HORSE with co-workers here from time to time, and knew it well. She'd never won a game, but she wasn't one to shy away from a challenge, especially not one posed by the overly aggressive dudes she worked with—the ones Donna and her friends at the firm called "the schmuck squad."

Donna lit another cigarette as she neared the chain-link fence that ran along the perimeter of the basketball courts. There were a couple of basketballs leaning against the fencing, and she stepped closer, trying to get a better sense as to where the house might be. She stared up into the sky, the small thicket of woody trees surrounding the court and saw nothing.

"What the . . . ?"

Then she saw it.

The sharp-pitched roof stabbing into the sky like a spear. But not in the position she saw it in earlier. It was as if the house had moved. Donna knew that she should have been able to see it just north of the basketball court, and now, staring at the point of the roof situated south, she was confused.

Did I have too much to drink? Donna thought, removing her glasses and wiping her eyes. She blinked a few times and looked back south.

The house remained.

As Donna walked through the small thicket of woods separating her from the strange structure, she did her best to keep her eyes on the pitched roof.

She sparked her lighter, using it the best she could to see in the encroaching darkness of the quarter acre of woodland she was walking through to make it toward the house. Within, she looked around, spotting two trees that were thicker than the others. On each there were ridges, not unlike a palm tree, sharp, pointing upward, each one like a small seal or scale. Thin, hair-like vines dangled, bristling in the light breeze as Donna walked underneath the home, staring upward into the abyssal darkness where the two trees holding the structure aloft disappeared.

Donna ran her hand along the ridges of one of the supporting trunks and it felt rough, like calloused flesh, spongy in places, but rough in others. She wondered if the trees were healthy and what kind they might be, as she'd never seen trees this thick before in her life. She knew redwoods grew incredibly thick, but that took decades, possibly centuries, to grow to such a thickness, but here in Sunset Park a tree so thick would be difficult to hide, let alone two. The parks department would surely make these ancient natural wonders a highlight of the park itself. An attraction of sorts.

The trees surrounding these two were nowhere near the same thickness. They were your average beeches, ashes, and poplars. Nothing too crazy in this part of the city.

Donna stared up into the darkness above her. She could make out something faint shifting in the inky void, but nothing specific. Just the slightest hints of movement. Enough to draw her eye, but not enough to discern anything truly visible. The darkness seemed to grow above her and she realized, as her heart began to race and a bead of sweat slid down her cheek, that the house, once aloft, had now begun to lower.

The enormous trees to her left and right began to bow, and Donna furrowed her brow, confused. A soft rustle of the trees around her drew her attention back skyward as the darkness enveloped her in warm, humid folds.

Did I drink too much? Am I home asleep? What the fuck is happening?

She found herself within gossamer nebulae, as if caught in a thousand spider webs, traces of silken thread gliding over her until finally, inevitably, a confusing, deep darkness. Dreamlike in its abstraction, but altogether crystalline beyond her eyes. As if the entire world had flipped the light switch, and she was still awake to see it.

The darkness of an empty room.

When Donna's eyes opened, she found herself staring at great wooden beams, stretching out widely from a pitched ceiling. She slipped her glasses off, wiped them, then rubbed her eyes hard, her head aching. When she slipped her glasses back on and the blurriness of the world gave way to clarity, she sat up on her elbows and looked around.

Flames crackled from a large, ornate stone fireplace. There were large graphical embellishments on some of the rocky slabs that Donna couldn't make out, and she was reminded of the old colonial homes she'd toured as a child in some of the more historic parts of Long Is-

133

land and upstate New York. The kind of places elementary school field trips go to give kids a sense of what it was like during the early, turbulent days of America.

A large dining-room table, also looking as though it emerged through a warp in time from the eighteenth century, sat to Donna's right, closer to the center of the room. It was adorned with a purple table runner and on the table itself, a great array of delights from succulent turkey to glistening fruit to freshly baked rolls, the scent of which wafted into Donna's nostrils and made her smile, remembering her youth in Queens, when her grandmother would bake fresh bread whenever Donna and her sister Laura would visit on weekends.

Slowly, Donna stood on her wobbly, tired legs. She felt as if she'd sprinted a mile, and yet . . . she was merely standing beneath the mysterious treehouse.

"Take it easy now," a voice came from behind her.

Donna spun and saw a woman. Ancient, tiny, seated upon a large stool, her gnarled fingers gripping an enormous pestle. The matching mortar was held in place by the woman's shrunken, shriveled feet, with toenails that had grown to absurd lengths, twisting violently in directions no human toenail should go, ribbon-like in their absurdity.

The woman's face was tiny, and in the dim lighting of the fireplace Donna could see that her nose was almost comically long. When the light caught it, it reflected almost metal in the darkness, and Donna wondered how such a small face could hold up such a long, preposterous nose.

"Oh. Hello," Donna said. "Where the hell am I?"

The woman recoiled at the vulgarity, waving a shriveled hand around as if to dismiss the word or its ghostly remnants from the air. "Please," she whimpered. "Please, no bad words. Nothing like that here, darling, please."

The tiny woman slipped off her stool and Donna got a better look at her. She wore a white dress adorned with dark stitching that ran across the sleeves and down the front. Symbology and shapes Donna didn't recognize. A crimson skirt ended just above the woman's ankles, and it too was adorned with various symbols. Small, rock-like objects dangled from a thick golden rope tied around the woman's waist.

Arm hair. Enormous lengths of arm hair ran off the woman, stretched across the floor to the left and right of herself, running up the walls and out the windows. Donna remembered the strings and vines below the house and shuddered, realizing now that it was the woman's hair.

The old lady stepped carefully, her toenails click-clacking across the wooden floor of the home. She used the pestle as a kind of cane, and it thudded before her with every step. There was a loftiness in the way the woman moved, as if her feet didn't truly touch the ground. Donna watched to ensure that they did, but in the fireplace lighting of the room she couldn't be sure.

Donna's eyes went wide as she watched the small woman move. There was a strange uneasiness that soaked through her as she watched the elderly figure shift in the dim light. There was something not altogether *natural* about the woman—and then it hit her.

The way she moved was almost uncannily real. Like something fake doing its level best to appear real. The only thing that came to mind was Jim Henson. The damn *Muppets,* of all things. Beings created by man that looked and acted real enough that you *believed* they were truly alive. Imbued with such personality that their actions, absurd as they may be, were actually happening.

This woman. From her small frame to her toenails, to the way she carefully walked around, looked like a damned Muppet.

The thought made Donna smile.

"What's funny, dearie?" the woman asked. Her voice was strangely deep. Masculine in a way.

"Nothing, something stupid," Donna said. "What is this place?"

"What do you think it is?"

"I think it's a dream because I'm talking to the smallest human being I've ever seen in my life who has arm hair so long it stretches out the damned windows," Donna said.

At the word "damned," the woman covered her ears and began muttering in a language Donna couldn't understand. It was vaguely Russian-sounding, but she wasn't sure.

"Please," the woman said. "Please, please, I beg you, you must stop with such vile words. Please!"

"All right," Donna said, holding her hands up to try and calm the woman down. "I'm sorry. I'm from New York, cursing is kind of in my blood, you know?"

"Is it?" the woman asked. "What else is in your blood?" She looked genuinely curious.

Donna stared at the woman, confused. "It's just an expression," Donna finally said after an uncomfortable silence between them. "Am I inside that treehouse?"

Suddenly, what she could see of the house shuddered and Donna felt herself lose her balance. She braced her hands against the large dining-room table and noticed that the food hadn't budged at all. The distant walls of the home were still shrouded in darkness, despite the flickering of the fireplace.

"What was that?"

"We're walking," the woman said, plucking a grape that was almost as big as her eyeball off the table and popping it into her mouth.

As the woman chewed, Donna could see her teeth. Like her nose, they looked metallic. Some of them sharp, others like normal human teeth, but made out of dark steel. Donna was reminded of the various bridges holding New York City together.

This woman's teeth were the same color as the Kosciuszko bridge.

"Where are we going?" Donna asked.

"Where do you *want* to go?" the woman replied after gulping down the vulgarly macerated grape.

"Home," Donna said. "To my bed in my tiny apartment. Where I can sleep off this dream and wake up and eat leftover Chinese food tomorrow for breakfast."

There was a silence as the house shuddered again, the flames dancing and sparking violently in the fireplace.

"It is already tomorrow," the woman said. "And breakfast will be soon."

Donna looked at all the delicacies on the table. "Looks like you're good on food."

"Oh, well, that's not *all* for me," the woman said. "It's for you, too. It's for my *guests*."

"Guests?"

"Yes, yes, of course!" the woman shouted, leaping into the air and clapping her hands. Donna thought for the briefest moment that she was held aloft by some unseen force if only for a moment before clicking back down on her toenails.

The room became brighter and Donna could see the walls with greater clarity. There were glass cases built into the walls, jutting out barely two inches, like an aquarium built into the home itself. In each glass case Donna could make out white-gray rocky pieces as the flames from the fireplace grew in intensity, her eyes adjusting to the increased lighting.

Sconces, round and white, sparked to life, mouths and eyes shimmering an intense shine. Glowing unnaturally, as if by conjuration.

The woman giggled, her tiny gnarled hands to her mouth.

Donna got closer to one such glass case and looked inside.

Bones.

She was staring at bones.

Donna stared at one of the skulls inside the glass case. It was small. A child's skull.

She looked at the sconces and noticed that they, too, were skulls. Some adult-sized, some smaller. The light within them glowed strangely, the color an unnatural pinkish-red.

"You're a monster," Donna said. "I know I'm dreaming."

The woman crept closer, and in the increased light of the room Donna could see that her captor was, in fact, floating. Her ribboned, fungal toenails scraped across the wooden floor as she moved.

"A dream?" the woman muttered, flashing her metallic teeth at Donna in an unnatural rictus. "You're adorable, darling. No. It's been three days, you're not dreaming."

Donna looked out the nearest window. Though the house was still rocking side to side, akin to a boat, she could barely see anything through the darkness outside. The occasional treetop. A smattering of stars.

"Three days? Maybe three minutes," Donna said.

"Time is like a game," the woman said, tapping a dirty, wrinkled finger against one of the bone-filled glass tanks. "It comes and goes; I can do whatever I want with it, you see. Things are different in here."

"And where is 'in here,' ma'am?" Donna asked.

"You saw my house," the woman said. "In the park. We picked you up."

"We?"

The woman nodded. Her gray hair bobbed around, almost as long as her entire body. As the woman moved, her arm hair dragged behind her. Donna watched it and could see it was still out the far left and right windows, no matter how much the creature before her fluttered around in the home.

"My hut," the woman said. "I say 'we,' but really it's just a part of me, like my arms or legs. The home is a *part* of me, you see? Is your home a part of *you*?"

"It's a sixth-floor walkup," Donna said, looking around for any way out of the room. She looked again out the window, bracing herself on the windowsill as the structure continued to move. "So . . . not really."

"Pity," the woman said, shifting closer to Donna. "Our homes are where we spend the most time, I think. Around the fire." She paused, gestured to the glass cases of bones. "With friends."

"Friends?" Donna asked. "You call these people friends? You killed them." She backed further away from the woman, moving in a half-circle toward one of the windows where the woman's lengthy arm hair still ran.

"*Killed* them?" the woman laughed. "No, no."

Moving quickly, the woman grabbed Donna by the wrist before

she could move further away. She sank her teeth hard into Donna's arm, the motorcycle jacket holding firm the best it could under assault from metal teeth. As Donna pulled away, she could feel the teeth tearing into her flesh and she stumbled backward, landing hard.

"*Ate* them, darling," the woman said, her mouth glistening with Donna's fresh blood. A thick, bulbous tongue emerged from her mouth and licked the blood from her lips. She dropped the pestle and it slammed hard to the floor.

Donna scrambled to her feet, holding her throbbing arm, and made a beeline for the window. She grabbed one of the sconces from the wall and pulled hard, tearing it loose with relative ease. Holding it, she was shocked by the warmth it gave off, as if the strangely colored fire within was putting out hundreds of candles' worth of light and intensity. She lowered it to the hair that lay her feet and hoped her plan would work.

"What are you?" the woman shouted, her voice going deeper, a vulgar unearthly sound.

The pinkish flame within the skull in Donna's hands caught the woman's arm hair quickly, and Donna watched as it snaked its way around the room, heading directly toward the tiny Muppet-woman.

Thinking quickly, Donna ran for the opposite window, where the other arm's hair was still draped over the sill and outward. She held the skull-sconce tightly and threw one leg over the lip of the window as the tiny woman thrashed around the home, her body engulfed in flame.

Donna knew she had only moments before the hair on the woman's other arm would catch ablaze, so she lobbed the glowing skull out the window and began her descent. The foul-smelling thick hair she used as a makeshift rope as the strange house continued to move through the darkness of Sunset Park.

She could see the baseball fields in the distance and knew she only had moments before the home would be out of the confines of the park and out onto the Brooklyn streets, where dropping off the side of this strange structure might result in injury or possibly worse.

Donna could hear the woman screaming above, a deep roar from within the confines of the home. It was smaller than she thought. The interior was a strange geometry to Donna. She pushed the thought out of her mind as she climbed further down, realizing there was still a twenty-foot gap between the bottom of her makeshift arm hair rope and the grass below.

She took a deep breath and let go.

By the time Donna's eyes opened, it was morning. A small crowd of men were around her, all wearing T-shirts, basketball jerseys, and gym shorts. As her eyes adjusted to the light around her, one of them stretched out his hand.

"Are you okay, ma'am?"

She reached up and took his grip, and he helped Donna to her feet.

"Oh, my god," another one said. "She's the woman on the posters."

"Posters?" Donna asked. She was holding her head and felt wobbly. Dehydrated. Exhausted. "What posters?"

One of the basketball players took off and the others escorted Donna to a nearby bench, where they sat her down and offered her squirt bottles full of ice-cold water. She couldn't remember a time when water tasted so good as she gulped down mouthful after mouthful.

The player who'd run off from the group returned with a piece of torn paper in his hands. A missing persons poster. With Donna's face on it.

"Says you disappeared three days ago," he said. "Is there someone you'd like us to call?"

Donna looked around. "My sister." Donna fumbled around in her jacket pocket for the small notebook she kept. She handed it to the man. "It'll be on the first page. Her name is Laura."

After recovering for two days in New York Presbyterian Hospital, Donna was wheeled out the front doors by her sister.

In the cab on the way back to Sunset Park, Laura wouldn't stop asking questions. She was almost as confused as Donna, but Donna knew that her sister was also mad because she thought she was lying.

About where she'd been for three days. Donna told her that she'd been drunk, that she must have hit her head or gotten lost in the park, but that didn't seem to be working.

Donna knew that the reality of what had happened was altogether too strange to tell her younger sister. What could she possibly say?

I was kidnapped by a witch for three days and almost eaten.

"Honestly, Laura, I'm fine, I just hit my head."

"Yeah, and I suppose you got those bite marks on your arm by bumping your head, huh?" Laura sighed. "I wish you'd tell me what really happened. You know, if some guy attacked you, we can go to the cops and—"

"Maybe it was a dog. Bit me while I was unconscious," Donna offered, cutting Laura off.

Laura shook her head. "They're human bite marks, ya creepo."

The cab pulled up to Sunset Park and they both climbed out. Laura paid the driver as Donna started walking into the park. She saw no evidence of the strange house. As she approached the basketball courts, she could hear the clip-clop of Laura's heels walking quickly behind her.

"I don't understand why we have to come back here," Laura said. "I wouldn't think you'd ever want to see this place again."

Donna stood near where she first encountered the home. In the daylight she could see clouds in the sky, the sun blazing above. Kids with their parents ran around the park, and a group of men played basketball behind the chain-link fence.

"Ma's gonna be pissed if we don't get there on time," Laura said. "She's ordering from that Portuguese place and you know the rush hour train'll be packed . . ."

The flickering of something pinkish-red in the verdant darkness of the woods caught Donna's eye, and she darted off deeper into the thick thatch of trees near the basketball courts.

"Donna, jeez, wait up!" Laura called after her.

Donna moved carefully through the woods, remembering her night-time visit. The glow was hard to see in the daylight, but it was there. As she approached, she knew exactly what it was—the skull-sconce. Still ablaze with its pinkish glow.

She pulled the skull from the patch of shrubbery it had fallen into and held it in her hands. There was warmth, but mostly there was light. The fire within grew a bit once freed from the darkness of the bushes. Donna smiled, the glow bathing her in pinkish light.

She heard her sister approaching behind her.

"What the fuck is that?" Laura asked.

Donna smiled. "The truth."

Donna and Laura sat opposite each other in the last car on the crowded Long Island Railroad train as it made its way through the tunnels under the East River. Donna held the skull in her hands, and as the car went darker the two sisters found themselves bathed in pinkish light.

"This thing's a trip," Laura said.

"I know," Donna said.

The crackle of the train car's sound system squawked to life as the train rumbled to a halt.

"Ladies and gentlemen, there appears to be a blockage on the line up ahead," the engineer spoke over the system. "Our crews are on-site already, and it shouldn't take longer than five minutes. We apologize for the delay."

The crowd aboard the busy LIRR car groaned loudly as Donna continued staring at the skull in her lap. She held it wrapped partially in her leather jacket to keep any curious onlookers at bay.

Donna looked up at noticed Laura staring out the window beside her.

"What's up?" Donna asked.

"Donna . . ." Laura whispered before trailing off. She raised a slender finger and gestured toward the rear of the train.

Donna turned and stared. In the distance behind the train, even in the darkness of the tunnel, she could make out a faint orange glow.

Fire.

A small house. On fire.

Walking on enormous legs.

Moving closer and closer as the train's lights came back on and began moving once more through the snake-like tunnels below the East River.

Donna jumped from her seat and ran to the rear of the car, pushing her way through the crowd and pressing herself against the rear metal doors of the car.

As the train broke into the light of day and emerged from the tunnel, Donna stared.

The house emerged after a moment, as the train sped further down the tracks. The legs stomped along the tracks; the house blackened from the fire.

Legs?

Enormous chicken legs.

After an excruciating few seconds that felt like hours, the train left the home safely in the dust.

Donna collapsed against the door of the train and saw the crowd staring down at her.

Laura emerged and helped her back to her seat. The skull sat, cradled in the motorcycle jacket, the left arm torn from where the woman had bit her days earlier.

The eyes and mouth of the skull glowed pink.

From *The Discoverie of Witches*

Matthew Hopkins

Querie. How can any possibly believe that the Devill and the Witch joyning together, should have such power, as the Witches confesse, to kill such and such a man, child, horse, cow, or the like; if we beleeve

they can doe what they will, then we derogate from God's power, who for certain limits the Devil and the Witch; and I cannot beleeve they have any power at all.

Answer. God suffers the Devill many times to doe much hurt, and the devil doth play many times the deluder and impostor with these Witches, in perswading them that they are the cause of such and such a murder wrought by him with their consents, when and indeed neither he nor they had any hand in it, as thus: We must needs argue, he is of a long standing, above 6000 yeers, then he must needs be the best Scholar in all knowledges of arts and tongues, and so have the best skill in *Physicke,* judgment in *Physiognomie,* and knowledge of what disease is reigning or predominant in this or that man's body, (and so for cattell too) by reason of his long experience. This subtile tempter knowing such a man lyable to some sudden disease, (as by experience I have found) as *Plurisie, Imposthume,* &c., he resorts to divers Witches; if they know the man, and seek to make a difference between the Witches and the party, it may be by telling them he hath threatned to have them very shortly searched, and so hanged for Witches, then they all consult with *Satan* to save themselves, and *Satan* stands ready prepared, with a *What will you have me doe for you, my deare and nearest children, covenanted and compacted with me in my hellish league, and sealed with your blood, my delicate firebrand-darlings.*[1] Oh thou (say they) that at the first didst promise to save us thy servants from any of our deadly enemies discovery, and didst promise to avenge and slay all those, we pleased, that did offend us; Murther that wretch suddenly who threatens the down-fall of your loyall subjects. He then promiseth to effect it. Next newes is heard the partie is dead, he comes to the witch, and gets a world of reverence, credence and respect for his power and activeness, when and indeed the disease kills the party, not the Witch, nor the Devill, (onely the Devill knew that such a disease was predominant) and the witch aggravates her damnation by her familiarity and consent to the Devill, and so comes likewise in compass of the Lawes. This is Satan's

---

1. *The Divelles Speech to the Witches.*

145

usuall impostring and deluding, but not his constant course of proceeding, for he and the witch doe mischiefe too much. But I would that Magistrates and Jurats would a little examine witnesses when they heare witches confess such and such a murder, whether the party had not long time before, or at the time when the witch grew suspected, some disease or other predominant, which might cause that issue or effect of death.

A Visit from the Shades

Im Bang

There was a minister in olden days who once, when he was Palace Secretary, was getting ready for office in the morning. He had on his ceremonial dress. It was rather early, and as he leaned on his arm-rest for a moment, sleep overcame him. He dreamt, and in the dream he thought he was mounted and on his journey. He was crossing the bridge at the entrance to East Palace Street, when suddenly he saw his mother coming towards him on foot. He at once dismounted, bowed, and said, "Why do you come thus, mother, not in a chair, but on foot?"

She replied, "I have already left the world, and things are not where I am as they are where you are, and so I walk."

The secretary asked, "Where are you going, please?"

She replied, "We have a servant living at Yong-san, and they are having a witches' prayer service there just now, so I am going to partake of the sacrifice."

"But," said the secretary, "we have sacrificial days, many of them, at our own home, those of the four seasons, also on the first and fifteenth of each month. Why do you go to a servant's house and not to mine?"

The mother replied, "Your sacrifices are of no interest to me, I like the prayers of the witches. If there is no medium we spirits find no satisfaction. I am in a hurry," said she, "and cannot wait longer," so she spoke her farewell and was gone.

The secretary awoke with a start, but felt that he had actually seen what had come to pass.

He then called a servant and told him to go at once to So-and-So's house in Yong-san, and tell a certain servant to come that night without fail. "Go quickly," said the secretary, "so that you can be back before I enter the Palace." Then he sat down to meditate over it.

In a little the servant had gone and come again. It was not yet broad daylight, and because it was cold the servant did not enter straight, but went first into the kitchen to warm his hands before the fire. There was a fellow-servant there who asked him, "Have you had something to drink?"

He replied, "They are having a big witch business on at Yong-san, and while the *mutang* (witch) was performing, she said that the spirit that possessed her was the mother of the master here. On my appearance she called out my name and said, 'This is a servant from our house.' Then she called me and gave me a big glass of spirit. She added further, 'On my way here I met my son going into the Palace.'"

The secretary, overhearing this talk from the room where he was waiting, broke down and began to cry. He called in the servant and made fuller inquiry, and more than ever he felt assured that his mother's spirit had really gone that morning to share in the *koot* (witches' sacrificial ceremony). He then called the *mutang*, and in behalf of the spirit of his mother made her a great offering. Ever afterwards he sacrificed to her four times a year at each returning season.

The Witch in the Graveyard

Clark Ashton Smith

Scene: A forsaken graveyard, by moonlight. Enter two witches.

FIRST WITCH
Sit, sister, now that haggish Hecate
Appropriate and ghastly favor sheds,
And with wild light forwards our enterprise;
And watch the weighted eyelids of each grave,
As never mother watched her babe, to mark,
At zenith of the necromantic moon,
The stir of that disquiet, when the dead,
From suckling nightmares of the charnel dark
Or long insomnia on a mouldy couch,
Impelled like wan somnambulists, arise—
Constrained to emerge and walk, or seated each
On his own tombstone, shrouded council hold,
Or commerce with the sooty wings of hell.
All omens of this influential hour
When all dark powers, thronging to the dark,
Promote enchantment with their wavèd wings,
And brim the wind with potency malign—
A dew of dread to aid our cauldron—these
Observe thou closely, while I seek afield
All requisite swart herbs of venefice
And evil roots unto our usance ripe.

(The first witch departs, leaving the other among the tombs, and returns after a time, in the course of her search.)

FIRST WITCH
Sister, what seest or what hearest thou?

149

SECOND WITCH
        I see
The moonlight, and the slowly moving gleam
That westers hour by hour on tomb and stone;
And shrivelled lilies, tossed i' the winter's breath
With their attenuate shadows, as might dance
Phantom with flaffing phantom; at my side,
The white and shuddering grasses of the grave,
With nettles, and the parching fumitory,
Whose leaves, root-trellised on the bones of death,
Will rasp and bristle to the lightest wind.

(The first witch moves on, and approaches again, after an interval.)

FIRST WITCH
Sister, what seest or what hearest thou?

SECOND WITCH
        I see
The mound-stretched gossamers, cradles to the dew;
Moon-wefted briers, and the cypress-trees
With shadow swathed, or cerements of the moon;
And corpse-lights borne from aisle to secret aisle
Within the footless forest. . . .
        Now I hear
The lich-owl, shrieking lethal prophecy;
And whimpering winds, the children of the air,
Lost in the glades of mystery and gloom.

(The first witch disappears, and passes again shortly.)

FIRST WITCH
Sister, what seest or what hearest thou?

SECOND WITCH
        I see

The ghost-white owl, with huge, sulphureous eyes,
That veers in prone, unwhispered flight, and hear
The small shriek of the moon-adventuring mole,
Griped in mid-graveyard. . . . And I see
Where some wild shadow shakes, though the pale wind
Of midnight stirs far off . . . and hear
Curst mandragores that gibber to the moon,
Though no man treads anigh. . . .
    (After an interval)
Some predal hand doth hold the wandering air;
Now dies the throttled wind with rattling breath,
And round about a breathing Silence prowls.
    (After another interval)
I hear the cheeping of the bat-lipped ghouls,
Aroused beneath the vaulted cypresses
Far off; and lipless muttering of tombs,
With clash of bones bestirred in ancient charnels
Beneath their shroud of unclean light that crawls. . . .
Earth shudders, and rank odours 'gin to rise
From tombs a-crack; and shaken out all at once
From mid-air, and directly 'neath the moon,
Meseems what hanging wing divides the light,
Like a black film of mist, or thickest shadow:
But on the tomb there is no shadow!

FIRST WITCH
Enough! 'twill be a prosperous night, methinks,
For commerce of the demons with the dead,
And for us too, when every omen's good,
And fraught with promise of a potent brew.

A Modest Enquiry into the Nature of Witchcraft

John Hale

Some Histories speak of strange *Extasies* of confessed Witches. *R. B.* of the kingdom of Darkness, tells us of a Woman confessing her self a Witch, who pretended she had been turned into a Wolf & killed a Sheep & Cow in that shape, and the Cow & Sheep were killed at that time. And of a man Wolf that was suspected in that shape, to devour Cattle, and his face had several scratches and hurts, which they said were given him by the Dogs that took him for a Wolf, and he confest himself, that twice a year he was changed from a man to a Wolf. But this change could not be real, but an abuse of Phantasie, either from a distracting Melancholy called *Lycanthropia,* whereby he imagined he was transformed into a Wolf. Or else, if he were indeed a Wizard, the Devil cast him into a profound trance, whereby he imagined he was killing Cattle as a Wolf; while the mischief done was other wise, and probably by a real Wolf.

But those that have been obsessed have had strange *Extasies;* as some of our afflicted persons have had their trance fits; in which they lay long time in a Swoon, and when they came out of them declared they had been carried to delectable places, and had seen glorious sights of Men and Angels; as is in part declared above, *Chapt.* 5. So that its easier to find a person possessed or distracted by such *Extasies,* than to prove a person hereby in voluntary league with the Devil.

A Witch's Den

Helena P. Blavatsky

Our kind host Sham Rao was very gay during the remaining hours of our visit. He did his best to entertain us, and would not hear of our leaving the neighbourhood without having seen its greatest celebrity, its most interesting sight. A *jadu wâlâ*—sorceress—well known in the district, was just at this time under the influence of seven sister-goddesses, who took possession of her by turns, and spoke their oracles through her lips. Sham Rao said we must not fail to see her, be it only in the interests of science.

The evening closes in, and we once more get ready for an excursion. It is only five miles to the cavern of the Pythia of Hindostan; the road runs through a jungle, but it is level and smooth. Besides, the jungle and its ferocious inhabitants have ceased to frighten us. The timid elephants we had in the "dead city" are sent home, and we are to mount new behemoths belonging to a neighbouring Râjâ. The pair, that stand before the verandah like two dark hillocks, are steady and trustworthy. Many a time these two have hunted the royal tiger, and no wild shrieking or thunderous roaring can frighten them. And so, let us start! The ruddy flames of the torches dazzle our eyes and increase the forest gloom. Our surroundings seem so dark, so mysterious. There is something indescribably fascinating, almost solemn, in these night-journeys in the out-of-the-way corners of India. Everything is silent and deserted around you, everything is dozing on the earth and over-head. Only the heavy, regular tread of the elephants breaks the stillness of the night, like the sound of falling hammers in the underground smithy of Vulcan. From time to time uncanny voices and murmurs are heard in the black forest.

"The wind sings its strange song amongst the ruins," says one of us, "what a wonderful acoustic phenomenon!"

"Bhûta, bhûta!" whisper the awestruck torch-bearers. They brandish their torches and swiftly spin on one leg, and snap their fingers to chase away the aggressive spirits.

The plaintive murmur is lost in the distance. The forest is once more filled with the cadences of its invisible nocturnal life—the metallic whirr of the crickets, the feeble, monotonous croak of the tree-frog, the rustle of the leaves. From time to time all this suddenly stops short and then begins again, gradually increasing and increasing.

Heavens! What teeming life, what stores of vital energy are hidden under the smallest leaf, the most imperceptible blades of grass, in this tropical forest! Myriads of stars shine in the dark blue of the sky, and myriads of fireflies twinkle at us from every bush, moving sparks, like a pale reflection of the far-away stars.

We left the thick forest behind us, and reached a deep glen, on three sides bordered with the thick forest, where even by day the shadows are as dark as by night. We were about two thousand feet above the foot of the Vindhya ridge, judging by the ruined wall of Mandu, straight above our heads.

Suddenly a very chilly wind rose that nearly blew our torches out. Caught in the labyrinth of bushes and rocks, the wind angrily shook the branches of the blossoming syringas, then, shaking itself free, it turned back along the glen and flew down the valley, howling, whistling and shrieking, as if all the fiends of the forest together were joining in a funeral song.

"Here we are," said Sham Rao, dismounting. "Here is the village; the elephants cannot go any further."

"The village? Surely you are mistaken. I don't see anything but trees."

"It is too dark to see the village. Besides, the huts are so small, and so hidden by the bushes, that even by daytime you could hardly find them. And there is no light in the houses, for fear of the spirits."

"And where is your witch? Do you mean we are to watch her performance in complete darkness?"

Sham Rao cast a furtive, timid look round him; and his voice, when he answered our questions, was somewhat tremulous.

"I implore you not to call her a witch! She may hear you. . . . It is not far off, it is not more than half a mile. Do not allow this short distance to shake your decision. No elephant, and even no horse, could make its way there. We must walk. . . . But we shall find plenty of light there. . . ."

This was unexpected, and far from agreeable. To walk in this gloomy Indian night; to scramble through thickets of cactuses; to venture in a dark forest, full of wild animals—this was too much for Miss X———. She declared that she would go no further. She would wait for us in the howdah, on the elephant's back, and perhaps would go to sleep.

Narayan was against this *parti de plaisir* from the very beginning, and now, without explaining his reasons, he said she was the only sensible one among us.

"You won't lose anything," he remarked, "by staying where you are. And I only wish everyone would follow your example."

"What ground have you for saying so, I wonder?" remonstrated Sham Rao, and a slight note of disappointment rang in his voice, when he saw that the excursion, proposed and organized by himself, threatened to come to nothing. "What harm could be done by it? I won't insist any more that the 'incarnation of gods' is a rare sight, and that the Europeans hardly ever have an opportunity of witnessing it; but, besides, the Kangalim in question is no ordinary woman. She leads a holy life; she is a prophetess, and her blessing could not prove harmful to any one. I insisted on this excursion out of pure patriotism."

"Sahib, if your patriotism consists in displaying before foreigners the worst of our plagues, then why did you not order all the lepers of your district to assemble and parade before the eyes of our guests? You are a *patèl,* you have the power to do it."

How bitterly Narayan's voice sounded to our unaccustomed ears. Usually he was so even-tempered, so indifferent to everything belonging to the exterior world.

Fearing a quarrel between the Hindus, the colonel remarked, in a conciliatory tone, that it was too late for us to reconsider our expedition. Besides, without being a believer in the "incarnation of gods," he was personally firmly convinced that demoniacs existed even in the West. He was eager to study every psychological phenomenon, wherever he met with it, and whatever shape it might assume.

It would have been a striking sight for our European and American friends if they had beheld our procession on that dark night. Our way lay along a narrow winding path up the mountain. Not more than two people could walk together—and we were thirty, including the torch-bearers. Surely some reminiscence of night sallies against the confederate Southerners had revived in the colonel's breast, judging by the readiness with which he took upon himself the leadership of our small expedition. He ordered all the rifles and revolvers to be loaded, despatched three torch-bearers to march ahead of us, and arranged us in pairs. Under such a skilled chieftain we had nothing to fear from tigers; and so our procession started, and slowly crawled up the winding path.

It cannot be said that the inquisitive travellers, who appeared later on, in the den of the prophetess of Mandu, shone through the freshness and elegance of their costumes. My gown, as well as the travelling suits of the colonel and of Mr. Y——, were nearly torn to pieces. The cactuses gathered from us whatever tribute they could, and the Babu's dishevelled hair swarmed with a whole colony of grasshoppers and fireflies, which, probably, were attracted thither by the smell of cocoanut oil. The stout Sham Rao panted like a steam engine. Narayan alone was like his usual self; that is to say, like a bronze Hercules, armed with a club. At the last abrupt turn of the path, after having surmounted the difficulty of climbing over huge, scattered stones, we suddenly found ourselves on a perfectly smooth place; our eyes, in spite of our many torches, were dazzled with light; and our ears were struck by a medley of unusual sounds.

A new glen opened before us, the entrance of which, from the valley, was well masked by thick trees. We understood how easily we might have wandered round it, without ever suspecting its existence. At the bottom of the glen we discovered the abode of the celebrated Kangalim.

The den, as it turned out, was situated in the ruin of an old Hindu temple in tolerably good preservation. In all probability it was built long before the "dead city," because during the epoch of the latter, the heathen were not allowed to have their own places of worship; and the temple stood quite close to the wall of the town, in fact, right under it. The cupolas of the two smaller lateral pagodas had fallen long ago, and huge bushes grew out of their altars. This evening, their branches were hidden under a mass of bright coloured rags, bits of ribbon, little pots, and various other talismans; because, even in them, popular superstition sees something sacred.

"And are not these poor people right? Did not these bushes grow on sacred ground? Is not their sap impregnated with the incense of offerings, and the exhalations of holy anchorites, who once lived and breathed here?"

The learned but superstitious Sham Rao would only answer our questions by new questions.

But the central temple, built of red granite, stood unharmed by time, and, as we learned afterwards, a deep tunnel opened just behind its closely-shut door. What was beyond it no one knew. Sham Rao assured us that no man of the last three generations had ever stepped over the threshold of this thick iron door; no one had seen the subterranean passage for many years. Kangalim lived there in perfect isolation, and, according to the oldest people in the neighbourhood, she had always lived there. Some people said she was three hundred years old; others alleged that a certain old man on his death-bed had revealed to his son that this old woman was no one else than *his own uncle*. This fabulous uncle had settled in the cave in the times when the "dead city" still counted several hundreds of inhabitants. The hermit, busy paving his road to Moksha, had no intercourse with the rest of the world, and nobody knew how he lived and what he ate. But a good while ago, in the days when the Bellati (foreigners) had not yet taken possession of this mountain, the old hermit suddenly was transformed into a hermitess. She continues his pursuits and speaks with his voice, and often in his name; but she receives worshippers, which was not the practice of her predecessor.

We had come too early, and the Pythia did not at first appear. But the square before the temple was full of people, and a wild, though picturesque, scene it was. An enormous bonfire blazed in the centre, and round it crowded the naked savages like so many black gnomes, adding whole branches of trees sacred to the seven sister-goddesses. Slowly and evenly they all jumped from one leg to another to a tune of a single monotonous musical phrase, which they repeated in chorus, accompanied by several local drums and tambourines. The hushed trill of the latter mingled with the forest echoes and the hysterical moans of two little girls, who lay under a heap of leaves by the fire. The poor children were brought here by their mothers, in the hope that the goddesses would take pity upon them and banish the two evil spirits under whose obsession they were. Both mothers were quite young, and sat on their heels blankly and sadly staring at the flames. No one paid us the slightest attention when we appeared, and afterwards during all our stay these people acted as if we were invisible. Had we worn a cap of darkness they could not have behaved more strangely.

"They feel the approach of the gods! The atmosphere is full of their sacred emanations!" mysteriously explained Sham Rao, contemplating with reverence the natives, whom his beloved Hæckel might have easily mistaken for his "missing link," the brood of his "Bathybius Hæckelii."

"They are simply under the influence of toddy and opium!" retorted the irreverent Babu.

The lookers-on moved as in a dream, as if they all were only half-awakened somnambulists; but the actors were simply victims of St. Vitus's dance. One of them, a tall old man, a mere skeleton with a long white beard, left the ring and began whirling vertiginously, with his arms spread like wings, and loudly grinding his long, wolf-like teeth. He was painful and disgusting to look at. He soon fell down, and was carelessly, almost mechanically, pushed aside by the feet of the others still engaged in their demoniac performance.

All this was frightful enough, but many more horrors were in store for us.

Waiting for the appearance of the *prima donna* of this forest opera company, we sat down on the trunk of a fallen tree, ready to ask innumerable questions of our condescending host. But I was hardly seated, when a feeling of indescribable astonishment and horror made me shrink back.

I beheld the skull of a monstrous animal, the like of which I could not find in my zoological reminiscences.

This head was much larger than the head of an elephant skeleton. And still it could not be anything but an elephant, judging by the skilfully restored trunk, which wound down to my feet like a gigantic black leech. But an elephant has no horns, whereas this one had four of them! The front pair stuck from the flat forehead slightly bending forward and then spreading out; and the others had a wide base, like the root of a deer's horn, that gradually decreased almost up to the middle, and bore long branches enough to decorate a dozen ordinary elks. Pieces of the transparent amber-yellow rhinoceros skin were strained over the empty eye-holes of the skull, and small lamps burning behind them only added to the horror, the devilish appearance of this head.

"What can this be?" was our unanimous question. None of us had ever met anything like it, and even the colonel looked aghast.

"It is a Sivatherium," said Narayan. "Is it possible you never came across these fossils in European museums? Their remains are common enough in the Himalayas, though, of course, in fragments. They were called after Shiva."

"If the collector of this district ever hears that this antediluvian relic adorns the den of your—ahem!—witch," remarked the Babu, "it won't adorn it many days longer."

All round the skull, and on the floor of the portico there were heaps of white flowers, which, though not quite antediluvian, were totally unknown to us. They were as large as a big rose; and their white petals were covered with a red powder, the inevitable concomitant of every Indian religious ceremony. Further on, there were groups of co-

159

coa-nuts, and large brass dishes filled with rice; and each adorned with a red or green taper. In the centre of the portico there stood a queer-shaped censer, surrounded with chandeliers. A little boy, dressed from head to foot in white, threw into it handfuls of aromatic powders.

"These people, who assemble here to worship Kangalim," said Sham Rao, "do not actually belong either to her sect or to any other. They are devil-worshippers. They do not believe in Hindu gods, but live in small communities; they belong to one of the many Indian races, which usually are called the hill-tribes. Unlike the Shanars of Southern Travancore, they do not use the blood of sacrificial animals; they do not build separate temples to their bhûtas. But they are possessed by the strange fancy that the goddess Kâlî, the wife of Shiva, from time immemorial has had a grudge against them, and sends her favourite evil spirits to torture them. Save this little difference, they have the same beliefs as the Shanars. God does not exist for them; and even Shiva is considered by them as an ordinary spirit. Their chief worship is offered to the souls of the dead. These souls, however righteous and kind they may be in their lifetime, become after death as wicked as can be; they are happy only when they are torturing living men and cattle. As the opportunities of doing so are the only reward for the virtues they possessed when incarnated, a very wicked man is punished by becoming after his death a very soft-hearted ghost; he loathes his loss of daring, and is altogether miserable. The results of this strange logic are not bad, nevertheless. These savages and devil-worshippers are the kindest and the most truth-loving of all the hill-tribes. They do whatever they can to be worthy of their ultimate reward; because, don't you see, they all long to become the wickedest of devils! . . ."

And put in good humour by his own wittiness, Sham Rao laughed till his hilarity became offensive, considering the sacredness of the place.

"A year ago some business matters sent me to Tinevelli," continued he. "Staying with a friend of mine, who is a Shanar, I was allowed to be present at one of the ceremonies in the honour of devils. No European has as yet witnessed this worship—whatever the missionaries may say; but there are many converts amongst the Shanars, who will-

160

ingly describe them to the *padres*. My friend is a wealthy man, which is probably the reason why the devils are especially vicious to him. They poison his cattle, spoil his crops and his coffee plants, and persecute his numerous relations, sending them sunstrokes, madness and epilepsy, over which illnesses they especially preside. These wicked demons have settled in every corner of his spacious landed property—in the woods, the ruins, and even in his stables. To avert all this, my friend covered his land with stucco pyramids, and prayed humbly, asking the demons to draw their portraits on each of them, so that he may recognize them and worship each of them separately, as the rightful owner of this, or that, particular pyramid. And what do you think? . . . Next morning all the pyramids were found covered with drawings. Each of them bore an incredibly good likeness of the dead of the neighbourhood. My friend had known personally almost all of them. He found also a portrait of his own late father amongst the lot. . . ."

"Well? And was he satisfied?"

"Oh, he was very glad, very satisfied. It enabled him to choose the right thing to gratify the personal tastes of each demon, don't you see? He was not vexed at finding his father's portrait. His father was somewhat irascible; once he nearly broke both his son's legs, administering to him fatherly punishment with an iron bar, so that he could not possibly be very dangerous after his death. But another portrait, found on the best and the prettiest of the pyramids, amazed my friend a good deal, and put him in a blue funk. The whole district recognized an English officer, a certain Captain Pole, who in his lifetime was as kind a gentleman as ever lived."

"Indeed? But do you mean to say that this strange people worshipped Captain Pole also?"

"Of course they did! Captain Pole was such a worthy man, such an honest officer, that, after his death, he could not help being promoted to the highest rank of Shanar devils. The Pe-Kovil, demon's house, sacred to his memory, stands side by side with the Pe-Kovil Bhadrakâlî, which was recently conferred on the wife of a certain German missionary, who also was a most charitable lady and so is very dangerous now."

161

"But what are their ceremonies? Tell us something about their rites."

"Their rites consist chiefly of dancing, singing, and killing sacrificial animals. The Shanars have no castes, and eat all kinds of meat. The crowd assembles about the Pe-Kovil, previously designated by the priest; there is a general beating of drums, and slaughtering of fowls, sheep and goats. When Captain Pole's turn came an ox was killed, as a thoughtful attention to the peculiar tastes of his nation. The priest appeared, covered with bangles, and holding a wand on which tinkled numberless little bells, and wearing garlands of red and white flowers round his neck, and a black mantle, on which were embroidered the ugliest fiends you can imagine. Horns were blown and drums rolled incessantly. And oh, I forgot to tell you there was also a kind of fiddle, the secret of which is known only to the Shanar priesthood. Its bow is ordinary enough, made of bamboo; but it is whispered that the strings are human veins. ... When Captain Pole took possession of the priest's body, the priest leapt high in the air, and then rushed on the ox and killed him. He drank off the hot blood, and then began his dance. But what a fright he was when dancing! You know, I am not superstitious. . . . Am I? . . ."

Sham Rao looked at us inquiringly, and I, for one, was glad, at this moment, that Miss X—— was half a mile off, asleep in the howdah.

"He turned, and turned, as if possessed by all the demons of Naraka. The enraged crowd hooted and howled when the priest begun to inflict deep wounds all over his body with the bloody sacrificial knife. To see him, with his hair waving in the wind and his mouth covered with foam; to see him bathing in the blood of the sacrificed animal, mixing it with his own, was more than I could bear. I felt as if hallucinated, I fancied I also was spinning round. . . ."

Sham Rao stopped abruptly, struck dumb. Kangalim stood before us!

Her appearance was so unexpected that we all felt embarrassed. Carried away by Sham Rao's description, we had noticed neither how nor whence she came. Had she appeared from beneath the earth we could not have been more astonished. Narayan stared at her, opening wide his big jet-black eyes; the Babu clicked his tongue in utter confusion.

Imagine a skeleton seven feet high, covered with brown leather, with a dead child's tiny head stuck on its bony shoulders; the eyes set so deep and at the same time flashing such fiendish flames all through your body that you begin to feel your brain stop working, your thoughts become entangled and your blood freeze in your veins.

I describe my personal impressions, and no words of mine can do them justice. My description is too weak. Mr. Y—— and the colonel both grew pale under her stare, and Mr. Y—— made a movement as if about to rise.

Needless to say that such an impression could not last. As soon as the witch had turned her gleaming eyes to the kneeling crowd, it vanished as swiftly as it had come. But still all our attention was fixed on this remarkable creature.

Three hundred years old! Who can tell? Judging by her appearance, we might as well conjecture her to be a thousand. We beheld a genuine living mummy, or rather a mummy endowed with motion. She seemed to have been withering since the creation. Neither time, nor the ills of life, nor the elements could ever affect this living statue of death. The all-destroying hand of time had touched her and stopped short. Time could do no more, and so had left her. And with all this, not a single grey hair. Her long black locks shone with a greenish sheen, and fell in heavy masses down to her knees.

To my great shame, I must confess that a disgusting reminiscence flashed into my memory. I thought about the hair and the nails of corpses growing in the graves, and tried to examine the nails of the old woman.

Meanwhile, she stood motionless as if suddenly transformed into an ugly idol. In one hand she held a dish with a piece of burning camphor, in the other a handful of rice, and she never removed her burning eyes from the crowd. The pale yellow flame of the camphor flickered in the wind, and lit up her death-like head, almost touching her chin; but she paid no heed to it. Her neck, as wrinkled as a mushroom, as thin as a stick, was surrounded by three rows of golden medallions. Her head was adorned with a golden snake. Her grotesque, hardly human body was covered by a piece of saffron-yellow muslin.

The demoniac little girls raised their heads from beneath the leaves, and set up a prolonged animal-like howl. Their example was followed by the old man, who lay exhausted by his frantic dance.

The witch tossed her head convulsively, and began her invocations, rising on tiptoe, as if moved by some external force.

"The goddess, one of the seven sisters, begins to take possession of her," whispered Sham Rao, not even thinking of wiping away the big drops of sweat that streamed from his brow. "Look, look at her!"

This advice was quite superfluous. We *were* looking at her, and at nothing else.

At first, the movements of the witch were slow, unequal, somewhat convulsive; then, gradually, they became less angular; at last, as if catching the cadence of the drums, leaning all her long body forward, and writhing like an eel, she rushed round and round the blazing bonfire. A dry leaf caught in a hurricane could not fly swifter. Her bare bony feet trod noiselessly on the rocky ground. The long locks of her hair flew round her like snakes, lashing the spectators, who knelt, stretching their trembling arms towards her, and writhing as if they were alive. Whoever was touched by one of this Fury's black curls, fell down on the ground, overcome with happiness, shouting thanks to the goddess, and considering himself blessed for ever. It was not human hair that touched the happy elect, it was the goddess herself, one of the seven.

Swifter and swifter fly her decrepit legs; the young, vigorous hands of the drummer can hardly follow her. But she does not think of catching the measure of his music; she rushes, she flies forward. Staring with her expressionless, motionless orbs at something before her, at something that is not visible to our mortal eyes, she hardly glances at her worshippers; then her look becomes full of fire; and whoever she looks at feels burned through to the marrow of his bones. At every glance she throws a few grains of rice. The small handful seems inexhaustible, as if the wrinkled palm contained the bottomless bag of Prince Fortunatus.

Suddenly she stops as if thunderstruck.

The mad race round the bonfire had lasted twelve minutes, but we looked in vain for a trace of fatigue on the death-like face of the witch. She stopped only for a moment, just the necessary time for the goddess to release her. As soon as she felt free, by a single effort she jumped over the fire and plunged into the deep tank by the portico. This time, she plunged only once; and whilst she stayed under the water, the second sister-goddess entered her body. The little boy in white produced another dish, with a new piece of burning camphor, just in time for the witch to take it up, and to rush again on her headlong way.

The colonel sat with his watch in his hand. During the second obsession the witch ran, leaped, and raced for exactly fourteen minutes. After this, she plunged twice in the tank, in honour of the second sister; and with every new obsession the number of her plunges increased, till it became six.

It was already an hour and a half since the race began. All this time the witch never rested, stopping only for a few seconds, to disappear under the water.

"She is a fiend, she cannot be a woman!" exclaimed the colonel, seeing the head of the witch immersed for the sixth time in the water.

"Hang me if I know!" grumbled Mr. Y——, nervously pulling his beard. "The only thing I know is that a grain of her cursed rice entered my throat, and I can't get it out!"

"Hush, hush! Please, do be quiet!" implored Sham Rao. "By talking you will spoil the whole business!"

I glanced at Narayan and lost myself in conjectures.

His features, which usually were so calm and serene, were quite altered at this moment, by a deep shadow of suffering. His lips trembled, and the pupils of his eyes were dilated, as if by a dose of *belladonna*. His eyes were lifted over the heads of the crowd, as if in his disgust he tried not to see what was before him, and at the same time could not see it, engaged in a deep reverie, which carried him away from us, and from the whole performance.

"What is the matter with him?" was my thought, but I had no time to ask him, because the witch was again in full swing, chasing her own shadow.

But with the seventh goddess the programme was slightly changed. The running of the old woman changed to leaping. Sometimes bending down to the ground, like a black panther, she leaped up to some worshipper, and halting before him touched his forehead with her finger, while her long, thin body shook with inaudible laughter. Then, again, as if shrinking back playfully from her shadow, and chased by it, in some uncanny game, the witch appeared to us like a horrid caricature of Dinorah, dancing her mad dance. Suddenly she straightened herself to her full height, darted to the portico and crouched before the smoking censer, beating her forehead against the granite steps. Another jump, and she was quite close to us, before the head of the monstrous Sivatherium. She knelt down again and bowed her head to the ground several times, with the sound of an empty barrel knocked against something hard.

We had hardly the time to spring to our feet and shrink back when she appeared on the top of the Sivatherium's head, standing there amongst the horns.

Narayan alone did not stir, and fearlessly looked straight in the eyes of the frightful sorceress.

But what was this? Who spoke in those deep manly tones? Her lips were moving, from her breast were issuing those quick, abrupt phrases, but the voice sounded hollow as if coming from beneath the ground.

"Hush, hush!" whispered Sham Rao, his whole body trembling. "She is going to prophesy! . . ."

"She?" incredulously inquired Mr. Y.———. "This a woman's voice? I don't believe it for a moment. Someone's uncle must be stowed away somewhere about the place. Not the fabulous uncle she inherited from, but a real live one! . . ."

Sham Rao winced under the irony of this supposition, and cast an imploring look at the speaker.

166

"Woe to you! woe to you!" echoed the voice. "Woe to you, children of the impure Jaya and Vijaya! of the mocking, unbelieving lingerers round great Shiva's door! Ye, who are cursed by eighty thousand sages! Woe to you who believe not in the goddess Kâlî, and you who deny us, her Seven divine Sisters! Flesh-eating, yellow-legged vultures! friends of the oppressors of our land! dogs who are not ashamed to eat from the same trough with the Bellati!" (foreigners).

"It seems to me that your prophetess only foretells the past," said Mr. Y——, philosophically putting his hands in his pockets. "I should say that she is hinting at you, my dear Sham Rao."

"Yes! and at us also," murmured the colonel, who was evidently beginning to feel uneasy.

As to the unlucky Sham Rao, he broke out in a cold sweat, and tried to assure us that we were mistaken, that we did not fully understand her language.

"It is not about you, it is not about you! It is of me she speaks, because I am in Government service. Oh, she is inexorable!"

"Râkshasas! Asuras!" thundered the voice. "How dare you appear before us? how dare you to stand on this holy ground in boots made of a cow's sacred skin? Be cursed for etern—"

But her curse was not destined to be finished. In an instant the Hercules-like Narayan had fallen on the Sivatherium, and upset the whole pile, the skull, the horns and the demoniac Pythia included. A second more, and we thought we saw the witch flying in the air towards the portico. A confused vision of a stout, shaven Brahman, suddenly emerging from under the Sivatherium and instantly disappearing in the hollow beneath it, flashed before my dilated eyes.

But, alas! after the third second had passed, we all came to the embarrassing conclusion that, judging from the loud clang of the door of the cave, the representative of the Seven Sisters had ignominiously fled. The moment she had disappeared from our inquisitive eyes to her subterranean domain, we all realized that the unearthly hollow voice we had heard had nothing supernatural about it and belonged to the

167

Brahman hidden under the Sivatherium—to someone's live uncle, as Mr. Y—— had rightly supposed.

Oh, Narayan! how carelessly, how disorderly the worlds rotate around us. . . . I begin to seriously doubt their reality. From this moment I shall earnestly believe that all things in the universe are nothing but illusion, a mere Mâyâ. I am becoming a Vedantin. . . . I doubt that in the whole universe there may be found anything more objective than a Hindu witch flying up the spout.

Miss X—— woke up, and asked what was the meaning of all this noise. The noise of many voices and the sounds of the many retreating footsteps, the general rush of the crowd, had frightened her. She listened to us with a condescending smile, and a few yawns, and went to sleep again.

Next morning, at daybreak, we very reluctantly, it must be owned, bade good-bye to the kind-hearted, good-natured Sham Rao. The confoundingly easy victory of Narayan hung heavily on his mind. His faith in the holy hermitess and the seven goddesses was a good deal shaken by the shameful capitulation of the Sisters, who had surrendered at the first blow from a mere mortal. But during the dark hours of the night he had had time to think it over, and to shake off the uneasy feeling of having unwillingly misled and disappointed his European friends.

Sham Rao still looked confused when he shook hands with us at parting, and expressed to us the best wishes of his family and himself.

As to the heroes of this truthful narrative, they mounted their elephants once more, and directed their heavy steps towards the high road and Jubbulpore.

Confession

Ann Putnam

I desire to be humbled before God for that sad and humbling providence that befell my father's family in the year about '92; that I, then being in my childhood, should, by such a providence of God, be made an instrument for the accusing of several persons of a grievous crime, whereby their lives were taken away from them, whom now I have just grounds and good reason to believe they were innocent persons; and that it was a great delusion of Satan that deceived me in that sad time, whereby I justly fear I have been instrumental, with others, though ignorantly and unwittingly, to bring upon myself and this land the guilt of innocent blood; though what was said or done by me against any person I can truly and uprightly say, before God and man, I did it not out of any anger, malice, or ill-will to any person, for I had no such thing against one of them; but what I did was ignorantly, being deluded by Satan. And particularly, as I was a chief instrument of accusing of Goodwife Nurse and her two sisters, I desire to lie in the dust, and to be humbled for it, in that I was a cause, with others, of so sad a calamity to them and their families; for which cause I desire to lie in the dust, and earnestly beg forgiveness of God, and from all those unto whom I have given just cause of sorrow and offence, whose relations were taken away or accused.

—[Signed] Ann Putnam

This confession was read before the congregation, together with her relation, Aug. 25, 1706; and she acknowledged it.

A Fowl Witch

Ambrose Bierce

Frau Gaubenslosher was strongly suspected of witchcraft. I don't think she was a witch, but would not like to swear she was not, in a court of law, unless a good deal depended upon my testimony, and I had been properly suborned beforehand. A great many persons accused of witchcraft have themselves stoutly disbelieved the charge, until, when subjected to shooting with a silver bullet or boiling in oil, they have found themselves unable to endure the test. And it must be confessed appearances were against the Frau. In the first place, she lived quite alone in a forest, and had no visiting list. This was suspicious. Secondly—and it was thus, mainly, that she had acquired her evil repute—all the barn-yard fowls in the vicinity seemed to bear her the most uncompromising ill-will. Whenever she passed a flock of hens, or ducks, or turkeys, or geese, one of them, with dropped wings, extended neck and open bill, would start in hot pursuit. Sometimes the whole flock would join in for a few moments with shrill clamor; but there would always be one fleeter and more determined than the rest, and that one would keep up the chase with unflagging zeal clean out of sight.

Upon these occasions the dame's fright was painful to behold. She would not scream—her organs of speech seemed to have lost their power—nor, as a rule, would she curse; she would just address herself to silent prayerful speed, with every symptom of abject terror!

The Frau's explanation of this unnatural persecution was singularly weak. Upon a certain night long ago, said she, a poor bedraggled and attenuated gander had applied at her door for relief. He stated in piteous accents that he had eaten nothing for months but tin-tacks and an occasional beer-bottle; and he had not roosted under cover for so long a time he did not know what it was like. Would she give him a place on her fender, and fetch out six or eight cold pies to amuse him while she was preparing his supper? To this plea she turned a deaf ear, and he went away. He came again the next night, however, bringing a written

170

certificate from a clergyman that his case was a deserving one. She would not aid him, and he departed. The night after he presented himself again, with a paper signed by the relieving officer of the parish, stating that the necessity for help was most urgent.

By this time the Frau's good-nature was quite exhausted: she slew him, dressed him, put him in a pot and boiled him. She kept him boiling for three or four days, but she did not eat him because her teeth were just like anybody's teeth—no weaker, perhaps, but certainly no stronger nor sharper. So she fed him to a threshing machine of her acquaintance, which managed to masticate some of the more modern portions, but was hopelessly wrecked upon the neck. From that time the poor beldame had lived under the ban of a great curse. Hens took after her as naturally as after the soaring beetle; geese pursued her as if she were a fleeting tadpole; ducks, turkeys and guinea fowl camped upon her trail with tireless pertinacity.

Now there was a leaven of improbability in this tale, and it leavened the whole lump. Ganders do not roost; there is not one in a hundred of them that could sit on a fender long enough to say Jack Robinson. So, as the Frau lived a thousand years before the birth of common sense—say about a half century ago—when everything uncommon had a smell of the supernatural, there was nothing for it but to consider her a witch. Had she been very feeble and withered, the people would have burned her, out of hand; but they did not like to proceed to extremes without perfectly legal evidence. They were cautious, for they had made several mistakes recently. They had sentenced two or three females to the stake, and upon being stripped the limbs and bodies of these had not redeemed the hideous promise of their shriveled faces and hands. Justice was ashamed of having toasted comparatively plump and presumably innocent women; and the punishment of this one was wisely postponed until the proof should be all in.

But in the meantime a graceless youth, named Hans Blisselwartle, made the startling discovery that none of the fowls that pursued the Frau ever came back to boast of it. A brief martial career seemed to have weaned them from the arts of peace and the love of their kindred. Full of unutterable suspicion, Hans one day followed in the rear of an exciting race between the timorous dame and an avenging pullet. They were too rapid for him; but bursting suddenly in at the lady's door some fifteen minutes afterward, he found her in the act of placing the plucked and eviscerated Nemesis upon her cooking range. The Frau betrayed considerable confusion; and although the accusing Blisselwartle could not but recognize in her act a certain poetic justice, he could not conceal from himself that there was something grossly selfish and sordid in it. He thought it was a good deal like bottling an annoying ghost and selling him for clarified moonlight; or like haltering a nightmare and putting her to the cart.

When it transpired that the Frau ate her feathered persecutors, the patience of the villagers refused to honor the new demand upon it: she was at once arrested, and charged with prostituting a noble superstition to a base selfish end. We will pass over the trial; suffice it she was convicted. But even then they had not the heart to burn a middle-aged woman, with full rounded outlines, as a witch, so they broke her upon the wheel as a thief.

The reckless antipathy of the domestic fowls to this inoffensive lady remains to be explained. Having rejected her theory, I am bound in honor to set up one of my own. Happily an inventory of her effects, now before me, furnishes a tolerably safe basis. Amongst the articles of personal property I note "One long, thin, silken fishing line, and hook." Now if I were a barn-yard fowl—say a goose—and a lady not a friend of mine were to pass me, munching sweetmeats, and were to drop a nice fat worm, passing on apparently unconscious of her loss, I think I should try to get away with that worm. And if after swallowing it I felt drawn toward that lady by a strong personal attachment, I suppose that I should yield if I could not help it. And then if the lady chose to run and I chose to follow, making a good deal of noise, I suppose it would look as if I were engaged in a very reprehensible pursuit, would it not? With the light I have, that is the way in which the case presents itself to my intelligence; though, of course, I may be wrong.

Géacspell

Adam Bolivar

Artful Géac was   an earl of songs,
Bane of giants,   his blade thirsty,
Spring-born and spry,   and special his wyrd,
A cuckoo's kin,   crafty by nature,
His feats followed   by fame and song.
He dared delving   in a dark hollow,
Hag-haunted in lore,   hiding evil,
Moonlit, misty   and mire-bottomed.
A pale lady   appeared to Géac,
Beaming beauty,   in bride's clothing,
Eager the hero   to enter her house.
In strange ruins   of stone she dwelt,
No fire burning   to furnish warmth,
Lighted only   by a languid moon.
As Géac dallied,   his yearning fierce
To dine deeply   on the damsel's feast,
A spectral glass   spied on his hunger,
A black devil,   bound in silver,
A fiend feeding   on fierce desire.
His swift iron   smashing the mirror,
The earl ended   the ancient curse;
The witch withered   to wan ashes,
Bone-chilling her keen,   like breaking glass.

[*Note:* Alliterative verse is the poetic form used in Old English poems such as *Beowulf* and in the Old Norse sagas and the *Poetic Edda*. Unlike rhyme, which is a repetition of the endings of words, alliteration repeats the beginnings of stressed syllables in accordance with complex metrical rules well known to the scops and skalds of old. The name *Géac*—a speculative Old English version of *Jack*—is pronounced 'yawk.']

Seeing Them

Darrell Schweitzer

I never knew Barry Atwood well. We moved in the same circles in college, but only because mutual friends led us to a casual acquaintance. We went to the same parties. We belonged to the same literary society.

And we both knew Laura Howard.

That was all. That was enough. Kismet, fate, inscrutable destiny. "There are no coincidences," Laura used to say. In the end, I believed her.

But the beginning was what we used to call a *flash from the past.* I had settled down to a quiet Sunday afternoon of marking test papers when the phone rang. Quasimodo, my terrier, yelped and ran in circles around the telephone stand.

A flash—

"Phil? It's Barry."

For a moment I didn't recognize the voice. "Barry *who?*"

"Barry Goldwater. Who do you think, old buddy? I'm running for president . . . and your contribution could make all the damn difference—" He faked a laugh, but even over the phone I could tell it was a fake. His voice was hoarse, strained. He sounded as if he'd been crying.

"Barry Atwood," I said. "I haven't heard from you in—what is it? Fifteen years, I think."

"Yeah. Look, Phil, I know I may be intruding, but if you have some time, I'd like to see you. It's *important.*"

I glanced at the pile of ungraded test papers, but some instinct told me this was indeed important. "Sure. Where are you?"

"Here. In Philadelphia. I can be over to your place in half an hour."

"Fine."

The year we graduated, Barry Atwood had moved to the West Coast. Los Angeles, undoubtedly. He'd wanted to get into films. I

174

think he actually had worked on a few commercials. Now he was back. It had indeed been fifteen years.

There are no coincidences.

Quasimodo barked with customary fierceness when the doorbell rang, then scooted under his favorite stuffed chair.

I opened the door.

Barry looked tired. That was the overwhelming impression I got. Stooped slightly, his hair thinning in front instead of going gray, but mostly *tired*, almost haggard. And he was thin. For most people, the difference between twenty-two and thirty-seven is at least twenty pounds, but he looked thinner than he had the last time I'd seen him. Not at all well, really.

"Phil?"

I noticed that he squinted.

"Come in, Barry."

He sat in the chair beneath which the dog had tactically withdrawn. Quasimodo kept still.

I fetched us a couple of beers. Barry sipped his occasionally. Then he started talking, nervously at first, and finally in a great torrent of words.

"It was really funny when it started," he said. "I mean, I laughed—"

He hesitated, as if he'd lost the train of thought.

I settled back, nursing my beer.

"What was funny?"

"Meeting Laura again after so long. This is getting to be a god-damn class reunion, Phil—"

"Laura *Howard*? Miss Occult USA 1970, teen witch, number one groupie of the ghost of Aleister Crowley, *that* Laura?"

He put down his beer, folded his hands in his lap, and said very quietly, "Don't joke about it, Phil. You went to her little sessions too."

"I mostly went to see her naked. Who could forget the sight of her crawling around by candlelight in her birthday suit, chalking circles on the basement floor at her mom's place. She had . . . a great ass."

175

"She still does."

I leaned forward and slapped my fist into the palm of my hand. "Hey, hey—know what I mean? Nudge-nudge? Wink-wink?"

He didn't laugh at my borrowed witticism.

"There's so much to fill in." He sighed. "It's been *such* a long time! There are things you're no doubt wondering, Phil. I'm wondering too. What have *you* been doing all this time?"

"Living. I think I'm the only member of the Villanova Literary Society to actually go off and commit literature. I even get published occasionally. But mostly I teach ninth grade in the public schools."

"Are you married, Phil?"

"Almost a couple of times, but no."

"Well I was. Her name was Anne Harris. You don't know her. After our divorce, she moved to New York. I'm in Philly so I can commute up every other weekend and see David, our son. He's five and the only good thing that came out of our marriage, which otherwise went very sour. Anne hates me."

"I'm sorry."

Suddenly I was very embarrassed, listening to this near stranger tell me such intimate things, and at the same time a little resentful that he had invited himself over to spill his guts on my living room rug, so to speak.

"Barry, aren't we off the subject?"

"No, we're not. It all has to do with Laura Howard. I met her just a block from here, a week ago yesterday, in Clark Park. I saw a poster about a rock concert, and I had this whim. I hadn't been to a real live *rock concert* in a long, long time, and—well, I actually put on a pair of genuine 1960s bellbottoms and a tastefully shrieking blue and red dashiki I hadn't worn in *decades*. But the concert was quite a disappointment."

"They always are. I've never been to a Clark Park event that wasn't—"

"*Tawdry*, Phil. That's what it was. A festival of some sort, but really an overblown flea market with some local group on a stage at the far end putting up a wall of noise. The whole thing was depressing. I realized how silly I'd been, dressing like an aging hippie when all the kids around me wore black leather, safety-pins, and Mohawks and carried boom-boxes the size of suitcases—as if the alleged music wasn't shattering eardrums quite efficiently enough.

"But I stayed long enough to flip through a record dealer's wares, boxes of albums on a table and on the ground underneath. It was underneath the table that I found myself face to face with a woman in her upper thirties. I didn't know who she was at first, but then she grinned hugely and said, 'Hey, man! Far out! We could be the Bobsey Twins!'

"I tried to stand up, but hit my head on the underside of the table. All I could say was, 'Huh?'

"When we got out from under the table, I could see what she meant. We were wearing identical dashikis.

"It was Laura Howard, unquestionably. The first thing she did was grab my wrist and say, 'Wait. Wait. Anachronism check. You're wearing a Timex. There were no digital watches in the Summer of Love—'

"'My God,' I said.

"'My God,' she said. 'You haven't seen me since the Upper Paleolithic. Hey—look what I found!'

"She waved a record in front of me. It was by the Fugs. *Golden Filth.* She read from the back of the sleeve in her finest mock-oratorical manner: *'If you hesitate to hear about the cold fork of naked reality . . . then you'd better flip this record back into the rack and go dig up some old Monkees albums—'*

"'Right on,' I said. 'Let's hear it for naked forks.'

"'Barry, give me a hug—'

"I did, and a kiss too, and pretty soon we both sort of *fell* down onto the curb, laughing hysterically. One or two of the teenagers glanced our way. The band let fly with another peal of electronic thunder.

"'Hey,' I said. 'People are *staring . . .*'

"'They probably wonder what us crazily garbed old farts are *on.* Or else they assume we're having heart attacks in stereo. I mean, *look* at us.

You're, what? Thirty-seven? Your hair's thinning. Mine's got a god-damn racing stripe down the middle—'

"'Laura, it's been a long time—'

"'Let's get out of here,' she said. 'This is getting maudlin.'

"She paid for the record and dragged me along toward a streetcar.

"'Were there any more treasures back there?'

"'Not unless you want old Monkees albums. Come on.'

I interrupted. "Barry, you loved her once, didn't you?"

He trembled slightly, then caught onto the arm rests, hard. Under-neath, Quasimodo started to whine. Barry didn't seem to notice.

"Yeah. Once."

"But not now." I said that as a statement, not a question.

"No, not in years. But for a moment there, I almost fooled my-self."

"Barry, level with me. It's great to see old school chums, but you don't suddenly come over here and—"

He stood up, as if to attention.

"I quite understand. I see. You're right, of course. Sorry to be of any bother. I'll just go now—"

I got up, caught him by the shoulder, and pushed him gently back into the chair.

"No, you don't have to go. But I do think you have to tell me the real story, the *whole* story. For friendship's sake, at least, I'll listen."

"Will you, for friendship's sake, *believe me?*"

That gave me a start. For the first time I was a little bit afraid.

"Has something happened? Involving Laura?"

He took a long draw on his beer, then said in a voice of the utmost sadness. "You could say that. Yes. No. Maybe. I'm not sure anymore, Phil."

"Just tell me everything," I said.

When we were on the subway [Barry said], I asked her where we were going, and she told me she had a business here in town. Would I like to see? Well, it did seem *wonderful* to meet up with her again. It brought back so many memories.

She took me to a part of the city I'd never even known existed before. Somewhere along the way, the subway burst out of the ground and became the elevated. It was sunset. I remember that distinctly. The sky was bright orange.

She told me a little of her own adventures in the intervening years, but I did most of the talking, about Anne, about David. Maybe I told her too much.

"Well, look at it this way," she said. "If you're not married, you're free. Like in the old days."

"It's fun to pretend," I said, "but you know perfectly well that we can't go back and be young again and make everything different—"

Then she looked at me sharply and said something I didn't understand, not then.

"What if we're not pretending?"

When our stop came, she led me down rusty stairs to a place where the El runs over Frankford Avenue like a roof and the stores are all blaring lights and iron bars. Every third one was boarded up. The street smelled like a subway tunnel, dirty and damp.

"You live here?"

"Like I said, my business. Opportunity is where you find it."

"A bit capitalistic for an over-the-hill flower child—"

She smiled ever so sweetly and said, "Well fuck you too. Here we are."

She got out a set of keys and unlocked a door I hadn't even noticed as we had come upon it, squeezed in between two vacant storefronts. A wooden sign swung overhead, a faded picture of a bare-breasted mermaid in a top hat waving a magician's wand, and slightly newer lettering that said merely *This is THE PLACE.* A plastic **CLOSED** sign dangled behind glass and bars.

Inside, she fumbled for a light. The switch clicked, but no light came on.

"Shit——"

We groped our way along in the musty dark, past crates and piles

179

of boards. Paint chips rattled from the walls at my touch. Once something scurried before us.

At the end of the corridor was another switch. This time the light worked, or at least one of the two uncovered bulbs came on, its harsh glare revealing a room filled with shelves of books and bottles and what looked like very peculiar pottery half hidden in the deep shadows. That was my first impression: a typical back-street junk shop. But then I followed her gaze upward and saw huge, brightly painted masks hanging from the walls.

"Isn't this *wild?*"

"Wild."

"Those are Mardi Gras masks. Some of them are very old. Once in a great while I sell one, but mostly they're my lares and penates."

"Larry *who?*"

"*Lares. Penates.* Guardian spirits. Never mind. Classical."

I started browsing and I saw at once that Laura Howard was still very much on her occult kick, as we used to call it. The books were all on witchcraft and "ancient mysteries," that sort of thing, including the inevitable *Necronomicon.* Packs of tarot cards hung from hooks on a pegboard. There was even a baggie of something labeled "Devil Dust."

I held it up to her. *"Devil Dust?"* I said.

"For them's that needs it, Devil Dust."

Amid the potions and herbs and black candles was a wide assortment of more conventional stage-magic paraphernalia: wands, hats, disguises, glasses with funny eyes, blindfolds, trick knives, and even a rubber chicken. Crystal balls gleamed in a locked case, each of them held in a pair of carved wooden hands.

"You sell this stuff?"

"The old guy I bought the place from used to supply Ernie Kovacs with gimmicks. I deal to an exclusive clientele."

On the wall at the end of an aisle was a huge poster that glowed in the semi-darkness: three flying disks and the legend *SEEING THEM by L. Allen Weinstein.* There were more books, mostly about UFOs, but also Atlantis, Bigfoot, the Bermuda Triangle, and a whole stack of the

Weinstein volume. I held up a copy quizzically.

"I haven't changed," she said softly.

"You don't still get yourself all yucky driving nails through rat hearts, do you?"

She didn't smile at that.

"You might as well ask me if I still suck my thumb. One *does* make progress over the years."

She took me by the arm and led me through a bead curtain. Behind us, something rattled. Glass fell and broke.

She jerked me around suddenly, back toward the shop room. *"Esmeralda!"* she hissed.

The only reply was a creaking, like the sound of an old house settling, followed by silence.

"Your cat?"

She didn't answer, but directed me back into the other room. I saw a lava lamp glowing in a corner, more posters of flying saucers on the walls, and a mattress on the floor. Beside the lamp was what looked like an altar, with a six-fingered wooden hand rising from it. Colored glass sparkled on the fingertips.

"Barry, I am sure it meant something that we met today."

"Destiny, my dear. It's written in the stars. Your sign is Scorpio. Mine is Right Turn Keep Moving—"

She put her finger to my lips. "Now don't be cynical about things you don't understand. It *meant* something. I *knew* to go to that place. I knew that I'd meet you—or someone else who mattered—there today."

"It's a wonderful coincidence, that's all."

"There are no coincidences, Barry Atwood. Not even this is a coincidence." She tugged her dashiki, then mine.

She knelt down on the mattress and pulled me down after her, then proceeded to demonstrate that not all her magic was of the ethereal, abstract kind . . . and as we lay there afterwards, sweaty with love, it was easy to pretend—to *forget* otherwise—that no time at all had passed since those nights we used to spend secretly together in the *Lynx* magazine office at Villanova University.

I remarked on this, and she said, "It's only in your mind that any time has passed, any distance. That's what I've learned over the past decade and more. That's why I don't need rat hearts and chalk circles anymore. It's hard to explain, but once your spirit has become attuned to . . . I suppose you'd call it cosmic energy, although there are different words the adepts use . . . you can see the Masters on other worlds, where there is no war or disease or death. You don't have to grow old. That's what you want, isn't it?"

"Like Peter Pan," I muttered, mostly to myself. I folded my hands behind my head and stared up at the ceiling. "I won't grow up, I *won't*——"

"You're so damned narrow-minded. You think you know everything with your goddamn *science*. I'm trying to give you the greatest gift you can ever receive. I can move you back and forth through time, like a needle through cloth, out of the reach of age and death. Once your eyes are opened, once you understand, you will be able to do it too. Once you *see them*——"

Barry stopped talking, as if he'd run out of words. He closed his eyes. For a moment I almost thought he was asleep. Then he suddenly sat bolt upright and all but shouted at me.

"I did something really stupid, Phil. Really stupid."

"Hey, calm down. What did you do? Just tell me."

"I *laughed* at her."

I knew I was being cruel [Barry went on], but I couldn't help myself. You know how it was back in college. We used to smirk about her being a witch and all. It was a big joke. You and me, Phil, we never took it seriously for an instant. And then, to hear her talk like that, so deadpan earnestly, it brought all the laughter back.

She glared at me, furious. As if on cue, the whole place shook. For a moment I thought it was an earthquake. A *lot* of merchandise fell in the next room. The lava lamp slipped in its base, sending jerky shadows over the walls and ceiling.

"That Esmeralda," I said somewhat nervously, "is going to put you out of business yet."

She crawled away from me, toward the lamp. Despite everything, the one thought that percolated into my brain was, *After all these years, she still has a great ass.*

I laughed again, but broke off in mid-chuckle when she flung my clothes into my face.

"I think you had better fucking *go*—"

I sat up. "I'm sorry," I said. "Really I am. I like you a lot, and I hope you'll always be my friend, but—it's just too much to listen to you offering to take me on a flying saucer-ride to see the perfect spiritual masters of Mars—"

The bead curtain rattled at the bottom, as if something small had just entered the room. But when I turned and looked, I saw nothing.

I dressed quickly and rose to go. "Look, I really am sorry. I apologize. Can I make it up to you? Take you out to dinner maybe?"

She just sat there, staring into space, oblivious to my presence. When she began to speak, it was as if to the whole universe.

"This is a very special day."

"I'm sorry I wrecked it for you. I've apologized. What more can I do?"

She got to her feet and walked toward me, still naked. She reached out to touch my face. I raised my hand to push hers away, but hesitated. She closed my eyes with two outstretched fingers.

"When it is the proper time," she said, "you will see everything. You will open your eyes. Yours will not be a fleeting glimpse, a mere streak across the heavens. For you, there shall be no mysteries. Open your eyes. Come to understand that we are bound together now, you and I, by the magic of the flesh. Understand the special meaning of this day, of this encounter. It is a kind of graduation for me. I have worked so many years to reach this point. Open your eyes. For you it is but a beginning, a first step. Open your eyes. *See them.* Open your eyes."

I drew back from her and stood in the doorway, gazing at her nakedness, her undeniable beauty. Still my mind entertained undergraduate-wolf thoughts, even though it hurt to see her angry.

And I told myself that on some level I still loved her. I couldn't explain the hurt any other way.

There was one thing more: she looked distinctly younger in the half-light. It was something about the way her skin gleamed. And something else, too, which didn't come to me until I was away from there.

Her hair was completely black. The white streak, the racing stripe as she'd called it, was definitely gone.

Barry paused again, as if he couldn't go on.

"Now wait a minute," I said after a while. "Parts of this are getting distinctly impossible. People don't *really* get younger now, do they?"

"I saw what I saw."

"It was the bad light. You said so yourself."

"Phil, I *saw* it."

"Okay," I said, sensing that it would be futile to pursue this point. "Tell me what happened next."

What happened next [Barry said] was I went home. The Indian summer daytime weather had given out, and it was quite cold. I shivered all the way in that damned dashiki.

Of course I couldn't sleep. I was rattled, to put it mildly. So I sat up listening to music. I tried to read. I tried to work on a script I'm doing. But I couldn't concentrate.

Eventually I lay on my bed in the dark, watching the hands move on the glowing face of my alarm clock. Regardless of what I tried to think about, I always came back to Laura, to what it had been like before with her, the sights and sounds and *scents*—the faint perfume she used to wear—and it was all so vivid I seemed to be reliving my youth. I was halfway moved to turn on the radio and see if I could pick up a 1970 newscast, but at the same time I was afraid that I might succeed.

Eventually I dozed off and had a dream. I *knew* I was dreaming, and it seemed that inside my dream, I awoke. Someone was rapping gently at the front door, almost like an animal clawing to get in.

I padded downstairs, barefoot, and opened the door.

A huge, orange, laughing face floated before me in the darkness. It was one of the Mardi Gras masks. It spoke to me in the voice of my five-year-old boy.

"Daddy, I'm lost. Daddy, it's dark here."

Then I realized that a child was wearing the mask. It covered his whole body. Untied sneakers stuck out beneath the orange chin.

"David?"

I snatched the mask away, but it wasn't David. It was Laura, her adult head on a little boy's body, distorted, gnarled, like a hideous dwarf. And her voice was cracked, grating.

"I am the way. I am the truth. I am the light of the other world. Come, follow me."

Then she laughed at me, a harsh, ugly laugh, and ran off my porch, down the steps, into the street. I ran after her in my bare feet, for blocks. The city was empty, silent, dark. The padding of my footsteps was the only sound, impossibly magnified, like the thunderous beating of an enormous heart. Still the huge-headed dwarf ran, vanished between two parked cars, then appeared again in the middle of the street only to disappear once more around a turn in an alley.

At last we reached an open place, bare ground, a vacant lot or maybe a park. The dwarf-child just stood there waiting for me to catch up.

Suddenly the sky was filled with blinding light. I looked up, shielding my eyes, into a glowing, whirling, humming disk, and I heard Laura's voice.

"Like a needle through the cloth of time. Forever and ever."

The light dimmed and the saucer had clock-hands on it, turning slowly at first, then faster, backwards, then forwards, then backwards again—

The alarm went off and I awoke in my bedroom, damp with sweat.

"That was quite some dream, Barry."

He sipped his beer, then gagged.

"You okay?"

"Yeah, yeah. I'm okay. Now you're thinking I woke up and found my pajamas torn and my feet dirty from running in the street, but it wasn't like that."

"It wasn't." A statement, not a question.

"But the dream was more than just mind-static. It was what occultists, sorcerers, or whatever call a *sending,* a message, clear as a phone call, from Laura—"

"You can't really believe—"

Now I was beginning to think I should stop Barry's story right there. This was not healthy for him to bring it up with such conviction.

He clearly believed every word he said. I thought he was truly going insane, just then.

But there was no stopping him.

"That Sunday—just a week ago—was visiting day, when I could go up to New York and see my boy. That was why the alarm had been set. I was exhausted. I'd had almost no sleep. But I got up anyway. I never wanted to let David down.

"I fell asleep once on the train and dreamed of Laura, scenes from our past, pleasant moments, but somehow they seemed forced to me, a kind of threat.

"'No,' I said in my dream. 'Get away from me—'

"Then the conductor was nudging me awake, a worried look on his face.

"'Hey buddy, dis your stop?'

"I thanked him, embarrassed, and hurried from the train. I was looking forward to seeing David. I was *dreading* seeing Anne. Whenever we met, we always ended up screaming at each other. I hoped she had left David in custody of the maid and gone shopping or something.

"Her apartment was in the East Nineties, right off Central Park. I—I——"

Once more Barry broke off. He put his hands over his face and sobbed.

I felt I had to say something, anything.

"Hey, East Nineties. You must have done very well for yourself—"

He pulled his hands away from his face and glared at me.

Instantly I felt like a total jerk for having said that.

"*She* did very well by me, that bitch-and-a-half!"

"But there was . . . there *is* your son."

"Yes, David. But, you know, Phil, I realize now that even David was bait. Anne used him as bait. And behind that, *Laura* was pulling all the strings like a fucking *puppet-master* . . . and I had to choose between *realities,* between *lives,* one with David in it, and Anne too, or else just Laura. Not that I had much choice."

"Barry, listen to what you're saying. This is seriously crazy. Paranoid. It'll destroy you."

He pounded hard on the arms of the chair. *"Not that I had any fucking choice!"*

Just then Quasimodo the terrier squealed as if he'd been stepped on and darted out from under the chair and into my lap, whining. Barry let out a yelp too, almost a scream, and jumped up, nearly tipping the chair over. It was like the stereotypical woman's reaction to a mouse. At any other time it might have seemed funny. But I didn't doubt that he had just mistaken my dog for Esmeralda the—what? Familiar? Semi-housebroken poltergeist?

Then Barry was laughing, humorlessly, desperately.

"*Jesus,* Phil, this *is* crazy. I'm acting like such an asshole. You have every right to toss me out on my ear—"

"No, Barry. I'm not going to do that. Meet Quasimodo."

"Hi, Quasimodo," Barry said, waving his hand feebly. "Nice to get to know ya.

"I went up to Anne's apartment and rang the bell. I knew where I was going, of course. I couldn't have gotten *lost.* No, I had stood in this very hallway and rung this bell many times before.

"But there was no answer. I rang again, waited, rang. At last the door opened with a jolt, hooked on a chain. A sixtyish woman I had never seen before in my life stared out at me suspiciously.

"'Yes? What do you want?'

"I was momentarily too startled to say anything.

"'What do you *want?'*

"At last I managed to say, 'I've come to pick up David. I'm—'

"*'Who?'* She almost spat the word.

"Somewhat more in control, I asked, 'Does Anne Harris live here anymore?'

"'I don't know anyone by that name.'

"'But . . . this is *her* apartment. Do you know where she's gone? Did you just move in here? The previous tenant—'

"The woman slammed the door in my face. I heard a bolt click. I raised my fist to knock, but staggered away and hit the opposite wall so hard I cracked the plaster, Then I realized I'd best be gone before someone called the police, so I hurried from the building.

"Outside, I sat on the garden wall and said over and over, *The bitch. The goddamn bitch.'*

"I thought I was talking about Anne, who had moved away without telling me, taking David with her. I thought my anger and my hurt came from the realization that I'd never see my son again.

"If it had really been Anne, if I'd truly believed she had moved, I would have called Information. I would have called my lawyer, or maybe even her lawyer.

"But I was actually talking about Laura.

"And I looked up in the sky and I *saw one,* a glowing disk, as clear a sign as any burning bush.

"I knew there was only one thing left for me. So I came back to Philadelphia on the next train. I didn't fall asleep this time. My mind turned endlessly in fantasies of revenge. By the time I reached Thirtieth Street Station my eyes were truly opened, and, just as Laura had predicted, I was *seeing them*—"

"Barry, what did you see? Think carefully."

"The saucers, Phil. Flying saucers, thousands of them at once, passing over the city like an incredible migration of suns. You didn't see anything unusual that day, Phil, nor did most people, but *I* did, because Laura had opened my eyes. She'd brought me that far, and my hatred and my fear provided the extra power I needed.

"I saw them, and I understood why the stupid Air Force with its Project Blue Book never turned up anything. They're not spaceships with little green men from Mars. They're spiritual *powers,* like angels, miraculous messengers, apparitions, but neither good nor evil. Most people never see them. A few catch a glimpse, just a glimpse, and they don't know what they've seen. But I *knew* that they're like the living cells in the bloodstream of the universe, all around us constantly, if only we can *see them.* That was what was happening. It was as if the painted backdrop of our reality were torn away, and I was seeing the bare stage behind.

"By the time I reached the Market-Frankford El, I was alone, no longer quite in *your* world, Phil, or at least perceiving it *very* differently. The city was deserted, the streets as empty and silent as in my dream, the flying saucers gliding overhead like a burning cloud.

"The train came just for me. There was no one in the attendant's booth, so I climbed over the turnstile and boarded. And that train didn't stop until it came to the place with the rusty stairs, where the street smelled like a damp tunnel.

"I got off, went down the stairs, and the saucers flickered through the tracks above me like a rain of fire. My footsteps echoed.

"Something ran ahead of me, something small and dark, rattling behind trash cans. Once a window flew open and a blast of air from within sent curtains flapping. I heard things falling in there, breaking.

"The door to Laura's shop was unlocked. I had expected that. I groped my way along the cluttered corridor, paint chips raining down on me. The main room seemed to be swaying like the cabin of a ship in a storm, glass tinkling, books tumbling from shelves.

"The masks on the walls swayed and rattled. Then they began to speak. One of them had my ex-wife's voice, Anne's.

"'Barry? Where are you? Goddammit—*Barry!*'

"And another screamed. It was David.

"'Daddy! Help me! I'm scared! *Daddy!*'

"I tore aside the bead curtain. Laura was sitting there, naked, on the edge of the mattress. She held a glowing disk in her hands. Then she released it and it floated in the air, expanding and whirling until it filled the room and its light was blinding. I staggered back into the shop room. The masks rattled.

"'Daddy! Daddy!' David screamed from behind one mask, then another, and another, as if he were running along a corridor behind them, shouting out of each mouth in turn.

"The room went dark. I rubbed my eyes. When I could see again, I went back into the bedroom, through the bead curtain. Laura was still sitting there.

"'It will be wonderful,' she said. 'The two of us together. We won't have to age. We won't have to die.'

"*Why?*' I said. 'Why are you doing this?'

"'I *take* what I *want* and I *want* you.'

"Furiously, I yanked on the bead curtain, tearing the curtain rod loose. Beads rattled to the floor. 'What about my *son?*'

"She smiled, and her smile was utterly malevolent. 'Think of the good old days, Barry, my love. You didn't have a son then. The needle passes in and out, back and forth, forward and back. That is all.'

"I was without words. 'You—you—*witch*—'

"Now it was her turn to laugh at me, and her voice was horrible, like the dwarf in my dream.

"*Do what thou wilt,*' she said. '*That is the whole of the law.* And I have done so.'"

The phone rang. Barry looked at it in absolute, abject terror. "Excuse me," I said.

"No, Phil—please! Don't answer it!"

The story had gone on for hours. I stood in the semi-darkness, flicked on a lamp, and went for the phone.

"*Phil!*"

Just then an avalanche of pots and pans fell in the kitchen. The phone kept ringing.

"Quasimodo? Is that you?"

But my dog peeked fearfully out of a nearby closet, whined, and retreated back in again.

The phone still rang. "*Phil!* For God's sake!"

Something rattled across the floor upstairs, like the hooves of a goat.

"*Phil!*"

He lunged for me, but I picked up the receiver and he froze where he was.

There was no voice on the other end of the line at first, just utter silence. Then, very faintly, something stirred. I thought of the sound of a crab scratching against the side of a bucket.

Finally there was a voice I had not heard in fifteen years. But I knew it certainly enough. It was Laura Howard.

"*I am the way. I am the door to the other world.* I have seen the frozen suns of Orion, and sailed on fiery ships into the darkness beyond, where there is no more suffering, only joy—"

I replaced the receiver carefully. I felt sick then, terrified. I grasped desperately at any possible rational explanation, and, not finding one, felt my own sanity fraying, about to snap.

"Phil," Barry said. "It was her." No question. Plain statement.

I nodded.

"I knew it would be."

"You knew?"

"Yes, because I killed her."

The lamp flickered, then went out. I could see out the window that the whole neighborhood had gone dark.

I regarded Barry Atwood with horror, and with awe.

And, sitting in the darkness, he told me the rest of the story.

"I hurled the glass part of the lava lamp at her. It shattered against her temple and she fell back onto the mattress. Then I grabbed the wooden hand-thing from the altar and beat her with it again and again, while the building shook and the floor heaved, and darkness flashed into brilliant light and back into darkness. Even then she wouldn't die. I had to strangle her.

"I felt like I was killing myself, but I had my hands around her throat for a long time.

"And, much later, I stumbled out into the silent, dark center room. I think some light came in through a skylight. I could see that all the masks had fallen. Many were broken. None of them spoke.

"I found the key to the shop in a drawer. I locked the door behind me as I left.

"Outside, the train rattled on its track overhead. There were people on the sidewalks, cars moving in the streets, and no flying saucers.

"I killed her, Phil."

"But *murder*—" I didn't know what to say. Just then I felt that Barry Atwood was far saner than I.

"It's been a week," he said. "The police haven't come looking for me. There was nothing in the papers. I don't think it was quite . . . murder."

"Is she really dead then?"

"In this world, in the body, she's dead all right. But I think it was all part of her plan. I think she *needed* me to somehow help her make the transition into . . . another state. Now she wants me to join her there. I know this, Phil, just like I knew it was her on the phone.

"When I got home that night, there was a single saucer hovering outside my window. It was for me, again, invisible to everyone else, I'm certain. And it has been there every night since. It isn't angry. It tells me, in her voice, how happy we were once and how we can be happy like that again. Together."

With great effort I asked, "Barry, do you want to go with her?"

"Part of me does, Phil, the same part that wants to be twenty-two forever. I'm not sure I can . . . stay away much longer. You understand?"

"I think so, Barry."

"That's why I came to you, Phil. I thought you would understand. I looked in the phone book, and you were the only one of my old friends I could find, the only one who knew Laura Howard. So I knew you would help me, even though we actually never knew each other very well. There are no coincidences, Phil. Somehow it has to be you. I want you to do something for me after I'm gone."

And for an instant everything snapped into a different focus, and I thought: *He's going to kill himself.*

But no, by the crazy logic of his story everything fit.

"What do you want me to do?" I asked quietly.

"Find my boy. Laura canceled David out somehow. She did something with time. Pulled a few stitches maybe. But he's out there somewhere. I know it. Help him find his way back, if you can."

"But *how?*"

Barry rose from his seat and closed my eyes with two extended fingers.

"When it is time, open your eyes."

"I'll try," I said.

"Thank you, Phil. Now, I think, Laura is waiting. Goodbye, Phil."

"Goodbye, Barry."

"You may need this."

He pressed a key into my hand, and he whispered an address.

I sat in the darkness and listened to him leave. He opened the door. The iron gate of the porch railing creaked. Then he was gone.

I opened my eyes, and after a minute there was light flickering in through the open doorway and through the Venetian blinds, as if the whole city were on fire.

I went to the doorway and looked out.

Barry was standing in the middle of the street.

And there in the darkness, as silent as falling snow, the flying saucers began to land.

Musings of a Conjurer

Michael Potts

Wind has wings tonight,
turning branches to threat.
Curses fly far to land
on victims asleep in their lies,
dreaming they will live another day.

Night of false hope grows
darker, palpable blackness
eating light. Tomorrow will be
a day of sorrow—families
of the cursed awaken next to chilled
skin, never to warm again.

I only pick the worst to curse—
my conscience clean of guilt,
Bud who stole a saw from Johnny's shed,
Ann, long married, slept with Bubba Shaw,
and Rob—he murdered children in their beds.

Now they boil in heat of Karma's eye.
I send them to the dark of death and hell,
and now all things once more are truly well.

The Old Lady

Eleanor Scott

Adela Young must have come up to Oxford at the same time as myself; but no one, in a way, knew that she had. She was one of those people whom one never notices, physically or mentally—the kind of person whose adjectives you always qualify with "-ish." She was small-ish, thinnish, palish, with dim brownish hair and pale scared eyes. She had a timid, withdrawing manner; she dressed always in rather dismal neutral tints—dull greys and dim greens and fawnish drab, and tussore silk, to match her sallow skin. She was a good deal ignored.

I should never have known Adela, or the old lady, if it hadn't been for a silly bet. One does these things in one's first year—risky, futile, daring things—rather caddish things sometimes—with perhaps half-a-crown on them. Someone had ragged me on my numerous acquaintance, and I'd retorted by saying that anyone could make friends with anyone else if they wanted to. Maude Evans caught me up at once.

"Rot!" she said, with her usual affectation of breezy brusquerie. "There's some people no one would ever know."

"I bet there's nobody in College I couldn't get to know if I wanted to," I asserted, with more assurance than was at all warranted. Maude had that effect on me.

Maude thought rapidly. I could see her, as I watched her challengingly, going over all the various types of people—the superior, the literary, the sporting, the fashionable, the "swots." I felt pretty safe. I was only a fresher, but I had possibilities of friendships with all these types.

"You'd never get to know little Whatshername—that washed-out little dishcloth—Young, that's it. I bet you'd never get thick with *her.*"

I had my doubts too, really. It was like betting you'd quarrel with a sofa-cushion. But of course I took her on.

"Bet I will," I said at once.

How much?" Maude caught me up. She always had rather an eye to the main chance.

"Oh—what you like." I expected the usual half-crown.

"Bet you a fiver you don't."

That stung me. Maude would never have risked such a sum—five pounds means a good deal to a girl undergraduate—if she hadn't felt certain of winning.

"Right," I said immediately.

Then we settled the terms of the bet. I was to have invited and been invited—the latter was, of course, the important point—to six walks or meals by the end of the term: to have got some sort of real confidence ("heart to heart talk," we called it) out of little Young, and have wangled an invitation to stay at her home before the end of the next term—the summer term.

Even as I took it on I felt a good deal of a cad. I felt much worse when I began the campaign. The college invitations were all right—one could take them as meaning a lot or as meaning nothing; but to fish for confidences and try to secure an invitation to stay with her people—rotten, both of them. I felt dimly even then that, even when tiresome, both are honours—often the highest honours one person can do another. But I'd been dared. Much as I wanted to win five pounds from the comparatively wealthy Maude Evans, little as I liked the idea of parting with any of my much smaller income to her, what really *mattered* was that I had been challenged and had accepted the challenge. So I set about the siege of Adela Young.

It was extremely difficult. Maude couldn't have chosen a more hopeless subject. Certainly if I could "make good" with her I could with anyone, I thought, as I studied her across the dinner-table that night. She looked permanently scared—she hardly raised her voice above a whisper, and her remarks, when audible, were merely hurried agreements with whatever the last speaker had said. She was silent whenever possible; her very movements were furtive and rapid, as if she had to get through the meal against time, and secretly. For the first time I felt rather *intriguée* about her. Plain, awkward, nondescript as she was, I felt something unusual, almost mysterious, about her. I was even rather thrilled by the idea of finding out more abut her.

I caught her up as she was silently scuttling to her room after dinner—I remembered, now that I came to think of it, that she almost never waited for coffee after dinner, nor, indeed, for any semi-social function like that.

"I say," I said, overtaking her, "you're taking Mods, this term, aren't you?"

"Y—yes," she breathed, looking terrified.

"I wonder if I might come in and go over the Plato with you?"

She said nothing, just goggled at me.

"You are taking the Plato set books, aren't you?"

"Oh, yes."

"I thought so. I've seen you at the classes."

"Yes."

We seemed stuck. I tried again.

"I meant to go over the stuff with Hanson and Phil Leamore, but they say they aren't going to revise at all. Shall you?"

"Oh, yes."

"When are you going to go over the Plato?"

She looked at me mutely, her mouth opening and shutting like a newly caught fish's. She seemed quite incapable of making any suggestion.

"Could you possibly do it to-night?"

"Oh, yes."

I began to wonder if she *could* say anything except "Yes" and "Oh, yes."

"Then may I come along now?" I pressed on.

She said nothing, but opened her door for me. She had the oddest manner as she did it—reluctant, almost, and yet half anxious. I wondered, rather cockily, if she was one of those people you meet sometimes who, when they want a thing, are half afraid of getting it.

As we entered I looked curiously round to see what ideas of decoration such a person (or thing—she hardly seemed to be a real person)

197

would have. She had apparently none. Not a picture, not a flower, not a cushion or a novel or a vase or a photograph was there. Just the usual regulation college furniture and the set books for Pass Mods. I've seldom seen anything so chilling, so absolutely impersonal. I began to regret the bet; Maude Evans was probably right—there were people you could never get to know, because there was nothing to know; and Adela Young was one of them. She had a nondescript face and figure, and inside—nothing. Nothing at all . . . However, I'd undertaken it, and I'd go on. I sat down—on a stiff college chair—you couldn't somehow sit naturally on the floor in that dead-alive room--and opened the "Apology" of Plato.

It was exactly like working with a well-informed gramophone—a hushed, husky voice with nothing alive behind it. But she'd quite obviously worked a lot. She was most useful. While we were working it wasn't so bad. But when I tried to get cheery and conversational afterwards—suggested making tea and so on—she was as palely noncommittal as ever. "Yes"—"No"—"Thank you"—"No, thank you"—"Yes"—"Yes, please"—"Oh, yes"—"Yes . . ." That was about the extent of it. But the very difficulty of it determined me. I fixed up a second *tête-à-tête*, and went away feeling quite astonishingly curious. She puzzled me completely. Pallid and dull and dusty and silent as she was, she somehow suggested a mystery. I found myself thinking of her constantly. She absorbed my thoughts as did no one else in the place, however brilliant or beautiful or witty. I could not get her out of my mind.

There wasn't much left of that term—only a few days—but I managed to see quite a lot of Adela Young. But "see" is the right verb. I saw her—occasionally heard her colourless voice whispering Greek verbs or Latin constructions—and that was all. I began to feel rather alarmed for my fiver. I didn't see how anyone could ever extract any confidences from that cobweb of a girl. I didn't believe she had any to make. As to an invitation from her people—hopeless. You simply couldn't imagine her as having any people or home or anything. I wondered vaguely, when I first thought of this, if she could be a foundling, a child from some orphanage or something, and, if so, whether that wouldn't cancel the bet. I rather jumped at the idea—I thought it would solve my difficulties so very nicely. So, rather tentatively, I broached the subject of families and homes and vacation plans to Adela.

"Shall you spend all the vac. at home?" I asked her one night when we'd "gone over" the work for the next day's paper—Tacitus, I think it was.

"Oh, yes."

"Shall you stay up for the viva, or go home in between?"

"Go home, I think." She paused, and then actually volunteered a remark. "I come so late on the list," she added.

"Yes. So do I, of course. Nuisance, beginning with a Y. But it's too expensive to go all the way to Ireland and back again. I shall have to stay up. Sickening," I added, "I shall be the only person in coll. except the dons."

That was as broad as I dared make it, but I began to fear that she wouldn't take the hint, she was so long before she spoke. She gave me the impression that she was trying to make up her mind to do something rather dreadful. At last she brought it out.

"I—that is, my guardian—she said—I mean, I—we—should be so glad—she said, if I had any friend—who would care . . ."

Her voice died away. It had been even more gasping and husky than usual—as if she were forcing herself to speak and her strength or courage wouldn't last out.

It wasn't exactly what you might call an invitation, but I eagerly took it as such.

"D'you mean that I could stay with you till the viva?" I asked with indecent haste.

"Oh, yes. She—she'd like you to . . ." Again her voice faded into silence.

"But does she know anything about me?" I asked.

"She wants me—make friends—my own age . . ." whispered Adela. She said nothing whatever, I noticed, about her own inclinations.

199

I twisted round—(we were in my room, and I was sitting on the floor, while Adela Young sat in an upright chair behind me)—I twisted round and looked at her curiously. Her face was dead white and her forehead was damp. Her pale eyes stared at me, terrified, above a handkerchief that she held with a shaking hand to her mouth.

What on earth could the girl be so scared about? At the very worst, I might be horribly rude—though she must have known me well enough to know that I shouldn't be. But I couldn't even then see how the grossest insolence could be as terrifying as that.

"Did she—your guardian—suggest that you should ask me?" I asked, curious.

She nodded dumbly.

"It's *awfully* kind of her," I said warmly, "I'd love to."

I expected to see her face clear at that; but it didn't. She looked as scared as ever, mutely terrified, with a kind of half-wistful, almost pitying look as well. I stared at her, rather obviously, I'm afraid, trying to think what the idea was that she suggested to my mind. She looked embarrassed—got up restlessly—moved to the door. But she was too late. I'd got it. She looked exactly like some one who has just been through some awful experience of pain telling the next victim that it's his turn . . . Relieved for herself, but knowing what she was sending me to . . . I was tremendously interested, too much so to speak.

At the door she turned.

"Shall I say you'll come?" she whispered.

"Oh, rather, please. May I send a note too? I mean—it's so awfully kind of your guardian to invite me. I'd like to thank her."

"Oh, I'll tell her," breathed Adela anxiously. "You needn't bother. I'll tell her. She'll be very pleased," she added; and at the words she did look a little easier.

When she was gone, I began to put things together. It came, I thought, to this—the kid must have been brought up in the firmest manner by a Tartar of a guardian of whom she was, even now, mortally scared. She had probably never been allowed to have a friend, or even a possession, of her own. Then, when she was grown up, the dragon had seen her mistake, and had sent her to Oxford with the idea of developing her. She was probably pathetically anxious to see Adela launching out, making friends, being a success, when, owing to the training she had given her, the poor kid was completely incapable of doing anything of the kind. And Adela was still so terrified of this tyrant of her childhood that she had dreaded my refusing—dreaded having to confess that she had, so far, failed to take advantage of her opportunities. That accounted, too, for her odd look at me. Dreading her guardian as she clearly did, she disliked having to hand me over to her. The Subconscious, no doubt, I thought rather grandly. Subconsciously she associated her guardian with whippings and supperless bedtimes and scoldings, and still feared, both for herself and for me, the iron discipline of her childhood. I felt very much pleased with his reconstruction, it fitted all the facts (so far as I knew them) so admirably. I was sure I was right!

I felt quite unwarrantably excited as I arranged my journey to he Bedfordshire village where, it seemed, Adela and her guardian lived, I'd already told Maude Evans where I was going, and rejoiced to see her scepticism change to disappointment and a kind of sulky admiration. If I could get the invitation, I was sure, I thought, to get the confidences in the end; and clearly Maude thought so too. She was obviously very much annoyed—though she could quite well spare the fiver. This added to my pleasurable excitement, which had been considerable in any case, for I was really interested, and very keen to find out what Adela's background really was. I was sure my guess was right in the main, and I also felt that I might, with luck, be able to do something to set things right for the poor kid. I hate to see people as crushed as that, and I had, then, almost unlimited faith in my powers to please and cajole people, especially oldish ladies. I had, then, not the smallest doubt that I should be able to soothe and tame this particular dragon and make life much easier for her aggravatingly timid charge.

On the way down, and especially during the inevitable and interminable wait at Bletchley, I tried to extract something more from Adela about her home conditions. I particularly wanted to know whether there were any other members of the household; my campaign would rather depend on that. But Adela seemed terrified afresh by the very tactful questions I asked. "No—no one else—now . . . We . . . there were more of us—at one time . . ." And here her voice quite gave out, and her pale eyes filled with horror, gazing past me in blank misery.

Again I guessed—some appalling family tragedy, of which she was the sole survivor. Experience, memory, or a "complex" due to an ancient terror—that accounted for a lot. And, on top of it, this probably severe guardian . . . I was getting on. Soon, I felt, I should know enough to extract confidences! I was almost sorry when the train struggled in.

It was pretty full—there had been some local market somewhere—and it was quite impossible to talk. But I watched, surreptitiously, and I saw the pale, vague face opposite me grow paler and the eyes more strained and blank with every stage of our slow, jolting progress.

We were met at our station by an odd old cumbrous carriage, "handsome" to look at, but most depressing. One felt that it was quite inevitably connected with highly respectable funerals; you could almost smell black kid gloves and expensive wreaths. And our dead silence, broken only by Adela's hoarse, uneven breathing and the splash as we rumbled through puddles, only made it worse. I've seldom felt so uneasy—not alarmed, nothing so definite, but just indefinably uncomfortable, with a rather quickened heart-beat as we moved, ponderously and silently, along deserted lanes, wet with the cold rains of March, and between hedges dripping with evening mist.

The house was as large, solid, respectable, and nearly as depressing as the carriage. As we got out, Adela startled me by a sudden, feverish clutch at my hand; hers was dead cold. But before I could respond, the huge front door had swung silently open, and we were inside the house.

It was quite different inside—warm, almost to oppression, well-lighted, roomy. I hardly had time to notice more than this before I saw my hostess.

One generally, though often unconsciously, makes pictures in one's mind of what a stranger will look like. 1 hadn't known that I had made such a guess about Adela Young's guardian (whose very name I had not yet heard); I think perhaps I had a sort of Lady Dedlock, or even a Mrs. Reid, in my mind; but, as we entered the hall, comfortingly warm and bright after the misty fields and lanes, and I had my first glimpse of her, I knew at a glance that whatever I guessed had been wrong, for I could never, never have pictured such a person as I saw.

She remained sitting by the fire—a tiny, tiny little old lady, wrapped in a marvellous Eastern shawl; and the first thing that I thought was that she was tremendously, incredibly old—not "old" as one generally uses the word of people, but "old" as the pyramids and Stonehenge are old—timeless, ageless, and vital. And she was also— not beautiful—fascinating is the only word I can think of to express her face—a face from which I could hardly take my eyes, it was at once so vivid and so inscrutable. When my first impressions settled into something more nearly approaching coherence, I thought I saw why that was. Her porcelain face was flushed, her tiny mouth scarlet, constantly moving, her motions all quick, precise, alert; but over her eyes she wore dark, blank glasses that gave her a secret look, rather dreadful.

As we came in, she moved round in her chair with one of the darting movements, between the movement of a bird and a snake, that, though they were startling at first, I soon got used to, they were so characteristic.

"Is that you, Adela? Have you brought Miss Yorke?"

Her voice was shallow, sweet and tremendously eager, but at the same time—what shall I say?—bodiless. From its eagerness I might have been a celebrity. Poor old thing, I thought, what a life she must lead when the visit of an Irish undergraduate thrills her like that!

"Yes," whispered Adela, hardly audibly. Her voice was so faint, so quavering, that I looked round at her sharply. Her face was ashen, her lips colourless, her eyes vacant as if with sheer naked panic. Her tongue passed incessantly over her white lips. She reminded me of a hypnotised rabbit.

"How very kind of her," murmured the old lady. "Bring her here,

Adela—I can't come to you, Miss Yorke, you must forgive me—I'm an old woman—lame and blind . . ."

And sick, too, I thought, as I took her tiny shrunken hand, for it was burning as if with fever, and tremulous with something that I did not think was age alone. It was more like the quivering of intense excitement. What a life, I thought! What a life they must lead, those two women in that big, lonely comfortable house, when the young one was a mass of terrors and alarms and the old one feverish with excitement over a visit from a girl she could not even see!

"I can't see you with my eyes," the old lady said then. "I wonder if you will let me see you with my fingers? Will you let me feel your face?"

"Of course," I said, and knelt down beside her.

If I had guessed at all what that ordeal would be like, I would never have assented. I cannot describe the utter loathing and repulsion that filled me as the tiny, soft, hot hands passed like feathers over my face. It was horrible, sickening—like allowing some dreadful unclean insect to crawl about one's face, up to the roots of my hair, down my cheeks, round my eyes, along my chin and neck . . . I could hardly restrain my utter disgust, although, when at last her hands dropped, and I rose, rather unsteadily, to my feet, I could not understand my own loathing. I shook myself impatiently, angry at my own folly.

Fortunately, I didn't have to remain beside her for very long. She kept Adela—her gesture was at once commanding and excited, as she asked her to stop for a few minutes, though her voice was as soft and sweet as ever—and I was given over into the charge of an elderly, most respectable-looking maid; but she, too, was odd. She was quiet, efficient, everything she should have been: but she had the face of a sleepwalker. There was not a flicker of expression on it. Her eyes were open, but wholly expressionless; they might have been made of glass, except that they were dull, like the eyes of a dead animal. Quiet, orderly, deft as she was, she made me shiver a little. It was like being waited on by an automaton, or a somnambulist. I got rid of her as soon as I could, saying that I preferred to dress myself, and turning at once to the dressing-table; and it was then that I got a real shock. For, looking in the mirror, my back to her, I saw that she turned at the door, and I caught a glance of a white face distorted by a look of such malignance as I had never dreamed possible. It was utterly inhuman, devilish.

I whipped round—but she had gone, the door closed silently behind her. I must have imagined it, I thought, taking up my brushes; some trick of reflection—some odd effect of the mingled twilight and electric light . . . I dressed quickly, though, and went downstairs as soon as I could. I felt I wanted company.

I remember practically nothing of that dinner, except the vivid, fascinating face of the old lady, surmounted by the terrible dark glasses. I don't remember even what we talked of, though I have a dim impression that the old lady did most of the talking and that her talk was extremely good. Adela, I think, said not one word. I remember nothing at all of her presence, except one glance, when, her guardian having turned aside to speak to a servant, I caught her eyes across the table and was shocked by the sheer despair of their terror. *Why?* What on earth was the matter with her? I felt impatient, almost angry; but the next moment I had forgotten her very existence in the charm (I use the word in its old sense) of the old lady's presence.

After I went to bed that night I could not sleep for thinking about this odd household. I lay for hours, it seemed to me, turning it over in my mind—that enchanting old lady, with the vivid face and blank eyes, the touch of her soft, wandering fingers on my face, the wonderful talk in the shallow, sweet, meaningless voice; Adela, scared, quivering and drab; the secretive, passive maid with that one malignant glance . . .

It had been a chilly month, but my room felt curiously close and warm. At home in Ireland, I always sleep out of doors, and, when I can, I get my bed out on a balcony even at college. I missed the cool freedom, I thought; so I got up to see if there were, by any chance, a balcony or even a ledge where I could sit for a bit.

There was—a narrow one, but wide enough to stand on. I got out of my window and stood there, enjoying the coolness. There must be central heating in the house, I thought, to get that oppressive heat . . . And then I heard voices.

". . . Midsummer. You must bring her, do you hear?"

"Oh, I can't! I *can't* . . ."

That, I knew, was Adela, though I had never before heard her voice so loud or so urgent. It was almost a wail.

"Be quiet, you fool! It's either that, or you . . ."

I stepped over my sill again. I couldn't stand and listen. But I was more wide awake than ever. The other voice, though it had been only a whisper, was, I felt sure, the old lady's. There had been in it something chill, menacing, that made me feel cold even now.

What could it all be about? I, no doubt, was the person who was to be "brought" at Midsummer. But *why?* And why had Adela broken through her scared neutrality to cry, in that anguished wail, "I *can't*"? And what would happen if she didn't? What was the choice suggested by that "It's either that, or you . . ."?

I am, I admit, curious by nature, and now I was thrilled, consumed by curiosity. My repulsion was gone in the sheer love of a mystery. For I felt sure that there was a real mystery here—it was not my imagination, but something real, actual, in this house—a mystery that concerned me, as well as Adela and the old lady. I must find out what it was. Adela was so docile, so entirely without the power of resistance; surely I could get it out of her? Surely I had a right to try, when it concerned myself? I determined, anyhow, that I would. Dawn had come when I fell asleep with that resolution.

Breakfast was brought to me in bed. I gathered, from the matter-of-fact way in which this was done, that it must be the rule of the house. I wasn't sorry; i was tired after my wakeful night, and besides I wanted to think things over, sort out my impressions, and, if it seemed necessary, get some sort of idea of what my plans should be. When I finally came down to the hall, I found the old lady in sole possession, established in her chair as she had been when we arrived. She might never have moved. I greeted her as cheerily as I could, and she called me over to her chair.

"Miss Yorke," she said, "I'm so glad to have you alone. I want to ask you something. You must forgive my springing things on you, but

I don't want Adela to hear and I might not have another opportunity."

I murmured vaguely.

"Tell me," said the old lady—and her voice was urgent—"has Adela ever said anything to make you think that she might marry?"

"Why, no!" I cried, astonished. *Adela* marry! You might as well suspect a faded lettuce of falling in love.

"Never? Not a hint?"

"Never. But we aren't at all—intimate, you know," I said. "She's never spoken at all of—of her personal affairs, her family or anything like that."

"No? No, perhaps she wouldn't. She's very shy," said the old lady, "and she had—a shock." Her voice was quite ordinary, sweet, compassionate a little; but for an instant Iler lips were parted in a tiny smile, furtive, malicious and cold, and her little scarlet tongue flickered over her lips. "Listen, Miss Yorke," she went on, very earnestly. "I'm anxious about Adela. She has no relations—no one but me. I can't explain now, there isn't time. But, you see, I'm very old. I want Adela to marry—to many *soon*," she added; and I could see her little wrinkled hands clutched on her stick.

"And is there any one . . . ?" I hesitated.

"Yes. There is. And I want it settled—at once."

Her voice was tense with her urgency.

"I want to lay my hands on her children," she added, in an extraordinary voice—"gloating" was the word that occurred to me. It ought to have been pathetic, her anxiety to feel, since she could not see, the children of the girl she had brought up; but it wasn't. It was sickening—nauseating. Why, I don't know—something in her voice or tone, or the greedy way in which her tiny aged hands tightened till the knuckles stood out like white pebbles.

"She's never said a word to me," I said, stupidly and coldly.

"No? Well, perhaps she will. If she does, Miss Yorke, urge her—urge her. Tell her she must, for her own sake."

It was the same voice I had heard last night—silky, cold and menacing. The voice that had said, "It's either that, or you . . ."

207

I said nothing. There seemed to be nothing to say. And in the stubborn silence I felt—enmity. It seemed to last for minutes. Then,

"Thank you," said the sweet, shallow voice. "Thank you very much, Miss Yorke. I am counting on you."

She smiled again, and again her smile sickened me, it was so triumphant and so ruthless. Or so it seemed at the time. A few seconds later, when, with a muttered excuse about looking for Adela, I had escaped into the damp garden, I thought I was a fool—over-tired, probably, with term—ready to read mysteries into the most ordinary things. For, after all, what was more natural than that the old lady should wish to see Adela's future safe before she died?—to touch, since she could not see, her children? What was there malignant in that? On the contrary, it was benevolent, rather pathetic. I felt very penitent over my own moodiness and (I feared) rudeness.

In fact, the more I thought of it, the more I saw how right the old lady was. Clearly, Adela's future would be pretty hopeless when her guardian was gone. Shyness, with her, was almost a mania. She would simply retire into herself, shut herself up here in the Bedfordshire house with the odd maid—go off her head, as likely as not. Myself, I should have thought marriage was an impossible idea for her; I could not imagine any man . . . But apparently there was one. She might be an heiress, you never knew. Not a very good motive for any one to want to marry her, perhaps; but even so a marriage that was at all reasonably happy would be better than solitude and craziness. Why on earth had I so loathed the idea when the old lady mentioned it? Why had I been so utterly repelled by her? I could not imagine. What a fool I had been!

I wandered about the neglected garden, vaguely, with no purpose. I was trying to sort things out in my mind, and I hardly noticed where I went. It was not a very big garden, but it seemed so because it had been allowed to run wild; the long, wet grass and overgrown borders and dripping evergreens gave a depressing effect of decay and neglect and age. There were tall hedges and clumps of laurustinus and box-elder that would have made h a fine place for hide-and-seek—only no one could imagine children laughing and romping there. It was dead, as gardens are when houses have long stood empty—dead, and yet somehow furtive. I disliked it more and more; but still I strayed there simply because I hated the house, and the blank-eyed, sweet-voiced old lady, even more. Things are never so bad out-of-doors, I thought; and I also thought that I could not imagine any one ever feeling really terrified out-of-doors—for I now admitted, although unconsciously, that in the house I had felt, suddenly and inexplicably, real fear such as I had never in my life known before.

The very next moment, I knew that I was wrong. Quite suddenly, without the least reason, I was cold and sick with sheer panic. It clutched my heart so that I could not breathe; sweat started out on my forehead and lips and arms. I heard my breath rasping in my throat, and the heavy, irregular thudding of my heart . . .

I stared round me wildly. If only I could see something, no matter how appalling—it would not be so bad. It was this terror of *nothing* that was so dreadful.

But there was nothing. Nothing. Long rank grass, hedged in by dark, dripping evergreens; a stone seat, low and broad and flat; the charred ring left by a weed fire, black in the long, rain-grey grass. Nothing else. Not a sound but the melancholy drip of the leaves— nothing. I stood there as if bewitched—I could not move, I could not even cry out. I felt soaked in evil . . .

And then, as suddenly, the charm was snapped. I heard a sound— a hurried, furtive, stumbling step, a little whimpering sobbing noise— and I could move again. I turned and ran, gasping and shaking, out of the silent, evil enclosure—and ran straight into Adela.

She shrieked—such a shriek as I never wish to hear again—and immediately clapped both her hands to her mouth, crushing back the sound. Her eyes stared, terrified, over her hands.

I caught at her as if she were my salvation.

"Adela," I gasped—I could not speak—"Adela—what is it—in there—in this house? *What is it?*"

She stared dumbly back. I shook her arm, dragging her hands down from her shaking lips.

"Tell me," I urged. "Who is she? What is it?"

"Oh. Honor, don't—I don't know—what do you mean? Oh, don't ask me—don't—I don't know . . ."

"You do know. What is it? What is going to happen at Midsummer?"

She still stared back, horror in her eyes, her white lips moving inaudibly.

"What do you know?" she whispered at last. I could only just hear the words.

"I know there's devilry going on in this house," I said, "and I know that I'm in it . . . Look here, Adela; we must work together. You must help me. We can stop it—we will. Only we'll have to be quick. Tell me. Who is she? What is it?"

She still stared back, too scared to speak.

I don't know what put the words into my head.

"It isn't only me," I said, "it's you, Adela—and your children."

She gasped at that, and her cold hands clutched at me.

"I know, I know!" she babbled in a whisper I could hardly hear. "She will, I know . . . Honor, what can we do? She's listening even now. She can hear and see everything we do . . . We can't ever get away from her. She—she wants another, Honor. It's the year—it's five years since . . . Listen. She got us when we were babies, my brothers and me. I don't know why. I was only three. Two years, later . . ."

She broke off, gulping.

I shook her arm again.

"Go on," I said.

She glanced at me, and then away, her eyes staring before her.

"He died—Phil, the youngest. He—they said he fell—on the shears—there, in the enclosure there. His throat—they said it was pierced. I think I knew even then—I was a baby, but think I knew—it wasn't as they said, I knew things, even then. Afterwards . . ."

Again she broke off, shaking all over.

"Five years after that," she went on—and again she stopped.

"Yes? Yes?" I urged her.

"It was Leslie next," she whispered. "It—an operation, she said—her own doctor—it satisfied people . . . But I knew, Honor, I *knew*—and he did, I think . . . And then, five years ago, Stephen . . . the one just older than me . . . They said it was suicide . . . Honor, oh, Honor, it wasn't, it *wasn't*. She . . ."

She sobbed, one deep, heavy sob.

"It was there—where you came from just now—oh, you frightened me so—I thought it was . . . It was there, Honor, one Midsummer night. I saw smoke. I guessed. I knew it was Stephen—the five years were over. I knew it was danger—oh, horrible, you don't know. I knew a good deal then . . . I was in bed, but I ran and ran . . . Stephen—I thought—I ran, hoping all the time . . . My feet were all cut next day . . ."

Her voice died away in a little sobbing whisper.

"It was—over . . . I saw her—and the fire—and the stone bench . . . Oh, Honor!"

She clutched at me again, staring as if she still saw that horror.

"She knew I was there," she went on at last. I could hardly hear her shaken whisper. "She never hid anything after that. I've seen everything . . . And now—she—the next five years are up."

I felt cold and very sick.

"It's to be me," I whispered.

Adela nodded.

"That's why I was sent," she said at last, "to get—some one. I tried not to, Honor, I did try. I couldn't help it. I had to do it . . . You see—she wants to keep me—she wants children—little children—ready . . ."

We stared at each other in hopeless horror.

"She knows everything I do and say and think," Adela went on in the same hurried gabbling whisper. "She knows we're here now, talking of it. She knows everything, Honor. We can't ever—oh what can I do? What can I do?"

Her despair roused me.

"We have till Midsummer," I said. "We'll be ready by then."

But she shook her head hopelessly.

"You don't know," she said. "You don't understand. She sees your thoughts. You can't plan against her."

"We can," I asserted, "and we will."

She looked up, a glimmer of hope in her questioning eyes.

"It'll be all right," I said. "I'll get you out of it." And linking my arm in hers I led her back to the house.

I can't find words to say how I dreaded entering it, facing the old lady who, according to Adela, knew all we had done and said. But Adela's presence made it easier. Anyhow I knew what I was up against, and I knew that some one weaker than I depended on me. You can't have better incentives to courage. So when we met the old lady face to face in the porch I was able to open my attack right away. I was astonished to hear how natural my voice was as I spoke.

"I did meet Adela, you see," I said, "and we've been having a lovely long talk. She's been awfully kind—she says she'd like me to come again. I wonder if I really may?"

"I should be delighted if you would," purred the old lady, with her polite, surface smile. I wondered with one part of my mind if she really could see into my mind and read my thoughts. "When can you manage it?"

"We go down on the twentieth of June," I said. "Could I come straight to you then—on the twentieth?"

I heard Adela give a terrified gasp, and her hand, tucked under my elbow, clutched my arm convulsively. The old lady's blank, black glasses above her shallow smile made me shiver a little; I had the impression that, owing to their very emptiness, they read me and concealed their knowledge. But I kept a hold on myself, thanks to Adela's trembling hand in my arm; I think there was not even a tremor in my voice as I made all the arrangements and polite speeches that one does make when one fixes up a visit.

We went back to Oxford that afternoon, and after that, I returned to Connemara for the rest of the vac. And, during those few weeks, I thought it all out. Finally I took my twin brother Conal into my secret. I knew he would know that I hadn't panicked over nothing and that he would help me to pull through. We spent long afternoons in the glens with a wise man. My family chaffed me about my sudden interest in fairy lore. I left Conal to carry on our preparations and went back to Oxford for the Summer Term.

One's first summer term generally seems to stand out in people's memory. Mine is a blank. I could think of nothing but what was to come on the day after term ended—on Midsummer Day. And I was not helped to forget it by Adela, who followed me round with mute, imploring, adoring eyes and half-begun, quavering sentences that she never completed. I nearly lost my patience with her more than once, and begged her not to destroy the little nerve I had left. After all it was my risk, not hers, and I'd seen—and, even worse, felt—quite enough to make it unnecessary and maddening to hear her constant appeals— "Oh, Honor, do take care—oh, don't try it—you don't understand . . ." I was determined to take every possible care, but I was equally determined to see the business through.

I don't believe Adela and I exchanged a single word on our journey down to Bedfordshire on that twentieth of June. It was a steamy, breathless day—not a leaf stirring on the heavy trees, the streams crawling sluggishly between the fields where the very grass was motionless. I hoped for thunder vaguely; and with all my might I hoped and prayed that Conal had managed his part of the business. I had said nothing about him, or our plans, to Adela, because I now believed that, owing to her long subjection and terror, her mind was really open to her terrible guardian even when they were apart. But my mind was free, my own; I was strong and independent; so I made my plans—and kept them entirely to myself. All I had said to Adela was that she was to slip out of the house at midnight and remain away from it. I had learnt that all the servants left it each evening—I could guess why.

The house seemed asleep, in a heavy, enchanted torpor that was, as it were, embodied in the thick flowery patens and sickly, pungent scent of the elder trees about it. It was silent, motionless. In the airless heat I felt my hands and feet dead cold. It was sinister—evil. It had not been like that before, I thought stupidly; it was as if the heat drew out some evil emanation as it drew the scent from the elder blossoms. My feet seemed turned to lead, heavy, cold. I could hardly drag them along. I felt drugged, stupefied, by the scent that enveloped the house and by the heat that only seemed to touch the outside of me and left an icy core of fear within. I kept thinking, all that dreadful evening, "Five hours more—only four hours now . . ." as the time loitered by and midnight approached.

I don't remember much of the evening except that. I heard my own voice making conversation, and remember being vaguely surprised to hear how easy and ordinary it sounded. I remember wondering if I had developed a dual personality. My mind felt like my body—giving normal reactions on the surface, while deep down in the centre it was frozen by sheer unnameable terror. I still dream sometimes of that hot, airless evening, with the smell of the elders outside the windows, and the smooth flow of mechanical talk concealing hatred and horror under a mask as smooth and thin as silk.

The sky darkened slowly, and at ten, I made my excuses. I said I was tired—the weather made me headachey—might I go to bed? I smothered a yawn convincingly. The old lady was very solicitous, and, I thought, relieved. I was urged to go to bed at once—she would send me hot milk and a mild sleeping draught. I thanked her, accepted everything, and went to my room.

I wondered, as I undressed, whether I should take that sleeping draught. Suppose Conal failed . . . I felt so sick at the thought that I had to sit down—I was trembling too much to stand. I felt despairing now. The house had sucked away my courage and my hope. I knew, now, that I was doomed as those others had been doomed . . . We would fail—we must. What could we do against—*that?* I would be sacrificed as Adela's brothers had been—as her children would be. Would I not be better drugged, only half aware of the final horror?

I stood hesitating, the draught in my hand. All my pluck was gone

. . . I can't describe the awful abyss of sheer terror that engulfed me. I heard myself whimpering a little, like a terrified dog, and felt my face twitching. I couldn't, *couldn't* do it—that terrible little enclosure, hedged by the secret shrubs—the fire—the stone bench—I couldn't—I couldn't . . .

Then the idea of Conal came into my mind. I mustn't let him down. I had my part to play. If I were a heavy, unconscious lump I might fail him just when he needed me. That braced me at once. I could do it now. I knew how I would have looked and felt if I had yielded to the temptation and taken the drug—I had seen myself as clearly as if I had stood beside my own drugged body. I could do it, and I would. I should not fail . . . I undressed and lay down in the bed. Somewhere in the silent house a clock tolled half past ten. My agony had lasted only a few minutes, and—I had to wait till midnight.

I can't attempt to describe those crawling minutes—the alternation of determination and overwhelming terror, of the picture of the secret, evil enclosure, and of my brother. At last I heard the heavy, boding stroke—a quarter to twelve. My time had come. Any minute now . . .

A step in the passage—light, shuffling, furtive. I relaxed every muscle; I half buried my face in the pillow, breathing slowly and heavily, and rejoicing that I had thought of smearing the edges of my lips with the pungent drug she had given me. The door opened inch by inch. I wondered if she could hear my heart thumping in the dead silence.

Not a sound. Had she gone? If only I dared look! It was awful, wondering and waiting. Had she gone? Or was she there, beside me, watching me? . . . No sound. I had to keep relaxing my muscles; they stiffened as soon as I listened. And I had to go on breathing steadily, quietly . . .

I nearly screamed when I felt a cold, light touch on my neck. I was just able to turn it into a restless sign and the little movement of a heavy sleeper settling again to slumber.

"Take the head," came a bodiless whisper. "We have only just time."

Hands were slipped under my shoulders; other hands—tiny, cold;

215

soft hands—took my feet. I could hardly bear that cold, soft ruthless touch. I knew whose hands they were . . .

They carried me downstairs. I think they were too heavily burdened—or perhaps too anxious—to notice how, twice, I forgot and found my muscles tense with loathing and terror. I lay, for most of that awful journey, limp and relaxed, breathing as if asleep, with my heart in my throat with terror.

We were out of doors. There was no stir of air, but it felt different, and the scent of the elders was heavier, more cloying than ever. On and on, through the rank grass that smelt of dew as they pressed it; over a path that gave a dull echo to their shuffling feet; through a gap in a hedge that smelt stuffily of evergreens . . .

They laid me on the stone bench. I could feel it, cold and rough, through my thin nightgown; and then—I can hardly bear to remember it—I smelt thick, heavy smoke and heard the rasp of steel on stone . . .

I could not endure another instant. I leapt up and shrieked—shrieked the words I had learned—heard a crash . . .

I don't remember anything more. All I know is that Conal had not failed me. He, outside that evil enclosure, had done his part as I had done mine within. It was over . . . An hour later the house was roaring in flame to the darkened sky, while lightning flickered overhead and Adela crouched weeping beside me . . .

I was ill after that, and went up late next erm. Almost the first person I met was Maude Evans.

"Hullo!" she said. "Better?"

I said I was all right.

"Fancy you being so upset about a fire!" she said. "But there was a death in it, wasn't there?" she added, as an extenuation.

"Yes," I said.

"You were there when it broke out, weren't you?" she went on.

"Oh yes. I was staying there. You've lost your fiver all right," I said, hoping that would make her sheer off. But it didn't. She had

clearly forgotten the fiver, and was rather crestfallen, but looking for a loophole at once.

"Well, but did the Young kid ever confide anything to you?" she demanded. "That was part of it, you know."

I shivered a little.

"Oh yes, she confided in me all right," I said.

"Really intimate?"

"Oh yes—very. Too intimate to tell you, Maude."

Maude scowled sulkily.

"Men?" she asked then.

Again I shivered.

"Well," I said, "marriage came into it."

Witchcraft

Edmund Clarence Stedman

I. A.D. 1692

Soe, Mistress Anne, faire neighbour myne,
  How rides a witche when nighte-winds blowe?
Folk say that you are none too goode
To joyne the crews in Salem woode,
When one you wot of gives the signe;
  Righte well, methinks, the pathe you knowe.

In Meetinge-time I watched you well,
  Whiles godly Master Parris prayed;
Your folded hands laye on your booke;
But Richard answered to a looke
That fain would tempt him unto hell,
  Where, Mistress Anne, your place is made.

You looke into my Richard's eyes
  With evill glances shamelesse growne;
I found about his wriste a hair,
And guessed what fingers tyed it there;
He shall not lightly be your prize—
  Your Master firste shall take his owne.

'Tis not in nature he should be
  (Who loved me soe when Springe was greene)
A childe, to hange upon your gowne!
He loved me well in Salem Towne
Until this wanton witcherie
  His hearte and myne crept dark betweene.

Last Sabbath nighte, the gossips saye,
  Your goodman missed you from his side.

He had no strength to move, untill
Agen, as if in slumber still,
Beside him at the dawn you laye.
    Tell, nowe, what meanwhile did betide.

Dame Anne, mye hate goe with you fleete
    As driftes the Bay fogg overhead—
Or over yonder hill-topp, where
There is a tree ripe fruite shall bear
When, neighbour myne, your wicked feet
    The stones of Gallowes Hill shall tread.

II. A.D. 1884

Our great-great-grandpapas had schooled
    Your fancies, Lita, were you born
In days when Cotton Mather ruled
    And damask petticoats were worn!
Your pretty ways, your mocking air,
    Had passed, mayhap, for Satan's wiles—
As fraught with danger, then and there,
    To you, as now to us your smiles.

Why not? Were inquest to begin,
    The tokens are not far to seek:
Item—the dimple of your chin;
    Item—that freckle on your cheek.
Grace shield his simple soul from harm
    Who enters yon flirtation niche,
Or trusts in whispered counter-charm,
    Alone with such a parlous witch!

Your fan a wand is, in disguise;
    It conjures, and we straight are drawn
Within a witches' Paradise
    Of music, germans, roses, lawn.

So through the season, where you go,
    All else than Lita men forget:
One needs no second-sight to know
    That sorcery is rampant yet.

Now, since the bars no more await
    Fair maids that practise sable arts,
Take heed, while I pronounce the fate
    Of her who thus ensnares men's hearts:
In time you shall a wizard meet
    With spells more potent than your own,
And you shall know your master, Sweet,
    And for these witcheries atone.

For you at his behest shall wear
    A veil, and seek with him the church,
And at the altar rail forswear
    The craft that left you in the lurch;
But oft thereafter, musing long,
    With smile, and sigh, and conscience-twitch,
You shall too late confess the wrong—
    A captive and repentant witch.

The Children of Glimbly

John Shirley

Before the great war, which you shall hear of soon enough, something rather sinister and appalling happened to me. I was kidnapped.

It wasn't the usual sort of child abduction. It was just as sinister, quite as appalling—but in quite a different way. In ways I had never heard of.

It was only toward the end of the kidnapping that I came to understand how appalling it was. Before then it was rather like being sent to a British public school . . .

Ten years ago, in a certain village centered in a broad valley in the least populous part of Britain, cell phones did not function. That's how it was in the suspicious and madly parochial Glimbly-on-the-Dimbly. I'm told the locals cleared their throats and looked at their shoes if strangers asked why cell phones and the internet did not operate thereabouts. Some muttered of electromagnetic peculiarities owing to ore deposits; others grimaced and declared that cell phones are a vile intrusion into the life of any sensible bloke, and "Why should we want them anyhow?"

Those who've spent some time in the area understood, by and by, that what the dark witches allowed, in those days, is what they allowed and what they didn't allow is simply what they didn't.

Glimbly is peculiar for many other reasons. When I was there, it was a place where crows were known to speak in sentences of grammatically perfect English, when they chose to; I heard one of them engage in a lengthy diatribe against "the patronizing disrespect embodied in the use of scarecrows." Even now, it is a village where each cottage has its own particular song, a fluting in its thatching and eaves when the wind is blowing from the east. The residents of that house know the words to the song, and they sing along. I learned a snatch of it:

> *Ever a leer, ever a fleer the squint-eyed ones demand*
> *For the godlings of the ancients made us serve them in their lands*
> *The Old Ones thunder, the seas are grumblier, and bones dance in stone*

And they who don't fall to their knees are found with broken bones
Aye and every bone is broken, not a single one forgot
Every bone a-broken, and eyes like wooden knots

The folk of Glimbly were in those days cowering under the knob-by thumbs of devil-sworn witches, in every wise, though the villagers rarely saw the enchantresses close-on. Yet the witch-power was made known, and the names of the powerful witches and warlocks well known too. The dark witches were the mistresses of industry in a significant portion of Dimblyshire, by deed and certification. A county unacknowledged by the government of the United Kingdom, Dimbly-shire was nearly one great plantation.

When travelers carelessly stumbled upon Glimbly, they didn't stay long. They reported nothing to the outside world except, "Those people are glum and unfriendly; their land is ugly, they have bleak weather, no comfortable beds, the water tastes septic and the inn meals are ghastly. We left as quickly as we could." None of their evaluation was strictly true—the beds, food and weather are not worse than elsewhere in England—but due to the enchantment laid on strangers to Dimbly, the place seemed repellent, and the traveler's reports always alike. For the witches wanted outsiders to quietly go away.

I know these things, because I had a different experience of Glimbly than casual visitors have. Upon my abduction I spent ten months in the pastures and sheds of Glengeelda's Stock Farm just north of Glimbly, and not far from the river Dimbly.

It wasn't so bad for us in some ways. There was a swing set, and a jungle gym. We had a shadow-play night in the child-sheds, and the food wasn't awful. We had a few toys and board games, but much of my experience was bearable only because of quite another spell that was upon me; that was upon all the children…

Any road, everything changed on the day Eloise was brought to our child-shed.

It was a balmy late-summer day, the elms nodding in a sweet breeze. The children of our shed, numbering seven, were gathered in the shade of a venerable oak tree that stood on a knoll in the center of

222

our fenced-in pasturage. We were Prudence, Glenn, Beatrice, Millie, Glum Gareth (as we called him), Penelope, and me. I'm Joel.

Near the compound side of the fence was our long narrow child-shed, and the water trough. The fence around the pasture and shed was of steel, topped with rusty barbed wire. The only gate in the fence, once unlocked, opened into a sizeable compound containing a large steel barn, several goodly outbuildings and the three-story Keeper House with its four twisty, ever-smoking chimneys. Beyond the gated compound were other pastures, other child-sheds. Our own shed was just as it sounds, a low-ceilinged thing of rickety wood, with bunkbeds, blankets and pillows, a low dining table and chairs.

I was sitting on a tree root, chewing a succulent sprig of fennel and trying to remember how old I was. I theorized that I was nine, almost ten. But it was a guess my blurred mind could not confirm. Some areas of my mind were clouded as was much of my past. Memories of my parents, of home, were almost entirely gone. I could not remember my last name. Certain feelings, too, seemed mostly numbed. One thing I'm sure of, though, is that I'm American. I know, because the other kids told me I sound American.

I heard the four crows high in the oak tree call a warning, a harsh caw and then one of the crows said, quite clearly, "The witches fly over, a phalanx of three; two hold hands, one trails free." (We've grown quite used to talking crows.)

I looked up and saw three witches, about thirty yards up, flying like swimmers in the air, legs stretched out behind them, the front two in fluttering red-trimmed black robes. The leaders flew side by side, their acolyte following a little behind. She wore a gray, frazzle-edged gown. The two women in front seemed old, long white hair streaming. They passed over the farm and suddenly blinked out—when they got to a certain distance from Glimbly, their cloaks made them invisible.

"They came and they went," said Glenn.

A few minutes passed, and I tried again to remember how old I was. Gareth sighed. He sighs a great deal.

"The new child is here," said Prudence, pointing.

"The eighth one, finally," said Glenn.

For eight was the normal number of child-shed residents. We knew this, as some of us had been moved from other sheds, on other parts of the property, beyond the high, opaque fences, so as to keep the number right. We were all about the same age. Now the eighth for our shed strolled up.

"I'm Eloise," she said as she approached, not seeming shy at all. She was perhaps a year older than me. Like the rest of us, she was wearing a blue and white uniform, very like the togs forced on British public-school children. She had her hair neatly cut with bangs, and trimmed clean at the nape of the neck—as we all did. "I was in shed five. A new child came in and the Keeper moved me into yours."

Millie, who had black hair and black eyes and pouting lips, whispered to me, "There's something odd about this girl. She has a strange look in her eye. The way she looks at us."

"You may as well know, that I have come among you to find out certain things," Eloise said. A pronouncement I'd never heard from any child.

"What things?" I asked.

"Things that could bring about your liberation. I have kept quiet for almost a week, since arriving in this compound, but last night I used the chicken bones for a casting. I have seen the signs, and I must act."

"Did you say liberation?" Glenn asked, frowning. He was a stocky grumpy boy, with plump freckled cheeks. "Liberation from what?"

"I don't suppose you remember how you came here," said Eloise. Adding matter-of-factly, "You were stolen away, and your minds have been clouded."

Glum Gareth, a short glowering boy who never spoke, but only made growling noises, made one now, and nodded.

Eloise nodded back to him. "And who are you?"

Garreth only growled again, touched his throat and shook his head.

"Garreth stopped speaking when they punished him for asking too many questions," Beatrice explained. She was a prissy little girl with a slight French accent.

"Here comes a Keeper," said Penelope, shading her eyes to look toward the compound. "It's the Second Most. Spleena." Penelope has blond hair, so blond it is almost white, and eyes like the blue paint on teacups. She has a pointed nose, fascinating because its tip would often move slightly as she talked.

Coming through the gate from the Keeper House was Spleena, a tall, narrow-shouldered woman in a green coveralls and mud-splashed wellies. She wore dark sunglasses, and a straw sunhat, and carried a staff that looked to be made of ebony. The staff was topped with the brass figure of a fanged monkey, its clawed fingers and toes holding on below its chin.

Clomping along behind her was The Ogle, as we kids called him: a mass of muscle with a severely hunched back, and dirty rubber-framed goggles he never removed. He had long thick arms that reached nearly to the ground. Wearing nothing but ragged, colorless trousers, he had no shoes, indeed no feet—he had hooves instead. His face was like a cross between a razorback boar and a man's face, but flattened. He was said to be the result of a breeding experiment. Ogle, and other deformed semihuman creatures, were used as muscle around the farm, as security and to carry massive haybales to the cows in the big red barns, and sometimes to carry children away, one child tucked under each arm. Those children were not seen again.

We were used to creatures like Ogle, in several shades of grotesquery. We were even used to Spleena's slithering eyes. For she had an extra set of eyes that moved around in her long gray-black hair; scuttling like beetles in the oily strands.

"She has come to weigh you," said Eloise, speaking with a strange self-assuredness.

We stood up, as we were trained to do, and passively waited for the ill-smelling Ogle and the vinegar-smelling Spleena. We saw our gawping faces reflected in Spleena's dark glasses as she smiled down at us.

"We will have weighing now," she said, in her unfitting melodious voice.

We could not help but groan. Getting weighed was very uncomfortable.

One of Spleena's eyes crept to a bare spot above her right ear and trained itself on Eloise.

Ogle stepped up to the nearest child—which happened to be me. I closed my eyes as his big, rough calloused hand closed around my throat. He lifted me off my feet, and I hung there, choking a little, my neck hurting, waiting. Hating this, but not much afraid—I'd been weighed several times since coming here. I'd always come through it alive.

Ogle's voice sound like gravel in a cement mixer. "Hez four n'er heff stone," said Ogle, dropping me. I fell coughing to the ground.

"Ah, four and a half stone," Spleena said. "He's getting rather plump, sitting around too much. We should run it off him. Perhaps a few days on the squirrel wheel."

Clutching my throat, I winced at her mention of the squirrel wheel. "No please. I fell and hurt my ankle on the squirrel wheel, last time, Ma'am Keeper," I pleaded.

"What I say will be, will be. And to remind you of that, you may all recite the Saying of Purpose."

We dutifully recited, *"I am fed and sheltered and given diversion, so that I may grow to add myself to the strength of his lordship Luciferus and his beautiful wives. For being of proper use is the very best we can be."*

The others were duly weighed, each with their measure of discomfort, but not without accuracy, and then it was Eloise's turn. She frowned, but had to submit.

"Shez eight n' a quarter stone!" Ogle declared.

"What?" Spleena exclaimed. "Impossible! Look at her! That's the weight of an adult woman! Put her down and weigh her again!"

He put Eloise down, then lifted her again. "Shez eight n' heff a stone, iz trooz!"

"She can't be!"

"She is, Ladysherp Missez! Bloody heavy tooz!"

"Oh, put her down! She's choking."

Ogle dropped Eloise. She got up, cleared her throat, and dusted herself off.

Spleena jabbed a finger at Eloise. "Eight and a half stone in a child that should weigh less than half that! There's bright-lodge witchery at work here!"

"Shall I *keel* herrrrr in the barrrrrn?" Ogle asked, licking his chops with an enormous blue phlegmy tongue.

"Perhaps—and then I will subject her to a soul vivisection!"

Eloise merely curtseyed. "As you please."

This made two of Spleena's eyes raise the eyebrows they carried about with them.

"However," Eloise went on cooly, "If I die, then shall Spleena die."

Two more of Spleena's eyes crept about on her head to stare down at Eloise. "What's that? A threat? I will see what you may be—here and now!"

She pointed the staff at Eloise. Its brass monkey-head glowed yellow, its eyes glowed red and a beam of mingled yellow and red fell upon Eloise...and faded out. The brass monkey lifted a clawed paw and scratched its head in puzzlement. Then it turned about on the staff, looked at its mistress—and shrugged.

"What!" Spleena said dumbfounded. "You can't see into her?"

The metal monkey shrugged again, and turned to grasp the staff, becoming an inert thing of brass once more.

Spleena stepped scowlingly back. "I will set a watch on you till I've consulted with Mistress Gleengelda. You could have a suicide spell upon you—they are dangerously explosive." She took another step back, adding thoughtfully, "When first I laid eyes on you I *thought* I sensed something awry!"

"The mistrezz, she's orff to them coven'n Edinburgh," rumbled Ogle

"She is on her way back now—but I shall send a message bidding her to haste." The witch turned to Ogle. "You stay here and watch these fat, troublesome little stew-rabbits, and punish them all if there's any trouble. But don't bruise them if you can avoid it. I shall go to the Farspeaker to consult with Gleengelda."

She stalked away, the staff over one shoulder. The brass monkey looked back at us, opening its mouth to leer with filed teeth.

I shivered at that, and looked at Ogle. He was scratching his rump and licking his lips, while ogling me and Eloise. "Yooz troublers, yooz two, I smellz it."

"You *smellz*, right enough," said Penelope.

The children tittered.

Ogle looked puzzled. "I gotz nose, yez? So I smellz."

More giggling.

Ogle sat in the shade under the tree with a grunt, legs crossed, scratching at his groin. "Too hotz, too hotz," he rumbled. "I sit, I watches yooz!"

I saw Spleena reach the gate to the compound. She told it to open, and it swung out of her way. The Keeper hurried through toward the house. The gate closed, locking behind her.

I stepped closer to Eloise, keeping my voice low to ask, "About these spells on us--on our memories, you say. Are you sure of that?"

"I am," she said. She was gazing at the fence on the other side of the pasture, where a flicker woodpecker was alighting on the barbed wire. The woodpecker gave us a significant look with one cocked eye and began to drum with its beak on the metal post holding the wire.

"There," Eloise whispered to me. "The signal. I must get closer to that fence. Something will burrow under it..." She started toward the fence.

"Stop!" Ogle shouted, shaking his head vigorously so that spittle flew from his drooping tongue. "I watches yooz here!"

Eloise paused and curtseyed to Ogle. "Sir, is it not time for our afternoon exercise? We are to run around the pasturage, are we not?" She was right, it was about that time.

Ogle banged a horny fist on the ground. "You stay here!"

"Oh *good*, I do want to stay here," I said. "It's getting *quite* hot outside, hotter and hotter, and we'll fairly *roast* if we run. We might collapse!"

As I'd hoped, Ogle liked the picture I'd painted. "You runz!" He kicked at the dirt with a hoof in emphasis. "I watches!"

"Right, right--if we must," I sighed.

Garreth growled, Penelope snorted and was genuinely annoyed. "Eloise, I don't think I like you. I don't care to run in this heat."

"It won't take long," Eloise murmured. "Come!" She led the way and the others trailed after her, jogging along toward the fence, and then along it. When we came to the woodpecker still drumming on the fence, it flew away. But then I saw a dark, shortish snout poke from the dirt under by a fence-post.

Eloise slowed, and whispered, "Children—kindly hide me for a few moments!"

Garreth and Millie and I stopped, as if to catch our breath, blocking Ogle's view of Eloise as she ran up to the badger, its head now emerging from the new hole, shaking dirt aside—and clasping something in its jaws: an amulet made of silver, on a silver chain. The amulet was in the shape of a star. The badger's eyes were all but closed against the sun but it thrust the pendant at Eloise, who said, "Thank you, my friend!" as she plucked it from the badger's jaws.

The badger snorted, and ducked away into the burrow, and I heard Ogle shouting, "Yooz! Why you stop running! Runz! Runz!"

Eloise hid the amulet in the pocket of her shorts and resumed running. "Come along, we must complete our run!"

"I don't know about any of this!" Glenn complained, grudgingly running after her. "Badgers waving baubles about! You're as witchy as them others!"

Once around the fence we trotted, and then back to the tree, where we panted, sweating in the shade.

"No!" Ogle grunted. "Yooz fatz runs five times more! Too many stones you is weigh! Lean, we likez! *Lean*!"

"Look what I've found, sir!" Eloise said. She stepped out into the sunlight so the amulet caught a glint—and it sent a ray right to Ogle's goggles.

"Ach!" He grunted. "Whatz thatz! It burns my seerz!"

"Then close your seerz," Eloise said, in a voice of syrupy persuasion. "Rest you in rest, slide into slumber!"

Ogle's head drooped, and he fell to snoring.

"Oooh!" cried Millie and Beatrice and Glenn. "It's truly magic!" Penelope said, awed.

"It is," said Eloise.

"What *are* you?" asked Glenn, looking at Eloise with a touch of suspicion. "What child knows magic?"

"I'm a bit compressed," Eloise said. "It's rather uncomfortable in a compressed body. If you don't mind, I'll decompress and you'll see more clearly what I am." With that, she held the amulet on its chain over her head. The silver star spun slowly there…and Eloise began to grow. She grew out and up, her clothes stretching, then bursting at the seams and almost falling off as she became a full-grown adult woman. Still Eloise, but all grown up.

She muttered words in a language I have never heard, and a mist shrouded her—then blew away in an anomalous breeze. She was now clad in robe of soft white linen, sewn with runes in green thread. On her feet were matching slippers.

The children gasped and started to back away.

"You have nothing to fear from me," Eloise said, now clasping the amulet around her neck. Her manner was much the same but her voice was a little deeper, quite grown-up. "I am Eloise Gupta Murti, a traveling seneschal of the Bright Lodge."

"Is that some sort of…of witch lodge?" I asked.

"Some sort," she said. "We are enchantresses, witches, and apprentices. We are *not* servants of Luciferus, like the dark witches. We serve the Great Organizer, a being called by many names. But they are all names that reflect her benevolence, and the nurturing warmth of her light. Still, she can wield a warrior's blade at need. The wives of Luciferus have for some time been more powerful in this world, than the Bright Lodge—until recently. Our numbers have grown, our power has grown, and we became aware that children were being kidnapped to Farms like this one…"

"I…don't remember that," said Glenn, shaking his head.

"I can help you remember," Eloise said. She closed her fingers over the amulet and light flared from the points of the star, to stream out between her fingers. Then the light spun like a pinwheel, so it flashed across all of us—and the drab haze evaporated from our memories. We remembered.

Suddenly I saw it flashing through my mind. Being taken by the witches, flown in a trance through the skies to a field where waited motor vehicles, vans and trucks, whose black-hooded drivers brought us here. I had been taken from my parents, when we were visiting England.

The spell had on the children our first names, and how to speak, and read, and how to play games and how to use a toilet and how to wash. And little else.

But it all came shimmering back now--and it brought pain with it. Anguish from the absence of our families flared up like hot flames within us. Some of us wept. Some prayed--and me, I quietly cursed the witches and looked about to see how I might escape this place…

Garreth glowered at Ogle. "Can I kick Ogle in the bollocks, Eloise?"

We stared. Millie burst out, "Gareth spoke! You can talk again!"

"Oh—I *can!*" Gareth said, a smile softening his glum face. "But—*can* I kick him in the bollocks, ma'am? He's helped keep us prisoner!"

"No, we don't want to wake him," said Eloise. "But I understand your feelings in the matter."

"Why have they brought us here, Eloise?" asked Beatrice tearfully.

Eloise shook her head sadly. She removed her hand from the amulet. The light died down; the children fell quiet, waiting for her answer. The only sounds were the distant calls of crows and Ogle's snoring. "You are free-range children," said Eloise.

"I don't understand!" Penelope said, wiping her eyes.

"Once a year, the dark witches have an annual feast, and their preferred meat is—I'm *so* sorry to say—children. Certain of the old fairytales are in some ways true, you see. The Luciferan witches feel the meat tastes best if you're allowed some freedom within the fences, until you're about ten years old. The preparations for the feast are carried out in a different place every year.

Now, the Bright Lodge now plans to stop the butchery and liberate the children. But we must learn where the butchery will happen this year, as many children are already there, awaiting slaughter—and that is why I've come here, among you...for Gleengelda is the chief chef of the feasts. She has chosen a new butchering site."

Most of the children were staring, mouths open, still assimilating the "they kill and eat us" part.

I asked, "Eloise—how were you able to arrange that you should be with us?"

"I used magic to disguise myself as a child. Then one of our allies, a nighthawk, came down and flew at a minion who was herding kidnapped children into a van—and while it attacked the minion's head, distracting him, I used that moment to mingle with the children. The crow flew away and the witch closed the van without knowing I was in it. Of course, I was in my child form then."

Just then a bird flew into the oak foliage shading us. A large crow-like bird but with curious yellow markings on their necks and head, it alit on a branch two yards above.

"I've never seen a bird like that," I remarked.

"*'I've never seen birds like that'*", repeated the bird mockingly, in almost exactly my voice.

We laughed and Eloise smiled. "That bird is my friend Krishna—he's a hill myna who came from India to help me spy on the witches. What have you to report, Krishna?"

The myna cocked its head to look down at Eloise and said, in quite another voice, "When I flew to the grove of the Dark One I found Gleengelda had arrived, at the behest of Spleena; I secreted myself in thick leaves, and listened, and here is what I heard..." Thereupon Krishna the myna spoke in two voices, alternately, first Spleena's and then Gleengelda's, reproducing the colloquy with undeniable plausibility:
"*. . . I have Ogle watching a creature I suspect may be a spy for the Bright Lodge.*"

Then, in Glengeelda's voice: *"Why did you not destroy her?"*

232

"I bethought me she might be tormented into revealing the secrets of her lodge--but I was not sure I had the power to overcome her."

"So! She made you afraid! Either she is powerful—or you are a coward!"

"O mother of us all, I could not risk magical combat. Struck down, I cannot warn you. I feel we must move the children to the flaying pens as quickly as we may!"

"It is so. We will transfer them to the Carpathian Center, near Borsec—it is readied for an influx of meat children. Go now and prepare them!"

Krishna cleared his throat and tilted an eye toward Eloise. "Thereupon I decided to fly to you, Eloise, and repeat what I heard. In truth I do not understand all, but this is how they spoke."

Eloise clasped her hands together and looked toward the house. "You've told me what I need to know. We have become aware of a property aswarm with dark witches, in Romania near Borsec. That is where they will bring the children from the farms! First go to the ground team, and tell them the time has come! Then tell the crows they will have their revenge this day!"

Krishna the myna flew away, and Eloise went softly to stand beside the sleeping Ogle. She bent, and whispered into his ear, words I could not hear, her hand cupping the amulet.

Suddenly he yawned, and sat up—and said, "I hear and obey!"

Getting awkwardly to his feet, Ogle turned and trotted toward the gate into the compound. Beyond it, I could see a group of four hooded men, each with spiky cattle prodders in hand. Blackhoods we called them. They were standing by an outbuilding, from which a large cargo truck of six wheels backed into view.

"That is how they'll transport us," Gareth said.

By then Ogle had reached the gate. When it opened for him, he redoubled his speed, like a bull charging. He ducked his head and plunged in amongst the hooded men, flailing with fists, pausing to kick his hooves out--smashing three of them down. One of the men kept his feet, and stabbed Ogle in the neck with the point of a prodder. Even at this distance I could see the red glint of spraying blood. But Ogle charged him, knocked him down, fell upon him, gnawing at the man's face. The blackhood screamed—and then both Ogle and the blackhood fell to dying, in clinging to one another as they quivered in death.

Two female figures in robes rose into the sky over the house, lightnings spraying from their hands—it was Spleena and Gleengelda, and a third witch I did not know. They were hovering, threatening figures, each with a brass-figured staff, discharging sulfur-yellow hatred formed into thunderbolts. The bolts struck the ground between us and the gate, making blackened craters.

Poised vertically, the three dark witches began flying toward us. Below them, on the ground, came three malformed creatures of the Ogle ilk, shambling toward us with hatchets in their hands.

An attack on us was coming by sky and by land.

"They're coming to kill us!" Millie cried.

A clamoring of caws came from above, and the sky was darkening. We looked up to see an enormous murder of crows, a flock bigger than any I'd ever seen.

I looked to Eloise, but she did not seem troubled. She had one hand on her amulet, and gazed with clinical interest as the great flock of crows converged on the oncoming witches. Electrical discharges shot from the brass-tipped staffs; burning black feathers were blasted to trail smoke, and half a dozen crows fell from the sky. But only a small number of the corvids were struck. The remainder swarmed aerially upon the witches, pecking at Gleengelda's eyes, clawing at Spleena's throat. More lightings cracked outward through the black-feathered host, and dying crows whirled away, burning--but still more arrived, redoubling the attack.

The ogles were getting close. Then hawks swooped down to tear at the ogles, who were quickly blinded, running away in confusion. Crows and hawks flapped furiously after them and soon the Ogles fell and were fed upon by a living morass of shiny feathers and probing beaks.

"There goes Spleena!" Penelope cried, clapping her hands together.

Spleena was turning head over heels, falling to the pasture, along with the unknown witch—

A great burst of purplish light exploded outward in the crows flapping and clustering about the hovering Gleengelda. Scores of crows were incinerated…revealing a blinded Gleengelda, red with her own blood, writhing in the sky, drifting slowly down…

A bolt of light shot from Eloise's amulet to strike Gleengelda, and the witch shrieked in pain and horror. Her body then fell like a stone—but I glimpsed something fluttering away from it, like a ragged cloth of burnt translucent black silk…it became lost in the smoke rising from the blast craters in the ground.

"The Keepers at this acreage are undone," announced Eloise. "Other farms will now be attacked by our allies, and the witches of the Bright Lodge. Bright Lodge forces will attack the base in the Carpathians. There are already children there, awaiting slaughter. But I believe we are in time to save them. Ah! Here—comes your transportation."

A big yellow school bus rammed through an outer gate into the compound. The children cheered at this. The bus passed through the inner gate, drove right to us and stopped close to the oak. A smiling Black woman waved to us from the driver's seat.

"All aboard!" called Eloise as the bus's door flew open. "We will take you to London…and from there, you will be returned to your families."

"Eloise—will all the dark witches be destroyed, this day?" I asked, looking at the crows feeding on what remained of Gleengelda.

"Oh no," she said sadly. "There are many, many more of them. They will congregate—and a great war will arise. A conflict that is long overdue. The Bright Lodge simply wasn't ready before. We can wait no longer."

But they did have to wait. The children were rescued, but after that the dark witches went into hiding. As I write this now, thirteen years later, I remember the hellishness and glory of the Witching War, and my own part in it. That is a tale I will tell—another day.

The Witch-Mother

Algernon Charles Swinburne

"O Where Will ye gang to and where will ye sleep,
  Against the night begins?"
"My bed is made wi' cauld sorrows,
  My sheets are lined wi' sins.

"And a sair grief sitting at my foot,
  And a sair grief at my head;
And dule to lay me my laigh pillows,
  And teen till I be dead.

"And the rain is sair upon my face,
  And sair upon my hair;
And the wind upon my weary mouth,
  That never may man kiss mair.

"And the snow upon my heavy lips,
  That never shall drink nor eat;
And shame to cledding, and woe to wedding,
  And pain to drink and meat.

"But woe be to my bairns' father,
  And ever ill fare he:
He has tane a braw bride hame to him,
  Cast out my bairns and me."

"And what shall they have to their marriage meat
  This day they twain are wed?"
"Meat of strong crying, salt of sad sighing,
  And God restore the dead."

"And what shall they have to their wedding wine
    This day they twain are wed?"
"Wine of weeping, and draughts of sleeping,
    And God raise up the dead."

She's tane her to the wild woodside,
    Between the flood and fell:
She's sought a rede against her need
    Of the fiend that bides in hell.

She's tane her to the wan burnside,
    She's wrought wi' sang and spell:
She's plighted her soul for doom and dole
    To the fiend that bides in hell.

She's set her young son to her breast,
    Her auld son to her knee:
Says, "Weel for you the night, bairnies,
    And weel the morn for me."

She looked fu' lang in their een, sighing,
    And sair and sair grat she:
She has slain her young son at her breast,
    Her auld son at her knee.

She's sodden their flesh wi' saft water,
    She's mixed their blood with wine:
She's tane her to the braw bride-house,
    Where a' were boun' to dine.

She poured the red wine in his cup,
    And his een grew fain to greet:
She set the baked meats at his hand,
    And bade him drink and eat.

Says, "Eat your fill of your flesh, my lord,
    And drink your fill of your wine;
For a' thing's yours and only yours
    That has been yours and mine."

Says, "Drink your fill of your wine, my lord,
    And eat your fill of your bread:
I would they were quick in my body again,
    Or I that bare them dead."

He struck her head frae her fair body,
    And dead for grief he fell:
And there were twae mair sangs in heaven,
    And twae mair sauls in hell.

The Old Witch Who Lived in a Forest

Alice Elizabeth Dracott

There was once a Brahmin who had five daughters, and after their mother died, he married another woman who was very unkind to them, and treated them cruelly, and starved them. So stingy was she that, upon one occasion, she took a grain of linseed, divided it into five pieces, and gave a piece to each child.

"Are you satisfied, sister?" they asked one another, and each replied: "I am satisfied," except the youngest, who said: "I am hungry still." Then the eldest, who had still a morsel of the linseed in her mouth, took it and gave it to her little sister.

Soon after their stepmother said to her husband: "These children must be sent away, or else I will go."

He did his best to dissuade her, but she insisted; so, taking the five girls, he went with them to the river, where he suggested they should all cross over to the other side. "Father, you go first, and we will follow you."

"No, my children, you go first, and I will follow; but, if you should see this umbrella which I carry floating upon the water, you will know that I am drowned and cannot come."

So the children crossed over, and waited for him; but soon, to their grief, they saw the umbrella floating down the stream, and then they knew that their father had been drowned.

After this they wandered about for many days, and passed through many cities. At last they came to a house in the woods, where a woman was sitting. She seemed very pleased to meet them, and invited them indoors; they went in, little knowing that she was a witch, and meant evil. Next day she told them to go and fetch wood, but kept back the eldest to sweep the house, and to keep her company.

In the evening when the other sisters returned, they found their eldest sister was missing; and the witch, who did not wish them to know that she had eaten the child, told them that she had run back to her parents. The next day she did the same thing, and detained the

239

second sister, and so on until only the youngest was left.

At last the old witch told her to stay at home that day to sweep the house, and look after it while she went out. The child swept the room, and then, out of curiosity, opened a box which stood in the corner, and, to her horror, she saw inside it the four heads of her sisters! They were all smiling, and she said: "Why do you smile, O my sisters?"

"Because you will also come here to-day," they replied. The poor child was much alarmed, and asked what she could do to escape.

"Take all the things in this room, and tie them in a bundle, and as you run, throw them on the road. When the old witch comes to look for you, she will see the things, and, while she is picking them up, you will have time to escape." The child quickly did as the heads told her, tied the bundle, and ran away.

"O Tree, shelter me!"

There was only a broom left in the room, and when the old witch returned she mounted upon it, and flew through the air in hot pursuit. As she went along she found her things strewn on the road, and began picking them up one after another. This gave the child time to run further and further away, until, at last, she came to a peepul tree, and said: "O tree, shelter me!" and the tree opened, and she was hidden within it, all but her little finger, which remained outside, as the tree closed. This the old witch saw and promptly bit off: while she ate it, she regretted more than once that such a dainty morsel had escaped, but she knew there was no getting out the child; so she went away disappointed.

Now, soon after, a man came to cut down the tree, but the child cried from inside: "Cut above, and cut below, but do not touch the middle, or you will cut me in half."

The voice so amazed the man that he went and told the Rajah about it; and forthwith the Rajah came with all his retinue, and heard the same thing; so they did as the voice advised, and, after carefully opening the tree, found the child, a beautiful young girl, who sat with her hands folded within.

"Girl," said the Rajah, "will you walk up to anybody here present to whose caste you belong?"

The girl came out and walked up to a Brahmin: this decided the question of her birth, and that she was fitted to become the wife of a Prince. So the Rajah had her taken to his Palace, where they were afterwards married with great pomp, and lived happily ever after.

Note.—It may interest my readers to know that the little native girl standing beside the peepul tree in my sketch is still living. She came to us during one of the great Indian famines, and we almost despaired of her life, for although seven years old at that time, she was a living skeleton, her calf measurement being exactly three-and-a-half inches, or *half of my wrist!* She is now a fine healthy child, and very devoted.—A.E.D.

The Eye of the Cyclops

Tony LaMalfa

> To die, to sleep; to sleep—perchance to dream. Ay, there's the rub!
> For in that sleep of death what dreams may come . . .
>
> —William Shakespeare, *Hamlet*

With the heaviest of hearts, I ran a pair of scarred fingers along the dusty lid of my cousin's solid oak casket and contemplated death—not for the first time, nor the last. In fact, there remained a certain comfort in propping the cold steel of my pistol against the cool skin of my veined temple, like friends reunited after having been long separated by inclement weather. This sensation accompanied innumerable other fragments of thought as I turned to consider my haggard reflection in a warped pane of stained-glass.

Being the solitary window to admit dusky light into the lonely mausoleum I now occupied, it created a blank canvas upon which dark imaginings painted one last picture in my mind: there I stood, interned within the head of a massive, one-eyed granite giant. From my stone prison I looked out upon the chaos of a broken world, as if through the ocular organ of that monolithic Cyclops. Only, I myself would soon find peace, alone within the confines of my consciousness . . . or so I thought.

The road that led my fractured life to such a desperate finality began in a humble village nestled among rolling foothills and Alpine greenery along a tributary of the Danube. Children of this convivial hamlet in the Kingdom of Bavaria carried not the woes of want or war. Burgeoning families enjoyed the safety of a community built upon glorious food, endearing customs, hard workers, and above all else, predictability. To recount my youth spent in this sacred place provokes waves of nostalgia I would prefer to avoid, for fear of showing frailty in the face of death; but at this interval it is necessary.

My younger cousin, Owen, and I were born three years apart on the very same day and raised like brothers, both bearing the surname

242

of von Stiehl. For as close as we might have been, our personalities were vastly different—he being quiet, clever, and of a bookish nature whilst I, rascally and charismatic, possessed the makings of a natural leader. During our adolescent years Owen wrote manifestos protesting the ever-increasing imperialism of the German Empire, whilst I regaled throngs of village children with minor acrobatic feats and self-taught legerdemain.

In 1910, Owen and his parents emigrated to the United States, crossing the Atlantic in search of greener pastures, which they allegedly found. Although divided by leagues of ocean, my cousin and I still corresponded on a regular basis. But in his absence, life in our little village was never the same. Adding to my dissatisfaction, the contents of Owen's letters became increasingly unusual over time. This circumstance, coupled with my own coming of age, began to tarnish the memories of our shared childhood.

When the *Weltkrieg* broke out across Europe, I leant into my loyalty to the state and rose through the ranks of the Royal Bavarian Army to lead a battalion of German artillery. On the contrary, my *Onkel* and *Tante* were stunned when Owen was drafted as an infantryman with the American Expeditionary Forces during the summer of 1917. It seemed the antithesis of poetic justice that a German native be enlisted by the enemy and pitted against his fatherland. Rather than conscientiously object to his conscription, as we assumed he would, Owen viewed this new assignment as a means by which he might combat the political corruption spread by Kaiser Wilhelm II—or so he indicated before we ceased our communications, for obvious reasons. I, on the other hand, would return home a changed man, less than whole.

War hardened me in ways none of my younger siblings, nor any village child, would ever understand. My will to survive killed the humanity within me whilst all around us our *Schlachtwerkzeuge* sowed seeds of destruction. From the safety of our firing platforms, my battalion took countless lives without hesitation or remorse until fate finally caught up with us.

Upon whittling down an entrenched troop of Allied soldiers in

Flanders for days on end, using artillery shells filled with chemical agents, we grew lax and arrogant. Trapped in a poor position with nowhere to flee, the harried troop chanced a gambit and ambushed us under cover of darkness. A veritable slaughter ensued.

Half-dead and bloody, I was pulled from a muddy ditch by my enemies. As a prisoner of war—and an officer, no less—I expected to be treated with *some* civility, but fear and hatred can numb even the kindest and most courageous of men, as evidenced by my own moral degradation. And did I truly get what I deserved? Perhaps.

Following the Treaty of Versailles, I was released from bondage and staggered home to find the Free State of Bavaria still recovering from a short-lived Soviet uprising. There I rotted for half a decade, having been violated by the ambitions of men and physically crippled by their tools of slaughter. To make matters worse, I learnt that Owen had been killed in action by mustard gas during the Battle of Ypres . . . in the same Flemish region of Belgium to which my battalion had been assigned. Long ago we played together in fields and forests; yet I could not help but wonder, did we ever meet on the field of battle? And more perversely, if we had, what if it were *my* artillery that ended his short life? Indeed, forces beyond our control sent us spiralling down opposite life paths, but how in God's name would I cope if it were *I* who murdered my own cousin and best friend?

Eventually I succumbed to bitterness and depression, bedridden for months on end. Concerned relatives tended to my scars, both seen and unseen, yet there remain some wounds even time cannot heal. Fortunately, a letter from America halted my descent into madness. Shortly after Owen's entombment in the family vault, his mother—my Tante—was sadly laid to rest alongside him after her life was taken by the Spanish Flu. For years my Onkel had grieved in isolation, but in the end it was sheer loneliness that drove him to write us.

Consequently, my parents encouraged *me* to answer the call, as a kind of messenger to mend past ties cut by distance and death. After days of protest, I realised there was nothing for it and agreed to cross the ocean to pay my Onkel a month-long visit in rural Connecticut, where his shrivelling offshoot of the von Stiehl family tree had once taken root. I was told the time away from home would do me good, but in my opinion this trip seemed a fool's errand. As an act of defiance, I secretly brought along my officer's pistol to help me retain a sense of patriotism, or at the very least, my identity.

In earnest, I was curious if the balding, pot-bellied brother of my father still harboured resentment at having lost his only son to the machine of war, or whether his resentment rivalled my own; for I, too, had been robbed a life of normalcy. Was it possible the German Empire's defeat had actually softened the blow for my Onkel through some strange twist of logic? Either way, I would soon find out.

After an awkward greeting and several days of terse conversation, he admitted how comforting it was to speak with someone from home, though this did not lift the veil of pain shrouding us both. By the end of the first week, he let down his guard enough to show me the vault where his wife and son were interred. Nary a step had he taken on that holy ground since the funeral of my Tante. Unsure of what else to do, I bought a bouquet of flowers, and together we went to pay our respects. However, my Onkel lacked the nerve to enter their tomb, so we returned to his house, leaving behind the flowers to allay the dead.

The following day I rose before sunrise and made my way to the von Stiehl vault with key in hand—set out by my Onkel, should I feel up to the task. As I departed for the thickly forested New England cemetery, instinct prompted me to conceal my pistol within the pocket of my trench coat. Whether out of fear or the need to bear something familiar, I did not question having the weapon in tow, as its weight provided a comfort beyond words.

Curling leaves crunched underfoot on that bleak autumnal morning whilst stinging frost hung in the air, threatening to cling permanently to those who lingered too long amongst the dead. I found this prospect rather welcoming as I wandered past weathered gravestones towards the dim clearing where my flesh and blood lay in eternal slumber.

Nearing my terminus, I spied the mausoleum and screwed my eyes shut, fighting off reveries of Owen and me enjoying without care the innocence of childhood. Rather, I embraced the chill of death and decay indicative of a world beginning its seasonal hibernation. As if in synchronicity with this natural dormancy, my extremities surrendered their warmth, and the ensuing numbness offered a momentary reprieve from my grief and guilt. Oh, but to fall asleep and never awake would be a kinder fate than carrying on, laden with loss and bearing the responsibility for my actions! Perhaps endless sleep was the very remedy I needed. . . .

I opened my eyes and was rewarded with a sliver of rising sun, which broke through the forest canopy and illuminated the mausoleum's lone, stained-glass window. The effect was truly remarkable, setting this monument apart from all others. To describe the von Stiehl vault as similar to the Cyclopean stone heads of Easter Island would be a fairly accurate assessment; granted, I saw the noble little granite building as its own metaphorical head, adorned with a single organ of sight. Its kaleidoscopic brilliance alone, in contrast to much duller surroundings, was proof that the right path lay before me. Inside I would surely find salvation by taking my own life, tucked in for the great sleep of death alongside my kinsman. I then nodded resolutely, brandished the key, and entered the vault to execute my plan.

And thus we arrive at the present, where I was surprised to find the courage to look myself in eye—through that dazzling stained-glass window—as I depressed the trigger of my firearm. To hold my own gaze seemed the least I could do to retain any real sense of honour. The hammer must have been only a hair's-breadth away from being released; but instead of the deafening roar of a gun to accompany my exodus to oblivion, I was stopped short by a soft noise amplified tenfold in the absence of all other sound: a weathered hinge bearing one of the mausoleum's rounded doors. Its rusty iron squeaked excruciatingly loud as the door was inched open by an unknown entity.

Who dared to interrupt my wretched swan song, my final act of free will?

I wheeled round and took aim at the intruder, heedless of the legal ramifications or social etiquette. And yet, not an arm or a leg, nor even a man appeared in the piercing crack of light that encroached upon the soothing darkness, but a curious form . . . a rodent, poking its delicate nose into my tragic affair! Its silhouette betrayed the mammal's true form. Ha! A mere rabbit! But wait!—had I not shut and bolted the mausoleum doors before moving on to exercise my right to no longer exist?

In frustration, I assaulted the cottontail with a string of unwholesome expletives, though it calmly stood its ground. It then crossed the threshold, hopping gracefully into the slanted rectangle of early daylight stretching across the floor—a mundane feature made menacing by the tiny hare's monstrous shadow. I froze, as if no longer the predator but the *prey*.

Leaning back on its hind legs, the rabbit raised both ears and sniffed the air whilst two petite paws dangled over its white paunch. For a woodland creature, it seemed rather well fed, but I deemed this detail trivial in light of the innocence with which it probed the solemn chamber. Satisfied with its reconnaissance, the furry little lookout twitched excitedly before exiting the mausoleum with a single bound. I was left mesmerised by the simple beauty of this subtle yet profound intercession and scuttled after the rabbit with as much curiosity as it surely had upon first entering that gloomy scene. However, I was afforded no more than a flash of greyish-brown as it darted behind a nearby stand of maples, leaves rustling in its wake.

Outside the mausoleum a blanket of hoarfrost covered the bouquet I laid there yesterday—yet another observation discounted in my singleness of purpose. Retrieving the sunlit flowers, I suddenly became spellbound by their elegance and, with the yearning of a lovelorn botanist, smitten with the sadness embedded in each melting ice crystal. As I slowly made my way back to town, a warm tear rolled down my cheek and fell from my chin, joining the stream of thawing frost which ran down my weary hands. To all else I was oblivious.

My Onkel could not understand this sudden change of heart and insisted I deposit the flowers back at the von Stiehl vault. I vowed to do so, though only after spending the remainder of that day in quiet reflection. As auspicious atoms of hydrogen and oxygen bonded together and frozen in time, were those icy patterns of geometric perfection inevitably fated to thaw? Other than to serve nature itself, for what reason did they exist? Were they not also meant for human witnesses, if only to take our breath away in anticipation of winter's impending kiss?

On and on I pondered such absurdities.

The next morning I returned to the cemetery with my bouquet but turned pale at the sight I came upon: the rounded doors of the mausoleum stood open, leaving its interior vulnerable to the elements! The chamber held all the earmarks of grave robbery, and I cursed myself for neglecting to secure the lock—which, again, I thought I had done but obviously did not. Nevertheless, the felonious interlopers were either too inept or simply unable to fulfil their scheme, as grubby hand prints in the dust covering my cousin's casket were just a few of the many traces left behind. A gooseneck crowbar and shattered candle lantern lay discarded next to muddy footprints lingering like unlucky accomplices left behind to take the blame.

Along the opposite wall, the funerary box of my Tante was—to my relief—free from any vandalism or burglary. And although it was clear that the lid of Owen's casket had been pried open, it now lay shut. My fingers trembled as they hovered over the lid's scuffed edges; I questioned whether or not I dared to defile the grave of my kinsman. Had I desired justice, I might have reported the incident to my Onkel—who would, in turn, alert the local authorities. Were it retribution I sought, I could have taken matters into my own hands. But my dignity gave way to emotional attrition, and ultimately I elected to open Pandora's Box.

As I slowly lifted the casket's lid, the pungent musk of death gushed forth to coalesce with the cool morning air. Despite this nauseating smell, I was shocked to find the body of my cousin still resting firm and fat in its tomb, as it surely had five years ago when sealed away. The most skilled mortician could not have performed such a feat of preservation, nor even the highest Egyptian priests who mummified mighty pharaohs and queens of the Old World. Every aspect of Owen's twenty-two-year-old body, including his blond hair and fair skin, displayed no outward sign of decomposition, whilst the fabric of his uniform remained as crisp and olive drab as the day it was dyed. Did the petty criminals who broke into the mausoleum wish to look upon this bodily marvel, or had they possessed ulterior motives?

The mere sight of my younger cousin's face in eternal sleep whisked me back to days of yore, when the world seemed larger and more colourful. That he should die and I should live drove a stake deep into my Draconian heart, and no longer could I hold back my sobs of sorrow suppressed over the past decade of war and peace. But on the precipice of accepting grief and releasing myself from guilt, I faltered and ultimately refused to surrender. My invisible wounds were not to be exposed, for fear of what weakness festered beneath. Instead, they scabbed over and hardened once more, becoming the scar tissue I relied upon to safeguard me through a life waylaid by one hellish enterprise after another.

Shaking myself free of this oozing pathos, I came to my senses and returned to the present, where I took note of the hard facts. As welcome a sight as it might have been under vastly different circumstances, the pristine state of the corpse was quite disturbing. Some extreme preservative or American embalming fluid must have been injected into the tissue to produce such an effect. The very thought revolted me. Moreover, the military identification tag listed the body as that of *Pvt. Owen Steele,* indicating my cousin had rejected our family name.

It seemed I knew him far less than I wanted to believe; however, I did not further entertain this notion and instead shifted my attention to another anomaly in the casket—a bronze placard which adorned the interior of its lid and bore the following passage in German:

No one tires for the sleep of death, yet some dream fitfully beyond its grasp.

What was the meaning of this anomalous epitaph? Why display these words *within* the casket, where no living person could appreciate them?

And because Owen had so ardently embraced his new homeland, why not inscribe the text in English?

As I pondered these questions, my gaze fell upon a heavy, leather-bound journal fit snugly between the dead youth's hands. I reached for the book and half expected the eyelids of the corpse to shoot open, revealing bright blue eyes staring daggers at me with mocking incredulity over my apparent disregard for the deceased. But such did not occur, and I was astonished when the journal began to slip free without resistance.

Just then a pair of ominous occurrences gave me pause. Whilst I breathed a sigh of relief at having retrieved the book without incident, I swore the unspoiled body before me exhaled in a similar manner. Simultaneously, my peripheral vision detected a flicker of shadow pass in front of the thin break of light between the mausoleum doors.

Usually a firm sceptic of the supernatural, I could not believe the haste with which I snatched up my cousin's journal, replaced the lid of his casket, and locked the vault behind me. I tripped along the trail from the cemetery with marked anxiety, stopping only once to look back. There in the centre of the path sat a small creature, poised and patient. Sure enough, I was in receipt of another visit from that elfin cottontail, and I soon found myself wondering if it had remembered our previous encounter.

My lips would have split into a smile were it not for something unsettling about the plump animal's ragged pelage—a result of moulting in preparation for its winter coat. The comfort I once felt in its presence was, all of a sudden, replaced by creeping doubt. And could it have been my imagination, or was this rabbit actually passing judgement on me for desecrating Owen's grave? Its beady black eyes bore down on me, penetrating my soul even as I hurried onward. Needless to say, my flight did not cease until I reached the safety of the temporary lodging whence I came.

Having established privacy behind closed doors, I opened the thick journal with as much care as I had its owner's casket. The countless entries, dating as far back as 1910, began with Owen and his parents settling in Connecticut, where they assimilated seamlessly, prospered financially, and ingratiated themselves into the upper echelons of immigrant society. Yet my cousin insisted they mingle with those *outside* their European heritage, and subsequently he fell in with an eccentric group of privileged but bored young Americans.

As time passed, the entries were written in increasingly comprehensive English, which I struggled more and more to grasp. All the while, the journal bore an equally increasing amount of notes from an obscure medieval grimoire, titled *Höllenzwang*, or 'Coercion of Hell.' Never before had I heard of this supposed spell book, nor its author, Doktor Johann Faust; but apparently, Owen and his band of erudite misfits held the manuscript in high regard.

Once the United States entered the *Weltkrieg*, however, the entries suddenly shifted to German. I could only assume my cousin made this linguistic deviation to protect something important. As I read on, I imagined a scenario in which the grave robbers had reached this same interval but could progress no further, seeing how they lacked the ability to interpret our mother tongue—though this musing merely proved a distraction.

Whilst fighting overseas, Owen catalogued in his journal several strange phenomena, but more important were those entries pertaining to a ritual he revered from Faust's book: *Schutz der Seele,* meaning 'protection of the soul.' Its lengthy description detailed the means by which a practitioner might suspend the animation of a living being, if performed correctly and with the proper material components as detailed below:

Ten candles, arranged in the shape of a star (see diagram)
A sprig of witch hazel
A pinch of bone meal
A handful of oak bark ashes
A lock of hair from the person to be protected
A scrap of metal (the purer, the better)
A dash of animal blood (fresh is best)

Conducting the ritual *exactly* at the stroke of midnight was yet another of the many requisites essential to obtaining accurate results. Also necessary was the correct delivery of the following incantation, which was to be spoken aloud by the practitioner during the invocation of each component:

> *Come skin and bone and ash to me, for this soul seeks immunity.*
> *It hides as steel and blood are mixed to call upon the gods of Nyx.*
> *Let night and day be intertwined as this enchantment slows down time.*
> *Each lighted candle leaves its mark whilst sleep meets death here in the dark.*

Sadly, it appeared that Owen had begun to dabble in some weird form of witchcraft. It begged the question, who was this mysterious relative of mine expressing an aptitude for the dark arts? Truthfully, I no longer recognised—nor retained any favourable connexion with—my once-beloved cousin, much to my chagrin. Surely his parents had no idea of their son's penchant for heathenism. And yet, one had to wonder if the occult exploits undertaken by Owen and his sadistic clique of amateur mystagogues actually amounted to some degree of success, as evidenced by the alarmingly fresh state of the corpse. . . .

Guarding this secret jealously, I feigned illness throughout the remaining weeks of my visit to America, during which time my Onkel persistently enquired about my having barred entry to his guest bedroom. Only when I needed more information concerning my cousin did I leave the confines of those quarters. Even then I took food and drink sparingly, for I had become obsessed with examining the entirety of his journal.

By conducting a thorough study of my kinsman, I gained a new lease of life. Even if I could not comprehend much of the contents set down betwixt the covers of his personal log, there remained one notion I understood all too well: Owen von Stiehl was deathly afraid of his own demise. From what I gathered, in the year leading up to his fall on the field of battle, he had ostensibly taken unspeakable steps to ensure the continuity of his life essence, should his body fail him.

During one of my abbreviated forays into town, I interviewed a host of locals in the hope of gleaning new evidence of Owen's true nature, but my attempts were met with either veiled absence of interest or sheer lack of knowledge. And not one of the families tied to those jaded youth with whom Owen fraternised could substantiate their child's association with him—nor any von Stiehl, for that matter. What I *did* accomplish, however, was covertly to procure an appropriate amount of each ritual component listed in the hefty journal.

A shadowy motive supplanted my newfound determination and drove me to a decision far beyond my usual convictions: to gain a more complete understanding of my cousin's psyche, I would attempt to replicate Schutz der Seele. Furthermore, if any appreciable results could be produced, I reasoned I might also shed the unwelcome horrors of my past and finally lay to rest the weights of war shackled round my heart. And although I could not abide placing my faith in notes taken from a book bearing the name *Coercion of Hell,* I remained committed to the cause.

Thus, upon the eve of my return trip to Germany, I carried out my plan. In preparation, I set my freshly wound pocket watch five minutes fast. This slight adjustment to the timepiece was necessary to maintain absolute certainty that the ritual would commence at midnight. Better to leave myself too much time than too little. Once my Onkel finished his customary bedtime bourbon and retired around eleven o'clock, I stole into the night bearing those accoutrements vital to the task: a paraffin lamp and matches, Owen's journal, each ritual component, and my resolve—such as it was. Into the sea of headstones I crept, past the occasional crypt or crumbling cenotaph erected by other wealthy families to honour the dead.

Outside the von Stiehl vault, a gentle wind whispered through the sparsely filled branches of old deciduous trees watching over the cemetery. My fingers trembled in anticipation, and the bronze key slipped from my grasp, tumbling out of the lock and onto the leaf-covered cement with a muted clink. I dropped to the ground and by lamplight scrabbled about on all fours to retrieve the key, then looked up in embarrassment—as if a crowd were watching me when, in fact, I was alone. How foolish of me to project fictional onlookers staring with cool indifference at my growing doubt! And yet, the wind failed to mask the unmistakable presence of a certain woodland creature come to spy on my progress: a curious cottontail, to be exact. But it could not have been the very same one, could it have?

Such trivialities were set aside as I located the palm-sized key, shouldered my rucksack, and opened the mausoleum. That was around half-past eleven. Only when my light source caught the withering flowers I had left those long weeks ago did I pause on the threshold. In truth, it brought me a great deal of comfort to see that the bouquet had indeed been subject to natural decomposition, in stark contrast to the extraordinarily well-preserved corpse I was about to disturb in the name of unfounded witchery.

Once inside the mausoleum, I locked its rounded doors behind me. A quick glance at the casket of my Tante made me ill at ease once more, for I could not help but imagine her disapproval at my course of action. Nevertheless, I turned towards the casket of my estranged cousin to steady my nerves and allowed myself to be whisked away aboard a train of speculation. What if this ritual actually *could* reanimate the sleeping dead? About which topics might the object of revival and I converse? Would the strained years between us slip away, admitting bittersweet pangs of longing for our shared youth? And what wisdom might be imparted by "he-who-had-travelled-beyond-death"? . . . by Owen.

I leant into this intensifying streak of optimism as I had once leant into my loyalty to the state of Bavaria and its Royal Army, only to find myself again seduced by the prospect of a happier, more hopeful tomorrow.

A familiar blend of malodorous putrescence and chilling air filled my lungs as I cracked open my cousin's funerary box. I gently placed the lid at an angle atop the sides of the casket for use as a makeshift shelf, with the body's inordinately fresh face exposed to the heavens. Once more I was confronted with the hidden epitaph which displayed that peculiar passage:

No one tires for the sleep of death, yet some dream fitfully beyond its grasp.

Bearing this in mind, I lit and arranged the ten candles at various heights around the sacred space of the mausoleum, adhering strictly to the points of the star diagram from Owen's notes. I then set the witch hazel, bone meal, and oak ashes on the lid of the casket, opposite a railroad spike and small vial of blood acquired from the local butcher—who claimed the fluid was from that day's cuts. The three dry goods and scrap of metal, along with a lock of the deceased's hair, were to be separated into the five triangular points surrounding the central pentagon, wherein I—the practitioner—was to stand whilst performing the ritual. Its instructions further described how, upon invoking the "dash of animal blood," the crimson liquid was to be spilled at my feet, directly onto the earth.

With much of the ritual's success depending on proper timing and delivery, I could not entrust reciting the incantation and its ordered sequence of offerings to memory alone. Therefore, I stood the journal upright next to my lamp, using the grave robbers' discarded lantern as a prop, and opened it to the pages detailing Schutz der Seele.

At a quarter of midnight, or ten to by my faster calculation, my preparations for the ritual were complete. I ran a clammy hand through my thinning hair and relaxed with a heavy sigh. Again, I convinced myself that a matching breath eked from the torpid lips of the corpse, but an unsuspecting breach of my mental acuteness—which lay dormant somewhere beyond the brink of insanity—coaxed me to embrace the supposed coincidence as if it were a good omen. Moreover, this prompted me to make a last-minute alteration to the components, removing the railroad spike in exchange for Owen's aluminium military tag. Doing so seemed apropos, and no doubt the more refined metal would improve the overall effectiveness of the ritual.

The hands of my pocket watch kissed at twelve, meaning my emergency reserve of five minutes had begun. Whilst I waited, the silence stretched on painfully, broken only by ambient noise from the soft wind outside and soothing hush of the paraffin lamp. But suddenly, when all seemed right with the world after so long, fate caught up with me for a second time—as it had in Flanders, when my battalion of artillery was ambushed by those Allied troops at wits' end.

To my ears, the sound of vegetation being chewed seemed quite harmless, albeit out of place in that solitary tomb; and yet, I failed to register its dire implications until after I met the source of this otherwise benign noise. All light in my life was then extinguished. Sitting rather smugly on the ground, within the triangular point of candles which previously held the sprig of witch hazel, was that cursed cottontail! The shabby hare must have scurried in unnoticed when I paused at the entrance to the vault.

I had no time for such nonsense. *Midnight was nearly upon us!*

Without hesitation, I sprang forwards and clawed at the irksome rodent, but its knowing, beady eyes were already wary of its offence, which helped propel it beyond my grasp. My one advantage over the rabbit was the limited floor space of the mausoleum, as the locked doors inhibited any chance of accidental escape.

All hell broke loose within a matter of seconds. Candles were overturned and other components disturbed as I closed in on my agile adversary. When finally I managed to snag the damned creature, it had all but devoured the witch hazel, leaving its gaping maw free to sink its teeth into my left forefinger before my grip tightened angrily around its scruff.

I glanced at my watch . . . just over a minute until the ritual was to commence!

If I could not retrieve the prized plant and rearrange the space accordingly, all would be for naught. Using my free hand and driven by the mad desire to succeed, both for the sake of my sanity and Owen's potential revival, I quickly restored order to the mausoleum. I then found myself struck by a singularly baffling stroke of genius: I would take the life of that troublesome vermin, not only to make use of what little time remained but also to improve the potency of the ritual with *fresh* animal blood. Furthermore, I estimated that enough witch hazel still sat in the rabbit's gullet to conduct Schutz der Seele to a passable degree.

The timing would be remarkably close—*too* close, in fact, for comfort or error.

As the witching hour struck, I began to chant the incantation whilst tufts of rabbit hair floated listlessly around me, as if suspended in animation. Wielding a shard of broken glass from the discarded lantern, I performed the deed with the skill of a surgeon, flinging a small clump of the bloody vegetation from the animal's throat into the vacant point of the candle star—careful not to spill any additional crimson liquid until the other components were invoked. I called upon the bone meal and oak ashes, then Owen's blond hair and military tag.

With each line I spoke, I felt an arcane authority coursing through my veins, surging from my very soul. Surely my cousin must have felt such absolute power when he himself performed this ritual. It gave meaning to the hollow shell I had become in recent years and rose with a crescendo matched only by the howling winds now whipping around the mausoleum like rushing water parted by a lowly rock. And from my quaking lips, I screamed the final phrase:

EACH LIGHTED CANDLE LEAVES ITS MARK
WHILST SLEEP MEETS DEATH HERE IN THE DARK!

It was pitch black and dead silent inside the von Stiehl vault.

I knew nothing and felt nothing yet remained certain I had known and felt *something* during those last moments leading up to the lamp and candles all blowing out of their own accord. I lay still for a long while, feeling . . . unclean, as if separated from the cycle of day and night—or any wholesome aspect of nature, for that matter.

I hoped this cognitive disembodiment would pass, but I kept drawing a blank when reaching for meaningful thoughts or experiences. Amidst lapses of memory, I eventually recalled delivering the conclusion of the incantation with great effect. Moreover, one might claim the ritual's success to have been elevated to an advanced degree, as evidenced by those final words being chanted by an additional voice: a melodious tenor speaking a familiar dialect of German.

Then a particular vision came to mind in which the mausoleum of my kin served as the head of a gigantic, granite Cyclops. As I reconstructed the scene in my imagination, I pictured myself residing therein. Through the lone and lovely window of that stone skull, I looked out upon the world, with all its sham and drudgery. Make no doubt about it, I *had* been imprisoned, but unlike the peaceful conclusion of that previous fantasy, I now lay in a fitful, never-ending state of helplessness.

All at once the silence was disturbed by a series of noises—far off and muffled at first, though distinct enough to place. Each sound reverberated throughout the chamber like proverbial nails in the coffin and confirmed a growing suspicion harkening back to when I hovered over the casket of my cousin, holding the barrel of a gun to my temple.

The first perceptible noise was the characteristic striking of a match and subsequent ignition of a paraffin lamp, despite the prevailing darkness. Next, I heard the whining of weighted metal scraped across concrete, as if an iron were being hoisted from the floor. The third noise came and went with outright finality, signalling the departure of whatever ethereal being had unlocked the mausoleum doors and paid its respects before taking their leave.

Other sounds may or may not have been produced during this sequence of events, but I dare not accept their existence. To do so would be to acknowledge the utter permanency of my current state, which punishes me day after day, like the perennial use of a faithful torture device. I fear I shall never again gaze upon the variegated colours of that sweet, sunlit stained-glass window . . . that eye of the Cyclops.

Those auditory blows that sealed my fate and banished my consciousness to a wakeful eternity of slumbering death landed as uneven footfalls echoed across the walls of the mausoleum, whose doors were then locked evermore. I made to stand and identify the person stumbling about with an alternating clip-clop but found my joints lacked voluntary locomotion. Each haunting step the visitor took drove the stake deeper still into that Draconian heart I call my own, yet no longer out of grief or guilt for Owen having died in battle whilst I lived, but for his obvious betrayal.

For you see, Schutz der Seele had more than worked its magic. And how exactly do I know this? Well, after recovering from my war wounds, I walked with a distinct limp. But it was not *I* who walked out of the mausoleum in my broken body on that terrible day, never to return. It was indisputably *he* who delivered those coolly spoken words in my own throaty voice:

'Look at it this way, dear cousin—at least you did one good thing with your life. . . .'

Lilith of Eld

Herman George Scheffauer

They tasted the sweet despair
    That flowed from her mortal kiss,
And they hung by one silken hair
    Above a black abyss!

For many had gone to wreck
    On the gleam of her coral lips,
By her shining finger's beck
    That boded no eclipse.

Then her smile had buried them
    As the waves the broken bark,
For what could bide or stem
    That magic dread and dark?

Deep down from her starry eyes
    The path led straight to hell,
And never the soul could rise
    That to their bottom fell.

She trod on the hearts of men,
    As they were pavement stones;
She danced, a light o' the fen,
    Across their charnel bones.

And the thoughts! the thoughts that rushed
    Like eagles from her eye—
And the smile—the smile that crushed
    The slaves it lured to die.

But a curse fell out of the night;
      It singled forth her head;
She vanished out of our sight
      And the world cried: She is dead!

She lived! she loved! she mourned!
      For a love she ne'er could own;
Her heart was racked and scorned
      With the vengeance she had sown.

And he, to whom this tale
      She told, lives doomed to write
The terror, tears and bale
      Of her—through night and night.

Sea Curse

Robert E. Howard

> And some return by the failing light
> And some in the waking dream,
> For she hears the heels of the dripping ghosts
> That ride the rough roofbeam.
> —Kipling.

They were the brawlers and braggarts, the loud boasters and hard drinkers, of Faring town, John Kulrek and his crony Lie-lip Canool. Many a time have I, a tousled-haired lad, stolen to the tavern door to listen to their curses, their profane arguments and wild sea songs; half fearful and half in admiration of these wild rovers. Aye, all the people of Faring town gazed on them with fear and admiration, for they were not like the rest of the Faring men; they were not content to ply their trade along the coasts and among the shark-teeth shoals. No yawls, no skiffs for them! They fared far, farther than any other man in the village, for they shipped on the great sailing-ships that went out on the white tides to brave the restless gray ocean and make ports in strange lands.

Ah, I mind it was swift times in the little sea-coast village of Faring when John Kulrek came home, with his furtive Lie-lip at his side, swaggering down the gang-plank, in his tarry sea-clothes, and the broad leather belt that held his ever-ready dagger; shouting condescending greeting to some favored acquaintance, kissing some maiden who ventured too near; then up the street, roaring some scarcely decent song of the sea. How the cringers and the idlers, the hangers-on, would swarm about the two desperate heroes, flattering and smirking, guffawing hilariously at each nasty jest. For to the tavern loafers and to some of the weaker among the straight-forward villagers, these men with their wild talk and their brutal deeds, their tales of the Seven Seas and the far countries, these men, I say, were valiant knights, nature's noblemen who dared to be men of blood and brawn.

And all feared them, so that when a man was beaten or a woman insulted, the villagers muttered—and did nothing. And so when Moll Farrell's niece was put to shame by John Kulrek, none dared even to put in words what all thought. Moll had never married, and she and the girl lived alone in a little hut down close to the beach, so close that in high tide the waves came almost to the door.

The people of the village accounted old Moll something of a witch, and she was a grim, gaunt old dame who had little to say to anyone. But she minded her own business, and eked out a slim living by gathering clams, and picking up bits of driftwood.

The girl was a pretty, foolish little thing, vain and easily befooled, else she had never yielded to the sharklike blandishments of John Kulrek.

I mind the day was a cold winter day with a sharp breeze out of the east when the old dame came into the village street shrieking that the girl had vanished. All scattered over the beach and back among the bleak inland hills to search for her—all save John Kulrek and his cronies who sat in the tavern dicing and toping. All the while beyond the shoals, we heard the never-ceasing droning of the heaving, restless gray monster, and in the dim light of the ghostly dawn Moll Farrell's girl came home.

The tides bore her gently across the wet sands and laid her almost at her own door. Virgin-white she was, and her arms were folded across her still bosom; calm was her face, and the gray tides sighed about her slender limbs. Moll Farrell's eyes were stones, yet she stood above her dead girl and spoke no word till John Kulrek and his crony came reeling down from the tavern, their drinking-jacks still in their hands. Drunk was John Kulrek, and the people gave back for him, murder in their souls; so he came and laughed at Moll Farrell across the body of her girl.

"Zounds!" swore John Kulrek; "the wench has drowned herself, Lie-lip!"

Lie-lip laughed, with the twist of his thin mouth. He always hated Moll Farrell, for it was she that had given him the name of Lie-lip.

Then John Kulrek lifted his drinking-jack, swaying on his uncertain legs. "A health to the wench's ghost!" he bellowed, while all stood aghast.

Then Moll Farrell spoke, and the words broke from her in a scream which sent ripples of cold up and down the spines of the throng.

"The curse of the Foul Fiend upon you, John Kulrek!" she screamed. "The curse of God rest upon your vile soul throughout eternity! May you gaze on sights that shall sear the eyes of you and scorch the soul of you! May you die a bloody death and writhe in hell's flames for a million and a million and yet a million years! I curse you by sea and by land, by earth and by air, by the demons of the oceans and the demons of the swamplands, the fiends of the forests and the goblins of the hills! And you"—her lean finger stabbed at Lie-lip Canool and he started backward, his face paling—"you shall be the death of John Kulrek and he shall be the death of you! You shall bring John Kulrek to the doors of hell and John Kulrek shall bring you to the gallows-tree! I set the seal of death upon your brow, John Kulrek! You shall live in terror and die in horror far out upon the cold gray sea! But the sea that took the soul of innocence to her bosom shall not take you, but shall fling forth your vile carcass to the sands! Aye, John Kulrek"—and she spoke with such a terrible intensity that the drunken mockery on the man's face changed to one of swinish stupidity—"the sea roars for the victim it will not keep! There is snow upon the hills, John Kulrek, and ere it melts your corpse will lie at my feet. And I shall spit upon it and be content."

Kulrek and his crony sailed at dawn for a long voyage, and Moll went back to her hut and her clam gathering. She seemed to grow leaner and more grim than ever and her eyes smoldered with a light not sane. The days glided by and people whispered among themselves that Moll's days were numbered, for she faded to a ghost of a woman; but she went her way, refusing all aid.

That was a short, cold summer and the snow on the barren inland hills never melted; a thing very unusual, which caused much comment among the villagers. At dusk and at dawn Moll would come up on the

beach, gaze up at the snow which glittered on the hills, then out to sea
with a fierce intensity in her gaze.

Then the days grew shorter, the nights longer and darker, and the
cold gray tides came sweeping along the bleak strands, bearing the rain
and sleet of the sharp east breezes.

And upon a bleak day a trading-vessel sailed into the bay and an-
chored. And all the idlers and the wastrels flocked to the wharfs, for
that was the ship upon which John Kulrek and Lie-lip Canool had
sailed. Down the gang-plank came Lie-lip, more furtive than ever, but
John Kulrek was not there.

To shouted queries, Canool shook his head. "Kulrek deserted ship
at a port of Sumatra," said he. "He had a row with the skipper, lads;
wanted me to desert, too, but no! I had to see you fine lads again, eh,
boys?"

Almost cringing was Lie-lip Canool, and suddenly he recoiled as
Moll Farrell came through the throng. A moment they stood eyeing
each other; then Moll's grim lips bent in a terrible smile.

"There's blood on your hand, Canool!" she lashed out suddenly—
so suddenly that Lie-Lip started and rubbed his right hand across his
left sleeve.

"Stand aside, witch!" he snarled in sudden anger, striding through
the crowd which gave back for him. His admirers followed him to the
tavern.

Now, I mind that the next day was even colder; gray fogs came
drifting out of the east and veiled the sea and the beaches. There
would be no sailing that day, and so all the villagers were in their snug
houses or matching tales at the tavern. So it came about that Joe, my
friend, a lad of my own age, and I, were the ones who saw the first of
the strange thing that happened.

Being harum-scarum lads of no wisdom, we were sitting in a small
rowboat, floating at the end of the wharfs, each shivering and wishing
the other would suggest leaving, there being no reason whatever for
our being there, save that it was a good place to build air-castles undisturbed.

Suddenly Joe raised his hand. "Say," he said, "d'ye hear? Who can be out on the bay upon a day like this?"

"Nobody. What d'ye hear?"

"Oars. Or I'm a lubber. Listen."

There was no seeing anything in that fog, and I heard nothing. Yet Joe swore he did, and suddenly his face assumed a strange look.

"Somebody rowing out there, I tell you! The bay is alive with oars from the sound! A score of boats at the least! Ye dolt, can ye not hear?"

Then, as I shook my head, he leaped and began to undo the painter.

"I'm off to see. Name me liar if the bay is not full of boats, all together like a close fleet. Are you with me?"

Yes, I was with him, though I heard nothing. Then out in the grayness we went, and the fog closed behind and before so that we drifted in a vague world of smoke, seeing naught and hearing naught. We were lost in no time, and I cursed Joe for leading us upon a wild goose chase that was like to end with our being swept out to sea. I thought of Moll Farrell's girl and shuddered.

How long we drifted I know not. Minutes faded into hours, hours into centuries. Still Joe swore he heard the oars, now close at hand, now far away, and for hours we followed them, steering our course toward the sound, as the noise grew or receded. This I later thought of, and could not understand.

Then, when my hands were so numb that I could no longer hold the oar, and the forerunning drowsiness of cold and exhaustion was stealing over me, bleak white stars broke through the fog which glided suddenly. away, fading like a ghost of smoke, and we found ourselves afloat just outside the mouth of the bay. The waters lay smooth as a pond, all dark green and silver in the starlight, and the cold came crisper than ever. I was swinging the boat about, to put back into the bay, when Joe gave a shout, and for the first time I heard the clack of oarlocks. I glanced over my shoulder and my blood went cold.

A great beaked prow loomed above us, a weird, unfamiliar shape against the stars, and as I caught my breath, sheered sharply and swept by us, with a curious swishing I never heard any other craft make. Joe screamed and backed oars frantically, and the boat walled out of the way just in time; for though the prow had missed us, still otherwise we had died. For from the sides of the ship stood long oars, bank upon bank which swept her along. Though I had never seen such a craft, I knew her for a galley. But what was she doing upon our coasts? They said, the far-farers, that such ships were still in use among the heathens of Barbary; but it was many a long, heaving mile to Barbary, and even so she did not resemble the ships described by those who had sailed far.

We started in pursuit, and this was strange, for though the waters broke about her prow, and she seemed fairly to fly through the waves, yet she was making little speed, and it was no time before we caught up with her. Making our painter fast to a chain far back beyond the reach of the swishing oars, we hailed those on deck. But there came no answer, and at last, conquering our fears, we clambered up the chain and found ourselves upon the strangest deck man has trod for many a long, roaring century.

"This is no Barbary rover!" muttered Joe fearsomely. "Look, how old it seems! Almost ready to fall to pieces. Why, 'tis fairly rotten!"

There was no one on deck, no one at the long sweep with which the craft was steered. We stole to the hold and looked down the stair. Then and there, if ever men were on the verge of insanity, it was we. For there were rowers there, it is true; they sat upon the rowers' benches and drove the creaking oars through the gray waters. *And they that rowed were skeletons!*

Shrieking, we plunged across the deck, to fling ourselves into the sea. But at the rail I tripped upon something and fell headlong, and as I lay, I saw a thing which vanquished my fear of the horrors below for an instant. The thing upon which I had tripped was a human body, and in the dim gray light that was beginning to steal across the eastern waves I saw a dagger hilt standing up between his shoulders. Joe was at the rail, urging me to haste, and together we slid down the chain and cut the painter.

Then we stood off into the bay. Straight on kept the grim galley, and we followed, slowly, wondering. She seemed to be heading straight for the beach beside the wharfs, and as we approached, we saw the wharfs thronged with people. They had missed us, no doubt, and now they stood, there in the early dawn light, struck dumb by the apparition which had come up out the night and the grim ocean.

Straight on swept the galley, her oars a-swish; then ere she reached the shallow water—crash!—a terrific reverberation shook the bay. Before our eyes the grim craft seemed to melt away; then she vanished, and the green waters seethed where she had ridden, but there floated no driftwood there, nor did there ever float any ashore. Aye, something floated ashore, but it was grim driftwood!

We made the landing amid a hum of excited conversation that stopped suddenly. Moll Farrell stood before her hut, limned gauntly against the ghostly dawn, her lean hand pointing seaward. And across the sighing wet sands, borne by the gray tide, something came floating; something that the waves dropped at Moll Farrell's feet. And there looked up at us, as we crowded about, a pair of unseeing eyes set in a still, white face. John Kulrek had come home.

Still and grim he lay, rocked by the tide, and as he lurched sideways, all saw the dagger hilt that stood from his back—the dagger all of us had seen a thousand times at the belt of Lie-lip Canool.

"Aye, I killed him?" came Canool's shriek, as he writhed and groveled before our gaze. "At sea on a still night in a drunken brawl I slew him and hurled him overboard! And from the far seas he has followed me"—his voice sank to a hideous whisper—"because—of—the—curse—the—sea—would—not—keep—his—body!"

And the wretch sank down, trembling, the shadow of the gallows already in his eyes.

"Aye!" Strong, deep and exultant was Moll Farrell's voice. "From the hell of lost craft Satan sent a ship of bygone ages! A ship red with gore and stained with the memory of horrid crimes! None other would bear such a vile carcass! The sea has taken vengeance and has given me mine. See now, how I spit upon the face of John Kulrek."

And with a ghastly laugh, she pitched forward, the blood starting to her lips. And the sun came up across the restless sea.

The Witch

Mary Elizabeth Coleridge

"I have walked a great while over the snow,
  And I am not tall nor strong.
My clothes are wet, and my teeth are set,
  And the way was hard and long.
I have wandered over the fruitful earth,
  But I never came here before.
O lift me over the threshold, and let me in at the door!

"The cutting wind is a cruel foe.
  I dare not stand in the blast.
My hands are stone, and my voice a groan,
  And the worst of death is past.
I am but a little maiden still,
  My little white feet are sore.
O lift me over the threshold, and let me in at the door!"

Her voice was the voice that women have,
  Who plead for their heart's desire.
She came—she came—and the quivering flame
  Sank and died in the fire.
It never was lit again on my hearth
  Since I hurried across the floor,
To lift her over the threshold, and let her in at the door.

From *The History of Magic*

Éliphas Lévi

Joan [of Arc] perished in her innocence, but the laws against Magic were vindicated soon after in the case of one who was chief among the guilty. The personage in question was one of the most valiant captains under Charles VII, but the services which he rendered to the state could not counterbalance the extent and enormity of his crimes. All tales of ogres and Croquemitaine were realised and surpassed by the deeds of this fantastic scoundrel, whose history has remained in the memory of children under the name of Blue Beard. Gilles de Laval, Lord of Raiz, had indeed so black a beard that it seemed to be almost blue, as shewn by his portrait in the Salle des Maréchaux, at the Museum of Versailles. A Marshal of Brittany, he was brave because he was French; being rich, he was also ostentatious; and he became a sorcerer because he was insane.

The mental derangement of the Lord of Raiz was manifested in the first instance by sumptuous devotion and extravagant magnificence. When he went abroad, he was preceded invariably by cross and banner; his chaplains were covered with gold and vested like prelates; he had a college of little pages or choristers, who were always richly clothed. But day by day one of these children was called before the marshal and was seen no more by his comrades; a newcomer succeeded him who disappeared, and the children were sternly forbidden to ask what became of the missing ones or even refer to them among themselves. The children were obtained by the marshal from poor parents, whom he dazzled by his promises, and who were pledged to trouble no further concerning their offspring, these, according to his stories, being assured a brilliant future.

The explanation is that, in his case, seeming devotion was the mask and safeguard of infamous practices. Ruined by imbecile prodigality, the marshal desired at any cost to create wealth. Alchemy had exhausted his last resources and loans on usurious terms were about to

270

fail him; he determined therefore to attempt the last and most execrable experiments of Black Magic, in the hope of obtaining gold by the aid of hell. An apostate priest of the diocese of Saint-Malo, a Florentine named Prélati, and Sillé, who was the marshal's steward, became his confidants and accomplices. He had espoused a young woman of high birth and kept her practically shut up in his castle at Machecoul, which had a tower with the entrance walled up. A report was spread by the marshal that it was in a ruinous state and no one sought to penetrate therein. This notwithstanding, Madame de Raiz, who was frequently alone during the dark hours, saw red lights moving to and fro in this tower; but she did not venture to question her husband, whose bizarre and sombre character filled her with extreme terror.

On Easter Day in the year 1440, the marshal, having communicated solemnly in his chapel, bade farewell to the lady of Machecoul, telling her that he was departing to the Holy Land; the poor creature was even then afraid to question, so much did she tremble in his presence; she was also several months in her pregnancy. The marshal permitted her sister to come on a visit as a companion during his absence. Madame de Raiz took advantage of this indulgence, after which Gilles de Laval mounted his horse and departed. To her sister Madame de Raiz communicated her fears and anxieties. What went on in the castle? Why was her lord so gloomy? What signified his repeated absences? What became of the children who disappeared day by day? What were those nocturnal lights in the walled-up tower? These and the other problems excited the curiosity of both women to the utmost degree. What all the same could be done? The marshal had forbidden them expressly even to approach the tower, and before leaving he had repeated this injunction. It must assuredly have a secret entrance, for which Madame de Raiz and her sister Anne proceeded to search through the lower rooms of the castle, corner by corner and stone after stone. At last, in the chapel, behind the altar, they came upon a copper button, hidden in a mass of sculpture. It yielded under pressure; a stone slid back and the two curiosity-seekers, now all in a tremble, distinguished the lowermost steps of a staircase, which led them to the condemned tower.

At the top of the first flight there was a kind of chapel, with a cross upside down and black candles; on the altar stood a hideous figure, no doubt representing the demon. On the second floor they came upon furnaces, retorts, alembics, charcoal—in a word, all the apparatus of alchemy. The third flight led to a dark chamber, where the heavy and fetid atmosphere compelled the young women to retreat. Madame de Raiz came into collision with a vase, which fell over, and she was conscious that her robe and feet were soaked by some thick and unknown liquid. On returning to the light at the head of the stairs she found that she was bathed in blood.

Sister Anne would have fled from the place, but in Madame de Raiz curiosity was even stronger than disgust or fear. She descended the stairs, took a lamp from the infernal chapel and returned to the third floor, where a frightful spectacle awaited her. Copper vessels filled with blood were ranged the whole length of the walls, bearing labels with a date on each, and in the middle of the room there was a black marble table, on which lay the body of a child murdered quite recently. It was one of these basins which had fallen, and black blood had spread far and wide over the grimy and worm-eaten wooden floor.

The two women were now half-dead with terror. Madame de Raiz endeavoured at all costs to efface the evidence of her indiscretion. She went in search of a sponge and water, to wash the boards; but she only extended the stain and that which at first seemed black became all scarlet in hue. Suddenly a loud commotion echoed through the castle, mixed with the cries of people calling to Madame de Raiz. She distinguished the awe-striking words: "Here is Monseigneur come back." The two women made for the staircase, but at the same moment they were aware of the trampling of steps and the sound of other voices in the devil's chapel. Sister Anne fled upwards to the battlement of the tower; Madame de Raiz went down trembling and found herself face to face with her husband, in the act of ascending, accompanied by the apostate priest and Prélati.

Gilles de Laval seized his wife by the arm and without speaking dragged her into the infernal chapel. It was then that Prélati observed to the marshal: "It is needs must, as you see, and the victim has come of her own accord." . . . "Be it so," answered his master. "Begin the Black Mass." . . . The apostate priest went to the altar, while Gilles de Laval opened a little cupboard fixed therein and drew out a large knife, after which he sat down close to his spouse, who was now almost in a swoon and lying in a heap on a bench against the wall. The sacrilegious ceremonies began.

It must be explained that the marshal, so far from taking the road to Jerusalem, had proceeded only to Nantes, where Prélati lived; he attacked this miserable wretch with the uttermost fury and threatened to slay him if he did not furnish the means of extracting from the devil that which he had been demanding for so long a time. With the object of obtaining delay, Prélati declared that terrible conditions were required by the infernal master, first among which would be the sacrifice of the marshal's unborn child after tearing it forcibly from the mother's womb. Gilles de Laval made no reply but returned at once to Machecoul, the Florentine sorcerer and his accomplice the priest being in his train. With the rest we are acquainted.

Meanwhile, Sister Anne, left to her own devices on the roof of the tower and not daring to come down, had removed her veil, to make signals of distress at chance. They were answered by two cavaliers accompanied by a posse of armed men, who were riding towards the castle; they proved to be her two brothers who, on learning the spurious departure of the marshal for Palestine, had come to visit and console Madame de Raiz. Soon after they arrived with a clatter in the court of the castle, whereupon Gilles de Laval suspended the hideous ceremony and said to his wife: "Madame, I forgive you, and the matter is at an end between us if you do now as I tell you. Return to your apartment, change your garments and join me in the guest-room, whither I am going to receive your brothers. But if you say one word, or cause them the slightest suspicion, I will bring you hither on their departure; we shall proceed with the Black Mass at the point where it is now broken off, and at the consecration you will die. Mark where I place this knife."

He rose up, led his wife to the door of her chamber and subsequently received her relations and their suite, saying that his lady was preparing herself to come and salute her brothers. Madame de Raiz appeared almost immediately, pale as a spectre. Gilles de Laval never took eyes off her, seeking to control her by his glance. When her brothers suggested that she was ill, she answered that it was the fatigue of pregnancy, but added in an undertone: "Save me; he seeks to kill me." At the same moment Sister Anne rushed into the hall, crying: "Take us away; save us, my brothers: this man is an assassin"—and she pointed to Gilles de Laval. While the marshal summoned his people, the escort of the two visitors surrounded the women with drawn swords; and the marshal's people disarmed instead of obeying him. Madame de Raiz, with her sister and brothers, gained the drawbridge and left the castle.

On the morrow, Duke John V invested Machecoul, and Gilles de Laval, who could count no longer on his men-at-arms, yielded without resistance. The parliament of Brittany had decreed his arrest as a homicide, the ecclesiastical tribunal preparing in the first place to pronounce judgment upon him as a heretic, sodomite and sorcerer. Voices of parents, long silenced by terror, rose upon all sides, demanding their missing children: there was universal dole and clamour throughout the province. The castles of Machecoul and Chantocé were ransacked, resulting in the discovery of two hundred skeletons of children; the rest had been consumed by fire.

Gilles de Laval appeared with supreme arrogance before his judges. To the customary question: "Who are you?" he answered: "I am Gilles de Laval, Marshal of Brittany, Lord of Raiz, Machecoul, Chantocé and other fiefs. And who are you that dare to question me?" He was answered: "We are your judges, magistrates of the Ecclesiastical Court."—"What, you my judges! Go to, I know you well, my masters. You are simoniacs and obscene fellows, who sell your God to purchase the joys of the devil. Speak not therefore of judging me, for if I am guilty, it is you, who owed me good example, that are my instigators."—"Cease your insults, and answer us."—"I would rather be hanged by the neck than reply to you. I am surprised that the president of Brittany suffers your acquaintance with matters of this kind. You question that you may gain information and afterwards do worse than you have done."

But this haughty insolence was demolished by the threat of torture. Before the Bishop of Saint-Brieuc and the President Pierre de l'Hôpital, Gilles de Laval made confession of his murders and sacrileges. He pretended that his motive in the massacre of children was an execrable delight which he sought during the agony of these poor little beings. The president found it difficult to credit this statement and questioned him anew. "Alas," said the marshal abruptly, "you torment both yourself and me to no purpose." "I do not torment you," replied the president, "but I am astonished at your words and dissatisfied. What I seek and must have is the pure truth." The marshal answered: "Verily there was no other cause. What more would you have? Surely I have admitted enough to condemn ten thousand men."

That which Gilles de Laval shrank from confessing was that he sought the Philosophical Stone in the blood of murdered children, and that it was covetousness which drove him to this monstrous debauchery. On the faith of his necromancers, he believed that the universal agent of life could be suddenly coagulated by the combined action and reaction of outrage on Nature and murder. He collected afterwards the iridescent film which forms on blood as it turns cold; he subjected it to various fermentations, digested the product in the philosophical egg of the athanor, combining it with salt, sulphur and mercury. He had doubtless derived his recipe from some of those old Hebrew Grimoires which, had they been known at the period, would have been sufficient to call down on Jewry at large the execration of the whole earth. Persuaded, as they were, that the act of human impregnation attracts and coagulates the Astral Light in its reaction by sympathy on things subjected to the magnetism of man, the Israelitish sorcerers had plunged into those enormities of which Philo accuses them, as quoted by the astrologer Gaffarel. They caused trees to be grafted by women, who inserted the graft while a man performed on their persons those acts which are an outrage to Nature. Wherever Black Magic is concerned the same horrors recur, for the spirit of darkness is not one of invention.

Gilles de Laval was burned alive in the *pré de la Magdeleine*, near Nantes; he obtained permission to go to execution with all the pageantry that had accompanied him during life, as if he wished to involve in the ignominy of his punishment the ostentation and cupidity by which he had been so utterly degraded and lost so fatally.

After François Queverdo (1748–1797), Départ pour le sabbat
(Leaving for the Sabbat)

Witch's Death Song

Oliver Smith

Now's time to leave behind the sun
    and follow the wild ravens' call
when tumbles down your witch's heart
    and death break its mortgaged walls.

Lay not beneath the cuckoo-pint
    nor yellow gorse nor jasmine white;
make your tomb where the old paths meet
    and ghosts cry in the restless night.

Where stunted oaks bend-in-the storm,
    lay your bones in the gibbet ground
garlanded in bizzom flowers,
    devil cursed and witchbane bound.

When you lie in your grave to sleep,
    an iron nail-will pin your feet;
a horseshoe hang above your head
    to quiet in your coffin keep.

You will not lie in shady nook,
    in the forest or church or sea,
but at the cross road, locked in chains
    under earth three fathoms deep.

A Plantation Witch

Joel Chandler Harris

The next time the little boy got permission to call upon Uncle Remus, the old man was sitting in his door, with his elbows on his knees and his face buried in his hands, and he appeared to be in great trouble.

"What's the matter, Uncle Remus?" the youngster asked.

"Nuff de matter, honey—mo' dan dey's enny kyo fer. Ef dey ain't some quare gwines on 'roun' dis place I ain't name Remus."

The serious tone of thee old man caused the little boy to open his eyes. The moon, just at its full, cast long, vague, wavering shadows in front of the cabin. A colony of tree-frogs somewhere in the distance were treating their neighbors to a serenade, but to the little boy it sounded like a chorus of lost and long-forgotten whistlers. The sound was wherever the imagination chose to locate it—to the right, to the left, in the air, on the ground, far away or near at hand, but always indistinct. Something in Uncle Remus's tone exactly fitted all these surroundings, and the child nestled closer to the old man.

"Yasser," continued Uncle Remus, with an ominous sigh and a mysterious shake of the head, "ef dey ain't some quare gwines on in dish yer naberhood, den I'm de ball-headest creetur 'twix' dis en nex' Jinawerry wus a year 'go, w'ich I knows I ain't. Dat's what."

"What is it, Uncle Remus?"

"I know Mars John bin drivin' Cholly sorter hard terday, en I say ter myse'f dat I'd drap 'roun' 'bout dus' en fling nudder year er corn in de troff en kinder gin 'im a techin' up wid de kurrier-koam; en bless grashus! I ain't bin in de lot mo'n a minnit 'fo' I seed sump'n wuz wrong wid de hoss, and sho' nuff dar wuz his mane full er witch-stirrups."

"Full of what, Uncle Remus?"

"Full or witch-stirrups, honey. Ain't you seed no witch-stirrups? Well, w'en you see two stran' er ha'r tied tergedder in a hoss' mane, dar you see a witch-stirrup, en, mo'n dat, dat hoss done bin rid by um."

"Do you reckon they have been riding Charley?" inquired the little boy.

"Co'se, honey. Tooby sho dey is. W'at else dey bin doin'?"

"Did you ever see a witch, Uncle Remus?"

"Dat ain't needer yer her dar. W'en I see coon track in de branch, I know de coon bin 'long dar."

The argument seemed unanswerable, and the little boy asked, in a confidential tone:

"Uncle Remus, what are witches like?"

"Dey comes diffunt," responded the cautious old darkey. "Dey comes en dey cunjus fokes. Squinch-owl holler eve'y time he see a witch, en w'en you hear de dog howlin' in de middle er de night, one un um's mighty ap' ter be prowlin' 'roun'. Cunjun fokes kin tell a witch de minnit dey lays der eyes on it, but dem w'at ain't cunjun, hit's mighty hard ter tell w'en dey see one, kase dey might come in de 'ppearunce un a cow en all kinder beas's. I ain't bin useter no cunjun myse'f, but I bin livin' long nuff fer ter know w'en you meets up wid a big black cat in de middle er de road, wid yaller eyeballs, dars yo' witch fresh fum de Ole Boy. En, fuddermo', I know dat 'tain't proned inter no dogs fer ter ketch de rabbit w'at use in a berryin'-groun'. Dey er de mos' ongodlies' creeturs w'at you ever laid eyes on," continued Uncle Remus, with unction. "Down dar in Putmon County yo' Unk Jeems, he make like he gwineter ketch wunner dem dar graveyard rabbits. Sho nuff, out he goes, en de dogs ain't no mo'n got ter de place fo' up jump de ole rabbit right 'mong um, en atter runnin' 'roun' a time or two, she skip right up ter Mars Jeems, en Mars Jeems, he des put de gun-bairl right on 'er en lammed aloose. Hit tored up de groun' all 'roun', en de dogs, dey rush up, but dey wan't no rabbit dar; but bime-by Mars Jeems, he seed de dogs tuckin' der tails 'tween der legs, en he look up, en dar wuz de rabbit caperin' 'roun' on a toomstone, en wid dat Mars Jeems say he sorter feel like de time done come w'en yo' gran'ma was 'specktin' un him home, en he call off de dogs en put out. But dem wuz ha'nts. Witches is deze yer kinder fokes wat kin drap der body en change inter a cat en a wolf en all kinder creeturs."

"Papa says there ain't any witches," the little boy interrupted.

"Mars John ain't live long ez I is," said Uncle Remus, by way of comment. "He ain't bin broozin' 'roun' all hours er de night en day. I know'd a nigger w'ich his brer wuz a witch, kaze he up'n tole me how he tuck'n kyo'd 'im; en he kyo'd 'im good, mon."

"How was that?" inquired the little boy.

"Hit seem like," continued Uncle Remus, "dat witch fokes is got a slit in de back er de neck, en w'en dey wanter change derse'f, dey des pull de hide over der head same ez if 'twuz a shut, en dar dey is."

"Do they get out of their skins?" askewd the little boy, in an awed tone.

"Tooby sho, honey. You see yo' pa pull his shut off? Well, dat des 'zackly de way dey duz. But dish yer nigger w'at I'm tellin' you 'bout, he kyo'd his brer de ve'y fus pass he made at him. Hit got so dat fokes in de settlement didn't have no peace. De chillins 'ud wake up in de mawnins wid der ha'r tangle up, en wid scratches on um like dey bin thoo a brier-patch, twel bimeby one day de nigger he 'low dat he'd set up dat night en keep one eye on his brer; en sho' nuff dat night, des ez de chickens wuz crowin' for twelve, up jump de brer an pull off his skin en sail out'n de house in de shape un a bat, en w'at duz de nigger do but grab up de hide, en turn it wrongsudout'ards en sprinkle it wid salt. Den he lay down en watch fer ter see w'at de news wuz gwineter be. Des 'fo' day yer come a big black cat in de do', en de nigger git up, he did, en druv her away. Bimeby, yer come a big black dog snuffin' 'roun', en de nigger up wid a chunk en lammed 'im side er de head. Den a squinch-owl lit on de koam er de house, en de nigger jam de shovel in de fier en make 'im flew away. Las', yer come a great big black wolf wid his eyes shinin' like fier coals, en he grab de hide and rush out. 'Twa'n't long 'fo' de nigger year his brer holler'n en sqwuallin', en he tuck a light, he did, en went out, en dar wuz his brer des a waller'n on de groun' en squirmin' 'roun', kaze de salt on de skin wuz stingin' wuss'n ef he had his britches lineded wid yaller-jackets. By nex' mawnin' he got so he could sorter shuffle 'long, but he gun up cunjun, en ef dere wuz enny mo' witches in dat settlement dey kep' mighty close, en dat nigger he ain't skunt hisse'f no mo' not endurin' er my 'membrance."

The result of this was that Uncle Remus had to take the little boy by the hand and go with him to the "big house," which the old man was not loath to do; and, when the child went to bed, he lay awake a long time expecting an unseemly visitation from some mysterious sources. It soothed him, however, to hear the strong, musical voice of his sable patron, not very far away, tenderly contending with a lusty tune; and to this accompaniment the little boy dropped asleep:

> "Hit's eighteen hunder'd, forty-en-eight,
>   Christ done made dat crooked way straight—
>   En I don't wanter stay here no longer;
>   Hit's eighteen hunder'd, forty-en-nine,
>   Christ done turn dat water inter wine—
>   En I don't wanter stay here no longer."

The White Witch

James Weldon Johnson

O brothers mine, take care! Take care!
The great white witch rides out to-night.
Trust not your prowess nor your strength,
Your only safety lies in flight;
For in her glance there is a snare,
And in her smile there is a blight.

The great white witch you have not seen?
Then, younger brothers mine, forsooth,
Like nursery children you have looked
For ancient hag and snaggle-tooth;
But no, not so; the witch appears
In all the glowing charms of youth.

Her lips are like carnations, red,
Her face like new-born lilies, fair,
Her eyes like ocean waters, blue,
She moves with subtle grace and air,
And all about her head there floats
The golden glory of her hair.

But though she always thus appears
In form of youth and mood of mirth,
Unnumbered centuries are hers,
The infant planets saw her birth;
The child of throbbing Life is she,
Twin sister to the greedy earth.

And back behind those smiling lips,
And down within those laughing eyes,
And underneath the soft caress
Of hand and voice and purring sighs,

The shadow of the panther lurks,
The spirit of the vampire lies.

For I have seen the great white witch,
And she has led me to her lair,
And I have kissed her red, red lips
And cruel face so white and fair;
Around me she has twined her arms,
And bound me with her yellow hair.

I felt those red lips burn and sear
My body like a living coal;
Obeyed the power of those eyes
As the needle trembles to the pole;
And did not care although I felt
The strength go ebbing from my soul.

Oh! she has seen your strong young limbs,
And heard your laughter loud and gay,
And in your voices she has caught
The echo of a far-off day,
When man was closer to the earth;
And she has marked you for her prey.

She feels the old Antaean strength
In you, the great dynamic beat
Of primal passions, and she sees
In you the last besieged retreat
Of love relentless, lusty, fierce,
Love pain-ecstatic, cruel-sweet.

O, brothers mine, take care! Take care!
The great white witch rides out to-night.
O, younger brothers mine, beware!
Look not upon her beauty bright;
For in her glance there is a snare,
And in her smile there is a blight.

From *The Witch-Cult in Western Europe*

Margaret Alice Murray

The exact order of the ceremonies is never given and probably varied in different localities, but the general rule of the ritual at the Sabbath seems to have been that proceedings began by the worshippers paying homage to the Devil, who sat or stood in a convenient place. The homage consisted in renewing the vows of fidelity and obedience, in kissing the Devil on any part of his person that he chose to indicate, and sometimes in turning a certain number of times widdershins. Then followed the reports of all magic worked since the previous Sabbath, either by individuals or at the Esbats, and at the same time the witches consulted the Master as to their cases and received instructions from him how to proceed; after which came admissions to the society or marriages of the members. This ended the business part of the meeting. Immediately after all the business was transacted, the religious service was celebrated, the ceremonial of which varied according to the season of the year; and it was followed by the "obscene" fertility rites. The whole ceremony ended with feasting and dancing, and the assembly broke up at dawn.

This was apparently the usual course of the ritual of the Sabbath; the Esbat had less ceremonial, and the religious service was not performed. The Devil himself often went round and collected the congregation; and, not being in his "grand army", he appeared as a man in ordinary dress. Instead of the religious service with the adoration of the god, the witches worked the spells and charms with which they bewitched or unbewitched their enemies and friends, or they exercised new methods which they learnt from their Master, or received instructions how to practise the arts of healing and secret poisoning, of causing and blasting fertility.

From L[awrence] P[rice], The Witch of the Woodlands *(1655)*

Witches on the Heath

Leah Bodine Drake

Three witches danced on the heath last night,
    Dancing widdershins round a tree.
    Wildly widdershins whirled the three
Under a wild and cloud-swept sky,
While a goblin moon rode high
Over the hill where the Old Stones lie;
    And their hats were peaked,
    And they twittered and squeaked
As they danced in the green moonlight.

And out of the boughs of the twisted thorn
    Came the wail of a violin,
    Queer and evil and sad and thin . . . . .
And though there was nobody one could see,
Somebody played in the twisted tree
Queer, sad tunes for the witches three,
    Till a lost wind crept
    From the hills and wept,

And the farm-cocks crowed up the morn.
I love the things that the most pass by,
The tree on the heath that leans awry,
    The wild black night and the lanterned owl,
    The bat that goes in a velvet cowl . . . .
O there's no doubt! a witch I must be
Who love with unholy ecstasy
The owl and the bat and the twisted tree
    And wind in a midnight sky!

The White People

Frank Belknap Long

Out of the grass when the dew is wet
  Their houses lean and their hoards are set
    Deep in the woods that are not yet.

Out of the earth when the night is cold
  Their worm-dogs leap and over the wold
    They fly with tales that are not told.

Out of the wold when the moon rides low
  Their witch-fires flicker and tapers glow
    To guide the goblins to and fro.

Out of the lake when the comets pass
  Their maidens rise; and over the grass
    They crawl like shadows on a glass.

Out of the East when the stars spin high
  They dance and dance and the years go by
    And the sun and moon fade out of the sky—

And still they dance.

The Witch of the Pit (Our Lady Endor)

Maxwell I. Gold

When the stars rang out, I saw above me hideous gods who walked the earth once more, slaves to some unknown melody. In the ruins of an old temple, spoken only in name where the deepest pit swallowed that which used to be flesh and blood, a haggard enchantress wandered from the sand and brittle woods. Shadow and swollen lips imbued her ancient countenance with an ivory glow by the dim spectral touch of the moonlight; and through fire and forgotten tongues she uttered bizarre voices and grotesque songs.

Helpless, I stood in her vile presence knowing something had changed within the fabric of existence while the hollowed gods swayed in the starless night; bereft of agency, deceived by the master who summoned them. All at once, drawn to the edge of the Pit, stone and sand-block perched precariously, I too was pulled closer and closer toward that harrowing abyss as the old witch of the Pit continued to dance wildly in the night.

Without warning, the heat-breath of the world exhaled with feverish and cataclysmic intent as the dirt and mud blasted into clay, sand became glass, and my brain beat with the witch's intense chant as if my very skull were cracked from the inside out. Her songs grew deeper with deadly crescendo, until I found my body without agency or will, transformed in mind and body like any false god when the stars rang out, a slave to the Witch of the Pit.

288

Witch's Brew

Dorothy Quick

A witch's brew is the Antic Sea
Of incantation and wizardry,
Of white foam edging a narrow shore
With breakers tumbling more and more.
Like a hundred horses with milk white manes
Rushing toward their promised gains,
Of Augean stables and horned meads
That are fit indeed for Neptune's steeds.

A witch's brew and a wizard's spell
Are the sea horses that ride the swell
And the storied waves which tower high
To link the water with the sky.
They bruise the land with a giant hoof
That is part of the darkling picture's woof.
For the sea must win in an equal fray
While the witch of time has her own wild way,
And stirs the brew that is tempest tossed
With the hand of a dead man long since lost.

The Necklace of Princess Fiorimonde

Mary De Morgan

Once there lived a King, whose wife was dead, but who had a most beautiful daughter—so beautiful that every one thought she must be good as well, instead of which the Princess was really very wicked, and practised witchcraft and black magic, which she had learned from an old witch who lived in a hut on the side of a lonely mountain. This old witch was wicked and hideous, and no one but the King's daughter knew that she lived there; but at night, when every one else was asleep, the Princess, whose name was Fiorimonde, used to visit her by stealth to learn sorcery. It was only the witch's arts which had made Fiorimonde so beautiful that there was no one like her in the world, and in return the Princess helped her with all her tricks, and never told any one she was there.

The time came when the King began to think he should like his daughter to marry, so he summoned his council and said, "We have no son to reign after our death, so we had best seek for a suitable prince to marry to our royal daughter, and then, when we are too old, he shall be king in our stead." And all the council said he was very wise, and it would be well for the Princess to marry. So heralds were sent to all the neighbouring kings and princes to say that the King would choose a husband for the Princess, who should be king after him. But when Fiorimonde heard this she wept with rage, for she knew quite well that if she had a husband he would find out how she went to visit the old witch, and would stop her practising magic, and then she would lose her beauty.

When night came, and every one in the palace was fast asleep, the Princess went to her bedroom window and softly opened it. Then she took from her pocket a handful of peas and held them out of the window and chirruped low, and there flew down from the roof a small brown bird and sat upon her wrist and began to eat the peas. No sooner had it swallowed them than it began to grow and grow and

290

grow till it was so big that the Princess could not hold it, but let it stand on the window-sill, and still it grew and grew and grew till it was as large as an ostrich. Then the Princess climbed out of the window and seated herself on the bird's back, and at once it flew straight away over the tops of the trees till it came to the mountain where the old witch dwelt, and stopped in front of the door of her hut.

The Princess jumped off, and muttered some words through the keyhole, when a croaking voice from within called,

"Why do you come to-night? Have I not told you I wished to be left alone for thirteen nights; why do you disturb me?"

"But I beg of you to let me in," said the Princess, "for I am in trouble and want your help."

"Come in then," said the voice; and the door flew open, and the Princess trod into the hut, in the middle of which, wrapped in a gray cloak which almost hid her, sat the witch. Princess Fiorimonde sat down near her, and told her, her story. How the King wished her to marry, and had sent word to the neighbouring princes, that they might make offers for her.

"This is truly bad hearing," croaked the witch, "but we shall beat them yet; and you must deal with each Prince as he comes. Would you like them to become dogs, to come at your call, or birds, to fly in the air, and sing of your beauty, or will you make them all into beads, the beads of such a necklace as never woman wore before, so that they may rest upon your neck, and you may take them with you always."

"The necklace! the necklace!" cried the Princess, clapping her hands with joy. "That will be best of all, to sling them upon a string and wear them around my throat. Little will the courtiers know whence come my new jewels."

"But this is a dangerous play," quoth the witch, "for, unless you are very careful, you yourself may become a bead and hang upon the string with the others, and there you will remain till some one cuts the string, and draws you off."

"Nay, never fear," said the Princess, "I will be careful, only tell me what to do, and I will have great princes and kings to adorn me, and all their greatness shall not help them."

Then the witch dipped her hand into a black bag which stood on the ground beside her, and drew out a long gold thread.

The ends were joined together, but no one could see the joins, and however much you pulled, it would not break. It would easily go over Fiorimonde's head, and the witch slipped it on her neck saying,

"Now mind, while this hangs here you are safe enough, but if once you join your fingers around the string you too will meet the fate of your lovers, and hang upon it yourself. As for the kings and princes who would marry you, all you have to do is to make them close their fingers around the chain, and at once they will be strung upon it as bright hard beads, and there they shall remain, till it is cut and they drop off."

"This is really delightful," cried the Princess; "and I am already quite impatient for the first to come that I may try."

"And now," said the witch, "since you are here, and there is yet time, we will have a dance, and I will summon the guests." So saying, she took from a corner a drum and a pair of drum-sticks, and going to the door, began to beat upon it. It made a terrible rattling. In a moment came flying through the air all sorts of forms. There were little dark elves with long tails, and goblins who chattered and laughed, and other witches who rode on broom-sticks. There was one wicked fairy in the form of a large cat, with bright green eyes, and another came sliding in like a long shining viper.

Then, when all had arrived, the witch stopped drumming, and, going to the middle of the hut, stamped on the floor, and a trap-door opened in the ground. The old witch stepped through it, and led the way down a narrow dark passage, to a large underground chamber, and all her strange guests followed, and here they all danced and made merry in a terrible way, but at first sound of cock-crow all the guests disappeared with a whiff, and the Princess hastened up the dark passage again, and out of the hut to where her big bird still waited for her, and mounting its back she flew home in a trice. Then, when she had stepped in at her bedroom window, she poured into a cup from a small black bottle, a few drops of magic water, and gave it to the bird to drink, and as it sipped it grew smaller, and smaller, till at last it had quite regained its natural size, and hopped on to the roof as before, and the Princess shut her window, and got into bed, and fell asleep, and no one knew of her strange journey, or where she had been.

Next day Fiorimonde declared to her father the King, that she was quite willing to wed any prince he should fix upon as a husband for her, at which he was much pleased, and soon after informed her, that a young king was coming from over the sea to be her husband. He was king of a large rich country, and would take back his bride with him to his home. He was called King Pierrot. Great preparations were made for his arrival, and the Princess was decked in her finest array to greet him, and when he came all the courtiers said, "This is truly a proper husband for our beautiful Princess," for he was strong and handsome, with black hair, and eyes like sloes. King Pierrot was delighted with Fiorimonde's beauty, and was happy as the day is long; and all things went merrily till the evening before the marriage. A great feast was held, at which the Princess looked lovelier than ever dressed in a red gown, the colour of the inside of a rose, but she wore no jewels nor ornaments of any kind, save one shining gold string round her milk-white throat.

When the feast was done, the Princess stepped from her golden chair at her father's side, and walked softly into the garden, and stood under an elm-tree looking at the shining moon. In a few moments King Pierrot followed her, and stood beside her, looking at her and wondering at her beauty.

"To-morrow, then, my sweet Princess, you will be my Queen, and share all I possess. What gift would you wish me to give you on our wedding day?"

"I would have a necklace wrought of the finest gold and jewels to be found, and just the length of this gold cord which I wear around my throat," answered Princess Fiorimonde.

"Why do you wear that cord?" asked King Pierrot; "it has no jewel nor ornament about it."

"Nay, but there is no cord like mine in all the world," cried Fiorimonde, and her eyes sparkled wickedly as she spoke; "it is as light as a feather, but stronger than an iron chain. Take it in both hands and try to break it, that you may see how strong it is;" and King Pierrot took the cord in both hands to pull it hard; but no sooner were his fingers closed around it than he vanished like a puff of smoke, and on the cord appeared a bright, beautiful bead—so bright and beautiful as was never bead before—clear as crystal, but shining with all colours— green, blue, and gold.

Princess Fiorimonde gazed down at it and laughed aloud.

"Aha, my proud lover! are you there?" she cried with glee; "my necklace bids fair to beat all others in the world," and she caressed the bead with the tips of her soft, white fingers, but was careful that they did not close round the string. Then she returned into the banqueting hall, and spoke to the King.

"Pray, sire," said she, "send some one at once to find King Pierrot, for, as he was talking to me a minute ago, he suddenly left me, and I am afraid lest I may have given him offence, or perhaps he is ill."

The King desired that the servants should seek for King Pierrot all over the grounds, and seek him they did, but nowhere was he to be found, and the old King looked offended.

"Doubtless he will be ready to-morrow in time for the wedding," quoth he, "but we are not best pleased that he should treat us in this way."

Princess Fiorimonde had a little maid called Yolande. She was a bright-faced girl with merry brown eyes, but she was not beautiful like Fiorimonde, and she did not love her mistress, for she was afraid of her, and suspected her of her wicked ways. When she undressed her that night she noticed the gold cord, and the one bright bead upon it, and as she combed the Princess's hair she looked over her shoulder into the looking-glass, and saw how she laughed, and how fondly she looked at the cord, and caressed the bead, again and again with her fingers.

"That is a wonderful bead on your Highness's cord," said Yolande, looking at its reflection in the mirror; "surely it must be a bridal gift from King Pierrot."

"And so it is, little Yolande," cried Fiorimonde, laughing merrily;

"and the best gift he could give me. But I think one bead alone looks ugly and ungainly; soon I hope I shall have another, and another, and another, all as beautiful as the first."

Then Yolande shook her head, and said to herself, "This bodes no good."

Next morning all was prepared for the marriage, and the Princess was dressed in white satin and pearls with a long white lace veil over her, and a bridal wreath on her head, and she stood waiting among her grandly dressed ladies, who all said that such a beautiful bride had never been seen in the world before. But just as they were preparing to go down to the fine company in the hall, a messenger came in great haste summoning the Princess at once to her father the King, as he was much perplexed.

"My daughter," cried he, as Fiorimonde in all her bridal array entered the room where he sat alone, "what can we do? King Pierrot is nowhere to be found; I fear lest he may have been seized by robbers and basely murdered for his rich clothes, or carried away to some mountain and left there to starve. My soldiers are gone far and wide to seek him—and we shall hear of him ere day is done—but where there is no bridegroom there can be no bridal."

"Then let it be put off, my father," cried the Princess, "and tomorrow we shall know if it is for a wedding, or a funeral, we must dress;" and she pretended to weep, but even then could hardly keep from laughing.

So the wedding guests went away, and the Princess laid aside her bridal dress, and all waited anxiously for news of King Pierrot; and no news came. So at last every one gave him up for dead, and mourned for him, and wondered how he had met his fate.

Princess Fiorimonde put on a black gown, and begged to be allowed to live in seclusion for one month in which to grieve for King Pierrot; but when she was again alone in her bedroom she sat before her looking-glass and laughed till tears ran down her cheeks; and Yolande watched her, and trembled, when she heard her laughter. She noticed, too, that beneath her black gown, the Princess still wore her gold cord, and did not move it night or day.

The month had barely passed away when the King came to his daughter, and announced that another suitor had presented himself, whom he should much like to be her husband. The Princess agreed quite obediently to all her father said; and it was arranged that the marriage should take place. This new prince was called Prince Hildebrandt. He came from a country far north, of which one day he would be king. He was tall, and fair, and strong, with flaxen hair and bright blue eyes. When Princess Fiorimonde saw his portrait she was much pleased, and said, "By all means let him come, and the sooner the better." So she put off her black clothes, and again great preparations were made for a wedding; and King Pierrot was quite forgotten.

Prince Hildebrandt came, and with him many fine gentlemen, and they brought beautiful gifts for the bride. The evening of his arrival all went well, and again there was a grand feast, and Fiorimonde looked so beautiful that Prince Hildebrandt was delighted; and this time she did not leave her father's side, but sat by him all the evening.

Early next morning at sunrise, when every one was still sleeping, the Princess rose, and dressed herself in a plain white gown, and brushed all her hair over her shoulders, and crept quietly downstairs into the palace gardens; then she walked on till she came beneath the window of Prince Hildebrandt's room, and here she paused and began to sing a little song as sweet and joyous as a lark's. When Prince Hildebrandt heard it he got up and went to the window and looked out to see who sang, and when he saw Fiorimonde standing in the red sunrise-light, which made her hair look gold, and her face rosy, he made haste to dress himself and go down to meet her.

"How, my Princess," cried he, as he stepped into the garden beside her. "This is indeed great happiness to meet you here so early. Tell me why do you come out at sunrise to sing by yourself?"

"I come that I may see the colours of the sky—red, blue, and gold," answered the Princess. "Look, there are no such colours to be seen anywhere, unless, indeed, it be in this bead which I wear here on my golden cord."

"What is that bead, and where did it come from?" asked Hilde-brandt.

"It came from over the sea, where it shall never return again," an-swered the Princess. And again her eyes began to sparkle with eager-ness, and she could scarcely conceal her mirth. "Lift the cord off my neck and look at it near, and tell me if you ever saw one like it."

Hildebrandt put out his hands and took hold of the cord, but no sooner were his fingers closed around it than he vanished, and a new bright bead was slung next to the first one on Fiorimonde's chain, and this one was even more beautiful than the other.

The Princess gave a long low laugh, quite terrible to hear.

"Oh, my sweet necklace," cried she, "how beautiful you are grow-ing! I think I love you more than anything in the world besides." Then she went softly back to bed, without any one hearing her, and fell sound asleep, and slept till Yolande came to tell her it was time for her to get up and dress for the wedding.

The Princess was dressed in gorgeous clothes, and only Yolande noticed that beneath her satin gown, she wore the golden cord, but now there were two beads upon it instead of one. Scarcely was she ready when the King burst into her room in a towering rage.

"My daughter," cried he, "there is a plot against us. Lay aside your bridal attire and think no more of Prince Hildebrandt, for he too has disappeared, and is nowhere to be found."

At this the Princess wept, and entreated that Hildebrandt should be sought for far and near, but she laughed to herself, and said, "Search where you will, yet you shall not find him;" and so again a great search was made, and when no trace of the Prince was found, all the palace was in an uproar.

The Princess again put off her bride's dress and clad herself in black, and sat alone, and pretended to weep, but Yolande, who watched her, shook her head, and said, "More will come and go before the wicked Princess has done her worst."

A month passed, in which Fiorimonde pretended to mourn for Hildebrandt, then she went to the King and said,

"Sire, I pray that you will not let people say that when any bride-groom comes to marry me, as soon as he has seen me he flies rather than be my husband. I beg that suitors may be summoned from far and near that I may not be left alone unwed."

The King agreed, and envoys were sent all the world over to bid any who would come and be the husband of Princess Fiorimonde. And come they did, kings and princes from south and north, east and west,—King Adrian, Prince Sigbert, Prince Algar, and many more,—but though all went well till the wedding morning, when it was time to go to church, no bridegroom was to be found. The old King was sadly frightened, and would fain have given up all hope of finding a husband for the Princess, but now she implored him, with tears in her eyes, not to let her be disgraced in this way. And so suitor after suitor continued to come, and now it was known, far and wide, that whoever came to ask for the hand of Princess Fiorimonde vanished, and was seen no more of men. The courtiers were afraid and whispered under their breath, "It is not all right, it cannot be;" but only Yolande noticed how the beads came upon the golden thread, till it was well-nigh covered, yet there always was room for one bead more.

So the years passed, and every year Princess Fiorimonde grew lovelier and lovelier, so that no one who saw her could guess how wicked she was.

In a far off country lived a young prince whose name was Florestan. He had a dear friend named Gervaise, whom he loved bet-ter than any one in the world. Gervaise was tall, and broad, and stout of limb, and he loved Prince Florestan so well, that he would gladly have died to serve him.

It chanced that Prince Florestan saw a portrait of Princess Fiori-monde, and at once swore he would go to her father's court, and beg that he might have her for his wife, and Gervaise in vain tried to dis-suade him.

"There is an evil fate about the Princess Fiorimonde," quoth he. "Many have gone to marry her, but where are they now?"

"I don't know or care," answered Florestan, "but this is sure, that I will wed her and return here, and bring my bride with me."

So he set out for Fiorimonde's home, and Gervaise went with him with a heavy heart.

When they reached the court, the old King received them and welcomed them warmly, and he said to his courtiers, "Here is a fine young prince to whom we would gladly see our daughter wed. Let us hope that this time all will be well." But now Fiorimonde had grown so bold, that she scarcely tried to conceal her mirth.

"I will gladly marry him to-morrow, if he comes to the church," she said; "but if he is not there, what can I do," and she laughed long and merrily, till those who heard her shuddered.

When the Princess's ladies came to tell her that Prince Florestan was arrived, she was in the garden, lying on the marble edge of a fountain, feeding the gold fish who swam in the water.

"Bid him come to me," she said, "for I will not go any more in state to meet any suitors, neither will I put on grand attire for them. Let him come and find me as I am, since all find it so easy to come and go." So her ladies told the prince that Fiorimonde waited for him near the fountain.

She did not rise when he came to where she lay, but his heart bounded with joy, for he had never in his life beheld such a beautiful woman.

She wore a thin soft white dress, which clung to her lithe figure. Her beautiful arms and hands were bare, and she dabbled with them in the water, and played with the fish. Her great blue eyes were sparkling with mirth, and were so beautiful, that no one noticed the wicked look hid in them; and on her neck lay the marvellous many-coloured necklace, which was itself a wonder to behold.

"You have my best greetings, Prince Florestan," she said. "And you, too, would be my suitor. Have you thought well of what you would do, since so many princes who have seen me have fled for ever, rather than marry me?" and as she spoke, she raised her white hand from the water, and held it out to the Prince, who stooped and kissed it, and scarcely knew how to answer her for bewilderment at her great loveliness.

Gervaise followed his master at a short distance, but he was ill at ease, and trembled for fear of what should come.

"Come, bid your friend leave us," said Fiorimonde, looking at Gervaise, "and sit beside me, and tell me of your home, and why you wish to marry me, and all pleasant things."

Florestan begged that Gervaise would leave them for a little, and he walked slowly away, in a very mournful mood.

He went on down the walks, not heeding where he was going, till he met Yolande, who stood beneath a tree laden with rosy apples, picking the fruit, and throwing it into a basket at her feet. He would have passed her in silence, but she stopped him, and said,

"Have you come with the new Prince? Do you love your master?"

"Ay, better than any one else on the earth," answered Gervaise. "Why do you ask?"

"And where is he now?" said Yolande, not heeding Gervaise's question.

"He sits by the fountain with the beautiful Princess," said Gervaise.

"Then, I hope you have said good-bye to him well, for be assured you shall never see him again," said Yolande nodding her head.

"Why not, and who are you to talk like this?" asked Gervaise.

"My name is Yolande," answered she, "and I am Princess Fiorimonde's maid. Do you not know that Prince Florestan is the eleventh lover who has come to marry her, and one by one they have disappeared, and only I know where they are gone."

"And where are they gone?" cried Gervaise, "and why do you not tell the world, and prevent good men being lost like this?"

"Because I fear my mistress," said Yolande, speaking low and drawing near to him; "she is a sorceress, and she wears the brave kings and princes who come to woo her, strung upon a cord round her neck. Each one forms the bead of a necklace which she wears, both day and night. I have watched that necklace growing; first it was only an empty gold thread; then came King Pierrot, and when he disappeared the first bead appeared upon it. Then came Hildebrandt, and two beads were on the string instead of one; then followed Adrian, Sigbert, and Algar, and Cenred, and Pharamond, and Baldwyn, and Leofric, and Raoul, and all are gone, and ten beads hang upon the string, and to-night there will be eleven, and the eleventh will be your Prince Florestan."

"If this be so," cried Gervaise, "I will never rest till I have plunged my sword into Fiorimonde's heart;" but Yolande shook her head.

"She is a sorceress," she said, "and it might be hard to kill her; besides, that might not break the spell, and bring back the princes to life. I wish I could show you the necklace, and you might count the beads, and see if I do not speak truth, but it is always about her neck, both night and day, so it is impossible."

"Take me to her room to-night when she is asleep, and let me see it there," said Gervaise.

"Very well, we will try," said Yolande; "but you must be very still, and make no noise, for if she wakes, remember it will be worse for us both."

When night came and all in the palace were fast asleep, Gervaise and Yolande met in the great hall, and Yolande told him that the Princess slumbered soundly.

"So now let us go," said she, "and I will show you the necklace on which Fiorimonde wears her lovers strung like beads, though how she transforms them I know not."

"Stay one instant, Yolande," said Gervaise, holding her back, as she would have tripped upstairs. "Perhaps, try how I may, I shall be beaten, and either die or become a bead like those who have come before me. But if I succeed and rid the land of your wicked Princess, what will you promise me for a reward?"

"What would you have?" asked Yolande.

"I would have you say you will be my wife, and come back with me to my own land," said Gervaise.

"That I will promise gladly," said Yolande, kissing him, "but we must not speak or think of this till we have cut the cord from Fiorimonde's neck, and all her lovers are set free."

So they went softly up to the Princess's room, Yolande holding a small lantern, which gave only a dim light. There, in her grand bed, lay

Princess Fiorimonde. They could just see her by the lantern's light, and she looked so beautiful that Gervaise began to think Yolande spoke falsely, when she said she was so wicked.

Her face was calm and sweet as a baby's; her hair fell in ruddy waves on the pillow; her rosy lips smiled, and little dimples showed in her cheeks; her white soft hands were folded amidst the scented lace and linen of which the bed was made. Gervaise almost forgot to look at the glittering beads hung round her throat, in wondering at her loveliness, but Yolande pulled him by the arm.

"Do not look at her," she whispered softly, "since her beauty has cost dear already; look rather at what remains of those who thought her as fair as you do now; see here," and she pointed with her finger to each bead in turn.

"This was Pierrot, and this Hildebrandt, and these are Adrian, and Sigbert, and Algar, and Cenred, and that is Pharamond, and that Raoul, and last of all here is your own master Prince Florestan. Seek him now where you will and you will not find him, and you shall never see him again till the cord is cut and the charm broken."

"Of what is the cord made?" whispered Gervaise.

"It is of the finest gold," she answered. "Nay, do not you touch her lest she wake. I will show it to you." And Yolande put down the lantern and softly put out her hands to slip the beads aside, but as she did so, her fingers closed around the golden string, and directly she was gone. Another bead was added to the necklace, and Gervaise was alone with the sleeping Princess. He gazed about him in sore amazement and fear. He dared not call lest Fiorimonde should wake.

"Yolande," he whispered as loud as he dared, "Yolande, where are you?" but no Yolande answered.

Then he bent down over the Princess and gazed at the necklace. Another bead was strung upon it next to the one to which Yolande had pointed as Prince Florestan. Again he counted them. "Eleven before, now there are twelve. Oh hateful Princess! I know now where go the brave kings and princes who came to woo you, and where, too, is my Yolande," and as he looked at the last bead, tears filled his eyes. It was brighter and

302

clearer than the others, and of a warm red hue, like the red dress Yolande had worn. The Princess turned and laughed in her sleep, and at the sound of her laughter Gervaise was filled with horror and loathing. He crept shuddering from the room, and all night long sat up alone, plotting how he might defeat Fiorimonde, and set Florestan and Yolande free.

Next morning when Fiorimonde dressed she looked at her necklace and counted its beads, but she was much perplexed, for a new bead was added to the string.

"Who can have come and grasped my chain unknown to me?" she said to herself, and she sat and pondered for a long time. At last she broke into weird laughter.

"At any rate, whoever it was, is fitly punished," quoth she. "My brave necklace, you can take care of yourself, and if any one tries to steal you, they will get their reward, and add to my glory. In truth I may sleep in peace, and fear nothing."

The day passed away and no one missed Yolande. Towards sunset the rain began to pour in torrents, and there was such a terrible thunderstorm that every one was frightened. The thunder roared, the lightning gleamed flash after flash, every moment it grew fiercer and fiercer. The sky was so dark that, save for the lightning's light, nothing could be seen, but Princess Fiorimonde loved the thunder and lightning.

She sat in a room high up in one of the towers, clad in a black velvet dress, and she watched the lightning from the window, and laughed at each peal of thunder. In the midst of the storm a stranger, wrapped in a cloak, rode to the palace door, and the ladies ran to tell the Princess that a new prince had come to be her suitor. "And he will not tell his name," said they, "but says he hears that all are bidden to ask for the hand of Princess Fiorimonde, and he too would try his good fortune."

"Let him come at once," cried the Princess. "Be he prince or knave what care I? If princes all fly from me it may be better to marry a peasant."

So they led the new-comer up to the room where Fiorimonde sat. He was wrapped in a thick cloak, but he flung it aside as he came in, and showed how rich was his silken clothing underneath; and so well

303

was he disguised, that Fiorimonde never saw that it was Gervaise, but looked at him, and thought she had never seen him before.

"Next morning when Fiorimonde dressed she looked at her necklace and counted its beads, but she was much perplexed, for a new bead was added to the string."

"You are most welcome, stranger prince, who has come through such lightning and thunder to find me," said she. "Is it true, then, that you wish to be my suitor? What have you heard of me?"

"It is quite true, Princess," said Gervaise. "And I have heard that you are the most beautiful woman in the world."

"And is that true also?" asked the Princess. "Look at me now, and see."

Gervaise looked at her and in his heart he said, "It is quite true, oh wicked Princess! There never was woman as beautiful as you, and never before did I hate a woman as I hate you now;" but aloud he said,

"No, Princess, that is not true; you are very beautiful, but I have seen a woman who is fairer than you for all that your skin looks ivory against your velvet dress, and your hair is like gold."

"A woman who is fairer than I?" cried Fiorimonde, and her breast began to heave and her eyes to sparkle with rage, for never before had she heard such a thing said. "Who are you who dares come and tell me of women more beautiful than I am?"

"I am a suitor who asks to be your husband, Princess," answered Gervaise, "but still I say I have seen a woman who was fairer than you."

"Who is she—where is she?" cried Fiorimonde, who could scarcely contain her anger. "Bring her here at once that I may see if you speak the truth."

"What will you give me to bring her to you?" said Gervaise. "Give me that necklace you wear on your neck, and then I will summon her in an instant;" but Fiorimonde shook her head.

"You have asked," said she, "for the only thing from which I cannot part," and then she bade her maids bring her her jewel-casket, and she drew out diamonds, and rubies, and pearls, and offered them, all or any, to Gervaise. The lightning shone on them and made them shine and flash, but he shook his head.

"No, none of these will do," quoth he. "You can see her for the necklace, but for nothing else."

"Take it off for yourself then," cried Fiorimonde, who now was so angry that she only wished to be rid of Gervaise in any way.

"No, indeed," said Gervaise, "I am no tire-woman, and should not know how to clasp and unclasp it;" and in spite of all Fiorimonde could say or do, he would not touch either her or the magic chain.

At night the storm grew even fiercer, but it did not trouble the Princess. She waited till all were asleep, and then she opened her bed-room window and chirruped softly to the little brown bird, who flew down from the roof at her call. Then she gave him a handful of seeds as before, and he grew and grew and grew till he was as large as an ostrich, and she sat upon his back and flew out through the air, laughing at the lightning and thunder which flashed and roared around her. Away they flew till they came to the old witch's cave, and here they found the witch sitting at her open door catching the lightning to make charms with.

"Welcome, my dear," croaked she, as Fiorimonde stepped from the bird; "here is a night we both love well. And how goes the neck-lace?—right merrily I see. Twelve beads already—but what is that twelfth?" and she looked at it closely.

"Nay, that is one thing I want you to tell me," said Fiorimonde, drying the rain from her golden hair. "Last night when I slept there were eleven, and this morning there are twelve; and I know not from whence comes the twelfth."

"It is no suitor," said the witch, "but from some young maid, that that bead is made. But why should you mind? It looks well with the others."

"Some young maid," said the Princess. "Then, it must be Cicely or Marybel, or Yolande, who would have robbed me of my necklace as I slept. But what care I? The silly wench is punished now, and so may all others be, who would do the same."

"And when will you get the thirteenth bead, and where will he come from?" asked the witch.

"He waits at the palace now," said Fiorimonde, chuckling. "And this is why I have to speak to you;" and then she told the witch of the stranger who had come in the storm, and of how he would not touch her necklace, nor take the cord in his hand, and how he said also that he knew a woman fairer than she.

"Beware, Princess, beware," cried the witch in a warning voice, as she listened. "Why should you heed tales of other women fairer than you? Have I not made you the most beautiful woman in the world, and can any others do more than I? Give no ear to what this stranger says or you shall rue it." But still the Princess murmured, and said she did not love to hear any one speak of others as beautiful as she.

"Be warned in time," cried the witch, "or you will have cause to repent it. Are you so silly or so vain as to be troubled because a Prince says idly what you know is not true? I tell you do not listen to him, but let him be slung to your chain as soon as may be, and then he will speak no more." And then they talked together of how Fiorimonde could make Gervaise grasp the fatal string.

Next morning when the sun rose, Gervaise started off into the woods, and there he plucked acorns and haws, and hips, and strung them on to a string to form a rude necklace. This he hid in his bosom *then,* and went back to the palace without telling any one.

When the Princess rose, she dressed herself as beautifully as she could, and braided her golden locks with great care, for this morning she meant her new suitor to meet his fate. After breakfast, she stepped into the garden, where the sun shone brightly, and all looked fresh after the storm. Here from the grass she picked up a golden ball, and began to play with it.

"Go to our new guest," cried she to her ladies, "and ask him to come here and play at ball with me." So they went, and soon they returned bringing Gervaise with them.

"Good morrow, prince," cried she. "Pray, come and try your skill at this game with me; and you," she said to her ladies, "do not wait to watch our play, but each go your way, and do what pleases you best." So they all went away, and left her alone with Gervaise.

"Well, prince," cried she as they began to play, "what do you think of me by morning light? Yesterday when you came it was so dark, with thunder and clouds, that you could scarcely see my face, but now that there is bright sunshine, pray look well at me, and see if you do not think me as beautiful as any woman on earth," and she smiled at Gervaise, and looked so lovely as she spoke, that he scarce knew how to answer her; but he remembered Yolande, and said,

"Doubtless you are very beautiful; then why should you mind my telling you that I have seen a woman lovelier than you?"

At this the Princess again began to be angry, but she thought of the witch's words and said,

"Then, if you think there is a woman fairer than I, look at my beads, and now, that you see their colours in the sun, say if you ever saw such jewels before."

"It is true I have never seen beads like yours, but I have a necklace here, which pleases me better;" and from his pocket he drew the haws and acorns, which he had strung together.

"What is that necklace, and where did you get it? Show it to me!" cried Fiorimonde; but Gervaise held it out of her reach, and said,

"I like my necklace better than yours, Princess; and, believe me, there is no necklace like mine in all the world."

"Why; is it a fairy necklace? What does it do? Pray give it to me!" cried Fiorimonde, trembling with anger and curiosity, for she thought, "Perhaps it has power to make the wearer beautiful; perhaps it was worn by the woman whom he thought more beautiful than I, and that is why she looked so fair."

"Come, I will make a fair exchange," said Gervaise. "Give me your necklace and you shall have mine, and when it is round your throat I will truthfully say that you are the fairest woman in the world; but first I must have your necklace."

"Take it, then," cried the Princess, who, in her rage and eagerness, forgot all else, and she seized the string of beads to lift it from her neck, but no sooner had she taken it in her hands than they fell with a rattle to the earth, and Fiorimonde herself was nowhere to be seen. Gervaise bent down over the necklace as it lay upon the grass, and, with a smile, counted thirteen beads; and he knew that the thirteenth was the wicked Princess, who had herself met the evil fate she had prepared for so many others.

"Oh, clever Princess!" cried he, laughing aloud, "you are not so very clever, I think, to be so easily outwitted." Then he picked up the necklace on the point of the sword and carried it, slung thereon, into the council chamber, where sat the King surrounded by statesmen and courtiers busy with state affairs.

"Then he picked up the necklace on the point of his sword and carried it, slung thereon, into the council chamber."

"Pray, King," said Gervaise, "send some one to seek for Princess Fiorimonde. A moment ago she played with me at ball in the garden, and now she is nowhere to be seen."

The King desired that servants should seek her Royal Highness; but they came back saying she was not to be found.

"Then let me see if I cannot bring her to you; but first let those who have been longer lost than she, come and tell their own tale." And, so saying, Gervaise let the necklace slip from his sword on to the floor, and taking from his breast a sharp dagger, proceeded to cut the golden thread on which the beads were strung, and as he clave it in two there came a mighty noise like a clap of thunder.

"Now," cried he, "look, and see King Pierrot who was lost," and as he spoke he drew from the cord a bead, and King Pierrot, in his royal clothes, with his sword at his side, stood before them.

"Treachery!" he cried, but ere he could say more Gervaise had drawn off another bead, and King Hildebrandt appeared, and after him came Adrian, and Sigbert, and Algar, and Cenred, and Pharamond, and Raoul, and last of the princes, Gervaise's own dear master Florestan, and they all denounced Princess Fiorimonde and her wickedness.

"And now," cried Gervaise, "here is she who has helped to save you all," and he drew off the twelfth bead, and there stood Yolande in her red dress; and when he saw her Gervaise flung away his dagger and took her in his arms, and they wept for joy.

The King and all the courtiers sat pale and trembling, unable to speak for fear and shame. At length the King said with a deep groan,

"We owe you deep amends, O noble kings and princes! What punishment do you wish us to prepare for our most guilty daughter?" but here Gervaise stopped him, and said,

"Give her no other punishment than what she has chosen for herself. See, here she is, the thirteenth bead upon the string; let no one dare to draw it off, but let this string be hung up where all people can see it and see the one bead, and know the wicked Princess is punished for her sorcery, so it will be a warning to others who would do like her."

So they lifted the golden thread with great care and hung it up outside the town-hall, and there the one bead glittered and gleamed in the sunlight, and all who saw it knew that it was the wicked Princess Fiorimonde who had justly met her fate.

Then all the kings and princes thanked Gervaise and Yolande, and loaded them with presents, and each went to his own land.

And Gervaise married Yolande, and they went back with Prince Florestan to their home, and all lived happily to the end of their lives.

Hex House

Wade German

Off track in twilight I had found the place—
A ruined house in deep, remotest woods;
Alone for centuries it must have stood,
Forgotten like some tomb by time effaced.
Inside, those worm-worn, wooden walls were traced
With cryptic symbols drawn in ash and mud—
And hieroglyphics in black ink of blood
Were scrawled on every inch of surface space.

I shuddered as the evening gathered gloom;
Transfixed, the sigils held me in a spell
As shadows rose from corners of the room
Like spectral emissaries out of hell—
As if that warlock writing had been read
And some dark other's work had raised the dead.

From *The History of Witchcraft and Demonology*

Montague Summers

In the popular imagination the witch is always associated with the broomstick, employed by her to fly in wild career through mid-air. This belief seems almost universal, of all times and climes. The broomstick is, of course, closely connected with the magic wand or staff which was considered equally serviceable for purposes of equitation. The wood whence it was fashioned was often from the hazel-tree, witch-hazel, although in De Lancre's day the sorcerers of Southern France favoured the "Souhandourra"—*Cornus sanguinea,* dog-wood. Mid hurricane and tempest, in the very heart of the dark storm, the convoy of witches, straddling their broomsticks, sped swiftly along to the Sabbat, their yells and hideous laughter sounding louder than the crash of elements and mingling in fearsome discord with the frantic pipe of the gale.

There is a very important reference to these beliefs from the pen of the famous and erudite Benedictine Abbot, Regino of Prüm (A.D. 906), who in his weighty *De ecclesiasticis disciplinis* writes: "This too must by no means be passed over that certain utterly abandoned women, turning aside to follow Satan, being seduced by the illusions and phantasmical shows of demons firmly believe and openly profess that in the dead of night they ride upon certain beasts along with the pagan goddess Diana and a countless horde of women, and that in those silent hours they fly over vast tracts of country and obey her as their mistress, whilst on certain other nights they are summoned to do her homage and pay her service." The witches rode sometimes upon a besom or a stick, sometimes upon an animal, and the excursion through the air was generally preceded by an unction with a magic ointment. Various recipes are given for the ointment, and it is interesting to note that they contain deadly poisons: aconite, belladonna, and hemlock. Although these unguents may in certain circumstances be capable of producing definite physiological results, it is Delrio who best sums up the reasons for their use: "The Demon is able to convey them to the Sabbat without the use of any unguent, and often he does so. But for several reasons he prefers that they should anoint themselves. Sometimes when the witches seem afraid it serves to encourage them. When they are young and tender they will thus be better able to bear the hateful embrace of Satan who has assumed the shape of a man. For by this horrid anointing he dulls their senses and persuades these deluded wretches that there is some great virtue in the viscid lubricant. Sometimes too he does this in hateful mockery of God's holy Sacraments, and that by these mysterious ceremonies he may infuse, as it were, something of a ritual and liturgical nature into his beastly orgies."

Although the witch is universally credited with the power to fly through the air to the Sabbat mounted upon a besom or some kind of stick, it is remarkable in the face of popular belief to find that the confessions avowing this actual mode of aerial transport are extraordinarily few. Paul Grilland, in his tractate *De Sortilegiis* (Lyons, 1583), speaks of a witch at Rome during whose trial, seven years before, it was asserted she flew in the air after she had anointed her limbs with a magic liniment. Perhaps the most exactly detailed accounts of this feat are to be found in Boguet, than whom scarcely any writer more meticulously reports the lengthy and prolix evidence of witches, such evidence as he so laboriously gathered during the notorious prosecutions throughout Franche-Comté in the summer of 1598. He records quite plainly such statements as: "Françoise Secretain disoit, que pour aller au Sabbat, elle mettoit un baston blanc entre ses jambes & puis prononçait certaines paroles & dés lors elle estoit portée par l'air iusques en l'assemblée des Sorciers." (Françoise Secretain avowed that in order to go to the Sabbat she placed a white stick between her legs & then uttered certain words & then she was borne through the air to the sorcerers' assembly.) In another place she confessed "qu'elle avoit esté vne infinité de fois au Sabbat . . . & qu'elle y alloit sur vn baston blanc, qu'elle mettoit entre ses iambes." (That she had been a great number of times to the Sabbat . . . and that she went there on a white stick which she placed between her legs.) It will be noticed that in the second instance she does not explicitly claim to have been borne through the air. Again: "Françoise Secretain y estoit portée [au Sabbat] sur vn baston blanc. Satan y trasporta Thieuenne Paget & Antide Colas estant en forme d'vn homme noir, sortans de leurs maison le plus souuent par la cheminee." "Claudine Boban, ieune fille confessa qu'elle & sa mère montoient sur vne ramasse, & que sortans le contremont de la cheminée elles alloient par l'air en ceste façon au Sabbat." (Françoise Secretain was carried [to the Sabbat] on a white stick. Satan, in the form of a tall dark man, conveyed thither Thieuenne Paget & Antide Colas, who most often left their house by way of the chimney. . . . Claudine Boban, a young girl, confessed that both she and her mother mounted on a besom, & that flying out by the chimney they were thus borne through the air to the Sabbat.) A marginal note explains *ramasse* as "autrement balai, & en Lyonnois coiue."

Glanvill writes that Julian Cox, one of the Somerset coven (1665), said "that one evening she walkt out about a Mile from her own House and there came riding towards her three persons upon three Broom-staves, born up about a yard and a half from the ground. Two of them she formerly knew, which was a Witch and a Wizzard." It might easily be that there is some exaggeration here. We know that a figure in one of the witch dances consisted of leaping as high as possible into the air, and probably the three persons seen by Julian Cox were practising this agile step. A quotation from Bodin by Reginald Scot is very pertinent in this connexion. Speaking of the Sabbat revels he has: "And whiles they sing and dance, euerie one hath a broome in his hand, and holdeth it vp aloft. Item he saith, that these night-walking or rather night-dansing witches, brought out of *Italie* into *France,* that danse which is called *La Volta*." Sir John Davies in his *Orchestra or A Poeme on Dauncing* (18mo, 1596) describes the lavolta as "A loftie iumping, or a leaping round." De Lancre observes that after the regular country dance at the Sabbat the witches sprang high into the air. "Après la dance ils se mettent par fois à sauter." At their assembly certain of the Aberdeen witches (1597) "danced a devilish dance, riding on trees, by a

315

long space." In an old representation of Dr. Fian and his company swiftly pacing round North Berwick church withershins the witches are represented as running and leaping in the air, some mounted on broomsticks, some carrying their besoms in their hands.

There was discovered in the closet of Dame Alice Kyteler of Kilkenny, who was arrested in 1324 upon the accusation of nightly meeting a familiar Artisson and multiplied charges of sorcery, a pipe of ointment, wherewith she greased a staff "upon which she ambolled and gallopped thorough thicke and thin, when and what manner she listed." In the trial of Martha Carrier, a notorious witch and "rampant hag" at the Court of Oyer and Terminer, held by adjournment at Salem, 2 August, 1692, the eighth article of the indictment ran: "One *Foster,* who confessed her own share in the Witchcraft for which the Prisoner stood indicted, affirm'd, that she had seen the prisoner at some of their *Witch-meetings,* and that it was this *Carrier,* who perswaded her to be a Witch. She confessed that the Devil carry'd them on a pole, to a Witch-meeting: but the pole broke, and she hanging about *Carriers* neck, they both fell down, and she then received an hurt by the Fall, whereof she was not at this very time recovered."

In many of these instances it is plain that there is no actual flight through the air implied; although there is a riding a-cock-horse of brooms or sticks, in fact, a piece of symbolic ritual.

The Beldame

Katherine Kerestman

The silk-shod foot slips in the clay.
Surprised, I leap out of its way.
The lass, careening through the glen,
Has wandered from the realm of men.
I draw in air and puff my face
And bellow out a belch in bass.
My fellow toads heed my alarm
And carry it from swamp to farm,
 Croaking a swelling tympany,
"Harrumph Brrrackk"—foul symphony
 With which soprano plaints do merge:
"Alas, alack! What evil scourge
 Doth beset a maiden's virtue?"
The raven's caw, opossum's mew
The beldame of the Black Wood hears,
Having lived sixteen thousand years.
I leap from twig to branch to leaf,
Hurrying to watch the mischief
That awaits a foolish maiden
Who hath strayed into the black glen
Where dwells the awful sorceress.
Sprawled lies the damsel on the moss,
Tripped up by gnarled roots which cross
The forest floor, her ankle broken.
"Ambrosia, sweet," her name spoken
 She looks around and sees four score
 (Or more) red pairs of eyes before
 Her and behind her in the gloom
 And listens to our dour croaking,
 Fearing what the night is cloaking.

A bent, old crone repeats, "Ambrosia,"
Slithering closer to the girl
Whispering, "I've caught a squirrel,
A tasty morsel I shall roast.
Of all of you I like the most
Your dainty fingers that I'll wear
Around my neck, strung with your hair."
The wood enlivens with the song
Of mouse and frog and buzzard throng.
The crescent moon smiles crookedly,
Glows on the damsel luridly.
The Black Wood is a festal place
For those of an unearthly race.

From Richard Head, The History of Mother Shipton *(1715?)*

[Ir]reversible
(three vignettes and a poem)

Anna Taborska

Graffti on a Wall in Southfield

One by one the youths were done,
Screaming, dying—every one.
Victims of the witch's ire,
Taken by her to hellfire.

For every scream of feline fear
She avenged those she held dear.

Should have lived a decent life,
Not put innocents to the knife.
Eternal suffering the youths' new home,
While Southfield cats are safe to roam.

One by one the killers fell,
Wrongdoers condemned to hell.

Vignette 3

In the fading light of early evening, the shapes standing in the middle of Southfield Park could have been anything. From a distance, the five rough, upright sticks with something ragged perched on top seemed like an unsettling art installation, unusually placed to provoke thought. Some passersby, catching them out of the corner of their eye while hurrying along the paths of the small park in West London, might have thought they were scarecrows for some odd, temporary display or even the remnants of strange, exotic plants. Others might have dismissed them as discarded pieces of trash, caught in the wind and snagged on sticks left by unsupervised children.

But curiosity pulled a few people closer. A couple of joggers slowed their pace, squinting in the burgeoning gloom as they tried to make sense of what it was that they were looking at. Dogwalkers paused, pets tugging frantically at their leashes. As people neared, the outlines became sharper, the details clearer, and a sense of unease began to creep in. The things skewered atop the sticks were not sculptures or weird plants, but something much more disturbing.

They were heads—human heads—impaled on the coarse, splintered wood. The hair, matted and dark with clotted blood, clung to the scalps like the brittle legs of dead insects, rustling faintly in the breeze. The skin, pulled tight over the skulls, reflected the dim streetlights with a sickly, unnatural sheen, like the exoskeletons of massive beetles. What first appeared to be hollow sockets in a bizarre piece of art revealed themselves to be sunken eyes, staring out blankly into the growing night.

In front of the morbid, congealing tableau lay the remains of a large tabby cat, lovingly placed on its side. If it wasn't for the dried blood where its head had been positioned in a gentle but futile attempt to reattach it to its body, the animal might have been mistaken for having fallen into a deep snooze among the autumn leaves.

The first few onlookers, drawn by morbid curiosity, approached with hesitant steps. They exchanged nervous glances, their faces reflecting a mixture of confusion and dawning horror. As they peered closer, the grotesque reality became impossible to ignore: the gaping mouths, frozen in silent screams, no longer seemed like the imagined maws of creatures, but a horrifying testament to a brutal act.

A murmur spread through the small group that had gathered, a low, uneasy buzz of disbelief. Then, as the horror of what they were seeing fully sank in, someone screamed—a sharp, shrill sound that pierced the cool evening air. The scream shattered the fragile calm, and panic rippled through the crowd. People stumbled back, their faces contorted with fear, some turning away in terror, others frozen in shock. Finally the smartphones came out and, before the police arrived and cordoned off the area, photographs of the infamous Acton

Wrecking Crew's severed heads were posted on every social media platform whose curators or policy guideline bots didn't remove them fast enough.

Vignette 2

It was nearly midnight by the time Hillbilly, Eddie, Makko, Squid, and Chance finally left The Organ Grinder. Too late to go to another watering hole and too early to head for the cemetery.

"Fuck off, you stupid cunt!" Eddie threw a final insult at the barwoman who'd been trying for some time to usher them out.

They'd been sitting in the old pub for a couple of hours, getting drunk on the allowance that Hillbilly, despite being twenty-two, still got from his father, and thrashing out the finer points of the night's entertainment.

Hillbilly—William or Billy Hillson to all but fellow members of his Crew—had what they call the luck of the devil. He and his gang had gotten away with two homicides, one rape, and countless acts of robbery and vandalism. No matter what crimes the five of them perpetrated, events—and the crack team of lawyers hired by Billy's wealthy father—conspired to see them walk away scot-free. But tonight the devil was finally going to claim his own.

Billy's mother was a homemaker-turned-amateur-historian, with a particular interest in local burial grounds, and she knew—quite literally—where the bodies were buried. Hillbilly rarely heard a word his mother said, but even he couldn't fail to notice her excitement when she convinced herself—rightly, as it would turn out—that she'd finally worked out who was interred in the furthermost corner of the Old Southfield Cemetery.

Delighted in the interest her son was finally showing in what she had to say, Margaret Hillson had shown him a photocopy of a map of the cemetery and explained where she thought a woman accused of witchcraft in the seventeenth century was probably buried.

Margaret had found the old map in the archives of Acton Library—yellowed and fragile, but still legible—and it revealed startling details about the oldest part of the cemetery: an area that had been left untouched, its graves unmarked. According to an annotation on the map, this was the resting place of those who were considered too sinful or too dangerous to be buried among the innocent. But despite the lack of gravestones or other markers on the graves themselves, the names of the interred were noted on the map. All of them but one. The grave in the furthermost, northwestern corner of the cemetery was marked on the map, but unnamed.

Margaret knew that a woman called Annie Carver had been hanged in what was now Southfield Park, and she was aware of the rumours that a witch was buried somewhere in the adjacent cemetery. If what they said was true, chances were that Annie was buried somewhere in the part of the cemetery that dated back to the seventeenth century. And there was now only one grave in that section left unaccounted for.

Finding the map, and the key to the unmarked graves, was a historian's wet dream—one that would finally get Margaret a publisher for her book on the history of Southfield from the sixteenth century right up to its incorporation into Greater London. Identifying Annie Carver's grave was the icing on the cake and perhaps a history award. For her son Billy, Margaret's theory about a witch in their local cemetery meant only one thing: the possibility of unearthing an occult item for his Hitler altar.

Ever since his teens, Hillbilly had a thing about Nazis. He fantasised about what it would have been like to be a member of the SS and purchased online any memorabilia he could afford. But what really fascinated Hillbilly were documentaries about the Nazis' interest in the occult. He devoured stories of how Hitler had in his possession the Spear of Destiny, used by the centurion Gaius Longinus to pierce Jesus Christ's side as he hung on the cross, and how this magic-imbued spear had granted the Führer power over his enemies.

Now there was a chance, a possibility, that the witch in his own West London backyard might have been buried with some occult item that would grant him power over his enemies too. Or at least look good on the corner table in his bedroom, where he kept his photograph of Adolf H. and an alleged SS dagger he'd bought via a neo-Nazi website years earlier.

So there they all were—West London's answer to the Hitlerjugend, two spades and three torches ready and waiting in the trunk of Hillbilly's car, holed up in The Organ Grinder, backs to the wall in the darkest corner they could find, knives hidden in their jackets, observing the other drinkers with barely concealed malice and waiting for the witching hour to arrive.

Before they could stop it or hurt it, the pub cat, which had been eyeing them coldly since they entered the pub, rubbed past them, marking their jeans with a few sand-coloured hairs before disappearing into the gloom of the bar area once more.

"Let's fucking kill it," said Eddie, trying to ascertain where it was exactly that the cat had gone.

"Later," Hillbilly replied absently, deep in thought about what they might find in the witch's grave: a grimoire, perhaps, or a piece of jewellery with a demonic attachment.

"Well, I wasn't suggesting we smash its head in in front of the whole pub," Eddie quipped.

"Fuck off," snapped Hillbilly, "or I'll smash *your* fucking head in."

After an hour of hanging out in Hillbilly's car, Eddie and Makko took the spades, Squid, Chance, and Hillbilly the torches out of the boot, and the five of them headed for the Old Southfield Cemetery. The lock on the gate had been broken for some time and, despite petitions from the local community, government cutbacks meant that Southfield Council had not prioritised fixing it. Soon they were heading through the newer part of the cemetery, towards their final destination.

The Old Southfield Cemetery—full to the brim and not used for new burials for many years—was creepy at the best of times, and 1 A.M. on a misty autumnal night was definitely not one of those. The moon hung low over the twisted oaks of the ancient burial ground, its pale light casting long, ghostly shadows across the uneven ground. The gravestones, if they hadn't already fallen, leaned at odd angles, their inscriptions long worn away by rain and time. The scent of decaying leaves and wet earth was overpowering. Hillbilly took the lead, while Squid and Chance helped light the way for the others. Although they'd waited until they figured everyone else would be asleep, they kept their voices down and their banter to a minimum. After a few minutes, the eldritch atmosphere started getting to them and they fell completely silent.

Annie Carver's grave lay hidden in the oldest, most forsaken part of the Old Southfield Cemetery, far beyond the reach of the better-tended plots, tucked away in a corner by the furthest wall where the ground sloped unevenly and moss clung to fallen branches. The graves here were little more than mounds of earth, slowly being reclaimed by nature, with no stones to mark their existence. Only wild grasses and creeping brambles grasped at the soil, entangling anything that dared to grow or remain. A scattering of leaves, brown and crumpled, rustled with each faint gust of wind, catching in the coarse undergrowth. Here the air was thick with the weight of forgotten souls—the unwanted, the unloved, and those no one cared to remember.

As with the others buried here, there was no marker for Annie Carver, no sign that a grave lay beneath the tangled weeds and shifting soil. Only a subtle rise in the earth indicated that anyone had been buried there at all, the ground slumping with the slow collapse of the forgotten coffin below. The wood, once strong, had rotted away over the centuries, leaving behind only fragments, waterlogged and crumbling into the earth.

Over Annie's grave stood a gnarled pussy willow, its long, spindly branches hanging low, almost scraping the earth. In the spring it would be dotted with delicate silver-grey catkins, soft and silky to the touch. Legend had it that the buds, soft as kitten fur, were created when a mother cat cried out to the willows to save her kittens from drowning, and the tree's branches bent to rescue them. Now, in the heavy dampness of autumn, the tree was stark and bare, its branches misshapen, dark, and tired, as if weighed down by the passage of time. What few leaves remained were brittle and yellowed, clinging stubbornly to the thin limbs before finally surrendering to the ground below.

The pussy willow's branches swayed slightly in the wind, though they seemed more burdened than graceful, like something long dead but still lingering out of habit. There was no sign of care or remembrance here, only neglect—a place meant to be forgotten. This part of the cemetery felt heavy, oppressive, as if the weight of the years pressed down on it, choking out any sign of life. The graves here were not tended, not visited; they were left to rot beneath the creeping fingers of nature. The world around Annie Carver's grave seemed frozen in a kind of bleak, perpetual autumn, with nothing to soften the bite of time. Here, where the forgotten lay, there was no hope, no promise of peace. Only the slow, inevitable pull of the earth reclaiming what it had buried.

Hillbilly and his little gang picked their way among the ancient tombstones and twisted shrubs. As they approached the oldest part of the cemetery, the atmosphere grew even heavier, the air thick with something none of them could name. Perhaps it was just the weight of the history beneath their feet—the countless bodies buried here, forgotten by time. A low mist started to roll in and, as they neared the far wall along which the shunned were buried, a ghastly shriek pierced the night somewhere ahead of them.

"What the fuck!" Chance stopped dead and hugged himself against the sudden chill. The others paused too. The jagged, bone-chilling wail came again—half screech, half growl—echoing among the graves like the cry of something caught between agony and fury.

"Probably just a fox," said Squid. He and Makko moved on ahead of the others, then stopped abruptly as the sound came again. Now it was clear that it was the yowl of a cat, but warped, feral, rising in sharp, ragged pitches. As the five of them listened, the caterwauling clawed at the silence, raw and unnatural, like nails scraping across a tombstone, its echoes lingering long after the cry itself ceased.

"Come on," said Hillbilly. "This way." He took the lead again, stepping over a fallen tombstone before heading for the far wall.

"They all look the same," said Chance, shining the light of his torch over the row of overgrown mounds of slightly raised earth. "None of them have any names. How do you know which one it is?"

"My mother has a map of the cemetery," Hillbilly explained. "It has the names." He stopped by the grave in the furthermost corner. "This is it."

As Hillbilly swung his flashlight toward the mound, a loud guttural hiss cut through the stillness and he recoiled in shock. The others froze behind him. A second later, Squid and Chance joined Hillbilly in pointing their torches at the grave. There, crouching on top of it, was a huge cat, eyes gleaming in the light like twin embers, its fur standing on end, tail bristling. It stood defiant, staring at the intruders, and then it yowled—the vicious, desperate sound they'd heard earlier.

Before anyone knew what was happening, Eddie, ever on edge, raced forward, swinging the shovel in a hard, sharp arc. The blade caught the cat clean across the neck, and in one swift, brutal motion the animal's head came clean off, landing with a soft thud in the tall grass. The body twitched once, blood spraying across the mound, then went still.

There was stunned silence for a moment, then Makko broke the spell.

"Eddie, what the hell?" he whispered, trying to shake off the unease that crawled down his spine.

"Cool!" Squid giggled nervously.

"The cat killer strikes again!" added Chance, patting Eddie on the back.

"Nicely done!" Hillbilly chuckled darkly. He kicked the cat's headless body off the grave, then stood back and gestured for Eddie and Makko to clear away the weeds and get digging. "Now let's get to work."

Makko's eyes lingered a moment longer on the cat's remains, now lying in a patch of nettles nearby, then he joined Eddie at the mound. The five of them took turns with the spades and torches, the physical labour helping to keep them warm.

They dug in quick, jerky movements, the rhythmic sound of metal on earth breaking the silence. It had been raining over the past week and the frosts had not yet set in, so they made good progress. Sometime between three and four in the morning they made a breakthrough. Chance was the first to hit something other than soil. It was wet, dark, and spongy. They shined their lights on it and Chance pulled it out. It was a piece of ancient wood. As they worked, more remnants of the old coffin began to surface—splintered and rotten, barely holding together. But as they cleared away the dirt, the flashlight that Eddie was now holding caught something else: a curved, rusted shape, half buried in the soil.

"What the fuck!" Squid exclaimed. Hillbilly pushed him out of the way and knelt, brushing the loose earth from the item as Makko shined a light on it. Despite centuries of corrosion, the sharp crescent shape was unmistakable. It was a sickle, its iron blade rusted and pitted but still intact. Hillbilly grinned, his hand curling around the handle.

"It's perfect." He tugged it free from the earth, holding it up for the others to see.

"Perfect for what?" asked Makko, shivering as a cold wind picked up around them, whistling in the surrounding oak trees and animating the pussy willow under which they'd been digging.

"My collection," Hillbilly replied, placing the sickle to one side and peering into the grave once more.

Eddie had been clearing more of the earth away and spotted something else of interest. There were bone fragments immediately underneath where the sickle had been. Most of them had disintegrated with time, but some still remained, their edges stained a deep, reddish-brown from the iron of the sickle that had lain across them. The rust had seeped into the porous bone, leaving a faint, bloody-looking mark across the vertebrae of what had been the woman's neck.

"Give them here," Hillbilly demanded.

"I want one too," said Chance.

"Get them out and we'll divide them up later," said Hillbilly. "And keep digging. The skull should be in there somewhere."

They worked a while longer, pulling out a few skull fragments and a piece of jaw bone, but the cold mist that had been rolling in was steadily thickening and the temperature seemed to be dropping by the minute. Something shrieked nearby—a startled bird perhaps, and the wind seemed to pick up even more.

"I'm done," said Eddie, glancing over his shoulder into the nearby bushes.

"Okay," Hillbilly agreed, "let's tidy up a bit and go." He tucked the rusted sickle into the belt of his jeans, stuffed the dirty bone fragments into his pockets, and shined his flashlight at the grave as his friends hurriedly shovelled some earth back into it. Chance and Makko stood beside him with the other two torches.

"Why did they bury her with a—a—?" asked Chance. Hillbilly shrugged.

"A sickle," said Makko. "To stop her coming back." The others stared at him in surprise. "That's what they used to do with witches in Poland. And vampires. Put a sickle over their necks to stop them rising from the grave."

"Poland?" Eddie looked up from covering up the hole. "I hate fucking Polacks."

"I'm not fucking Polish!" Makko was a little too quick to defend himself. "I hate them too."

"Your gran's Polish." Hillbilly wanted to laugh, but something about the jerky movements of the pussy willow branches was making him nervous.

"That doesn't make me a Polack," squirmed Makko. "Look, all I'm saying is that my gran told me that when they buried a witch, a long time ago like, they put a sickle over her neck to stop her from coming back."

"You're not in Poland now, fucktard!" Eddie had finished at the gravesite and was winding himself up.

"Fuck's sake, Eddie." Makko was wishing he'd kept quiet. "I'm just saying that Southfield is full of Polacks, right?"

328

"And they should all fuck off back to Poland!" Eddie was on a roll.

"Yes," sighed Makko, "I agree. But what I'm saying is that maybe there was already Polacks here when the witch was buried and maybe it was their idea to put a sickle over her neck."

"Frankly, fucktard," Eddie concluded philosophically, "I don't give a shit."

Another animal shriek, much closer this time, made them jump. The wind, which had died down a little, now picked up again with a hollow whistling sound, and with it came a sudden, creeping sense of being watched.

"Let's go!" Hillbilly made sure the sickle was properly secured in his belt and slapped his failing torch against the palm of his hand.

"Wait!" Squid, pointed his flashlight into the tall grass nearby and grinned. A moment later he was bending down, picking up the cat's severed head and dangling it by the fur. "Witch wants her friend back."

"Gross," said Makko. The others laughed as Squid placed the cat's head atop Annie's reconstituted mound. It sat there, grotesque and defiant, eyes still open and wide, reflecting the moonlight in a dull, lifeless gleam.

"Nice headstone!" cackled Chance, giving the dirt one final kick.

"Okay, let's go," repeated Hillbilly.

But as the five of them turned to leave, Makko thought he heard a soft hiss behind them, faint and far too close for comfort:

"You killed my cats."

Vignette 1

The bitter wind whipped through the village of Southfield, scattering the last autumn leaves, already browned and brittle from the cold. A restless, malevolent energy crackled in the air, like the moments before a lightning strike, as the villagers closed in, their faces lit by the fitful glow of torches, eyes wild with bloodlust. An angry murmur swept through the crowd like the rumblings of an oncoming storm.

At the centre of it all knelt Annie Carver, wrists bound with rough rope, skirts muddied and torn. Her long hair clung to her face, damp with sweat and blood from the cut on her brow, eyes wide with fear and despair, heart broken. Around her, bloodied and lifeless, lay her cats—her beloved strays, her babies. Six of them in all, their fur matted with dirt and streaked with red. The villagers had pinned Annie down and made her watch.

"You evil bitch," hissed one of the men holding her firm.

"Let's see how you fare without your familiars!" shouted a woman standing opposite. Annie's breath came in shallow gasps. She struggled to free her hands, desperate to touch her babies, to offer them some scant comfort in their final moments, but she could not.

"They were innocents!" she cried out as she was pulled to her feet and dragged towards the great oak that stood at the edge of the village green, its ancient branches stretching out like dark, skeletal fingers against the twilight sky. "As am I!" The noose of a hangman's rope was forced over her head, scratching, stinging. "All I ever did was offer you kindness and the healing power of my herbs in your times of need."

A couple of the villagers shifted uncomfortably, but it was too late. Thomas Barker threw the other end of the rope over a low, sturdy branch and pulled it taut. A couple of other men joined him at the tree, ready to help him pull.

Before the men could hoist her up, and just when it seemed that Annie's fear would kill her before the rope did, it came. The first cat's cry echoed through the night. It was faint but unmistakable—a long, drawn-out wail of sorrow and rage. Another followed, then another, until the woods beyond the village were alive with the sound of cats crying out for their lost kin and the woman who'd given them sanctuary.

Annie's terror turned to hate, fury, and a thirst for vengeance that would never be sated. She looked at her neighbours, her eyes blackened with shadow, glistening in the dying light. Her voice changed; her features suddenly unrecognisable, alien.

"My death will bring more ruin than you can imagine." She smiled—a sinister, broken smile. "I will not rest. I will haunt you—every last one of you. I will haunt you and all who spill innocent blood." Then despair and heartbreak returned to Annie's voice, and yet something about the desolate accusation in her final sob was even more chilling than the wrathful curse that preceded it:

"You killed my cats."

Notes on Contributors

The Editors

S. T. Joshi is the author of *The Weird Tale* (1990), *H. P. Lovecraft: The Decline of the West* (1990), and *Unutterable Horror: A History of Supernatural Fiction* (2012). He has prepared corrected editions of H. P. Lovecraft's work for Arkham House and annotated editions of Lovecraft's stories for Penguin Classics. His exhaustive biography, *H. P. Lovecraft: A Life* (1996) was expanded as I *Am Providence: The Life and Times of H. P. Lovecraft* (2010). He has edited the anthologies *American Supernatural Tales* (Penguin, 2007), *A Mountain Walked: Great Tales of the Cthulhu Mythos* (Centipede Press, 2013), *The Madness of Cthulhu* (Titan Books, 2014), and the ongoing *Black Wings* series (PS Publishing, 2010f.). Joshi has won the World Fantasy Award, the British Fantasy Award, the Bram Stoker Award, and the International Horror Guild Award.

Katherine Kerestman (B.A. English and History, John Carroll University; M. A. English, Case Western Reserve University) is the author of *Cultes des Goules* (WordCrafts Press, 2025), *Lethal* (Psychotoxin Press, 2023), *Creepy Cat's Macabre Travels: Prowling around Haunted Towers, Crumbling Castles, and Ghoulish Graveyards* (WordCrafts Press, 2020), and *Haunted House and Other Strange Tales* (Hippocampus Press, 2024). She is co-editor (with S. T. Joshi) of *The Weird Cat* (WordCrafts Press, 2023) and *Shunned Houses: An Anthology of Weird Stories, Unspeakable Poems, and Impious Essays* (WordCrafts Press, 2024). More than 80 of her Lovecraftian and gothic poems, essays, and short stories have been featured in *Black Wings VII, Penumbra, Journ-E, Spectral Realms, Illumen, Retro-Fan, Dissections, Off-Course, Lovecraftiana* and other discerning publications. Katherine thinks *Dracula* and *Wuthering Heights* are the greatest books ever written, and is wild about *Dark Shadows* and *Twin Peaks*. Her name is etched forevermore among the inscrutable glyphs of the Esoteric Order of Dagon and the Dracula Society. She invites her fans to stalk her at www.creepycatlair.com.

Dmitri Akers is a writer and poet of the weird tradition, living on Kaurna country. His poesy and prose have appeared in *La Piccioletta Barca*, *Spectral Realms*, *Spawn 2*, and *Penumbra*. Through an admixture of modes and rhythm, he wishes to resurrect the decadent sweetness of the Python below Parnassus.

Im Bang (1640–1724) was a leading Korean writer of fables, folk tales, poetry, and other matter. He served in the government for many years, including being governor of Seoul.

L. Frank Baum (1856–1919) was an American author who gained celebrity with *The Wonderful Wizard of Oz* (1900), the first of sixteen books about Oz he wrote during his career. Baum also wrote several other series of children's books. The Oz books, although ostensibly written for children, employ a complex series of symbols and metaphors that reflect the social and political concerns of the period.

Ambrose Bierce (1842–1914?) was an American journalist (chiefly for William Randolph Hearst's *San Francisco Examiner*, 1887–1906) and short story writer, best known for his tales of the Civil War (collected in *Tales of Soldiers and Civilians*, 1891) and of supernatural and psychological horror (collected in *Can Such Things Be?*, 1893). His prodigious output also includes essays, poetry, fables, and *The Devil's Dictionary* (1906/1911).

Helena P. Blavatsky (1831–1891) was a Russian writer who, after engaging in extensive travels throughout the world, devised a religion or philosophy she called Theosophy, embodied in such works as *Isis Unveiled* (1877) and *The Secret Doctrine* (1888). She also wrote short fiction, included in *From the Caves and Jungles of Hindistan* (1892) and *Nightmare Tales* (1892).

Henri Boguet (1550–1619) was a French judge who gained celebrity with a treatise on witchcraft, *Discours exécrable des sorciers* (1602; usually translated as *Examen of Witches*), which gives advice on how to try witches.

Adam Bolivar is a poet and writer of weird and folkloric fantasy, as well as a playwright for marionettes. He is the author of *The Lay of Old Hex* (Hippocampus Press, 2017), *The Ettinfell of Beacon Hill* (Jackanapes Press, 2021), *Ballads for the Witching Hour* (Hippocampus Press, 2022) and *A Wheel of Ravens* (Jackanapes Press, 2023). A native of gambrel-roofed Boston, Massachusetts, he now resides in the gloomy dream-lands of Portland, Oregon.

The *Oxford Companion to English Literature* describes **Ramsey Campbell** as "Britain's most respected living horror writer," and the *Washington Post* sums up his work as "one of the monumental accomplishments of modern popular fiction." He has received the Grand Master Award of the World Horror Convention, the Lifetime Achievement Award of the Horror Writers Association, the Living Legend Award of the International Horror Guild, and the World Fantasy Lifetime Achievement Award. In 2015 he was made an Honorary Fellow of Liverpool John Moores University for outstanding services to literature. The two volumes of *Phantasmagorical Stories* offer a sixty-year retrospective of his short fiction. *The Village Killings* collects his novellas, and *Ramsey's Rambles* his film reviews. His latest novel is *The Incubations* from Flame Tree Press, who have also recently published his *Brichester Mythos* trilogy.

Mary Elizabeth Coleridge (1861–1907) was a British novelist and poet and the great-grandniece of the poet Samuel Taylor Coleridge. Her most celebrated novel was *The Seven Sleepers of Ephesus* (1893). She published several volumes of poetry, including *Fancy's Guerdon* (1897); her collected poetry appeared as *Poems* (1908), published posthumously.

Mary De Morgan (1850–1907) was a British writer who published three volumes of fairy tales: *On a Pincushion* (1877), *The Necklace of Princess Fiorimonde* (1880), and *The Windfairies* (1900). A close friend of William Morris and other Pre-Raphaelites, De Morgan advocated woman suffrage and denounced capitalism. Some elements of these views can be detected in her fairy tales.

Little is known of British writer **Alice Elizabeth Dracott** (d. 1939) aside from her authorship of *Simla Village Tales* (1906) and *The Voice of Mystic India: My Psychic Experiences* (1930), recounting the influence of Indian religion and culture upon her outlook.

Leah Bodine Drake (1904–1964) was an American writer who published a book of weird verse with Arkham House, *A Hornbook of Witches* (1950). But this slim volume is only the tip of the iceberg of her work. She published a second poetry volume, *This Tilting Dust* (1955), coedited (with Charles Arthur Musès) the poetry anthology *The Various Light* (1964), and wrote several tales of fantasy and terror. Her collected writings were assembled by David E. Schultz in *The Song of the Sun* (Hippocampus Press, 2020).

Euripides (480?–406? B.C.E.) was the youngest of the three celebrated tragic playwrights in fifth-century Greece, along with Aeschylus and Sophocles. He is reputed to have written more than ninety plays, of which nineteen survive. Aside from *Medea* (performed in 431 B.C.E.), he wrote *Alcestis, Andromache, Electra,* and *Iphigenia in Aulis.*

Debra K. Every is an author of horror, thrillers, and stories with twisted perspectives. Her debut novel, *Deena Undone,* has won multiple awards including an American Fiction Award, a Storytrade Book Award, and a Page Turner Award. A Spanish edition of *Deena Undone* will be released in 2025. Additionally, her short stories have appeared in numerous publications and anthologies. Debra lives in Upstate New York, where she endlessly strives to write one perfectly balanced sentence.

Wade German's most recent full-length poetry collection is *Psalms and Sorceries* (Hippocampus Press, 2022). His first collection, *Dreams from a Black Nebula,* is also available from Hippocampus Press. Other titles include four slim volumes of his selected poems with Portuguese translation: *Incantations, Apparitions, Phantasmagorias,* and the latest, *Chapel of Celluloid* (Raphus Press, 2023).

Maxwell I. Gold is a Jewish-American multiple award-nominated author who writes prose poetry and short stories in cosmic horror and weird fiction with half a decade of writing experience. He is a five-time Rhysling Award nominee and two-time Pushcart Award nominee.

John Hale (1636–1700) was a Puritan pastor in Beverly, Massachusetts, and participated in the Salem witch trials of 1692. Initially an eager advocate of witchcraft persecution, he ultimately modified his views to the degree of asserting that the accused witches were demons in disguise. His treatise *A Modest Enquiry into the Nature of Witchcraft* appeared posthumously in 1702.

Joel Chandler Harris (1848–1908) was an American writer who lived most of his life in Atlanta, where he absorbed legendry from the African Americans in the area and began writing the Uncle Remus stories, first published in book form as *Uncle Remus: His Songs and His Sayings* (1880). He went on to write eight further volumes about Uncle Remus, Br'er Rabbit, and other characters, as well as a score of other books.

Robert Herrick (1591–1674) was a British poet and Anglican cleric whose poetry fuses secular love and religious faith. The only book of his verse published in his lifetime was *Hesperides* (1648), which includes more than a thousand poems.

Matthew Hopkins (1620?–1647) was an officially designated witchfinder (1644–47) whose treatise *The Discoverie of Witches* (1647) provides detailed information on how to determine whether a suspect is a witch. His book influenced witch trials in both England and New England.

Robert E. Howard (1906–1936) was an American writer who published weird, adventure, and other types of fiction in the pulp magazines of his day. Most celebrated for the creation of such heroic figures as Conan the Cimmerian, King Kull, Solomon Kane, and Bran Mak

Morn, Howard also wrote tales of pure supernaturalism. All his books appeared posthumously, many issued by Arkham House, beginning with *Skull-Face and Others* (1946). His correspondence with H. P. Lovecraft was published as *A Means to Freedom* (2009).

James Weldon Johnson (1871–1938) was a leading African American writer of his era, publishing several books of poetry (*Fifty Years and Other Poems,* 1917; *God's Trombones,* 1927), the anthologies *The Book of American Negro Poetry* (1922), *The Book of Negro Spirituals* (1925), and *The Second Book of Negro Spirituals* (1926), and the novel *The Autobiography of an Ex-Colored Man* (1912), among others. He was also a vigorous advocate of civil rights for African Americans.

John Kachuba's most recent book is *The Bottle Conjuror,* an historical fantasy novel. *Haycorn Smith and the Castle Ghost* is a paranormal novel for middle-grade readers. Other novels are *Dark Entry* and *The Savage Apostle.* His *Shapeshifters: A History* was a 2020 Bram Stoker Award finalist.

Heinrich Kramer and Jakob Sprenger were the purported authors of *Malleus Maleficarum* (1487; The Hammer of Witches), one of the most notorious of the many witch-hunting manuals produced during the Middle Ages and Renaissance. It was written after Pope Innocent VIII issued a papal bull in 1484 ordering the Inquisition to pursue witchcraft cases. Sprenger's name was only added in a 1519 reprint, and there is now doubt as to whether he was involved in the book's writing.

Tony LaMalfa's original stories and poetry have been included in respected anthologies, such as *The Weird Cat* and *Shunned Houses* from WordCrafts Press, as well as publications by Elvelon Press, Weird House Press, and the Horror Writers Association. In 2023 Hippocampus Press published his literary debut *Forbidden Knowledge: Two Tales of Lovecraftian Terror.* Tony lives in Upper Michigan with his young family and is grateful to S. T., Katherine, and Derrick for their friendship and virtuosity.

Éliphas Lévi was the pseudonym of French writer Alphonse Louis Constant (1810–1875), who became devoted to ceremonial magic and wrote a score of books on the subject, including *Histoire de la magie* (1860; translated as *The History of Magic*), *La science des esprits* (1865; *The Science of Spirits*), and *Clefs majeures et clavicules de Salomon* (1895; *Major and Minor Keys of Solomon*).

Frank Belknap Long (1901–1994), American novelist, short story writer, and poet, was a protégé of H. P. Lovecraft and published many stories in *Weird Tales* and other pulp magazines, as well as the poetry volumes *The Man from Genoa* (1926) and *The Goblin Tower* (1935). Later in his career he wrote several novels of horror, the supernatural, and science fiction, including *Journey into Darkness* (1967) and *The Night of the Wolf* (1972).

Simon MacCulloch lives in London and contributes poetry to a variety of print and online publications.

Cotton Mather (1663–1728) was a Puritan clergyman in Boston whose most notable work was *Magnalia Christi Americana* (1702), an account of the advance of Christianity in the American colonies. He defended belief in witchcraft in two treatises—*Late Memorable Providences Relating to Witchcrafts and Possessions* (1689) and *Wonders of the Invisible World* (1693), the latter written in the wake of the Salem witch trials of 1692. These are among hundreds of works he wrote over his lifetime.

Margaret Alice Murray (1863–1963) was a British anthropologist who wrote prolifically on ancient Egyptian history and culture, among other subjects. But she gained celebrity with *The Witch-Cult in Western Europe* (1921), which propounded the theory that the European witch-cult was a holdover of a pre-Christian fertility cult. She followed up this work with *The God of the Witches* (1931). Although some anthropologists and historians accepted her theory, it has been rejected by many scholars in recent decades.

Robert P. Ottone is the Bram Stoker Award–winning author of *The Triangle* and is also the best-selling author of *Curse of the Cob Cob Man*, *The Sleepy Hollow Gang*, *The Vile Thing We Created*, and *Nocturnal Creatures*. His short fiction has been collected in *Wrapped in Plastic and Other Sweet Nothings* as well as *Her Infernal Name and Other Nightmares*.

Michael Potts is the author of three novels: *End of Summer*, *Unpardonable Sin*, and *Obedience*, all published by WordCrafts Press. He also has published three volumes of poetry: *From Field to Thicket* (winner, 2006 Mary Belle Campbell Poetry Book Award, North Carolina Writers Network), *Hiding from the Reaper and Other Horror Poems*, and *Slipknot and Other Dark Poems*. He serves as Professor of Philosophy, Methodist University, Fayetteville, North Carolina.

Ann Putnam (1679–1716) was one of the leading accusers during the Salem witch trials of 1692, accusing sixty-two people of witchcraft. In 1706 she recanted her testimony, blaming it on her chronic ill-health and claiming that she was "deluded by Satan."

Dorothy Quick (1896–1962) was befriended by Mark Twain when he met her on a boat trip across the Atlantic in 1907. She later wrote the memoir *Enchantment: A Little Girl's Friendship with Mark Twain* (1961). As an adult she wrote tales and poems of fantasy and terror for *Weird Tales* and other pulp magazines. Her work has now been gathered in *The Witch's Mark and Others* (Sarnath Press, 2024).

Stephen Mark Rainey is the author of numerous novels, six short story collections, approximately 200 works of short fiction, and the scripts to several *Dark Shadows* audio productions from Big Finish Studios, which feature members of the original ABC-TV series cast. For ten years he edited the award-winning *Deathrealm* magazine. He has also edited several anthologies, including the recent *Deathrealm: Spirits* from Shortwave Publishing. His latest novel, *The House at Black Tooth Pond*, is now available from Crossroad Press.

Nicholas Rémy (1530–1616), sometimes referred to by the Latinized form of his name, Remigius, was a French magistrate who claimed to have executed as many as 800 suspected witches during his lifetime. He wrote *Daemonolatreiae libri tres* (1595; Three Books of Demonolotry) as a guide to witch-hunting.

Herman George Scheffauer (1876–1927) was a German-born American poet and translator who published several volumes of poetry—*Of Both Worlds* (1903), *Looms of Life* (1908), among others—under the tutelage of Ambrose Bierce. In later years he moved to England, then Germany, where he translated the work of Heinrich Heine and Friedrich Nietzsche. Becoming friends with Thomas Mann, he published some of the earliest translations of that author into English.

Darrell Schweitzer has been publishing weird or fantastic poetry for decades. Not counting comic verse (e.g., *They Never Found the Head: Poems of Sentiment and Reflection,* 2001) his two previous collections of (mostly weird) verse are *Groping Toward the Light* (2000) and *Ghosts of Past and Future* (2008). Hippocampus Press will issue a new volume of previously uncollected and selected poems, *Dancing Before Azathoth*, in 2025. His most recent story collection is *The Children of Chorazin* (Hippocampus, 2023) and his most recent anthology is *Shadows out of Time* (PS Publishing 2023).

Eleanor Scott is the pseudonym of British writer Helen Madeline Leys (1892–1965). She is the author of a single volume of horror tales, *Randalls Round* (1929).

William Bell Scott (1811–1890) was a Scottish painter associated with the Pre-Raphaelites. He also wrote a volume of poetry, *Poems* (1875), much influenced by the English Romantic poets. He followed it up with the volume *A Poet's Harvest Home* (1882). He also wrote treatises on Albrecht Dürer, William Blake, and other artists.

William Shakespeare (1564–1616) was a British actor and playwright whose dozens of plays—tragedies, comedies, and histories—have made him the most renowned author in English literature. Aside from *Macbeth* (first performed in 1606), supernatural elements are present in *Hamlet* and other plays.

John Shirley won the Bram Stoker Award for his book *Black Butter-flies: A Flock on the Dark Side*. His first poetry collection, *The Voice of the Burning House*, has been nominated for the Elgin Award for poetry.

Clark Ashton Smith (1893–1961) was an American writer who first gained prominence with the poetry collection *The Star-Treader and Other Poems* (1912), published when he was nineteen. After issuing several other poetry volumes, Smith turned to writing fantasy, horror, and science fiction stories for the pulp magazines, including *Weird Tales* and *Wonder Stories*. These tales—as well as his poetry—were later gathered in book form by Arkham House. Today Smith is regarded as a pioneering figure in weird and cosmic poetry.

Oliver Smith is a writer from Cheltenham, UK. He is inspired by Tristan Tzara, J. G. Ballard, and Max Ernst; by the poetry of chance encounters, by frenzied rocks towering above the silent swamp; by unlikely collisions between place and myth and memory. His poetry has been published in *Spectral Realms, Penumbra,* and *Radon Journal* and has twice been nominated for the Pushcart Prize. He holds a Ph.D. in Literary and Critical Studies.

Edmund Clarence Stedman (1833–1908) was an American poet, critic, and editor who wrote such treatises as *Victorian Poets* (1876), *Edgar Allan Poe* (1881), *Poets of America* (1885), and *The Nature and Elements of Poetry* (1892), as well as the notable poetry anthology *An American Anthology* (1900?). Among his poetry volumes are *Poems, Lyrical and Idyllic* (1860), *The Blameless Prince and Other Poems* (1869), and *Hawthorne and Other Poems* (1877).

Montague Summers (1880–1948) was an English clergyman who converted from Anglicanism to Catholicism. He wrote numerous treatises on Elizabethan literature, but gained greatest celebrity by a series of books on witchcraft and related subjects, including *The History of Witchcraft and Demonology* (1926), *The Geography of Witchcraft* (1927), *The Vampire: His Kith and Kin* (1928), *The Werewolf* (1933), and several others. He also compiled the notable weird anthology *The Supernatural Omnibus* (1931). He appears to have believed in the reality of witchcraft, vampirism, and the like.

Algernon Charles Swinburne (1837–1909) was a leading British poet of the later nineteenth century, challenging the moral norms of Victorian poetry. He wrote three series of *Poems and Ballads* (1866–89) along with *Songs Before Sunrise* (1871), *Astrophel and Other Poems* (1894), and other volumes. He also wrote verse plays, including *Rosamond* (1860) and *Mary Stewart* (1881). He wrote critical studies of Shakespeare, Ben Jonson, Victor Hugo, William Blake, George Chapman, and Charlotte Brontë.

Anna Taborska writes horror stories and screenplays, with tales appearing in over forty anthologies and three single-author collections: *Bloody Britain* (Shadow Publishing, 2020), *Shadowcats* (Black Shuck Books, 2019), and *For Those Who Dream Monsters* (Mortbury Press, 2013, 2020). She has been nominated for a British Fantasy Award three times, and for a Bram Stoker Award five times, and has won the Dracula Society's Children of the Night Award. Anna has also directed five films.

Mary A. Turzillo won a 2000 Nebula for *Mars Is No Place for Children*. Her poetry collection *Lovers & Killers* won the 2013 Elgin Award. Her collaboration with Marge Simon, *Sweet Poison,* also won an Elgin. She is presently (2024) a Pushcart nominee. Her latest two books are *Cast from Darkness,* also with Simon, and *Cosmic Cats and Fantastic Furballs*. In a Kent State Trumbull production of *Macbeth,* she played the first witch.

Donald Tyson is a Canadian writer who lives and works in Nova Scotia. He is the author of dozens of nonfiction books on all aspects of

Western esotericism, and also numerous novels and short stories of horror and the supernatural. His latest work of fiction is *The Old Gods Awaken* (Weird House Press, 2024), a collection of linked short stories centered around the return of Lovecraft's Old Gods and their conquest of planet Earth.

Lady Wilde (Jane Francesca Agnes Wilde, 1821–1896), mother of Oscar Wilde, was an Irish writer who also wrote under the pseudonym "Speranza." She was the author of *Poems* (1864, 1871) and *Notes on Men, Women, and Books* (1891), as well as *Ancient Legends, Mystic Charms, and Superstitions of Ireland* (1888), a collection of folktales and legends.

Acknowledgments

"Beautiful Baby Bianka" by Deborah K. Every. Original to this volume. Copyright © 2025 by Deborah K. Every. Printed by permission of the author.

"The Beldame" by Katherine Kerestman. *Illumen Magazine,* ed. Tyree Campbell (Spring/April, 2023); reprinted in *Beauty in Darkness* (Dark Moon Rising Publications, 2025). Printed by permission of the author.

"The Children of Glimbly" by John Shirley. Original to this volume. Copyright © 2025 by John Shirley. Printed by permission of the author.

"Confession" by Ann Putnam, written 1706; first published in Charles Wentworth Upham, *Salem Witchcraft* (Boston: Wiggin & Lunt, 1867).

Demonolatry by Nicholas Remy (1595), translated by E. A. Ashwin (London: John Rodker, 1930).

The Discoverie of Witches by Matthew Hopkins (1647; rpt. London: Cayne Press, 1928).

"Dollhouse" by Mary A. Turzillo. Original to this volume. Copyright © 2025 by Mary A. Turzillo. Printed by permission of the author.

"Donna and the Yaga" by Robert P. Ottone. Original to this volume. Copyright © 2025 by Robert P. Ottone. Printed by permission of the author.

An Examen of Witches by Henri Boguet (1602), translated by Montague Summers (London: John Rodker, 1929).

"Foragers" by Stephen Mark Rainey. Original to this volume. Copyright © 2025 by Stephen Mark Rainey. Printed by permission of the author.

"A Fowl Witch" by Ambrose Bierce, first published in *Fun* (22 February 1873); rpt. in Bierce's *Cobwebs from an Empty Skull* (George Routledge & Sons, 1874).

"The Necklace of Princess Fiorimonde" by Mary De Morgan, from De Morgan's *The Necklace of Princess Fiorimonde and Other Stories* (London: Macmillan, 1880).

"The Old Lady" by Eleanor Scott, from Scott's *Randalls Round* (London: Ernest Benn, 1929).

"A Plantation Witch" by Joel Chandler Harris, from Harris's *Uncle Remus: His Songs and Sayings: The Folk-lore of the Old Plantation* (New York: D. Appleton & Co., 1880).

"Sea Curse" by Robert E. Howard, first published in *Weird Tales* (May 1928).

"The Search for the Wicked Witch" by L. Frank Baum, from *The Wonderful Wizard of Oz* (Chicago: G. M. Hill Co., 1900).

"Seeing Them" by Darrell Schweitzer. Original to this volume. Copyright © 2025 by Darrell Schweitzer. Printed by permission of the author.

"Song of Fae-Land" by Dmitri Akers. Original to this volume. Copyright © 2025 by Dmitri Akers. Printed by permission of the author.

"A Visit from the Shades" by Im Bang, from *Korean Folk Tales* by Im Bang and Yi Ryuk, translated by James S. Gale (London: J. M. Dent; New York: E. P. Dutton, 1913).

"The White People" by Frank Belknap Long, first published in *Weird Tales* (November 1927), rpt. in Long's *The Goblin Tower* (Cassia, FL: Dragon-Fly Press, 1935).

"The White Witch" by James Weldon Johnson, first published in the *Crisis* (March 1915); rpt. in Johnson's *Fifty Years & Other Poems* (Boston: Cornhill Co., 1917).

"Why We Don't Dig Up Witches" by John Kachuba. Original to this volume. Copyright © 2025 by John Kachuba. Printed by permission of the author.

"The Witch" by Mary Elizabeth Coleridge, from Coleridge's *Fancy's Following* (Oxford: Daniel, 1896; as by "Anodos").

The Witch-Cult in Western Europe by Margaret Alice Murray (Oxford: Clarendon Press, 1921).

"The Witch in the Graveyard" by Clark Ashton Smith, first published in Smith's *Ebony and Crystal: Poems in Verse and Prose* (Auburn, CA: Auburn Journal, 1922).

"The Witch Mother" by Algernon Charles Swinburne, first published in Swinburne's *Poems and Ballads: Third Series* (London: Chatto & Windus, 1889).

"The Witch Who Lived in a Forest" by Alice Elizabeth Dracott, from Dracott's *Simla Village Tales; or, Folk Tales from the Himalayas* (London: John Murray, 1906).

"Witch's Brew" by Dorothy Quick, first published in *Weird Tales* (March 1954).

"Witch's Death Song" by Oliver Smith. Original to this volume. Copyright © 2025 by Oliver Smith. Printed by permission of the author.

"A Witch's Den" by Helena P. Blavatsky, from Blavatsky's *From the Caves and Jungles of Hindostan,* [no translator given] (London: Theosophical Publishing Society, 1892).

"Witchcraft" by Edmund Clarence Stedman, first published in *Harper's* (December 1884); rpt. in Stedman's *Poems Now First Collected* (Boston: Houghton Mifflin, 1897).

Wonders of the Invisible World by Cotton Mather (1693; rpt. London: John Russell, 1862).

www.ingramcontent.com/pod-product-compliance
Lightning Source LLC
Chambersburg PA
CBHW060941030726
47503CB00003B/680